STRAP YOURSELF IN FOR A BOLT OF

BLUE LIGHTNING

CHARLES STELLA served in Vietnam as a search-and-rescue pilot for downed airmen and later became a flight instructor and intelligence officer.

BLUE LIGHTNING

A NOVEL
Charles Stella

WARNER BOOKS

A Time Warner Company

WARNER BOOKS EDITION

Book design: H. Roberts
Cover design: Mike Stromberg
Cover illustration: Edwin Herder

Warner Books, Inc.
666 Fifth Avenue
New York, N.Y. 10103

 A Time Warner Company

Printed in the United States of America

This book was previously printed in hardcover by Warner Books.
First Printed in Paperback: August, 1991

10 9 8 7 6 5 4 3 2 1

To Lt. Paul C. Charvet, MIA; AX3 Clayton C. Kemp, MIA; AX3 Wayne C. Reinecke, MIA; and to all aviators and air crewmen who gave so much and asked so little

ACKNOWLEDGMENTS

I wish to thank the following for their help and guidance: Harrison E. Salisbury, Wendy Grubbs, Tad Arbuckle, Jim Robertson of Combat Jets, Col. Dale Hainley, Dr. Dave Watkins, Sally Boyd, Audrey Guild, Connie Fox, Dawn Ireland, Bill Hord, Mel Parker, and Robert Gottlieb. And a special thanks to my wife, Rachel, for her patience and understanding during the completion of the manuscript.

PROLOGUE

"Three one switch to button six!"

Lt. Jim Campbell rotated his radio switch four clicks and adjusted his power slightly, locking his A-4 in behind the starboard wing of the lead bomber. He listened for the flight lead to check in with Red Crown, code name for the USS *Chicago*, the guided-missile cruiser somewhere to the north of them. Red Crown controlled all flights going in and out of North Vietnam, maintaining a fixed position off the port of Haiphong. With her surface-to-air missiles and a captain itching to use them, she maintained constant vigilance over any aircraft the North Vietnamese launched as well.

Campbell felt tense as the two Douglas A-4s descended below the last cloud layer into clear air below. His muscles ached from being cooped up in the cramped cockpit for nearly two hours. His four-plane flight had bombed a petroleum site east of Hanoi, and whatever had caused two of their flights to discontinue their approach to the carrier had to be important.

The pilot of the lead aircraft, Lt. Larry Jordan, squeezed his mike button. "Red Crown, this is Blackbeard two seven with three one, squawking ident, and three one is taking the lead, over."

Campbell rocked forward in his ejection seat, then sat up straight. The sudden appointment to flight leader caught him by surprise and his neck tensed again. Though now leader of the flight, he didn't know where they were going or why they were going there. He realized Jordan was offering him the opportunity for some experience, but it seemed strange not to be following another aircraft into combat. As Jordan maneuvered his aircraft aft to assume wing, Campbell could see the other pilot grinning at him.

The chief controller on the cruiser jotted down the lead change then called, "Three one, this is Red Crown. Your vector is two eight four and target area sixty-four miles. An air force F-4 recon went down about thirty-five minutes ago trying to nurse their bird out over the water. An SH-3A from the *Bennie* is talking to the back seater. Remain this freq and contact Loosefoot five one. Call when feet dry. Over."

Campbell acknowledged the call, then looked back over his shoulder. He could see Jordan flying loosely behind his starboard wing, then heard Jordan click his mike twice. Their two-plane flight had no air-to-air missiles or bombs on board, only full loads of 20 millimeter, good for strafing trucks and troops. To the north were airborne fighters serving as barrier patrols against any unidentified aircraft coming out of North Vietnam, but they were armed only with air-to-air missiles. Flights weren't usually pulled out of the landing pattern after a bombing run and sent off on a secret mission, and Campbell guessed the situation was desperate and that they were the only ones available; normally the slower prop-driven Spads were used for escort duty with the rescue helos. Campbell stopped trying to figure it out and gazed at the coastline coming up. They were flying into the setting sun, making it hard to see. If they didn't locate the crew soon, it would be dark and the downed pilots would have to spend the night on the ground.

Campbell expected to see antiaircraft fire as they crossed the beach, but only silence enveloped the two aircraft as they flew westward. They were well south of the point where they had crossed inland earlier and been fired upon. Here the land was flatter, mostly rice fields and small hamlets with no significant military targets that he knew of. He hesitated for a moment, then squeezed the mike button. "Loosefoot five one, this is Blackbeard three one, over." Campbell waited for an answer, heard nothing, then tried again.

There was a long pause before the helicopter pilot answered. "Three one, this is Loosefoot five one. I'm picking up one of the pilots now. Key on my tone." The busy helo pilot transmitted, holding down his mike button while he held the 19,000-pound Sikorsky helicopter in a stable hover.

Campbell selected the UHF homer position and watched the needle swing to the left of his nose, pointing in the direction of the helicopter. "Got it. What's your situation?"

"So far no opposition—picking one up now, but haven't heard from the other pilot." The helicopter was hovering eighty feet above a large patch of jungle that grew like an island bounded by rice paddies. The brush was dense and some of the trees soared well above the top of the helicopter, making it hard to spot anyone on the ground below. The downblasts of air from the giant rotor were bending the tops of the nearby trees, breaking branches and sending them flying through the air. The pilot fixed his eyes on a large tree to hold his position while his rear crewmen operated the hydraulic rescue hoist. The third-class sonarman was slowly reeling in the steel cable attached to a "jungle penetrator," a device designed to crash through dense foliage and provide a downed pilot a ride up.

"How much longer?" Lt. Craig Prattles called over the intercom system. He gripped the cyclic stick firmly, making almost invisible movements to keep the twin-engined helicopter motionless. He was nervous, sweat dripping off his chin, and he wanted to wipe his eyebrows in the worst way. It was his first rescue mission in North Vietnam, and Prattles had elected to cross inland without fixed-wing air cover because of the urgency of the situation. Now he felt as if every soldier in North Vietnam were taking aim on the vulnerable helicopter as he hovered above the trees.

His copilot was just as nervous, rapidly shifting his eyes from the cockpit instruments to the jungle floor, scanning for any signs of enemy troops that might have been pursuing the pilot. He pressed back into the armor-plated seat for greater protection.

"He's almost in the hatch—coming up—okay—we got him," Rusty St. Clair, the hoist operator, said. Along with the second crewman he grabbed the bewildered-looking pilot by his torso harness and hauled him in through the cargo hatch. Shaking but grinning, the pilot stood up in the rear cargo bay, and St. Clair helped him to the troop seat, handing him a thermos of water. The shaken pilot eagerly grabbed the container, gulping down the cool water and spilling it down the front of his flight suit. He had been running blindly through the thick jungle, evading a group of farmers for twenty minutes, and he drank as if he had been running for hours.

"Bring the pilot up here and give him a headset," Prattles said.

St. Clair helped the stunned air force officer to his feet, pointing toward the cockpit. He handed him a spare headset and walked forward with him, plugging it into the ICS system, then returned to the rear and manned the door gun while he listened in on the radio chatter. He could hear the lead pilot of the inbound A-4s calling them on the UHF.

"Red Crown, this is three one, feet dry, over," Campbell said, continuing the descent, trimming his nose to hold 450 knots. "Loosefoot five one, this is Blackbeard three one with two seven. You read, over?" Then he called again after failing to hear from the helicopter pilot.

"Loud and clear, three one. Sorry, we were a little busy. I've got one of the pilots and looking for the second. What's your posit, over?"

"Less than five minutes."

"Roger, we're at a huge rice field that has an island with a very thick growth of trees in the middle. Call when you're overhead. No opposition so far, out." The helicopter pilot turned to the air force officer and grinned at him, keying the ICS. "Welcome aboard, which one are you, and do you know where your partner is?" Prattles rocked the nose over and pulled in a handful of collective, transitioning to forward flight. He would feel better when they were moving again.

The pilot was still breathing hard and gripped the back of the flight seat to steady himself. "I'm Capt. Jim Sullivan. I'm the radar intercept officer and I don't know where Jerry is." His face had a look of desperation and he leaned forward to see through the Plexiglas windscreen. "A bunch of rice farmers found us almost as soon as we hit the ground, and we've been running from them ever since. None of them had guns, but each seemed to have his own machete. When we fired a few shots, the little bastards would back off, then come after us again. Somehow Jerry and I managed to become separated. Thank God, the radio was working. He's still running from the farmers as far as I know. If you spot them, he'll be close." He suggested they search along the treeline, in case the pilot ran outside the small plot of forest inside the enormous rice field. Anxiously he pointed in the direction he thought his friend might be.

He scanned the terrain below, eagerly trying to identify where they had been and where the other pilot could be. Suddenly recognizing a small clearing, Sullivan pressed the ICS button of his headset. "There—that's where we got split up. I think the farmers went after him and lost me where the jungle opens up." He leaned forward, pointing toward a small dry field that opened up inside the expanse of trees. He gripped the backrest of the pilot's seat as the helicopter banked and they headed into the field. It was several hundred meters long, and about half as wide, and was covered with short, knobby grass. Tall, spindly trees staked out the edge, plainly marking the beginning of the dense jungle.

"Three one, this is Loosefoot. We're going in to investigate this open field inside the island. Can you make a pass down it before we arrive?"

Campbell listened to the helicopter pilot as he leveled the jet at 500 feet several miles to the east, letting the speed bleed down and looking at the terrain below him. All he could see were miles of rice paddies dotted with islands of jungle that he supposed would eventually be cleared and converted into more rice paddies. He signaled for Jordan to spread out, and each armed his guns. The island of trees was straight ahead, and he could see the helicopter searching along the edge. With the sun sinking fast, good daylight wouldn't last much longer.

"Have you in sight, five one. Rolling in now."

The two A-4s banked steeply, until they were lined up with the field and just above the treetops. Jordan was about 200 meters out to the side, matching Campbell's speed. They both spotted a group of men at one end of the field, a sight that quickly blurred as the two jets passed overhead and rolled into a climbing, banking turn for another pass.

"Looks like three or four men at the end of the field. Suggest you proceed with caution."

"You can count on it," Prattles assured him.

The second helicopter crewman was manning the door gun behind the copilot and looking out the side, holding binoculars on the distant figures at the end of the field. They were approaching at 100 knots, and both pilots strained their eyes trying to make out the men moving away from them.

"It's the pilot," the crewman said.

"How do you know?" Prattles asked, barely making out the figures nearing the edge of the field.

"Looks like he's wearing a flight suit and torso harness and three farmers are leading him away. They've got a rope around his neck. Don't see any guns, just machetes and some kind of spear. These guys must be pretty primitive."

"The ones chasing me had no guns, just machetes," Sullivan repeated, watching intensely as they approached.

They could see the captured pilot between two men while the third, the captor, held the rope. They were running, looking back at the approaching helicopter. The helo pilot jerked the cyclic stick back and dropped the collective handle to the bottom, causing the rotor blades to autorotate. The nose cocked up at a steeply uncomfortable angle, and Prattles began pulling in collective, loading the blades again and slowing his forward speed. The air quickly filled with grass and dust from the rotor wash as the helicopter transitioned into a hover. Prattles air-taxied to the other side of the running group, blocking their exit from the field. The loose grass, in the meantime, was making visibility difficult. Each time Prattles blocked their exit, they would start off in a different direction. Finally they stopped running, facing the hovering helicopter. Prattles gently lowered the collective and the Sikorsky settled to the ground, bouncing slightly on the tail wheel. Visibility quickly returned as debris settled, and they could now see that the North Vietnamese holding the rope had his machete raised over the American's head. For what seemed like an eternity, the two groups remained motionless, each studying the other.

St. Clair trained his door gun on the Vietnamese. They seemed pitiful to him, each wearing a tattered, sweat-stained shirt, dark pants rolled up above the knees, open-toed sandals, and the typical conical hat. He wished he had a loudspeaker system and could speak Vietnamese, but he realized it would be risky to approach. If the farmers decided to kill the pilot, he might not be able to kill all of them in time to save him.

Suddenly the group took off, jerking the pilot with them. Prattles quickly picked the helicopter up and air-taxied to the other side, again blocking their route, then settled back to the ground.

"What's going on down there?" Campbell asked, passing over the field and looking down on the helicopter below. Flying low and fast, he couldn't tell if they were moving or stopped. The two aircraft pulled up at the end of the field and banked steeply to repeat the pass.

Prattles keyed his mike. "We've got three farmers holding the pilot and it's turning into a Mexican standoff. If you can give me a strafing pass from south to north, just to the right of the helo, I think that will distract them enough for us to get the pilot. They're armed with machetes and spears—no guns."

"I can give you a low, slow pass that should get them looking when the ground starts coming apart," Campbell transmitted. "Spook, take up an orbit overhead and cover me." Campbell watched Jordan pull away, then turned for the south of the field and waited for Prattles to call him in. He would slow his aircraft to 200 knots for the pass.

Prattles twisted around to face Sullivan. "Are you up to going out there? We can't just sit here forever and wait."

"If you cover me!" Sullivan said, then pulled out his government-issue pistol and reloaded it.

"We'll cover you with the door gun. St. Clair will go with you. When you're outside, I'll signal the lead A-4 and he's going to come in and put on a strafing show off to the right. When the farmers look up, do what you have to do, but get the pilot. Picillo, you man the door gun."

St. Clair removed his pistol from its holster, then he and Sullivan cautiously stepped outside, watching the farmers standing motionless just beyond the path of the rotor blades. Each had a machete and one was holding a long spear that seemed tipped with a metal point. With Sullivan leading and their pistols pointed at the group, the two moved to the perimeter of the rotor blades and stopped, staring at their enemy a few feet away. They saw fear in the eyes of the North Vietnamese farmers.

"Okay, three one, give me a good show now," Prattles called to the approaching A-4 as he watched the two groups facing each other. He could see Sullivan motioning to them to let the pilot go.

Campbell acknowledged Prattles's call. He was less than a half mile out and descending at a shallow angle and holding 200 knots. He intended to keep his guns firing just to the right of the helicopter and stir up a lot of dust, giving them a better chance of retrieving the air force pilot. At 500 yards he opened up, firing in bursts as he descended. At that speed, he would be abeam in four to five seconds. He watched the cloud of dust rising from the ground, then watched the group standing in front of the helo, barely distinguishable from each other and mostly a blur to him. He thought he could make out one without a hat as he got closer.

The first shells struck the ground about eighty meters away, causing everyone to look up. Two of the farmers immediately went to their knees and raised their hands above their heads, letting their weapons drop to the ground beside them. The third farmer was mouthing something in Vietnamese, but was drowned out by the noise of the plane. He still held the end of a rope tied around the neck of the pilot, who stood motionless and wide-eyed. He saw that the two Americans were looking away. If they had been looking at him, they would have seen his eyes widen and the veins in his arms suddenly bulge as he brought the blade of his machete down, sinking it into the back of the pilot's neck, severing the head from its torso.

Campbell quit firing at 100 yards out and rammed the throttle forward. In an instant he swept past, rapidly accelerating. The scene had been a chaotic blur as he passed, but from the screaming he had heard on Prattles's radio, he sensed that something awful had happened down there. He banked the A-4 hard and began to climb.

Prattles blinked his eyes hard, his stomach suddenly in his throat as the reality of what had happened hit him. Prattles and his copilot were speechless as they watched the pilot slump to the ground, landing on his knees and then falling over, his arms twitching, blood gushing onto the grass. As the severed head lay at the feet of Sullivan, St. Clair just stood there, confused, unable to believe what was happening. He was looking down at the corpse lying on the ground, a large pool of blood gathering near its neck. The third-class sonarman had a dazed look on his face and his drawn pistol was pointed at no one. Suddenly, Sullivan began unloading his .38 into the two farmers, pulling the trigger several times even after the gun was empty. He grabbed St. Clair by his arm and jerked him to the ground, snapping him out of his daze.

"Picillo, get him. Picillo, fire, damn it!" Prattles screamed at the door gunner.

Picillo fired the 7.62-millimeter machine gun mounted in the doorframe, but the farmer had already moved past its firing line. With wild eyes, the North Vietnamese charged the helicopter with the spear he had retrieved. His arm extended back with the spear high overhead, and he ran screaming forward.

The copilot shielded his eyes and bent down as the iron-tipped spear ripped through the Plexiglas windscreen, embedding itself in the bulkhead behind the copilot's head, missing him by inches. The door gunner was still firing, but the swivel mount prevented the gun from tracking far enough right. The farmer ran around the helicopter out of sight.

"What's going on down there?" Campbell asked over the UHF.

Prattles disregarded the call and screamed at Picillo, *"He's coming around the side. Get him!"*

Picillo still held the door gun and Prattles drew his pistol. The door gunner turned just in time to see the crazed farmer leap up into the open cargo hatch at the side of the helicopter in the rear. He saw him grab the machine gun mounted at the cargo door and swivel it around, aiming it at them, but then he heard the sound of a gun going off beside him, followed by several more reports. He opened his eyes in time to see the farmer falling out the cargo hatch, clutching his chest.

"Let's get the fuck out of here, Picillo! Get out there and help them with the pilot." Prattles set his gun down on top of the Doppler screen, watching the crewman jump down from the helicopter and run to Sullivan. Prattles waited impatiently as the three struggled to load the dead pilot into the cargo hatch. As soon as the door was secured, he picked up into a hover and rocked the Sikorsky over on its nose, transitioning to forward flight.

Jordan had rejoined Campbell and the two A-4s were crisscrossing above the helicopter. "Is the guy down there dead?" Campbell asked over the radio, thinking back to the hazy but violent scene he'd barely witnessed.

After a moment's silence, Prattles finally answered, "Yeah, the fucking farmer put a machete into his neck. Now let's get the hell out of this place."

The flight lapsed into complete silence as Campbell and Jordan flew above the helicopter until it was safely over the water and heading for the *Bennington*. Then they turned away and headed for their own carrier, the *Barbary Coast*.

Two weeks later...

With a measure of defiance, the World War II vintage aircraft carrier steamed north, inching closer to the North Vietnamese shoreline as she ghosted along through the smoky black water of the Gulf of Tonkin. The immense ship was veiled in darkness, illuminated ever so faintly by the impending dawn creeping in from the east. Only the blinking of the signalman's light revealed her presence as a third-class petty officer communicated silently with the destroyer escorts a thousand meters off her beam.

The carrier's position was not unknown. She was constantly watched by the Chinese radars on Hainan Island at the north end of the gulf and the ever-present Russian trawlers that dogged the fleet day and night, gathering intelligence and reporting to Hanoi.

The quarter moon hung just above the horizon, barely visible and preferring to hide behind the remnants of the weak front that enveloped the area surrounding the South China Sea. A few stars shone down upon the *Barbary Coast* through the breaks in the clouds as she made her way into the waters known as Yankee Station, a fixed spot off the coast of North Vietnam.

A feeling of peace shrouded the carrier as she slipped lazily through the water as dawn approached. In a few short hours, she would turn into the wind and launch her aircraft against a target approved by members of the White House planning staff, who would soon be sitting down to dinner in Washington, D.C.

On the darkened bridge, the commander of the *Barbary Coast*, Capt. William Pearson, sat languid in his command chair, bathed in the soft-red glow of the night lighting. He wore his hat tilted slightly back, yet still covering the long scar just below his curly black hair. The gold braid on the bill was showing the first signs of the effects of the tropical climate. One leg was propped up, his arm was on the armrest, and he held his second cup of coffee, occasionally taking a sip and surveying everything around him.

A Filipino steward had awakened him earlier, ending nearly two hours of sleep, his longest period of uninterrupted rest in the last several days. He preferred catnapping throughout the night and hesitated to be away from the bridge for long periods of time. Satisfied that everything was running smoothly under his officer of the deck, he relaxed in his chair, savoring the calm. His thoughts slipped to times past, times of another place and another war. Times when the *Barbary Coast* was newly commissioned and he was a green ensign fresh from the training command wearing the wings of a young naval aviator. He had been proud to serve aboard the last carrier to see combat in World War

II, and in these early morning hours the events were still fresh in his mind. Even as they steamed northward into the war zone, the wind whistling through the superstructure sometimes made him wonder if the ghosts of the Japanese still dwelled there. The spirits of the pilots who found them that night, crashed into the deck and spread fire and death everywhere. The memories were still vivid and real, but he shared them with no one. Pearson blinked, wiping away the vision, his mind returning to the present.

He knew the Russians, the Chinese, even the North Vietnamese, knew where the carrier was, but still he insisted on a darkened ship at night. Russian and Chinese submarines were suspected to be in the area, but only to observe and remain undetected. He thought the other carriers sometimes looked like cruise ships operating in the Caribbean.

"Captain, Captain Pearson," the officer of the deck called again.

Pearson blinked again, then faced the radar scope, stepping down and walking over to it. "What do you have?" he said, bending over the scope, staring down into the glowing screen. He watched the sweep line hurry around the circle, illuminating ships and fishing vessels alike. The subdued glow of the radar screen bathed his face, intensifying the wrinkles of his leathery skin and causing his bushy black eyebrows to appear even more prominent. Each member standing watch seemed wrapped in an unnatural tinge, their features distorted or amplified, adding to the eeriness created by the special night lighting on the bridge.

"Thought you might want to take a look at the trawler. Looks like she's breaking off and following us." The lieutenant took a grease pencil and circled the dot on the screen.

"What does Combat say?"

"Same thing, sir."

"They're just jockeying for a better position when we launch." Pearson went back to his command chair and the bridge became silent again. Only the low volume of some ship-to-ship radio chatter broke the stillness. Pearson stared through the misted side windows at the destroyer off the starboard quarter. He watched a white light blink on and off as the signalman on the destroyer talked to them silently. Pearson studied the blinking light for a moment, then looked away and resumed sipping his coffee, deciding the message was only routine. He turned and leaned closer to the side window, looking down at the flight deck. He watched the men below preparing for the upcoming launch.

Below the bridge and behind the island superstructure, an SH-3A Sikorsky helicopter was parked next to the edge of the flight deck, its tail pylon hanging over the rim and its enormous rotor blades folded aft. Later that morning it would be pulled out on the flight deck and launched, fulfilling its role as the plane guard or "angel" while the fixed-wing aircraft launched.

Some of the attack jets slated for the morning launch had their fuselages opened and were undergoing last-minute maintenance. The Douglas A-4 attack jet, the smallest jet in the navy, was originally designed as a one-shot delivery system for nuclear bombs. Known as Skyhawk, scooter, or, in engineering circles, Hinnenman's hot rod after its designer, it was the workhorse of the fleet. Clusters of long green shapes hung from wings that seemed no larger than a Piper Cub's. Underneath the wing, red-shirted ordnancemen inserted fuses into each bomb, installing safety wires to prevent them from arming until released during the bombing run. They worked feverishly to finish their task before going below for breakfast, now being served.

Several decks below in the enlisted mess, the oncoming watch was up. Sailors moved slowly through the line, sleepily eyeing a large selection of foods as vapor curled upward from the steam tables. Carrying overloaded trays, the sailors moved to tables set with pitchers of cold milk made from powder, which only added to their increasing desire for fresh milk. The dining space was rapidly filling up as sailors going off watch entered to grab a quick breakfast before getting some sleep.

The *Barbary Coast* had been at sea for a month since its last port visit and nearly two months since leaving Hawaii. She had joined the *Bon Homme Richard* on station, and another carrier, the *Coral Sea*, was due shortly, making a total of three attack carriers plus the USS *Bennington*, an antisubmarine warfare—or ASW—carrier hosting a stable of helicopters and fixed-wing aircraft.

Weather throughout the Gulf and overland had been bad, preventing the desired all-out air strikes wanted by the task force commander. Because of the weather, few aircraft had been lost—and none from the air wing of the *Barbary Coast*—only three to hostile fire and two more to accidents. But the dry season was coming and with the anticipated breakup of the weather, a full strike was planned to interdict supplies being moved south out of Haiphong and Hanoi.

The hangar deck was jammed with aircraft and Lt. Jim Campbell picked his way across, ducking around parked aircraft until he reached the starboard elevator. The naval aviator eased his lanky frame in and out of the shadows until he reached his favorite spot forward of the elevator and facing the sea. It was vacant, and he stopped opposite an oversize cleat and looked out over the water, his short, light-brown hair ruffling in the breeze.

He was wearing his green Nomex flight suit and scuffed steel-toed boots, and his survival vest hung down, unfastened and sagging under the weight of his service .38 pistol. The suit was unzipped to the waist and his dog tags hung outside his T-shirt, revealing the onset of a greenish mold from accumulated sweat. At twenty-five Campbell seemed young to be fighting this kind of war, his face now narrow and exposing high cheekbones from the weight he had lost on the cruise. The hot, balmy weather had curbed his appetite, and only early in the morning before the sun was up did he feel like eating. He was twelve pounds below his normal 178 pounds.

He sipped from the cup of coffee he'd brought with him from the aircrew flight mess, then moved over to the oversize cleat next to the railing. Campbell propped his leg up on an aircraft chock and looked out across the sea. It was black with no sign of whitecaps, almost as flat as San Diego Bay. He could make out the destroyer riding off the beam, backlighted by a warm glow forming on the horizon. At first he saw only the tip, then more of the sun appeared as it rose from the water, molten and glowing, growing larger with each degree of ascension. A wisp of gray cloud, long and slender, sliced it into two separate halves of a sphere. He never tired of the sight of the rising sun, no matter what part of the world he found himself in. As he watched, he wondered if his wife was up, looking out from her hotel window, watching the same sun rise over the steep roofs of the Buddhist temples in Bangkok. Campbell carefully folded her latest letter, slipping it into his left breast pocket. He crumpled up the paper coffee cup and stuffed it into a pocket below his knee, then headed toward the squadron ready room.

After working his way up through the myriad assortment of passageways, he entered the ready room of Attack Squadron 47, the home of the "legendary bombing bastards from hell," as they liked to call themselves. He was early and could only make out the duty officer and the air intelligence briefing officer in the dim light. Campbell reached for his flight gear, checking to make sure it was still hanging from its hook, then proceeded to the front of the room.

The small ready room was crammed with seats not unlike those found in pocket-size movie theaters. Olive-green G suits hung from hooks lining the gray walls on both sides, dangling limp and lifeless, waiting for their owners. Torso harnesses and flight bags also hung there, completing the ensemble for combat. The room was lit by the single lamp on the desk of the squadron duty officer and a light modeling the large map of North Vietnam. A tall, thin officer wearing glasses that seemed as thick as Coke bottles stood close to the map, marking red and black crosses on the Plexiglas covering, updating the enemy defenses prior to the briefing. The aroma of freshly brewed coffee permeated the space, spreading from the large coffee urn beneath a rack of coffee mugs emblazoned with the squadron emblem.

"Hey, Soupy."

Campbell turned around, looking for the speaker, his eyes still adjusting to the dimness.

"Back here—in the corner. Jesus, it ain't that dark in here."

Campbell looked but saw only empty seats. Suspecting it was Pete Gonzales, he walked to the back row of seats and looked down at the figure lying in a sleeping bag. Gonzales looked up, grinning.

The Mexican American from Edna, Texas, sat up, his face contorted by an exaggerated yawn as he stretched his arms, then leaned back against the bulkhead and lit up a cigarette. He extended the pack to Campbell, then retracted it as he remembered Campbell didn't smoke. Chubby-jowled, he wore a huge black mustache whose tips extended almost beyond his cheeks, his squadron mates having given him the name Pancho as soon as he started growing it. Pancho was the shortest pilot on the ship, barely five foot seven, and ideal for the minuscule jet aircraft they flew. He liked to brag that he had room to spare in the cockpit of the A-4, chiding the larger pilots, who felt the tiny cockpit was a snug fit at best. Gonzales was forever complaining about the hot and muggy weather, and he could usually be found sleeping in the rear of the air-conditioned ready room.

"Morning, Pancho." Campbell strained his eyes to see into the darkened corner. "You in on this one?"

Gonzales pulled his knees up to his chest, then eased into one of the seats, still clad only in his underwear. He rubbed his eyes, then reached for a flight suit draped over the back of a seat. "Not me, man, I'm free and clear—just trying to get some rest before we hit Bangkok. Then it's four whole days of women and booze and no sleep." He stepped into the flight suit, his cigarette dangling from the corner of his mouth. "You going to meet your wife there?"

"Yeah," Jim said. "Karen, Patricia, and some other wives are supposed to be there."

"That's great. Hey, aren't you due to quit being Jordan's wingman and get your own?"

"You guessed right, señor. The skipper promised me one fresh out of the training command. The personnel officer tells me he'll be flying out to the ship ferrying in a replacement aircraft in the next few days. He'll probably meet us on the way into Bangkok. Anyhow, I've got to go. Try to be up by noon."

Gonzales folded his hands behind his back, watching Campbell turn and walk toward the front of the room. "You're one lucky son of a bitch, man—a honeymoon in every port. Good luck on this one," he added.

At the other end of the room, a young airman apprentice was putting on a set of earphones as a link between the flight deck and the duty officer in anticipation of upcoming flight operations. New to the service, he looked disgruntled at having to get up so early and sat there with his eyes closed. Directly in front of him, the squadron duty officer sat slumped at his desk, drinking a fresh cup of coffee, having been up for several hours.

At the front of the room a large map of North Vietnam was mounted on the bulkhead. A plastic overlay with black and red grid marks was tacked over it, locating antiaircraft gun emplacements and surface-to-air missile sites according to the latest intelligence. It was there for the pilots to look at and they always did, each time noting the additional red and black marks as the Russians and Chinese moved in more weapons. They would look at the map, then shake their heads in frustration. The Vietnamese were constantly moving their weapons around to keep the Americans guessing. One thing was known—no matter how many installations were destroyed, somehow there would always be two in their place every time they went back to a target.

Standing off to one side, the briefing officer, Stan Podowski, pored over his briefing materials. Campbell greeted the young lieutenant junior grade, who had close-cropped black hair with shades of gray peppering the sides. Nearsighted, he wore thick glasses, which only added to his gawky appearance. Campbell felt Podowski's eyesight was probably bad enough to get him discharged medically, but the skipper liked him and he was the best briefing officer on the ship. Stan had been assigned to the squadron after finishing the air intelligence course at Alameda NAS in San Francisco and had less than three years of service. A loner, he spent little time in the bars with his squadron mates. Most of the squadron members knew him as "Professor," and he readily answered to it.

Campbell stopped in front of the map, staring at the numerous red marks and shaking his head. "Well, Professor, is it Canh Tra?"

Stan tilted his head down, peering over his thick glasses, and nodded his head. "I'm afraid so. The admiral wants to make an impression with the buggers before we go off-line."

Campbell turned away from the map and looked to make sure no one else had entered the room. "If the old fart wanted to make an impression, we should be bombing the stuff before they even unload it." He moved in closer to Podowski. "We even let them assemble it and ship it out before we can go after it. Now, does that make any sense?" Campbell didn't expect an answer from Stan, but he couldn't help venting his frustrations. The rules of engagement, set down by a group of civilians in Washington, irritated him and most of his squadron mates as they constantly risked their lives trying to comply with them.

Stan only shrugged and went back to his clipboard full of papers.

Campbell turned away and dropped into a front-row seat. He pulled out the letter from his wife and began reading it again.

Dearest darling,

It seems like only yesterday we were lying on the beach together at Waikiki, adrift from the war and the world and all its problems. When your carrier pulled out of sight and I realized you were really gone, it hit me so hard that my eyes misted over every time I thought of you. It took me days before I could go down to the beach again. Now it's only a few days before I'll be able to see you, to touch you again. It seems like a thousand years since we were together. It will be a honeymoon all over again for us.

Patricia Jordan and I have been sharing a room together here at the Ambassador Hotel in Bangkok. She is as excited as I am about you two guys coming here. Don't worry, we've got a second room reserved and we'll be alone. Some of the other wives have begun to show up, and to keep busy a bunch of us have been touring

the sights. Seems like it's all temples and Buddhist monks.
And it is so hot here. I know you must be used to it by
now, but I don't think I ever will.

Rumor has it that the *Barbary Coast* will have to
anchor out and row you guys in. I'll be waiting for you,
but if I miss you, look for me in the Thai Room at the
Ambassador. In case you've forgotten what I look like,
I'll be the horniest-looking girl at the bar.

> Please be careful.
> My love,
>
> Karen

Campbell carefully folded the letter, tucking it into the
breast pocket of his flight suit. He slouched down in his
seat, closed his eyes, and let images of his wife dance in
front of him, tantalizing him with her presence. The de-
mands of his squadron had often blurred the image, pushing
it back, only to be recalled during lulls in the bombing
missions they made against the North. Now the image
sharpened itself again, cropping up more frequently.

"Hey, sport, are we going to get 'em today?"

Campbell opened his eyes and Karen disappeared. Standing in her place was Lt. Larry Jordan, his roommate and
section leader. Jordan piled into the next seat, throwing his
helmet bag down beside him. The two attack pilots had been
friends for years, their friendship going back to their college
days at San Diego State, where Jordan had been a year
ahead of Campbell. They had met at a party when Jordan
had been attracted to Campbell's blind date. Jordan was
daring where Campbell was more laid-back, and for some
reason they had hit it off and become close friends. Jordan
had been the wild one, a magnet for girls, and he drove a

yellow 1955 Chevrolet convertible that he and Campbell frequently double-dated in. Jordan's dad owned a small plane he kept at Brown Field in San Diego, and they would often go for flights around the area with Jordan instructing Campbell. It took nearly a year before Jordan thought Campbell could safely solo. Campbell's flying ended when Jordan graduated and signed up for the naval flight program and moved to Pensacola that summer.

Jordan was sometimes called Spook, a name he'd picked up at a squadron party some years back. He was at least two inches shorter than Campbell and seemed to maintain his stocky build throughout the cruise, never losing weight as nearly everyone else did. He had dark, close-cropped hair and coal-black eyes that flashed and lay back in a head that seemed almost too small for his thick, muscular neck. His military bearing was everything that Campbell's wasn't, and even when he slumped, Jordan's posture seemed correct. Though he didn't look intelligent, he was, with a mischievous personality to match.

Jordan moved closer to Campbell and said in a lowered voice, "Man, you should read this letter I got from Patricia." He dangled a folded piece of paper in front of Campbell, then jerked the letter back as Campbell reached for it. "No, maybe you'd better not."

"Come on, Spook, what could she possibly say about your private life that the whole ship doesn't already know?"

Jordan dangled the letter out again. "It's not what she says about us," he said, pausing for a moment. "It's what your wife has been telling her about you two."

Campbell lunged for the letter but missed as Jordan expertly snapped it back just out of his reach.

"I'll let you read it when we get back. If I let you read it now, you'd just get hornier than you probably already are, and that would mess up your concentration on dropping a bridge span today." Jordan held the letter beneath his nose, inhaling what little remained of the fragrance Patricia had sprayed on it, still grinning at Campbell.

"Who's horny? When we get to the hotel in Bangkok, I'm going to hang three do-not-disturb signs on the doorknob and come out three days later."

"Yeah, yeah—after ten minutes you'll probably be ready to go check out all the libraries in town." Jordan put his hands behind his head and leaned back, his mind drifting to thoughts of his wife, waiting in Bangkok with Karen.

It had been a last-minute thing, a spur-of-the-moment idea after drinks one evening several months before the deployment began. Patricia had mentioned that several of the wives were planning to take out huge loans to finance their plan to meet their husbands in port. Both Campbell and Jordan tried to convince their wives that it wasn't a good idea and that the navy frowned on it, but their arguments did little to dissuade them. They felt they had been separated from their husbands for too long. And as the air war intensified, many of those husbands never came back.

"Attention on deck!"

Campbell and Jordan jerked upright, opening their eyes as they were jolted from memories to reality. They stood at attention as Comdr. Ben Lorimar, the skipper of their squadron, charged into the room leading several officers. The squadron duty officer held the door open as Captain Briggs, the admiral's chief of staff, walked in, followed by Admiral Laceur. Everyone in the room seemed a little surprised by this unexpected visit by the admiral. Laceur and his staff officer took seats next to Campbell and Jordan.

Commander Lorimar was suffering from blocked sinuses and was unable to fly. He wanted to make sure that this last mission before R and R went smoothly. He was short, as were many A-4 pilots, and his once-thick mop of hair had receded to the top of his head. Lorimar was considered an able leader by the officers and men of his command. Craters of sweat stained his underarms, and he wished he could have changed shirts before the flag officer appeared. Lorimar stepped up to the podium at the front of the room, asking everyone to be seated, then announced that the admiral would like to say a few words on today's mission at the conclusion of the briefing.

"Lieutenant Podowski, begin the briefing." Lorimar stepped back from the podium, found a seat, and the air intelligence briefing officer stepped up.

Looking as if he would be more comfortable teaching classes in a medium-sized high school, he laid a stack of folders on the podium, then took out a collapsible briefing pointer and pulled on the end, extending it to its three-foot length. He stepped over to the large map behind him. "Admiral, Commander Lorimar, gentlemen." He nodded to the seniors in the room as he acknowledged them. "As you probably know, today's target is the much-bombed bridge at Canh Tra. The mission will consist of a four-plane flight of A-4s from the *Barbary Coast* and another four-plane flight from *Bon Homme Richard*. MiG Cap will be provided by VF-164 giving you F-8 coverage in case their fighters want to come up and play. For some reason they have been holding their fighters on the ground and using only their SAMs and triple A on us."

"How come we're going in without the fighters?" asked the flight leader, a pilot who seemed too old to be flying jet aircraft, his face too red from booze and sun. Known as Smokin' Joe because of his differing point of view on nearly everything and his adamant arguments, the slightly overweight pilot minced few words with anyone. To some he was considered opinionated to the point of rudeness. To others he was a man who spoke his mind when he felt he was right. He was also considered the best flight leader in the squadron in spite of his forty-three years.

Admiral Laceur turned around, staring at Porter for a moment, then smiled at him. "You aren't going to be bare. The fighters will be just offshore, just out of SAM range waiting for the first opportunity to get in fast and take out any fighters that show up. Maybe if we're lucky, it will tempt the little bastards to launch and then we can rip them up. Just like in the old days, right, Porter?" Laceur looked at Porter for a moment, then turned around.

Lieutenant Commander Porter leaned forward in his seat again. "What happens if they launch their MiGs at us and we're inbound to the target? Can we expect the F-8s to appear instantly? And why aren't the F-8s going in with us for flak suppression?" Porter's craggy face became redder by the minute. He had flown fighters against Chinese MiGs in the Korean War, and Laceur had been his flight leader during the landings at Inchon. Porter didn't think much of Laceur then and even less now. He completely tuned Laceur out, choosing instead to think back to the last flight in Korea when he was flying wing on Laceur and they were jumped by a flight of MiGs. They had become separated, and he still felt Laceur had abandoned the fight, fleeing to safety out over the ocean, leaving Porter to get shot up. He could never prove it, but he never liked Laceur after that.

Podowski stood silent for a moment, unsure of why Porter kept butting in, then continued, "An airborne tanker will remain offshore along with the E-1 for anybody with fuel shortages. Red Crown will control you to the beach and give you the green flag to cross. You have the frequencies and bomb loads on your briefing cards, the same as last time. Expect to join up with Gator flight en route to Red Crown. It's been over two weeks since we hit the bridge, and gun emplacements and the weather have prevented any decent pictures. We don't know what they've put in there. However, word is that the Russians have been shipping in a hell of a lot of stuff lately, and it's going south across that bridge and about four others.''

Podowski paused for a moment and watched their reaction. Sometimes he could sense the frustrations radiating from the pilots, who had to fly the missions under restrictive rules of warfare. He adjusted his glasses and stepped up to the map, placing the tip of the pointer over an X marked over a small inlet, the initial point. ''This is your first IP. You will form up in bombing formation and proceed inbound along this small river until you reach the bend. Then swing north and proceed inbound until you reach your target. You have the first flight, followed by Gator flight from the *Bonnie Dick*. We expect the weather to be breaking up by the time you are over the target. Their radar-controlled guns are well established above and below the bridge, as you already know. Does anybody have any questions?''

There were none and Podowski stepped back from the map, closing up his pointer.

Admiral Laceur stepped up to the podium. His gray hair was parted down the middle, and he looked as if he could be a senior executive at General Motors. Placing one hand on the podium edge, he began, ''Gentlemen, this is the last mission you will fly before we go off-line for Bangkok. Up to now the weather has slowed down operations and we haven't been able to hit them like I would like to. We are approaching a period when weather should be in our favor, and you can expect a proportionate increase in sorties flown.'' He paused then continued, ''When we joined the *Bonnie Dick*, I was briefed on some of the problems they encountered operating in the north. One of those problems is that everyone—that is, the fighter community—is relying entirely too much on air-to-air missiles. Several of their pilots got into an engagement with a couple of MiGs, and a total of eleven missiles were fired with one MiG being hit. One of the F-4s was shot up so badly by 23 millimeter that he had to eject over the sea. The Vietnamese must have had a good laugh over that one. We think the MiGs were probably piloted by non-Vietnamese pilots except for this particular one who keeps showing up every time there is a major confrontation. Every war seems to produce one pilot on the opposite side that's heads above the rest, and this war is no exception. If we send the F-8s in with you, the North Vietnamese are not going to risk any of their shiny new Russian MiGs, and besides, the Crusader boys won't be able to spot AAA fire through the cloud cover.'' Laceur paused again. ''Anyway, I didn't come down here to lecture you, only to wish you good luck.'' He stepped down and headed for the door, followed by Captain Briggs.

Commander Lorimar called the room to attention as they left: ''Attention on deck!''

Lieutenant Commander Porter jerked upright, then made a halfhearted effort to stand at attention. Lorimar added a few things then wished them good luck.

Before the pilots left the ready room, each one deposited personal photos and letters into a special box maintained by the squadron duty officer. They would retrieve them upon return. Campbell deposited his letter from Karen, but Jordan stuck his back into his pocket.

On the flight deck, the plane captains patiently waited for their pilots, checking and rechecking the aircraft for any problems. Linemen scurried about, rolling start carts into position. Ordnancemen stood by if needed to assist with the weapons loads slung underneath the aircraft.

Several decks below, the catapult officer was going through launch procedures with his assistants, ensuring that the steam pressure was sufficient to send the heavily loaded aircraft off the end of the deck at the right speed. Even farther down in the ship, where temperatures sometimes reached 140°, the engine gang was superheating steam, bringing pressure up to the maximum to give the launch officer all the pressure he needed.

On the landing signal officer platform, Lieutenant Corbousier checked out the arresting gear, then the Fresnel-lens mirror the pilots would use to get back aboard. After their launch, the COD—carrier on-board delivery—flight bringing in a load of mail and passengers from Da Nang would land.

Campbell stepped out into the bright sunlight beaming down through partially clouded skies, locating his aircraft at the end of the pack. His would be the last aircraft launched, and he would be tail-end Charlie as number-four man in the flight. Campbell spotted his aircraft captain standing by his aircraft, waiting for him.

A tall black youngster from Philadelphia stood watching Campbell approaching from across the flight deck. With his smile revealing perfect white teeth, Cecil Washington patiently waited until the pilot neared, then saluted him. "Good morning, sir," he said, emphasizing the *sir* and bringing his hand down, taking Campbell's helmet bag from him.

"How's the bird look?" Campbell asked.

"Fine, sir. I had maintenance add a little air to that starboard tire though. You been driving off the main roads lately?"

Campbell continued his walk around the aircraft, pushing and pulling, shaking some items for security, ensuring that ordnance had placed the wires into the fuses so they would be armed upon release. He could find nothing wrong and quickly climbed up the boarding ladder of the A-4, followed by Washington.

The plane captain positioned the harness straps over Campbell's shoulders, then plugged in his oxygen mask. Next he pulled the ejection seat safety pin from behind the aviator's head and handed it to him, along with the red-flagged gear safety pins.

Campbell placed them in a side pocket and shook Washington's hand as the airman started down the ladder. Now ready, he sat there patiently with both hands resting on the canopy rails watching the activity around him. Moments later, the start-engines signal was given and all four aircraft simultaneously commenced their start sequence.

From the bridge above the flight deck, Captain Pearson gave the order to bring the ship into the wind and increase speed. The helicopter was airborne and flying in circles off the starboard beam, awaiting the launch. Pearson watched Lieutenant Commander Porter following the lineman's direction as the aircraft moved up to the number one catapult where several youngsters with goggles and earmuffs ran out to hook up a steel bridle. A blast deflector immediately raised behind the small jet, designed to protect other aircraft and personnel during launch. Smokin' Joe Porter looked over to his left at his wingman in position on the port cat. He could see him giving him a thumbs-up and he returned the signal. Making one last adjustment to his shoulder straps and squirming into the seat, he looked up at the island superstructure. He could see a signalman running up the launch flag, followed by the Jolly Roger. His stomach tightened. He was at war again.

Lieutenant Campbell was slightly aft of Porter as he waited for him to launch. He could sense Porter's engine was at full power by the vibration working its way up through the airframe. He watched as the A-4 hunkered down slightly as the bridle pulled it down the track. Instantly it was over the end of the deck, and Porter was rotating the aircraft's nose upward, clawing at the humid air. A moment later the other aircraft shot forward. Campbell followed the linemen's signals as he taxied into position. He could see Jordan already in position and two men underneath his aircraft struggling to attach the bridle. Campbell braked to a stop and waited, turning the air-conditioning to full although he knew it would do little good until the engine was running at a higher speed. Knots began to form in his stomach as he prepared himself for the launch, going over the checklist, adjusting and readjusting his straps. In his mind he went over the steps he would take if the catapult failed and he couldn't stop or hadn't enough airspeed to take off. Though he didn't like to think about it, he always made himself do it.

The radio crackled, jarring him back to the launch.

"Blackbeard three one, this is Blackbeard two seven. You ready, Soupy?" Jordan called.

Campbell pressed the mike button on the throttle and acknowledged. He could hear Jordan's engine spinning up and was soon doing the same as he followed the signals of the launch officer. His stomach tightened even more.

The two aircraft strained against the steel bridles holding them back as their engines ran at full power. A moment later Jordan was launched and struggling for altitude with the heavy bomb load. Campbell saluted the launch officer and braced for the jolt. The launch officer pressed a button and tons of superheated steam sent a large piston screaming down its tunnel, dragging behind it the cables that tensioned, instantly jamming Campbell into the backrest of his aircraft as he accelerated forward. He was flying.

★ 2 ★

Black, oily smoke belched from the Russian Likhachev as the Vietnamese driver downshifted through the heavy transmission. The truck driver was nervous. He was late, out on the open road in daylight and a prime target if an American jet caught him with his load of replacement surface-to-air missiles. He gunned the diesel again, jamming the gearshift and double-clutching as he reached the turnoff in the road. In his rearview mirror he could see someone on a motor scooter trying to pass him, then deciding against it. The driver straddled the middle of the road with his wide load, seizing the space essential to execute the sharp turn. Let him wait. I have been driving all night and am late, he thought to himself.

The Czech-built motor scooter weaved back and forth

behind the big two-and-one-half-ton truck as its driver slowed, then braked to a stop. The North Vietnamese officer put both feet on the ground, balancing the scooter and eyeing the load in front of him.

The truck's tall exhaust stack was still spewing enormous clouds of dense black smoke into the air, covering everything around it. Large branches covered with tropical leaves protruded from the netting covering the rig from front to back, meant to camouflage it when parked in the forest, but now making it a conspicuous prey for the probing eyes of American bomber pilots. This make of truck, manufactured by the Likhachev factory in Moscow, was a common sight on the busy roads around Hanoi.

Sticking out from beneath the layers of tropical foliage were tail fins of a surface-to-air missile, a Russian-built SA-2 Guideline destined for a SAM site somewhere in the woods. The missiles were assembled in a factory in downtown Hanoi, put together from the pieces shipped in by Bulgarian freighters docked at the port of Haiphong. Once assembled, the missiles were loaded on large trucks and quickly dispersed throughout the country to replace ones already fired at American bombers. The trucks moved at night, in convoys or alone, starting their runs soon after dark, their drivers experiencing the worst driving conditions imaginable. Running with darkened lights, the North Vietnamese drivers faced greater risks from accidents than bombings.

As he waited for the truck to move, Maj. Quac To Quang twisted the throttle grip of his scooter, revving the one-cylinder engine to a throaty pitch and preventing it from coughing to a stop on the low-octane Russian gasoline. He paused and lifted his hat above his head, then ran his hand across his black hair, smoothing it down. He could hear the driver shifting gears as the truck disappeared into the forest. He waited a moment, then pulled his hat down on his head and gunned the motor scooter. The bike wobbled as he pushed off with both feet, then quickly gained speed. The road ahead was clear and he steered down the middle, avoiding piles of fallout debris scattered over the thinly asphalted highway. In the last two weeks he had patched the front tire several times after driving over the shrapnel of exploded missiles and pieces of spent shells fallen back to earth. He passed several men pushing bicycles with baskets attached to the sides, loaded with six-hundred-pound cargos. They strained to handle the heavy loads over a freshly repaired section of recently bombed highway. Workers wearing tropical pith helmets were finishing the repairs, smoothing over a layer of clay soil in the recent crater. Piles of clay and gravel were cached along the roads all over Vietnam for future repair work.

Quang eased around the workers and drove a short distance before slowing to turn onto the street than ran past his house. Someone had tacked up new posters on the fence at the intersection showing directions to the latest air raid shelters. The city was becoming one big catacomb of public bomb shelters. Along his street, one-man shelters were randomly spaced, allowing anyone caught in the open to dive into the sunken concrete tubes.

It was too early for the few children who lived in his neighborhood to be out and on their way to school. He missed seeing the mobs of children who once gathered in large groups noisily walking to the school, talking and laughing. Many of the children had been taken to the country by parents anxious over the increasing bombing. Every month the bombers edged closer into Hanoi itself as the American president tightened his invisible ring around the city. Some areas were off limits to all bombing; others had limited restrictions. Even the parks that dotted Hanoi were empty, the voices of the children and their protective grandparents long absent.

Large shade trees, heavy with foliage, lined the sides of his street. The trees were planted long ago by Vietnamese working under the French. Quang lived in an older section of Hanoi on the northeast side, a residential area far from any factories. A few of the houses on his street had low plaster fences, painted white and showing signs of age. Most of the houses had been built during the French occupation and were now occupied by Vietnamese families. The houses were roofed with cement tiles that showed signs of chipping from the falling metal that rained down after the antiaircraft crews expended their rounds. The one thing Quang feared most was that something would come crashing down through the roof on his family. He felt he was too far away from any military target to worry about bombings, although his house was not far from a road that suffered occasional damage.

Quang closed the throttle and pulled to a stop in front of his house, killing the engine. He got down and pushed the motor scooter inside the fence, then paused for a moment, straightened his hat, and walked to the front door. Quang watched the door open as he reached the first step and waited as his wife stepped through the doorframe, throwing her arms around him.

"I could hear your motor scooter as you turned down the road." She took his hat and kissed him on the cheek. "I hope you are hungry. Mother has gone to much trouble to obtain your favorites."

"I am hungry enough to eat even your mother's cooking." Before his wife could say anything, the Vietnamese pilot put his arm around his wife's tiny waist and guided her through the doorframe. She turned and grinned at him, then grabbed his hand, pulling him forward. Her fetching smile revealed almost perfect teeth.

Major Quang felt himself lucky to have married Kwan Chi. Even after the birth of their two children—a boy and a girl—she still had the same lithesome figure she'd always had, a slim waist and small, firm breasts. Her husband especially liked her long black hair, which he would stroke at night when they were alone in bed and she was curled up in his arms. Those times were becoming rarer as the war intensified.

Kwan Chi backed against the doorframe as her husband walked into the kitchen and spotted his four-year-old son. As usual Le Doc was struggling, resisting the efforts of his grandmother to prepare him for school. The major watched, amused, as his wife's mother held the wriggling tyke by the ear and drew a washcloth down over his eyes. "He is just like I was as a boy," observed the proud father. "Resists any authority."

Quang went to the rear door and looked into the backyard where he knew his daughter would be with her grandfather. He shouted to her, watching her break away and run to him. He nodded to the old man, then grabbed his daughter as she jumped into his arms and hugged him around his neck.

Quang held Mai Ling for a moment then put her down and placed his military hat on her head and spun her around, pushing her into her grandfather at the door. The old man pulled the hat down even farther over her head until the rim rested below her ears, eliciting giggles from her.

Major Quang bowed respectfully to the white-bearded old man, of whom he was very fond, treating him like the father he'd lost years ago. Quang towered above Kwan Chi's father by nearly a foot, as he did most Vietnamese. He'd inherited his height from his French father and his features from his Vietnamese mother, the combination producing an extremely handsome man. He'd known his father but for a short time. He had died in a boating accident in Marseille, and Quang's mother had taken him back to her family in

Hanoi. Then during the war with the French his mother was killed, and he was taken in by his grandparents. A year later Quang's grandparents were arrested and never seen again.

For a while, Quang wandered the streets seeking work or begging, anything to stay alive. Then he was taken in by the government and put in school, where he did well, continuing his studies until he was selected for further education in Russia.

Quang had wanted a teaching career, but at the government's request he went to Russia for flight training along with twenty-three other North Vietnamese high school graduates. Upon completion of the intensive course, Quang returned to Hanoi with no combat experience and 117 hours in jet aircraft.

The major sat down at the kitchen table. He watched his wife as she scurried about between the cookstove and the table, ignoring her son and concentrating on preparing a splendid breakfast for her family. Kwan Chi would see her husband but once or twice a week, and she knew any time might be the last.

"Will you fly today?" asked Kwan Chi's father. He had taken his seat at the other end of the table, next to his adoring granddaughter.

Quang looked away from his son and faced the old man. He paused, then answered, "I don't know. Only the Americans can answer that."

The old man's face tensed. "The weather is lifting and you will fly, I know it." He clenched his jaw, staring straight through his son-in-law. "Ho Chi Minh," he said.

"What did you say, grandfather?" Quang asked.

"Ho Chi Minh—Ho Chi Minh!" He raised his voice as he repeated the name of their leader. "That old bastard will get us all killed. Him and his power-hungry snakes." The weathered old man continued his diatribe, even though no one listened but his young granddaughter. Mai Ling listened to everything he said, although being only seven she understood little. In addition to her father, she adored the old man, who allowed her to pull his long white beard while he feigned pain and anger, which seemed to delight her even more. The long lines in his face fascinated her, and she would sometimes trace them with her fingers as if she were reading a map. Kwan Chi's father, outspoken and cantankerous, had contempt for anyone in power or any foreigner living in his country. His daughter feared he would say something to the wrong person and tried to keep him at home whenever possible.

Quang continued to ignore the old man as Le Doc ran to take his seat beside his father, waiting as his mother and grandmother set the last bowls of steaming rice before them. He set his small toy plane on the table in front of him. His father had made it from a piece of the wreckage of his first kill. Le Doc began making noises like the jets he heard fly over the city.

"You must not play with your toys at our table, my son. There will be plenty of time after you have finished your breakfast."

Le Doc obediently set his prized model on the floor and hungrily eyed the meal set before him. He knew that the special food was prepared only when his father could come home, but he was too young to connect his father's absence with the fighter interceptor duty at the nearby base.

"Sit down, Kwan Chi, I am famished." Quang grinned as she took her place next to him.

Kwan Chi had outdone herself that morning. Some of the foods were either extremely hard to find or very expensive. Kwan Chi picked up the plate containing the slices of freshly smoked fish and held it before her husband.

"Sometimes I think it is worth going on alert duty just so I can come home to these meals," Quang said. "All I ever have at the base is *com nep* and *banh bo*."

Kwan Chi nodded as he selected two pieces of the prized fish and placed them atop a pile of rice on his plate. She passed the plate down to her father as her son eyed the delicious fish.

"Don't worry, Le Doc," the old man said, "there will be some left for you."

Mai Ling giggled when she saw her grandfather slip an extra piece into his lap. She had seen him play this game with her brother before, and it delighted her to see the small boy protest when his portion always seemed to be missing. She suspected the boy knew but humored the old man whenever he hid a piece and then produced the missing food just before his grandson got upset.

Major Quang was savoring every bite of the tasty fish, knowing his wife had gone to much trouble to obtain it. His young son and daughter happily consumed their meal, oblivious to the war, but Quang was concerned for their safety and wanted to move them into the country. It was Kwan Chi who argued against the idea, saying she preferred the city. Quang pushed away from the table and stood up, his son looking up at him as he did.

"Are you leaving, Father?" the small boy asked.

"No, not yet."

His son seemed satisfied with his answer and went back to his breakfast. Kwan Chi got up from the table and followed her husband out of their small kitchen into the yard. Quang stopped at the garden the grandmother cultivated daily, admiring the budding plants.

"Your mother will soon have more melons than we can eat," he said.

Kwan Chi took her husband's hand and stared at the flowering plants. "Yes," she said, "many melons. My mother has always grown the best, and she will be able to trade some for other things we need."

The major looked at his wife, taking both her hands in his. "I think soon you will have to move into the country."

"But why?" she asked. "We are safe here. The Americans only bomb the bridges and railyards. Even you said their own leaders have tied the bombers' hands."

"I know I did." Quang led her around the garden plot, walking slowly as he held her hand. "But things are changing. Their leaders are frustrated and becoming more aggressive. Soon they will be attacking even more targets. Haven't you noticed the effort in expanding our defenses around the city?"

Kwan Chi continued to walk with her husband, saying nothing for the moment. She could not answer his last question. She had paid little attention to the weapons installed around the city or even to the jets when they flew over or the bombs exploding in the distance. She sometimes heard the weapons being fired at the attacking Americans, but the sound was tempered by earth above her, for she and her children and parents would always be in the bomb shelters during an attack, and then the explosions were muffled and distant.

Suddenly Le Doc ran through the door clutching his prized plane. "Father, someone wants to talk to you on the telephone."

"Did he say who he was?"

"Yes," the small boy said.

"Well, who is it?"

Le Doc stood at his father's feet, his head lowered. "I don't know." He began flying his airplane again, making noises he thought sounded like his father's jet.

"Wait here for me, Kwan Chi. I will be right back." Major Quang let loose his grasp on his wife's hand and headed inside.

"Major Quang," he answered.

The voice on the other end sounded excited and hurried.

"This is Captain Vo, Major. You must return to base immediately. Radar has reported a large flight of American warplanes headed inbound from the sea. We think they are going after the bridge at Canh Tra."

Quang could hear the captain breathing over the phone as he waited for Quang's reply. His heart rate quickened as he mentally prepared himself. "I will be there in less than ten minutes. Have my mechanic start the engine for me." Quang waited for the captain to acknowledge his order, then hung up the phone. He dashed outside, beckoning to his wife.

"Is it an attack?" his wife asked.

"Yes, gather the children and your parents and go to the shelter. I must go immediately." He quickly kissed his wife and children good-bye, ran through the house, and mounted his small scooter. In the early morning hours, sound traveled far. He thought he could already hear the jet engines being started as he turned onto the dirt road leading to the base.

3

Jim Campbell tilted his head slightly and stared at the breaks in the solid-white overcast below him. He could see gaps and canyons forming near the tops of the rapidly thinning cloud formation and knew the weather was breaking up. The weather guessers had been right for a change and for a brief moment he admired the scattered patches of blue water of the Gulf of Tonkin.

Twelve thousand feet above the tops of the highest layer, Campbell's A-4 hung back, flying loose wing position on Jordan, who was also managing an occasional glimpse through the cloud buildups. The air was velvety smooth, not even a bump to disturb the tranquil flight inbound to the North Vietnamese coastline. Campbell's oxygen mask hung loosely to the side, imprints of its rim still marking his face. In a few minutes they would be crossing the beach and turning inbound. Campbell gently eased the throttle lever up, nudging the nimble jet closer to Jordan's wing, then reset the power to hold him in position. He was close enough to see Jordan smoking a cigarette, the white tip hanging from his lip as he flew just to the right and aft of the flight leader. Campbell could never decide who was the bigger smoker of the two—Larry or his wife, Patricia.

"Blackbeard," a voice boomed into Campbell's earphones. "This is Red Crown, over." He pulled himself up and reattached his mask, then moved in closer to Jordan. "You are cleared through the gate. No posses are airborne, over." He listened to the voice broadcasting from the guided-missile cruiser five miles below him. He heard Lieutenant Commander Porter acknowledge the call. For a moment Campbell wondered who was attached to the distant voice that cleared them in and out of North Vietnam. Each time he flew a sortie into the North, it was the same voice, calm and detached, his last contact with the world he lived in. If Campbell was lucky enough to come back, he could always count on that same voice to be there, clearing him to his home or directing a rescue helicopter to him if he was in trouble. Someday he hoped to meet this navy chief, and he would buy him a drink, maybe a whole bottle. One thing he knew: The controller had the reputation of being able to spot MiGs when they taxied out for takeoff.

Campbell took one last look behind him as they approached the coastline of North Vietnam, then lined himself back up with Jordan. Out of the corner of his eye he spotted a flash, causing him to flinch. Then he relaxed as he realized the sun was glancing off the wing of an aircraft skimming the tops of the clouds well below him, playing hide-and-seek with the blue sky around it. Only the large round dome mounted atop the aircraft was visible as it ghosted just under the peaks, creating the illusion of a hovering flying saucer.

"Hey, Spook, look down at your four."

Jordan twisted around, as did most of the rest of the flight, and looked behind his wing. "Martians." He watched the Grumman E-1B for a moment, then turned around.

The E-1B was a slow, prop-driven aircraft loaded with the most advanced electronic snooping and jamming gear produced by the free world. Its immense radar dome mounted atop the aircraft housed a powerful search radar that complemented the USS *Chicago* in keeping an eye on things during their mission. The pilot of the E-1B banked the aircraft, turning away from land, disappearing completely into the clouds. For the duration of the mission he would remain just offshore, out of range of the ground-launched surface-to-air missiles. Its sensors silent, the E-1B flew seaward, continuing its scan for radiation from the Vietnamese Spoon Rest A acquisition and Fansong fire-control radars.

Campbell knew the silence wouldn't last nor did he expect it to. Already powerful Soviet-supplied Vietnamese search radars were probing, seeking them out and coordinating their well-planned defense. Like a well-orchestrated game, each side probed the other's defenses, then shielded itself behind walls of silence.

Over the coastline Lieutenant Commander Porter initiated a turn to port, starting a routine of jinking to throw off any Vietnamese gunners taking aim on his aircraft. The two flights of A-4s moved out, setting up a looser formation and beginning to bob and sway, making changes in altitude and heading. The intelligence reports indicated little or no defenses in the area they were crossing, motivating each man to jink even harder.

Campbell eased the stick over, dropping his wing so he

could see the small flashes coming from the beach. A young teenager was firing a 37-millimeter antiaircraft gun recently supplied to his village and undergoing its first test. Even though the flight was well above the gun's effective range, the boy and several of the village's appointed militiamen continued firing, hoping to be the first to bring down one of the jets they saw overhead nearly every day. Campbell could see the shells exploding harmlessly below even as larger guns began firing farther down the beach, looking for his altitude. The flashes soon ended as Campbell's flight flew out of range, continuing inland toward their target.

Lieutenant Commander Porter squeezed his mike button. "Red Crown, this is Blackbeard—feet dry, over." The call announcing the flight's presence over enemy territory was required of any aircraft crossing into North Vietnam.

"Roger, Blackbeard, this is Red Crown. Good hunting, out." The chief petty officer marked down the time and place they had crossed, then continued squinting into the green glow of his scope. He ordered a fresh cup of coffee from a seaman apprentice without even looking up.

Campbell, maintaining position, could see Larry had his mask on and was no longer smoking. Jordan looked back at him, shooting him the finger, as he liked to do to everybody. Several hundred yards to the side he could see the second flight of A-4s, spread out and closing in on their leader. He knew several of the pilots in the squadron from the *Bon Homme Richard* and had attended flight school with two of them. Almost a year had passed since he had last seen them, and he was unlikely to see them again for some time. Although there were at least three carriers on station and sometimes more, it was unusual for two to be in an overseas port at the same time.

Campbell looked at the terrain below, noting the river they would use for a turning point. In a few minutes they would turn back to the north, heading directly for their target. Nervously he scanned his instruments again, assuring himself everything was working, then readjusted the air-conditioning knob. The midmorning sun was beaming brightly through the clear plastic canopy, warming up the cockpit like a greenhouse.

"Blackbeard flight, this is Blackbeard three six, listen up." Porter summoned his flight to attention as he prepared for the upcoming attack. "Check over your systems and arm your aircraft; we'll be going in in flights of twos. Move into attack formation now. Gator lead acknowledge."

"This is Gator lead. Acknowledge flight of twos and arming now. Gator two four, move in on me. Three nine, pick up your wingman and move back, over."

Campbell looked over at the other flight. He could see them quickly moving into their preplanned attack formation as his own flight did the same. He knew that Gator flight would split off, taking their flight in from a different angle but still perpendicular to their target for the morning—the bridge at Canh Tra. The attack procedure was dictated by the White House to prevent any stray bombs from walking past the bridge and hitting any civilians living nearby. Most of the civilians had long ago moved away from such high-priority targets as the bridges. In the backyards of their homes, antiaircraft guns now stood where chickens and pigs had once roamed. Smokin' Joe was especially incensed at the bombing procedure, but as usual, his voice fell on deaf ears. If they were lucky, someone would drop a bridge span. The odds were more in favor of missing altogether and splashing water on the gun crews along the riverbanks.

Campbell flipped on the wing station arming switches, carefully moving his right thumb off the bomb pickle button as he raised the master arm switch. He rechecked his harness and wriggled from side to side, making himself as comfortable as possible in the tiny cockpit. Each pilot went through procedures not unlike a baseball pitcher's on the mound. The junior airmen tucked underneath the more senior section leaders' wings, each man silently rechecking his torso fittings, pulling them tighter, fingering the lower ejection handle, reassuring themselves it was there. Droplets of sweat began to appear on some of the aviators; others flew in cold silence.

The air in the concrete underground bunker was quickly growing stagnant and humid. Fans placed along the passageway strained to bring in outside air to cool the rows of electronic consoles. The heart of North Vietnam's defense capability lay underground, undetected and concealed from the probing eyes of reconnaissance aircraft, a secret even from many who lived nearby. This central core controlled when and where their intercepters flew and the antiaircraft guns fired. This hub received information through spokes that led to the myriad and diverse facilities that made up the countrywide reporting system. Similar to the one Britain used in World War II, the system of spotting and reporting every U.S. aircraft that crossed the coast enabled the North Vietnamese to coordinate their defenses to maximum advantage—whether it was radar-controlled guns or a group of teenagers shooting straight up into the air on command.

At the same time every day, the air-conditioning system would break down and fans were put in place until the system was up and running again. It was vital to keeping the radar system working.

Maj. Pham Van Bhi hovered over the shoulders of the enlisted operator monitoring the radar scope. He drew his hand across his brow as the heat soared, wiping away the first sign of sweat. Silently he cursed the Russians' inability to build a simple cooling system. He was thirty feet below ground just outside Hanoi. The radar complex was encased in massive layers of concrete with heavy steel reinforcement rods laced within and additional layers of bamboo covered with dirt. As soon as American aircraft had been detected, land lines to every sector were activated and checked. On Bhi's desk were several phones. One went direct to the small house where Ho Chi Minh and his staff would be until the actual bombing began. Bhi remained silent as phone operators smoothly went through their routine, taking calls of enemy sightings. He continued staring at the blips on the radar screen for a moment then stood up straight.

"At last," he said. A sudden rush of cool air from the overhead vents brought a smile to his face. The heated air had made the major feel faint, and he thought he would have to leave and go above ground for relief. Actually the air-conditioning was both a blessing and a curse to him. The cool air caused his crippled arm to throb, constantly reminding him of his last air battle—one he had lost. He knew he was lucky to be alive, although he would never fly again. His valuable talents were now used controlling the MiG fighters against the American incursions. His expertise as a fighter pilot was invaluable to the green pilots sent up against the Americans. They flew by his orders—launched when he ordered, went into afterburner at his command, fired air-to-air missiles when he signaled, and returned when he said to. The ones that didn't usually failed to return.

Bhi lit a Russian cigarette with his good hand, secretly wishing it were one of the American brands. He could never understand how the Russians could put a satellite into orbit and yet never seemed to master producing any of the everyday things in life that were any good. But at least their aircraft were first-rate fighters, he thought to himself. Ah, how nimble in the air they were. He smiled at the thought of being able to turn inside anything the Americans had, and shooting down their more complex Phantom aircraft, which was faster. Even though the Phantom had a second man whose sole job was to operate the weapons system and act as a second pair of eyes, he felt he had been their equal. The thought made him smile again. He had loved to make head-on passes, firing his guns as he flew through the enemy formations, scattering them and causing some to prematurely drop their bombs. He knew they had no guns, only missiles, and only when they got on his tail could they fire a heat-seeking missile at him. The one time he had gotten careless and let an F-8 Crusader get on his tail, it had cost him the use of his arm. The bullets had exploded his canopy, then destroyed his engine. Before he could eject from the disabled aircraft, his arm was destroyed along with any chance of ever flying again. The thoughts were triggered every time the Americans crossed the beach.

The room was cooling down and Bhi leaned over the controller's shoulder again, staring at the blips on the screen, watching the Americans' feint to the south. They were always doing that, he thought. Did they think the Vietnamese were stupid? It wasn't hard to guess where the attack would end up—in one or two places. Bhi knew the Americans were permitted only a few main targets in the country. Continuing to think to himself, Bhi remembered the French defeat. "In time we will have our Dien Bien Phu," he quietly whispered to himself. Bhi picked up the special phone on his desk and called in to his defense commander, updating him on the situation.

The big Spoon Rest A acquisition radars were turned on as the Americans flew inward. The flight was following a route that had the least known defenses. Bhi's narrow face grew tense as he watched the tiny blips on the screen rapidly moving northward after their last turn. He stood up and turned to the captain seated across the room who was wearing a set of earphones.

An enlisted orderly standing next to the captain nudged him, pointing to the major. The officer slipped one of the earphones up over his ear. "Yes, Major," he responded.

"Are the MiGs on the runway and ready?"

"Yes sir, they're ready for takeoff—armed and fully fueled." He looked up at his status board to reassure himself. "They are talking to Ground Control Intercept now."

Bhi picked up a headset from the table, cupping one of the earpieces to his ear. He recognized Major Quang's voice as the flight leader, then turned once again to the main scope, studying it for a moment. "Order the MiGs aloft," he said. "Give them vectors for the bridge at Canh Tra, but make sure they hug the ground all the way. I want GCI to bring them up right into and through the American bomber formation. I don't think they brought their fighters with them." Major Bhi clutched his crippled hand as he issued orders, continuing to watch the screen.

The intercept officer acknowledged, then turned back to his desk, relaying the order to the controller. Major Quang and his flight were quickly ordered into the air, with further information and vectors provided as they rolled down the runway. It was Vietnamese policy to provide all solutions to the pilots from GCI control, their word being final. Only Major Quang, a former squadron mate of Major Bhi, was given the latitude to make his own decisions in the air. The others were expected to follow GCI orders explicitly.

The clouds were breaking up into clusters, forming large canyons and valleys between them. The A-4s would be visually shielded from the ground gunners at least until they rolled in for the bombing run. Smokin' Joe rechecked his map, confirming that the bend in the river matched the one on his briefing card. Satisfied, he took one last look at the flight. Passing over the preplanned initial point, he turned to the briefed heading and flew toward the target. He could see the bridge coming up underneath his nose and he rolled the A-4 onto its back, pulling the nose into a sixty-degree dive angle. The perpendicular bomb run was perfect for the ground gunners waiting for them to fly into range. Smokin' Joe had argued with the commanding officer and the admiral himself, pointing out that the only way to drop bombs on a bridge target was to aim for one end and walk them down to the other, with a degree or two offset on the run in. That would provide the best odds of hitting the bridge. Today they were aiming for one spot, the center span. A miss would only splash the bridge and wet the gun crews lined up on the riverbanks.

Campbell was the last plane in the flight and had an excellent view of the strung-out aircraft now forming a graceful arc as each aircraft rolled into the steep dive angle for the target. Patches of smoke appeared around them as the antiaircraft gunners on the ground opened up. The puffs of gray smoke soon changed to white as they flew lower into the range of the smaller guns. Campbell jinked even harder. Now it was merely a matter of luck. The sky had so much metal in it, there was hardly an empty space to fly through. The gunners that had survived other attacks knew which direction the jets would come from and at what point they would release their bombs. The odds were usually in favor of the gunners.

The firing stopped. Campbell blinked his eyes. He could feel a cold chill running through his body as he continued his attack run. Something isn't right, he thought. They can't be out of ammunition.

"MiGs, head on," was all he heard Lieutenant Commander Porter say as two MiG-17s knifed through the attacking flight, pouring 23-millimeter rapid-fire cannon into them. He had no way of knowing the first shells tore through Porter's aircraft, destroying his radios and pressurization system. Nor did he know that Porter continued his run on the target, lining up the first span of the bridge in his gunsight and releasing his load of bombs. Campbell didn't see the MiGs as they flashed by, but felt the concussions in the air as the ground gunners opened up again. As usual everything was happening superfast, and when the bridge briefly crossed his gunsight, he released. Pulling back on the stick, the G load built rapidly and his G suit quickly filled with air, clamping around his legs and holding blood in his upper body. He called off target and began looking around for other aircraft. A midair was just as much a hazard as the ground gunners. Twisting his head back, he make a quick check to his rear to look for the MiGs he knew were around somewhere. The other flight was already rolling in from another direction and would probably receive the same treatment from the MiGs as they had. He began closing on Jordan.

"Red Crown," the second flight leader shouted into his mask after failing to hear Porter make the call. "We have MiGs in the area, repeat, MiGs in the area, at least two seventeens, over."

"Roger, Gator, acknowledge your MiGs. Enfield flight is inbound and will be there shortly, over." The controllers aboard the USS *Chicago* had not spotted the MiGs taking off from their air base, nor had the controllers in the E-1B flying just offshore.

"We may not have a *'shortly,'* " an anonymous voice announced.

The MiGs quickly broke up the second wave of A-4s. Using the same tactics, they forced some to punch off their bomb loads immediately and others to miss the target. The bridge remained standing as the armed bombs fell short, exploding in the water. As soon as the MiGs cleared, the gunners received orders from the underground complex at Hanoi to resume firing.

Major Quang's wingman rejoined him as Quang pulled into a vertical climb after passing through the last wave of attackers. The two MiGs were inverted as Quang's nose fell through the horizon, allowing him a quick glimpse of two A-4s several thousand feet below them and heading for the coast. He rolled upright, all the time listening to his GCI controller advising him on what action to take next. He continued watching the two A-4s below.

The Vietnamese controller was frantic. "We have in-bound jets at high speed approaching from the coast, probably American fighters, probably Crusaders. You are cleared for one pass and then you are ordered to return to base. Acknowledge, over."

Major Bhi stood behind the controller, intensely watching the gaggle of American bombers, reduced to innocent green blips on a radar screen. They were heading for the safety of the sea without fighter cover and he wanted them. Not yet, he thought, not yet. He yearned to be back in the air pursuing the escaping jets.

Major Quang put his hand on the electronic armament panel, flipping a switch that armed his Atoll air-to-air heat-seeking missile. The Atoll was an almost exact duplicate of the American Sidewinder and had been copied from one stolen and sold to the Russians. A humming noise hissed in his headset as he tested the circuitry of the missile. He knew he would have only one chance at the Americans. If he missed, there would have to be another time. He also knew that unless he wanted to engage the incoming American fighters, he would have to land immediately after making the one pass. Once he touched down at his base, he could not be fired upon by the Americans. Another of their president's rules. It seemed like a children's game he played as a boy, where one could not be tagged unless one crossed the line marked off in the schoolyard. If the Americans wanted to make rules that were to their disadvantage, that was fine with him.

Quang pushed the press-to-test button on the armament panel again, causing a tone in his headset, indicating the missile circuitry was working. If he could maneuver behind the American and obtain the same tone, then the missile would lock on to the high heat from the jet's exhaust and he could fire and have a high probability of a hit. He remained at the same altitude, several thousand feet above the two jets heading out to sea. They were alone.

Campbell's headset crackled as he heard Gator flight checking in with a flight of four. Good, he thought, everybody made it. He anxiously scanned over his shoulder for any enemy aircraft. Then, looking up, he spotted the two MiGs high above his right wing. "Hey, Spook, I got a couple of bandits high at our four, over." Campbell's gut tightened as he watched the two MiGs with their sleek swept-back wings and high trademark vertical stabilizer that sliced through the air like a predator shark.

Jordan twisted around, tilting his head upward to look, only to see the two MiGs rolling in on them. Like a hawk going after a rabbit, he thought. "Break right, Soup!" He realized they were in a bad position and rolled his aircraft hard, turning into the diving MiGs and hoping it would force them to overshoot.

The MiG pilot expected the American to break into him and slowed his aircraft as he descended, falling in behind the fleeing A-4 just out of the envelope to fire the Atoll. Quang jammed the power back up and tightened his turn, forcing the MiG to the inside of Jordan's turn, gaining on him. The MiG was hard to turn at high speeds, a weakness sometimes used to advantage in a dogfight, but now it turned like a rabbit. Quang was inside the A-4s' radius of turn, and the two A-4s rolled inverted into a split S as they realized the MiGs were still with them. Quang's wingman was having a hard time staying with his leader.

"I'm going to pull out and see if I can get behind whoever stays." Campbell rolled upright and pulled high into a vertical, hoping the MiGs would hesitate on whom to go after. "If they both come after me, you get on them." He watched the second MiG peel off from his leader and initiate a climb behind him. Campbell ruddered over at the top of his vertical climb, letting the nose fall through, then accelerating rapidly as he screamed downward toward the hills below. "Okay, Larry, I got one following me, but I'm coming around on yours."

The MiG following Campbell hesitated, then pulled through, putting him farther away from Campbell. Campbell swiveled his head back and forth, rapidly moving his eyes as he searched for Jordan. He couldn't see him but he knew he had to be there, invisible against the ground as he screamed downward. Without looking, he flipped on the arm switch for the single Sidewinder missile he had on board. Come on, Spook, hang in there, he thought to himself. He spotted Jordan down low, screaming across the landscape with the MiG almost close enough to open up. He could tell Jordan must be just out of the firing envelope or the MiG would have already fired. But the MiG was gaining and Jordan was in serious trouble. Quang seemed as if he were playing with him, countering his every move.

"He's in range, Soupy, he's got his nose on me—get him off." Jordan was trying everything he knew but couldn't shake the agile MiG. Come on guys, Jordan thought to himself, where are you fighter jocks when I need you? He broke left and then right, hoping to prevent the MiG from shooting. Jordan was getting frantic. He could see the sea over the hills ahead and knew if he could hang on a little longer he would be safe.

"Hang in there, Spook, I'm setting up." Campbell rolled

the A-4 to set up a firing shot, ignoring the MiG moving in behind him. He was too far away to use his guns and would have to chance firing the heat-seeking missile, hoping it would lock on the MiG and not his friend. "Okay, Spook, pull up into a hard vertical and then cross back for the deck. Drag him out for me, I'm almost in position to . . ."

Quang was trying to ignore the orders screaming through his earphones. The GCI controller was getting frantic as he reported the inbound fighters minutes away. A loud tone drowned out the screaming controller, alerting Quang as the A-4 flew inside the concentric target rings of his gunsight. Instinctively he pressed a button on the control stick between his legs. Instantly the Russian missile came to life, and its infrared homing device locked onto the A-4. It was guiding to the Skyhawk.

"Break, Spook, break," Campbell yelled into his oxygen mask. "He fired." Campbell's attention to his lead was diverted as bright tracer shells from the second MiG began sailing past his cockpit. "Holy shit," he said into the mike. He pulled on the control stick harder than he ever had before and grunted as the sudden G force hit him. The stream of tracers moved aft and away from the cockpit.

Quang briefly watched the missile fly right up the jet's tailpipe and explode, tearing the tail section off the plane. He watched in fascination as the canopy of the tumbling A-4 blew off, followed by the pilot ejecting from the aircraft. He sped by less than 200 feet away as Jordan tumbled through the air. Quang pulled up and away, swiveling his head from side to side as he remembered the other A-4. He could hear the ground controller still ordering them away. As he rolled his aircraft, he spotted the American not far from him with his wingman in pursuit. He was not in position to fire and Quang pulled up into a barrel roll, passing above the A-4, inverted and looking down at him for a brief moment. For an instant he stared into the cockpit of Campbell's aircraft. Continuing the roll, he headed back for his base.

It was over in a moment, but Campbell was able to glimpse into the cockpit of the MiG as it crossed over him. It was the first time he had seen one up close and he was amazed at how small it was. The high swept-back tail was unmistakable. He thought he saw the flash of a scarf but was unsure. He was sure that the MiG had several rows of what looked like crosses painted just beneath the canopy. He hoped he was wrong. Tracers streaming above his wing ended his admiration of the MiG as he realized the other MiG was still pursuing him.

"Return to base now, return to base now!" Major Bhi had taken the mike away from the young Vietnamese controller and was screaming into it himself.

Quang was already heading for the air base at full power. He called to his inexperienced wingman several times to follow him and receiving no answer, continued homeward. He would fight them another day when the odds were better. The MiG pilot looked over his shoulder, squinting into the sun, searching for his wingman. He spotted him still pursuing the A-4, trying to gain a firing position on the American. Quang called to him again and again but it was no use. The young pilot was too intent on his quarry and didn't see the two F-8 fighters rolling in behind him. He never knew what hit him as his MiG-17 instantly turned into a flaming mass of metal, the Crusader's armor-piercing shells penetrating the engine and volatile fuel tanks. Quang was too far away for them to pursue him, and he continued away to the safety of his air base.

* * *

Campbell shoved the stick over. For a brief moment he watched the burning MiG quickly disappear from sight as it hurled downward, then saw another explosion as it hit the ground.

"Has anybody seen Larry's chute?" Campbell asked, banking his aircraft, hoping to spot Jordan descending safely to the ground. With careless abandon he rolled the A-4 from one side to the other, his eyes searching the landscape for any signs of his friend. With the sun behind him, he spotted the parachute just before Jordan landed at the bottom of a hill, the chute collapsing around him.

"I've got a chute—at the bottom of that small hill." Campbell pulled back on the power, dropping his nose and descending. Though it was dangerous, he hadn't received any AAA fire and hoped there wasn't any nearby. The silence was almost deafening. The sound of the air rushing by the canopy filled the cockpit as he descended farther, down to the level of the ridges just above where Jordan had landed. He had heard nothing since Jordan was hit, not even the automatic signal emitted by the emergency radio as soon as the seat is ejected from the cockpit. Campbell began to wonder if it might be the MiG pilot he was circling. He switched over to the emergency channel and listened for a sign that his friend was still alive.

"Anybody heard anything?"

"This is Enfield twenty-one—negative, nothing. We'll remain overhead and cover you. The MiG pilot never got out, by the way." The lead F-8 and his wingman pulled out of the flight of four, leaving the two remaining fighters to run interference for any remaining MiGs in the area. The higher-flying Crusader contacted Red Crown again. He was told a SAR helicopter recovery team was inbound, accompanied by a couple of A-1 Skyraiders.

Campbell turned up the volume of his radio and flew up

the hill perpendicular to the small stream at the bottom. At his speed, the figure on the ground was blurred and he couldn't tell whether it was Jordan or a soldier. Only the presence of the chute gave him hope. He rocked his wings to acknowledge his sighting and was rewarded with a loud noise in his earphones as Jordan made his first transmission.

"Blackbeard three one, this is Blackbeard two seven, over."

Campbell turned the volume down and pressed the mike button. "Is that you, Spook?" He had to make sure it was Jordan and not a North Vietnamese soldier trying to lure him into a trap. "Spook, this is Soupy. Where are we going to be this weekend?" Campbell challenged Jordan.

"At the Bangkok Ambassador, sloshed to the gills; now get me outta here, will ya?"

"It's him, it's Blackbeard two seven," Campbell transmitted excitedly. "Enfield, this is Blackbeard three one, I have a positive confirmation of Blackbeard two seven. He is at the bottom of the hill near the stream, over." Campbell banked his jet, flying just up the hill from Jordan. He could see a crumpled-up parachute half-pulled into some shrubbery and assumed Jordan was nearby. "Hey, Spook," he called. "If you are with your chute, pull it in some more. The slopes can see it for miles."

For a moment Jordan sat on the ground watching the A-4 streaking by, then hobbled over and pulled in the exposed parachute, rolling it into a heap and stuffing it underneath a row of leafy bushes.

"Are you hurt?" Campbell asked.

"My leg." Jordan paused for a moment. "Might be broken, or at least sprained pretty bad."

Campbell flew down the hillside, looking for any signs of troops looking for his friend. He passed near a village on the other side of the hill.

Jordan raised the hand-held radio to his mouth, lowering his voice in case troops were nearby. "Soupy, this is Jordan. I think my leg is broken." He paused for a moment to catch his breath as he ran his hand over the bulge next to his kneecap. "It's hard for me to walk and it hurts like hell. If you can get the chopper in here and lower a sling, I'll manage to get into it somehow."

"Okay, buddy, just hang in there. Help is on the way." Campbell didn't mention the village he had sighted less than a mile from where Jordan was hidden. He knew that nearly every village in North Vietnam had its self-defense force of farmers and teenagers armed with a few old rifles and someone appointed to maintain order. Survival depended a lot on who got to the pilot first: an angry farmer or disciplined troops. If they did get to Jordan, he hoped it would be the trained villagers and not one of the local farmers who would just as soon run a pitchfork through a downed pilot as capture him. The pilots all knew the leaders in Hanoi wanted the Americans captured alive and brought in so they could exploit them for propaganda.

Campbell flew down and away from the village and set up an orbit away from Jordan. He hoped the villagers would think the downed pilot was on the ground underneath him.

The search and rescue helicopter, Loosefoot 53, had started inbound at top speed as soon as he was notified by the USS *Chicago* that a pilot was down. This was his first time across the beach into North Vietnam, and his heart raced as he pushed the Sikorsky SH-3A to its limits. Flying alongside the faster A-1s assigned as his escort was impossible, and they flew gentle S-turns to keep him in sight. The SH-3A was capable of doing over 150 knots, but the stiff armor plating added to this machine limited its speed to 100 knots.

"Can't you make that thing go any faster, Loosefoot?" Though frustrated, the A-1 pilots knew the pilot was doing all he could. Only the air force CH-53s based in Thailand could reach greater speeds, up to nearly 200 miles per hour. The navy had been given the task of providing rescue service offshore and inland near the coast.

"I wish I could but the armor plating they stuck on here stiffened the frame so much that she goes into extreme vibrations." The Sikorsky SH-3A helicopter, known as Big Motha, was designed for antisubmarine warfare and carried a submersible dipping sonar along with torpedoes and depth bombs. As pilots got shot down, Admiral Laceur had advocated using the chopper for rescue work after he convinced his superiors there was little submarine threat in the Gulf. They ended up performing both missions. The helicopter pilot watched the strange terrain passing underneath him as his copilot tried to chart their progress on the map he had unfolded. It being hard to navigate at such low altitudes, they were depending on the A-1s up ahead to guide them safely to the site.

"Escort one, this is Red Crown. Your heading is two nine zero and fifteen miles. Transfer to the on-scene commander, over."

The A-1 pilot acknowledged, changing course and making contact with the F-8 circling the area. The chopper turned, trailing in behind the two Skyraiders.

"Loosefoot five three, this is Escort two two. Fly this track inbound. We are leaving you to check out the area and will call you when clear, over."

The helo pilot acknowledged, following the established routine of letting the heavily armed A-1s check out the area and establish the identity of the downed pilot. More than one helo had been lured into an ambush by a North Vietnamese soldier using a captured radio.

"Soupy," Campbell heard Jordan call. His voice sounded excited but subdued.

"I can hear voices coming from the other side of the hill, to the north."

Campbell could sense the anxiety in his friend's voice. "Are you still in the same place?"

"Yeah."

"Okay, don't move. Just stay hidden. The Spads are checking in with the F-8s now so the helo can't be far behind. How's the leg?"

"Hurts like hell." Jordan cautiously peered out from the brush, looking up the hill. He could see uniformed figures near the top. "Soup, I can see troops coming down the hill near the top of the ridge."

"Yeah, I can too. Stay where you are. I'm going to strafe up the hill just above you. Break, Escort flight, the downed pilot is just above the bottom of the hill I am about to strafe. Follow my lead." He rolled in after getting an acknowledgment from Enfield.

Jordan crouched down inside the clump of bushes growing above the stream below him and looked around. The stream looked shallow but he couldn't run. There seemed to be a trail running beside it. The brush thickened along the stream and thinned out up the hill. Jordan didn't think any of the Vietnamese had spotted him.

He took out his service .38-caliber Smith & Wesson and opened the chamber. Jordan noticed the shell rims were splashed with red markings—tracers. If he fired, it would give him away. Jordan snapped the gun closed and looked back up the hill. He could see two columns of men spreading out and working their way down the hillside, probing the brush looking for him. He was sure he hadn't been spotted, but if the helo didn't get here soon, he would be captured. "Give me your best shot, Soup, there's a bunch of them." He watched in fascination as Campbell wrapped the A-4 around to set up for a firing pass at the figures working their way down the hillside.

Campbell aimed at a point halfway up the hill and pressed down on the trigger on the stick, keeping the gunsight lined up. Jordan could not see the clouds of dust rising as the shells from Campbell's 20-millimeter cannon walked up the hill. The North Vietnamese had seen the A-4 circling and ran as soon as he rolled in. Two lay dead on the trail, their bodies cut in half by the large shells, but the others were regrouping. They started down the hill again as Campbell pulled off target to set up for another pass.

Jordan peered up the hill. "Nice pass, buddy, but they're spreading out. Can you get some of the fighter jocks to help out?" With one hand he held the radio to his ear as he crouched low in the brush, the pistol in his other hand.

The North Vietnamese were getting closer, cautiously probing each patch of brush with one eye on the circling aircraft. As the jets rolled in again, they scattered, running across the hill, diving under any cover they could find. As soon as the pass was completed they were up again.

Jordan watched two of the F-8s roll in behind. "Soup, they're spreading out across the hill. You better hose'em good this time." He knew that unless the helicopter showed up soon, they would win. He watched Campbell and the F-8s begin another strafing pass. Jordan could see dust flying up the hilltop but no soldiers.

As Campbell and the two F-8s pulled off, Campbell spotted the lead A-1 flying inbound toward Jordan and contacted the pilot, quickly briefing him on the situation.

Lieutenant Jacobson, the A-1 pilot, was taking no chances on bringing the helo into a trap. As he flew down the hill, he spotted Jordan waving at him. The Spad pilot contacted Jordan, verifying it was him, then contacted the helicopter, now crossing over the stream about a mile away.

When Jordan spotted the two A-1s flying low and heading straight for the hill, a feeling of relief came over him as he realized the helicopter couldn't be far behind.

"Okay, Loosefoot, this is Escort two two. Your pickup is at the bottom of the hill just above the stream. There are still troops trying to work their way down the hill, and we will continue to work them over while you make the pickup. We can hold them up a bit, but get in and get out, over."

As Campbell and the F-8s climbed above the SAR site, the two A-1s began making runs on the hillside, methodically walking a stream of shells up the hill. By now the troops were scattered and few were being hit.

The helicopter pilot acknowledged, then started his approach. His rear crewman was manning the 7.62-millimeter machine gun mounted in the open door, nervously sweeping the gun from side to side as he prepared for the rescue. The gun had a small protective shield of armor plating built behind the breech, and he crouched closer to it as the helicopter slowed. He could see soldiers up the hill out of range, and he fired ineffectively at anyone exposing himself.

The second helicopter crewman busied himself preparing the jungle penetrator, which the downed pilot would ride up to the waiting helo. He was prepared to get out and assist Jordan if necessary.

Jordan edged out from under his cover. He could see the two pilots in the helicopter cockpit as they approached his position. He felt safe with the Spads strafing the enemy, and he looked back at them running up the hill. Turning around, he watched the helo slowing, its nose pitching up. He moved away from the brush, kneeling on one knee and waving with one hand. "You're headed right, chopper. This is Lieutenant Jordan. I'm just above the flat sandy spot at the bottom of the hill. Make it snappy if—'' His voice stopped in midsentence.

Campbell heard Jordan stop transmitting as he orbited overhead. "Hey, Spook," he called.

The North Vietnamese sergeant slapped the radio from Jordan's hand, knocking it to the ground. Another soldier grabbed him around the neck, choking and pulling him into the brush where a short, lean soldier with ever-widening eyes quickly placed his rifle to Jordan's head. Jordan sat there in shock, not believing what was happening. His leg hurt from the shove to the ground.

"Jordan, this is Loosefoot. Repeat your last. You are breaking up, over." The big chopper stirred up a huge cloud of dust as it pulled its nose up to kill off forward speed. The aircraft commander couldn't seen any sign of the downed pilot, only the white chute lying across the ground next to a group of high shrubs. He called again, only to be interrupted by the Spad pilot.

"Loosefoot, get out of there! Something is not right. You copy? Get out of there!"

The helicopter pilot instantly pulled up on the collective and pushed forward on the cyclic stick at the same time, stopping the descent. The helicopter rocked forward, accelerating.

"Now," commanded the North Vietnamese sergeant. His troops stepped out from their hiding places and opened fire on the large dark-blue helicopter. Automatic fire raked the side of the chopper, penetrating the thin aluminum skin and instantly killing the crewman holding the rescue sling.

"We're hit," was all anybody heard as the helicopter crashed on the bottom of the hill and exploded in a huge ball of flame.

It was the first time the corporal had fired the Soviet-built rocket-propelled grenade in combat, and for a moment he just stood there with a look of astonishment on his face.

Suddenly he began jumping up and down, holding the weapon over his head and shouting as the helicopter burned. He had not expected such good results. Jordan's eyes flared with anticipation as a second soldier holding a bayonet-fixed rifle motioned for him to get up. He looked quickly over his captors, unsure of what to do, then pointed at his knee, his eyes now wide with fright. The soldier motioned for him to get up, gesturing with the razor-sharp tip of his bayonet. Jordan grimaced again and pointed to his knee, then howled as the top of the bayonet glanced off his ribs, drawing blood and a scream. Jordan hobbled up as the soldier grabbed him by the arm and jerked him upward, shouting something unintelligible to him in Vietnamese. Several of the other troops pointed their rifles at his head.

A chill went up Campbell's spine when he saw the helo explode. He didn't know if Larry had been aboard. For an instant he wanted to put the soldiers in the center of his gunsight and hold down the trigger until his guns were silent. But concern over Jordan's possible capture held him back and he circled lower for another look.

"Enfield flight, this is Escort. Terminate the SAR and return to home plate. The pilot has been confirmed as captured, over." The lead Spad pilot banked as he flew as close as he dared. Ground troops were firing at him. He could see the captured pilot and knew further efforts would be fruitless and risk other lives. He knew the navy pilot would soon be a new tenant of the Vietnamese prison system.

"Call in another helo," Campbell demanded. He felt so helpless, flying above his friend in air-conditioned comfort.

"Negative," responded the on-scene SAR commander. "They have him. I'm sorry. There were four people aboard that chopper that just bought it trying to save his life. That's all that can be done." The Spad pilot flew near the burning helicopter, looking for any sign of life. He knew there was none and banked sharply, taking a course that would take him to the sea. His wingman joined him in silence.

Campbell flew over his friend and rolled the aircraft from side to side. To remain any longer would be dangerous for him as well as for Jordan. He was afraid the soldiers would try something at Jordan's expense. Campbell added full power and turned toward the east. He would cross the beach under the escort of the fighters as they returned to their base at sea. Campbell had never felt as alone in all his life as he did during the short trip back to the *Barbary Coast*. On the way all he could think of was what he now had to tell Patricia Jordan.

4

Campbell leaned back in the ejection seat with his eyes closed and suppressed an increasing desire to throw up. The turbine whine was rapidly subsiding, the high pitch diminishing to a low hum, then nothing, as the jet engine wound down. He felt the tow bar locking onto his nose gear and he opened his eyes again. His hands were shaking now and a feeling of coldness was overtaking him. Campbell took several deep breaths, then secured his aircraft, shutting down the electrical system and waiting while Washington inserted the ejection-seat pins. He removed his helmet and handed it to the plane captain, then unhooked the fittings binding him to the seat. He could hear the rotor blades from the helicopter slowing behind him as Aggie secured from plane guard duties on the aft spot just forward of the fantail.

"Mr. Jordan not coming back?" Washington stood on the ladder attached to the aircraft waiting for his pilot to disembark. Descending the ladder with Campbell's helmet, he then stood to one side as Campbell climbed down from the A-4.

"I'm afraid not, Washington, he got bagged." Campbell regained his composure and began a walk-around of his aircraft, checking for battle damage. The plane captain walked alongside, carrying his helmet bag.

"Is he . . . is he dead?"

"No, he's not dead—he's a captive, a POW now." Campbell remained tight-lipped as he continued his walk around the Skyhawk. He stopped underneath the Sidewinder missile mounted on the side of the fuselage, then turned away and kicked an aircraft chock, planting the tip of his steel-toed boot squarely in the middle. It moved but a few inches, only adding to his frustration. The strain was showing in his face as he cursed, then turned away and headed for the island.

The plane captain was silent, sensing a burden that the pilot wouldn't share, and followed behind with his helmet bag.

Pancho was standing near the hatch holding a clipboard containing the maintenance-status, yellow-sheet forms. He was prepared to fill them out for Campbell, saving him the trouble. Word was quickly spreading that Jordan was down.

"What happened, man?" He scrutinized Campbell as he approached, then looked at his aircraft. He handed Campbell the yellow sheet. "Just sign it and put down the total time. I'll take care of the rest." He wanted to make things as easy for Campbell as possible.

Campbell took the clipboard and a pen from Pancho, hurriedly filling in flight times. "They shoved a missile right up his ass before I could shoot." He signed the form and handed it back to Pancho, then turned and took his helmet bag from Washington.

"A SAM?"

"No, a MiG—a seventeen—fired right in front of me before I could shoot—I was just about to take him off Larry's tail when he fired. Then he disappeared and the next thing I know a MiG is doing a slow roll over me like he's looking me over."

"Did you see a chute?"

"Yeah, I saw him captured on the ground. Listen, I've got to run, I'll talk to you later." Campbell turned and disappeared down the corridor, hurrying to the ready room.

Flight quarters had been secured and only the two ready-alert F-8s were positioned on the deck. The attack squadrons were standing down as the carrier headed south out of the northern war zone toward Thailand.

Inside the squadron ready room, the pilots had assembled to hear firsthand the account of the shoot-down. In the front of the room, Commander Lorimar and Lieutenant Podowski stood to one side, conferring with Smokin' Joe on the next course of action. Neither Porter nor the other flight members were witness to the engagement and could only speculate on what had taken place. Several of the squadron pilots leaned against the wall behind Porter, listening to him describe the attack against the bridge as he gestured with his hands.

Campbell entered the ready room through the rear door. Suddenly all conversation stopped as everyone watched him hang up his gear in the corner of the room. When he turned around, he was immediately besieged with questions. In the front of the room, several pilots from the other squadrons quietly slipped into the room unnoticed.

Campbell quickly moved to the front of the room,

stopping in front of Commander Lorimar. The flight surgeon handed him a cup of coffee heavily laced with brandy.

"Here, this will brace you up."

"Thanks." Campbell swallowed a slug of the lukewarm drink, then set it down on the SDO's desk and faced the gathered pilots. They listened quietly as Campbell reflew the mission with his hands, describing the position of the MiGs relative to his aircraft, twisting his body as he morosely explained how close he had been to firing at the MiG. The room grew even more silent as he continued, elaborating on the MiG he had seen and the markings on its side below the cockpit. In a few minutes he had recounted the entire mission.

Smokin' Joe listened attentively then described the MiGs as they attacked their flight, representing the attacking jets with his hands.

Podowski took notes as he listened, writing down as much as he could about the circumstances of the engagement. Later he would glean information from Campbell's written report to try to piece together recommendations for future missions.

"You said you saw a bunch of crosses painted on the side of his aircraft?" Tom McClusky, the Irish operations officer, was standing next to Commander Lorimar. His arms were folded and he was listening intensely. Suddenly he picked up the phone from the squadron duty officer's desk and began dialing the VF-112 ready room.

Podowski handed Campbell a clipboard with a debriefing form. "Here, you better fill this out while it's fresh in your mind."

Campbell took the board from the air intelligence officer and slumped into a chair. The events were still vivid in his mind and he could close his eyes and see the missile striking

Jordan's aircraft. The markings on the side of the MiG were as clear as if he were flying alongside him.

A pilot wearing a survival vest with a service .38 stuffed into a holster and hanging loosely to the side walked down the aisle, taking a seat behind Campbell. He was sweating and he wiped his hand across his brow. His light brown hair was cut short and clung to his head, still showing the marks of the flight helmet crease along the sides. He leaned forward over the seat in front of him.

Campbell stopped writing and turned to face Anson, then shrugged his shoulders. "There's no doubt, Ag. They had him surrounded. I guess you heard about the helo buying it?"

"Yeah, I knew the copilot back in flight training in Pensacola. Good kid." He paused a moment, not sure what to say. "Sure going to miss Jordan at our nightly smoke game."

"Yeah." Campbell continued to write, trying to explain on the form all the things that had happened in such a short time. He quickly filled in the blocks, turned the form over, and started on the back page.

Aggie waited patiently as long as he could, then asked, "What happened?"

Campbell set the clipboard on the seat next to him and turned around in time to see a tall, thin marine captain named Larue taking a seat next to Aggie. He was wearing pressed fatigues and smelled of gunpowder. Campbell guessed he had come from gunnery drill off the fantail. He watched the marine pull his cap off, revealing closely cropped, light brown hair.

"Jordan got bagged."

"I just found out. Damn, I hate to hear that. I really liked old Larry." The marine was shaking his head, his lips pressed together. Captain Larue was the officer in charge of the marine detachment aboard the ship and a regular at the nightly card game of smoke they played in the ward-room after dinner. Although Larue had yet to see combat, he seemed genuinely shocked upon hearing of Jordan's capture.

The rear door flung open and a lieutenant dressed in khaki walked into the ready room, stopping in front of the SDO's desk and asking who wanted to see him. The SDO pointed toward Lieutenant Commander McClusky.

"I'm Terry Steiler." He turned to the operations officer. "You wanted to see me." The fighter pilot shook McClusky's hand as the ops officer looked him over. The tall, lanky youngster who had turned twenty-three two weeks ago looked puzzled.

"I had a conversation with your ops officer a couple of weeks ago. He mentioned that some of his pilots had encountered this hot-shot North Vietnamese pilot that could hold his own with the best of them. He said they thought he was probably a Russian or a North Korean. He just in-formed me you had some stick time nose-to-nose with him. That true?" The slightly paunchy officer waited for Steiler to respond.

"Yeah, I had some eyeball-to-eyeball time with this guy. I just heard one of your guys got bagged—sorry to hear that. Wish I could have been on the scene—they should have had the fighters with them," he added.

"What about this hot shot?" McClusky came right to the point, ignoring the reference to the admiral's procedures.

"Mind if I get a cup of coffee first?"

"Help yourself. Take any cup."

Steiler stepped behind the SDO desk, helping himself, filling a cup to the brim. Several of the attack pilots who knew Steiler moved to the front of the room, abandoning Campbell to his task of filling in the details of the flight.

Steiler took a short sip, then turned around. "About three

weeks ago I was flying wing on my flight leader when Red Crown called a MiG scramble. The MiGs were after a recon flight, so we headed inbound looking for them. We spotted a loner and jumped him, thinking he was meat on the table. As soon as we did, another one showed up and started a run on us, forcing us to split, and I went after the newcomer. We fenced for a while, but it was him controlling the shots, and I realized I wasn't going to get a shot at him. I disengaged at the first opportunity, and the next thing I know, this guy is rolling around me.'' Steiler paused for a moment, his eyes glassing over as he visualized the scene again.

Campbell had stopped writing and was listening to the fighter pilot. He signed the form, then handed it to Podowski and walked over to Steiler and McClusky. He had met Steiler early in the cruise, talking to him briefly on the flight deck prior to a launch. "What did his plane look like—any special markings or anything?" Campbell asked.

"Yeah, the MiG had something special. It was like the planes you see in old WW Two footage—you know—rows of kills painted on the whole side of the aircraft. I briefly had a glimpse of rows of crosses, or something that looked like crosses. Could have been Xs."

Campbell's face lit up. "That's what I saw—rows of crosses. That son of a bitch must be one of their aces. I didn't think any of their pilots lasted long enough to become an ace."

Podowski was standing off to the side, listening to Campbell and Steiler. "I think I may have something on this guy. There's a report circulating about enemy fighter-pilot capability. I think the admiral's staff has it. I'll go see if I can borrow it." The AIO stepped through the door, disappearing down the corridor.

Steiler continued, trading comparisons with Campbell

until Podowski reappeared with a folder under his arm with several red SECRET labels stamped on the outside.

"What do you have, Professor?"

He opened the folder, pulling out a section marked DRV FIGHTER PILOT CAPABILITY, and set it on the podium, flipping through the pages. "They have a pilot over there that's got a reputation among the North Vietnamese. He's kind of . . . their Red Baron. His name—it sounds like Quan or Quang or something." He turned to the back section listing known pilots. "Ah, here he is, Quang—Maj. Quac To Quang. He flies a MiG-17, and believe it or not, he's coded 'Gray Ghost.' " Podowski continued reading from the file as the rest of the pilots gathered at the front of the room, anxious to hear more. For the first time the enemy had a name, one they might very well encounter in the future.

Campbell stood up and headed out of the ready room. He needed to be alone for a while. On the way out the flight surgeon slipped several of the miniature bottles of brandy into his pocket.

The corridors were empty and he worked his way to the forward part of the ship and his stateroom. As soon as he entered, he was overwhelmed by the absence of his roommate. Jordan's desk was open, revealing a framed photo of Patricia just inside. Another framed photo pictured Jordan and his dad standing in front of the old yellow Piper Cub that Campbell and Larry used to fly in college. In the slots were several letters from his wife, including one postmarked Bangkok.

Campbell flopped into a chair near his desk, slumping down and putting his feet up on the desk top. He spun the dial on the small safe and opened the door. Inside was a bottle of Jim Beam whiskey and a glass. He took out the glass, then opened one of the miniature bottles from his pocket and poured out half of it. He was alone in the two-man stateroom, and the room was dark except for the small lamp on his fold-down table.

Campbell drained the glass, then leaned back in his chair, propping his feet up on his desk and closing his eyes. Immediately, glimpses of the battle floated before him again. He began to see the MiG rolling over him, the rows of crosses perfectly clear.

The air-conditioning system was off again; only hot air poured from the duct inside the room. Beads of sweat were beginning to form on his forehead and he drew the back of his hand across his brow, causing a few drops to fall into his glass. He opened his eyes and the image disappeared. Campbell looked straight at the box sitting on the bunk bed, brought there for him to pack up Jordan's effects. The reality of war was taking hold, and he remembered a quotation he had once read in college. As he tried to remember it, the words slowly came back to him. Now they began to make sense and he remembered what the clergyman had written nearly two hundred years ago. Quietly he whispered to himself, " 'What distinguishes war is, not that man is slain, but that he is slain, crushed by the cruelty, the injustice, the treachery, the murderous hand of man.' "

A knock at the door jolted him and he sat erect, pushing the safe door shut. "It's unlocked," he shouted.

The door eased open. Pancho was leaning against the doorframe, grinning. "Thought you might feel like a little of this." He produced a bottle of Irish whiskey and set it on the desk.

"Don't you know booze is illegal aboard ship?" Campbell pulled out another glass and poured some in each, handing one to the Mexican American pilot. He slumped back into the chair, toying with the glass, then tossed down the liquor. Campbell stared at the glass, saying nothing for a few minutes, then looked up at Gonzales. "I should have got him."

"Got who?"

"The Gray Ghost, or whatever they call him."

"Quang?"

"Yeah—Quang. If I could have had another couple of seconds..."

"Listen, man, you did all you could. Uncle Sam pays us to bomb bridges and water buffalos and things, not get in shootouts with their best fighter pilots."

"I'm going to get the bastard—I'm going to plant a Sidewinder right up his ass."

"Yeah, and he's going to turn around and put one right up yours, too. You should have stuck around the ready room. Podowski got into some real shit about this guy." Pancho poured some of the whiskey into Campbell's glass, then some into his own. "Seems this Quang is willing to sacrifice his own wingman if it will get him a chance for a shot at an American. I bet he goes through a lot of wingmen that way." Pancho slugged down the liquor in his glass.

"Next time I'll be ready."

"You keep talking like that and you may be seeing Jordan sooner than you think. Speaking of wingmen—skipper told me to tell you that you are now a wing leader and you've been assigned a nugget that's due in tomorrow."

"A nugget?" Campbell feigned surprise.

"Yeah, a brand-new nugget fresh out of the training command. Congratulations."

"Due in tomorrow?"

"Tomorrow—the old man said he's in Da Nang picking up a replacement A-4 and ferrying it out to the ship. He'll catch us on the way to Bangkok." Pancho put the cap back on the bottle and slipped it into the desk. "Save me a little for some other time." He left, leaving Campbell alone again.

Campbell leaned back in the chair and placed his feet up on the desk top. He finished off the last of the glass, then closed his eyes, trying not to think of the events of the morning. Try as hard as he could, the images kept reappearing— Jordan's jet exploding, the MiG flashing by him. He opened his eyes and the images disappeared. Campbell reached into his pocket and pulled out the sleeping pill the flight surgeon had given him. He popped it into his mouth, swallowed, then climbed up into his bunk and leaned against the bulkhead at the end. To keep the battle scenes away he concentrated on happier scenes when he, Karen, Larry, and Patricia were together. Finally he drifted off, still wearing his flight suit and boots.

5

Someone was banging on the door. Campbell could feel the blows as if they were directed inside his head. Grudgingly he opened his eyes and peered down at the flight boots he'd slept in throughout the night. Then he realized he had on the flight suit he'd worn yesterday. He smelled of sweat and booze.

Above the stench of his own body he could smell the aroma of coffee. He pulled himself up and sat erect, rubbing his eyes. Pancho was standing by the bed, holding a cup of coffee.

"Doc said the booze and pills would make you wonder if life was worth living this morning. Here, I brought you this." He held out the cup of coffee.

Campbell took the cup, then climbed down from the bunk. "What time is it?"

"Almost noon. You get more sleep than I do in the ready room. Just come by to tell you that a message came in saying your boy will be launching out of Da Nang for a fifteen hundred overhead. If you want to catch the show, better get dressed and head for the flight deck." Gonzales waved, then turned and left the room.

Campbell took a sip of the coffee. His head was throbbing from the combination of booze and pills. The sleep had been good for him with no nightmares of yesterday's incident. He reached inside a drawer and pulled out an aspirin bottle and took three.

He wondered how the Brits did it—flying all day and then an open bar aboard ship. He decided he wasn't the drinking type and headed for the shower. He wanted to grab lunch and then be on the LSO platform when his new wingman came aboard.

The afternoon was hot, almost balmy, and too miserable to spend belowdeck. On the flight deck sailors and pilots alike were lying out in the sun, enjoying the breeze the carrier generated. It was Sunday, and the *Barbary Coast* was off-line and out of the battle zone for almost a week. Today was the first day in a week a combat mission had not been flown against the North Vietnamese. Flight operations had dwindled to almost nothing except for the occasional comings and goings of the helicopter. Only the two armed F-8s poised on the bow catapults connected the sailors lying in the sun to the war they were leaving behind, even if for a short period. The carriers remaining behind had already launched an attack against petroleum depots, taking advantage of the clearing weather.

Campbell liked to go up on the flight deck when the breeze freshened from the thunderstorms building up in the area. The hot, humid air would form into clouds, which when heated by the sun grew rapidly, turning dark and menacing as they expanded and rolled about each other. He leaned against the railing, looking out across the expanse of sea. On the flight deck below him, several jets were waiting to be towed to the elevator and taken below to the hangar deck. He watched the yellow-shirted linemen struggling to move the aircraft out of the way. With their goggles pulled back above their brows and with noise-suppression earphones hanging from their necks, they jockeyed the minuscule A-4s, wedging some behind the island and others onto the elevators. He could hear clicking coming over the PA system, then the call came announcing flight operations would commence in ten minutes. At the bow of the carrier each man picked up the straw mat he had been lying on and headed belowdecks, grumbling as only sailors knew how.

The cooling breeze was clearing his head and it felt good, a respite from the oppressive heat of the Gulf of Tonkin. The sun had already reached its zenith and was arcing into the west, hidden by the darkening clouds as they expanded and climbed upward. Campbell sensed his new wingman must be close by. The squadron LSO and his assistants were manning the platform in front of the Fresnel-mirror landing system. Campbell decided it was time for him to move out to the platform, where he planned to be when the A-4 arrived.

The LSO platform was manned by Lt. Mike Corbousier, an officer known as Pokey to everyone and the senior landing-signal officer aboard the carrier. He was the one LSO all pilots wanted on the platform when the weather was bad. His reassuring voice seemed to calm the pilots when the deck was pitching on a dark, moonless night. His face, red and scarred from adolescent acne, only got redder from standing out in the sun. His usual garb consisted of a baseball cap with a khaki handkerchief sewn to the back covering his neck. Sunglasses and white lip balm smeared across his lips, plus the regulation white LSO jacket, left no one to question who was manning the platform.

Pokey threw a headset at Campbell as he approached the platform. "Put that on when your boy shows up and you can listen in as I fearlessly guide him in for a perfect landing."

Campbell slipped the headset around his neck and climbed out on the small platform adjacent to the flight deck. They would be standing just a few feet from the wingtip of a landing aircraft as it screamed by groping for the exact touchdown point. Next to the platform was a net for them to jump into should an aircraft stray too far to the left.

"Got contact with him yet?" Campbell held one of the earphones to his ear but heard nothing.

"Approach is talking to him. They just gave him a hold while the admiral comes aboard." Pokey pointed to the bow of the ship and handed Campbell his binoculars.

Campbell adjusted the focus out to infinity and scanned to the south. He could make out the familiar shape of one of the carrier's helicopters as it approached, still a great distance away. He could not spot the A-4 that his new wingman was ferrying out from Da Nang.

"How far out is he?" Campbell asked.

"Your boy or the admiral?"

"Now you know I don't give a shit about flag officers."

"Our beloved admiral is about five minutes out—the new kid is about two if I could land him now." Pokey took the binoculars back from Campbell and pointed them toward the helicopter, which had been given a "Charlie" signal to land.

Campbell started to say something but didn't. He heard a voice over the loudspeakers ordering the deck cleared for the helo recovery. He turned and watched the helicopter growing larger, almost an illusion of motion as it appeared suspended in the sky, reminding him of an overgrown dragonfly. They were steaming south with the prevailing winds out of the northeast. The carrier would have to reverse course into the breeze to generate wind across the deck for the fixed-wing recovery. The helicopter could land from any direction and point into the wind, something Campbell could never understand and finally gave up trying. He looked down at the instruments providing relative wind direction and speed. The needle wavered at two to eight knots, averaging about ten degrees off the starboard quarter. The thunderstorms building up in the area were sending out winds of varying strengths and directions. He decided the helicopter pilot would figure it out and gave up thinking about it.

"Stand by to recover helo on spot five," the speaker boomed again.

Pokey pointed up at the island and Campbell looked amidship at the black, acrid smoke burbling from the stack, rolling around the island. Aggie had once told him that the combination of stack gas and the island's blocking the wind made landing his helicopter challenging. Campbell smiled.

Pokey leaned closer to Campbell. "I just read the new kid's training jacket. Looks like I've got my work cut out for me."

"What do you mean?" Campbell gave him a puzzled look.

"It appears that your boy can bomb the shit out of a target—but he isn't worth a damn when it comes to landing on a boat." The LSO gave Campbell his best "shit-eating grin," as he liked to call it.

"That's why he carries the nickname Ringer," Campbell countered. "I read his jacket, too."

They both turned and watched the helo as it got closer. Already the approach looked unusual to Campbell as the helicopter prepared to land in the opposite direction the carrier was heading. Aggie had reassured him that the helicopter always landed into the relative wind and it was perfectly routine. He was glad he was not a helicopter pilot.

Several miles off the starboard bow, Ens. Paul Swenson looked out of his aircraft at the heavy storm clouds forming in the area. They reminded him of the ones he used to see when he was a kid growing up in Kansas—not as big or as bunched together, but still he felt they had the same kind of menacing look. The storms fascinated him as he watched them rolling and boiling, the bottoms giving the appearance of an upside-down sea. They seemed endless and he could see bands of rain churning the water below into froth as the winds from the downdrafts pushed against the sea. Already the weather had forced the carrier to begin a series of course changes to avoid the worst of the building storms.

The naval aviator adjusted his power and continued flying the oval holding pattern as he waited for the helicopter to land. He was puzzled and for a moment wondered who was on board the helicopter that was causing him to use up his precious fuel. He decided they knew what they were doing and banked the aircraft, flying the outbound leg. He was burning little fuel, but it was his calculated reserves he was into now, the extra amount he counted on for delays. Swenson tilted his head down, focusing his eyes on the tiny fuel gauge on his instrument panel. Mentally he calculated how much longer he could remain aloft, then looked up again. Directly ahead he could see a large storm that was producing a lot of rain and wind. Probably my last chance at getting aboard in decent weather, he thought to himself.

Swenson listened to the helicopter pilot calling gear down. He didn't know helicopters could retract their gear and wondered what kind of helicopter was landing. He decided to call again. "Mother, this is Blackbeard two one," he called to the airboss up in the island overseeing all aircraft recovery operations. He used the call signs the ops officer back at Da Nang had given him, which he had copied onto a card. Swenson had made carrier landings before. The first time in Pensacola, when he made his first trip aboard the *Lexington* in a training-command single-engine Buckeye, and again in advanced training, it had both frightened and thrilled him. And later when undergoing transition training in the replacement training squadron, he had experienced the same feelings, both apprehension and elation simultaneously. The night landings had been terrifying, but the reassuring voice of a nearby instructor had steadied his nerves, and the seas had always been kind, giving him a steady deck. This was the first time Swenson had flown aboard a carrier when he wasn't in a training environment. He was nervous.

"Go ahead Blackbeard, this is Motha."

Swenson peered ahead at the darkening clouds directly in the path of the carrier and accompanying destroyers. "Are you aware of the large storms in the area, over?" He banked the aircraft and started a turn on the return leg of the circle he flew.

The slightly overweight commander twisted his head around, reexamining the approaching weather. The line of dark clouds in their path would be out of the way when they turned the ship into the wind, but there were equally menacing storms in the opposite direction. The tropical heat was building the cells rapidly. "We are aware of them, son. We plan to have you aboard before they reach us. What's your fuel state?"

Swenson glanced at his fuel gauge again. "Twenty-two hundred pounds." He eased the power back and gently raised the nose of the small jet. The A-4 locked onto the altitude and Swenson settled back into the seat.

Campbell could feel the ship beginning a turn into the wind. "I guess the helo pilot had second thoughts and decided to land headfirst.'' He shouted at Pokey, who couldn't hear him and pointed at his headset. Campbell pulled the earphones up over his ears, listening to the conversation between PriFly and the helicopter. As the carrier came around, the wind picked up and began blowing down the deck. Fixed-wing recovery would start soon and Campbell leaned into the wind trying to spot the tiny A-4. He tapped on Pokey's shoulder and pointed at the line of thunderstorms the new heading would take them directly into. The darkening clouds provided a better background to spot the silhouette of the A-4, circling at low altitude about a mile off the carrier's starboard quarter. He heard the ship's address system announce the arrival of Admiral Laceur's helicopter.

''Stand by to recover the helicopter. Welcoming party stand by,'' came another announcement over the ship's speakers. Near the island, six sailors in dress whites stood as they watched the admiral's helicopter pitch its nose up, slowing its descent. The Sikorsky SH-3A air-taxied forward, churning up an almost overpowering blast of air beneath its blades. Campbell braced himself as the helo air-taxied by him, following the directions of a lineman standing opposite the island. He wore sound suppressors cupped around his ears and had his arm extended, guiding the helicopter to its assigned landing spot. With both thumbs pointing downward the lineman lowered his arms, directing the helo to a smooth landing.

Campbell watched as the enlisted welcoming party ran to the port side of the helo and began struggling to unroll a red carpet, the wind whipping it up and down. Finally gaining control, the sharply dressed sailors lined up on both sides of the carpet, stood at attention, and placed their toes on the edge to hold it in place. Admiral Laceur stepped down from the helicopter.

"Isn't that a lot of garbage?" Campbell commented. He was frowning as he watched the spectacle unfold.

"Admiral Laceur arriving." The speaker was barely audible over the sound of the helicopter. A short, stocky first-class petty officer, with rows of hash marks sewn onto his sleeve, stood stiffly at attention and blew into his bosun's whistle. The sound was absorbed by the helicopter.

"That's bullshit," Campbell said. "My new wingman is out there burning up fuel while this pompous bastard has himself piped aboard."

"Stand by to launch helicopter." Pokey heard the call over his headset and punched Campbell. He pointed to the helo and then upward. They both braced themselves as the helo pilot raised up on the collective, lifting the helicopter into a hover. Again both Campbell and Pokey felt they were being shoved off the platform by the wind.

The nose of the helicopter dipped slightly and Aggie crept forward, slowly transitioning to forward flight. He flew forward about one hundred yards, then banked left and flew around behind the carrier, taking up a position off the starboard quarter to act as plane guard for Swenson.

"Stand by to recover fixed wing."

"It's about time." Campbell moved to the edge of the platform, watching Pokey and his assistant prepare to take Swenson aboard. Pokey was fingering the trigger housing that was hooked to the cut lights by a long black cable, testing each set of lights. Satisfied, he made one final adjustment to the intensity of the source light that formed the orange ball that the pilots used for a reference during their approach.

"Your signal is Charlie, Blackbeard two one. Say your fuel state." The commander in PriFly watched the A-4 through his binoculars.

"Nineteen hundred pounds," Swenson answered.

"Roger, two one, contact Paddles this freq, over."

Swenson missed the last call, pulling his torso harness straps tighter as he prepared to turn downwind for the landing approach. Already beads of sweat were beginning to gather around his eyes, seeping onto the oxygen mask cupped tightly to his face. He adjusted the temperature a bit cooler. His blond hair, bleached almost white by the sun, was matted and stuck to his helmet.

The junior pilot began his landing routine, completing the checklist and then sitting up straight, trying to find a comfortable position for his large frame in the tiny cockpit. He pulled on his gloves, yanking them up until they were snug, then readjusted the straps of his harness again as nervous tension began to build. He knew everyone would be watching him on his first landing aboard his new home.

"Blackbeard two one, this is Paddles. What's your fuel state?" The landing signal officer didn't wait for Swenson to call.

"Under . . . uh . . . under eighteen hundred pounds, sir." Swenson passed abeam the carrier and began a shallow turn to line up with the ship.

Campbell watched the A-4 begin its turn as he listened to the aerial conversation. He detected nervousness in the new pilot's voice and was glad the calm senior LSO was the one handling Swenson.

Pokey leaned over toward Campbell. "I looked at this kid's training record. He's had his share of problems landing aboard carriers—looks like his weapons scores got him assigned to an attack squadron."

"The kid's a pretty good bomber, huh?" his assistant asked.

"Yeah, better than good." Pokey pressed his mike button. "You're doing fine, Blackbeard two one. Call the ball."

Both men turned to look at the rapidly approaching storm

the carrier seemed to be zeroing in on. The deck was already beginning a slight roll as swells passed underneath.

"I don't like the weather we're heading into. Check with the bridge." Pokey turned to watch the approaching aircraft.

"Ball, A-4, one point six," Swenson called as he rolled wings level above the wake leading to the carrier. He had flown too far downwind before turning and was below the glide path. The round orange ball reflecting off the mirror of the Fresnel-mirror landing system looked low to him. He flew straight and level for a moment, allowing the ball to rise. As the ball touched the center of the mirror he lowered his nose, reducing power at the same time. The ball continued to rise even as his descent slowed, then stopped. Swenson sank below the glide path again and found himself adding and taking off big handfuls of power as he struggled with the illusive ball dancing on the polished mirror. He could see the huge ship pitching, causing the mirror to appear lower as the ship's bow climbed up over rolling swells. Swenson was trying not to overcontrol but it was becoming more difficult. He was getting behind.

"Settle down, Swenson," Paddles called. "You're chasing the ball. Set your attitude and quit making such big power changes." He slowed his words and lowered the tone, changing into his "Southern, way-out-in-the-country-sounding voice," as he liked to call it. Whatever it was, it usually had the right effect on pilots coming aboard at night in horrendous weather. "The old lady is shaking her fanny at ya—don't you pay her no attention. That's it, now drop your nose a hair and hold it," the LSO broadcast from his perch a few feet from where the jet would touch down. In older days, the landing signal officer would have his arms extended, holding a pair of yellow paddles for the pilot to use for a reference as to whether he was above or below the correct descent path. With the addition of the gyro-stabilized mirrored landing system, landing proficiency had improved, although landing on a pitching deck, especially at night, was more unnerving than any form of combat.

Pokey stood on the platform watching the approaching A-4. He could do little to help the pilot beyond giving advice, then waving him off if the approach looked unsafe. Pokey held the cut switch in his hand, ready to signal the red flashing lights. "He's not going to make it on this pass," Pokey told his assistant. "Notify PriFly that I'm going to send him around." The LSO in training called the commander in PriFly as Pokey pressed the wave-off button. A bank of red lights on both sides of the mirror came to life, flashing their warning.

The lights caught Swenson by surprise and he instantly added power, stopping his descent.

The four men on the platform swiveled their heads in unison as they watched Swenson fly overhead, accelerating as he flew upwind.

"No sweat, Swenson. I'll get you aboard this time, but you gotta steady up and stay off the power. You're light and causing yourself to go high in close and then diving for the deck. This time take off some of that power—you're overpowering yourself. What's your fuel state?"

"Roger," was all the LSO heard from the pilot. Swenson was sweating and shaking now. His breathing rate was too high and his pulse was too fast. He turned the air conditioner up full and loosened his mask. "Okay, Swenson, settle down now," he said out loud. "You've *got* to settle down. You've done this before. It's a piece of cake, just a piece of c-a-k-e."

"Fuel state, Swenson, fuel state. *Listen up now*." The LSO's voice brought Swenson back to reality and he looked at the gauge. The needle was buried in the lower part of the round fuel indicator. "Nine hundred pounds," he responded.

Campbell looked at Pokey, shaking his head in disbelief. "Pokey, you've got to get him aboard on this pass."

"I know, I know. He should have been brought aboard before the admiral, but the kid never indicated he was that tight on fuel." A light rain was beginning to fall, and the carrier was making a slight course change to miss the worst part of the storm, forcing Swenson to adjust to the new heading.

"A-4, ball, ah, seven hundred pounds," Swenson called. Campbell could sense the apprehension in his voice.

The LSO could sense it, too. "All right, Swenson, nice and easy now, ease off some of that power and fly the ball. You're looking good, but don't start chasing it. The old girl is shaking a little but just hold what you got." Pokey could see the A-4 nose pitch up and then back down again. He could hear the engine whine increase and then decrease several times as the jet neared the carrier.

"Come on, Swenson, quit jockeying with the power." The A-4 was high again and rain was beginning to fall as the carrier headed into a squall. If Pokey allowed the approach to continue, this nugget would miss the wires or dive into the deck. It was hopeless, and Pokey again initiated a wave-off. The bank of lights came on, flashing bright red against a background of darkening rain clouds. Everybody who had been observing Swenson watched in horror as the small attack jet continued. "He's not going around. Holy shit, he's not going to take the wave-off!" Campbell shouted. He went down on one knee, watching the A-4 as the nose suddenly dropped, then rose up again as Swenson groped for the deck.

A cascade of sparks showered down as the tail hook grazed the third arresting cable then snagged the last wire, slamming the jet down hard. Campbell watched with amazement as the jet stretched out the cable.

"He flies just like you do," Pokey said. "But when I get through chewing him out, he's going to wish he had stayed in Da Nang."

"The kid just needs a little practice, that's all," Campbell said as he heard the engine whine die down as Swenson pulled back the throttle. Swenson had hit hard, so hard that the gear would have collapsed had he not been low on fuel and at minimum landing weight. Campbell watched the A-4 rolling backward, the tail hook still holding on to the tensioned cable. The aircraft had landed left of centerline and was precariously close to the edge of the deck. He heard the young aviator shut down the engine and could imagine him staring at the blue-green water swiftly passing by sixty feet below. Now rain was beginning to fall in sheets, obscuring forward visibility to a few feet.

"Thank God." Captain Pearson leaned against his chair on the bridge and watched a flight-deck lineman disappear into the rain as he ran to place chocks against the wheels on the A-4. The commanding officer of the *Barbary Coast* turned around and faced his officer of the deck. "Lieutenant Farthing, turn starboard forty degrees and let's get out of this storm; and inform Treasure Chest of our intentions and execute." The Old Man, as he was known, sat down in his chair and twisted around to see the recovered aircraft, distinguishing only a dim shape as the rain poured down.

Lieutenant Farthing passed the order to the newly assigned quartermaster at the wheel, then got on the phone to AirOps, advising them to hold off on recovering the rescue helo stationed off the stern quarter until they were clear of the storm. He made the call to the destroyer following in trail and watched the compass begin to swing as the 33,000-ton ship started its turn slowly to starboard. The ship was still moving through the water at thirty knots and leaned slightly due to its high center of gravity.

Pearson could sense the turn even as he faced aft and quickly turned around, gripping the side railing of his chair.

He tried to focus on the position of the rudder indicator, hurriedly searching his pockets for his glasses.

Campbell jumped down from the catwalk, pulling the hatch shut behind him, intending to wait out the rain before going up to meet Swenson. He was soaking wet.

Swenson watched as the chocks went in around his wheels and waited for one of the small tow vehicles to hook up to him and pull his aircraft away from the edge. At first he felt only a small jolt as the aircraft's nose moved slightly left. Then another one and a series of small bumps. His gloved hands gripped the canopy rail tightly as he realized what was happening. He pushed hard against the brake pedals, lifting himself off the seat. The aircraft continued its slide.

Pokey was still on the LSO platform securing the equipment. When he realized the aircraft was sliding over the side, he screamed into his mike. The heel of the ship didn't seem excessive, but the jet was definitely going over. Somebody was turning the ship too hard and again he screamed over his phones to stop the turn. It was too late. The aircraft was inching its way toward the edge of the deck, its tailhook still gripping the cable.

Campbell cracked the hatch open to let in fresh air. The rain had almost stopped and he started to step outside, then heard a loud crunch followed by a tearing sound. As he stepped out onto the catwalk, his eyes widened when he saw the nose gear of the aircraft dangling over the edge of the flight deck, the plane's tailhook still attached to the cable, but slowly slipping. Campbell leaped from the catwalk up onto the deck, ignoring the tensioned cable strung out like a rubber band.

The linemen were frantic, throwing chocks and anything at hand in an attempt to stop the aircraft. They'd jumped out of the way at the last moment as the nose gear went over the side. Only the hook prevented the aircraft from falling off the deck as the arresting cable slowly played out. Nothing seemed to stop the slide.

"Get out of here!" Campbell heard Pokey shout at him. If the cable snapped, it could act like a great scythe, severing legs and arms as it whipped across the deck. Campbell ignored the warning and ran to the side of the aircraft. He could see Swenson sitting in the cockpit, both hands gripping the ejection handle, ready to pull it if the aircraft didn't stop. Aggie already had the helicopter in position, hovering abeam and slightly aft of Swenson, waiting to see what would happen.

As soon as Captain Pearson was informed of the situation, he ordered the turn reversed, and the ship was now leaning the other way. He hoped it would stop the aircraft from slipping any farther. The engineering watch, eight decks below, was ordered to put the propellors in reverse and was doing his best to get the huge propellor shafts slowed. Pearson knew it would take several miles before the ship would cease its forward motion. He prayed the pilot could hold on until then. The *Barbary Coast* had slipped from the storm and bright sunlight beamed down on them now.

Campbell looked across the flight deck. Already the cherry picker, the flight-deck crane, was being fired up to pull the aircraft back up on deck. Spotting Washington near the island, he ran across the deck. Together they jumped into the start cart and headed for the disabled A-4. Campbell leaped out just as Washington rammed the low vehicle into the leading edge of the front wing. The tug came to a stop resting against the starboard gear, halting the sliding aircraft.

Campbell stood back out of the way as Washington and several linemen wrapped a chain around the tailhook and attached it to the huge crane behind the aircraft. He looked up at the cockpit. Swenson still had his hands on the ejection handle, not sure if he was going over the side or not. Campbell looked at Washington and gave him a thumbs-up as the aircraft was secured to the crane. Campbell jumped up on the tightly wedged tug jammed under the wing. Stretching up as much as he could, he beat on the canopy until he saw Swenson release the face curtain and look down. He motioned for Swenson to open the canopy, waiting while he heard the motor engage, raising it.

Swenson unhooked his oxygen mask, then raised the dark visor. His face was ashen, almost colorless, and sweat was running off his brow. He had shut the engine down, securing the electrical system, as soon as he started the slide, failing to hear any of the calls made to him.

"Hand me the pins, sir."

Swenson looked around for the voice, unsure what to do.

"The pins, hand me your ejection seat pins." Washington was perched precariously on a ladder being held by several of the linemen. He took two pins from Swenson and inserted them in the ejection seat behind his head while Swenson inserted the other one in the yellow canopy-jettison handle. Washington helped him unstrap, and together, they carefully exited the A-4, its nose hanging precariously over the edge.

Swenson was unhurt and Campbell grabbed him by the arm, leading him toward the crowd waiting near the island. "My name is Lt. Jim Campbell and you're going to be flying wing with me. But you sure know how to make an entrance, don't you?

Campbell was grinning as he guided their newest aviator toward the ship's island, but he was having mixed emotions over Swenson. He was excited over the prospect of being a section lead, but he wondered if the accident would shake the ensign's confidence. Time would tell, he thought.

The *Barbary Coast* pulled gently against her anchor, stretching the heavy chain links that led below to the massive spike buried in the mud-encrusted bottom. A gentle breeze was brushing across her, slowly swinging her around in the shallow Gulf of Siam. A few sailors had spread woven reed mats out on the flight deck and were lying in the early-morning sun. The man-of-war was standing down, no longer a mobile airfield but a floating hotel, and her crew anxiously awaited their chance to go ashore and experience the delights of exotic Bangkok.

The officer of the deck had shifted his watch from the bridge to the starboard quarterdeck. Looking trim in freshly laundered whites, the OOD stepped up to the rail and adjusted his binoculars, focusing on the procession of World

War II vintage landing craft that were converging on the carrier. The venerable craft were strung out all the way from the boarding ladder below the quarterdeck to the shoreline.

The Gulf of Siam was shallow and the *Barbary Coast* was anchored as close to shore as her captain dared. Transporting the liberty parties back and forth fell to the Royal Thai navy, whose country was host to the complement of officers and sailors who would soon be overrunning the streets of Bangkok on a much-needed R and R.

Going ashore, Lieutenant Campbell pulled himself higher, wedging his shoes into the netting draped over the inside hull of the landing craft, and scanned the beach as they neared a Thai navy base. Spots of perspiration stained the back of his shirt, and the fresh air felt good to him in spite of the uncomfortable perch.

"Can you see ashore yet, Mr. Campbell?"

"Just ahead." Campbell was letting his mind wander as they approached the beach, rekindling visions of his wife. He remembered the honey-colored skin and the deep red she liked to put on her toenails. Karen seemed born with a tan and needed only a little exposure to the sun to achieve one. Unlike his wife, it took Campbell weeks of exposure before he could stay out in the sun without burning. To many of the pilots who had been encased inside the *Barbary Coast* for long periods, the sun seemed even more intense this morning.

Campbell looked down at Washington and smiled. The airman was on a special three-day liberty, a reward for having saved Swenson's A-4.

"Yeah, I see it. Hang on, Washington, we're almost there." Campbell squinted beneath the hot sun, trying to find a sign of Karen. Seeing nothing, he twisted around on the rope netting and looked down into the landing craft. He could see Pancho crammed into a sea of white, standing next to Paul Swenson at the rear of the hold. Swenson wore a small Band-Aid on his cheek to conceal the cut he'd received exiting his A-4. Both men were wearing civilian clothes, but Gonzales had on a bright red Hawaiian shirt he had purchased in Pearl at the beginning of the cruise, standing out among the sailors clad in all-white uniforms.

The scene on the beach was indeed taking on the appearance of a small invasion as the landing craft reached the shoreline. Sailors and officers from the carrier were scrambling out of the craft, stepping from the opened bows onto the beach.

Campbell clung to his perch as the Thai helmsman pointed the bow at an empty strand of beach, gunning the engine. He tightened his grip as the bow impacted, heaving some of the sailors into each other and drawing curses from a few. Immediately the landing platform that formed the bow split away, lowering itself down, creaking and groaning as the chain played out. It reminded Campbell of an ancient drawbridge being lowered.

Thai sailors tying lines to the beached craft broke into grins as hordes of white uniforms and a few multicolored shirts discharged onto the beach. The men of the *Barbary Coast* were ready for action and wasted little time as they headed for cold beers and the friendly Thai girls they had been dreaming about.

Outside the base, taxicabs were lining up in single file along the fence. Each driver had a pocketful of business cards advertising the pleasures of Bangkok. Eager sailors were piling into the taxis, encouraging the drivers to hurry up and leave. After speeding away, most cabs traveled only a short distance before the drivers were besieged to stop at roadside bars doing a land-office business selling the first beers the sailors had tasted in over a month.

Campbell probed the crowd of onlookers as he walked alongside Pancho and Swenson. Nearing the gate, he still hadn't spotted his wife.

"Don't worry, man, she'll be here." Pancho reassured Campbell.

"I hope so. I'd hate to spend four days here knowing my wife is somewhere in the city and being unable to find her." He continued looking as they walked, then paused. He could hear someone calling his name.

"Jim . . . Jim." The voice was coming from across the fence.

Campbell searched up and down the fence line, but still she eluded him.

"Is your wife blond and kind of tall, Mr. Campbell?" Swenson pointed toward a group of people.

"Yeah, but I'm not 'Mr. Campbell.' 'Jim' or 'Soupy' will do just fine." Before Swenson had a chance to respond, Campbell broke away. He ran through the security gate while returning a salute to the grinning Thai guard.

"Karen!" he shouted.

Karen handed her bag to Patricia, then broke away and ran toward her husband. Patricia Jordan dutifully held Karen's purse, watching Jim hoist his wife in his arms. Patricia's eyes misted over as she watched. The pain of her husband's being missing was still very much on the surface as she silently wished Larry could be there with her.

Jim and Karen stood kissing as uniformed sailors walked around them, heading for the platoons of waiting taxis. Washington was walking ahead of Pancho and Swenson when he slowed, giving his special mock salute as he passed near Campbell and his wife.

Gonzales stopped him. "Don't bother. Right now he's not on this planet. Kind of makes you want to get married, doesn't it, Swenson?"

"Yeah, I guess so." Swenson came to a stop, patiently waiting to be introduced to Campbell's wife, his smile seemingly permanently attached to his face.

Karen Campbell felt her husband loosen his grasp on her

and she slid to the ground. "You're embarrassing. Did you know that?" Stepping back, she looked him up and down, her eyes scrutinizing every inch as if she expected something to be missing.

"Don't worry. I'm all here, completely intact," he said.

Karen moved close to him again, taking his hand. "Jim, I was so worried when Patricia was notified. There was nothing about you, only Larry."

"Where is Patricia?"

Karen twisted around, pointing. "She wanted us to be alone before she came over."

"I understand. In the meantime, I want you to meet my new wingman," he said, guiding her over to the young ensign. "Karen, this is the famous Ringer Swenson, at least until we come up with a better name for him. He just checked in—we'll be flying together the rest of the cruise." He decided not to mention the landing incident. "Paul, this is my wife, Karen."

Swenson blushed as Karen extended her hand. "I'm glad to know you, ma'am."

Her hand was dwarfed by his and she giggled upon hearing the word "ma'am." "It's a pleasure meeting you. I hope you're going to take good care of my husband." Karen let her hand drop and for a brief moment stared at him, wondering if this young pilot was capable of making sure her husband returned to her. Then she turned back to her husband. "Patricia is standing over there. I think it's time we went over."

Swenson and Pancho fell in step behind them, holding back as Campbell approached Larry Jordan's wife. All during the night Campbell had lain awake, trying to think of what he would say to her. A feeling of helplessness washed over him as Jim walked up to Patricia and put his arms around her, knowing all he could do was recount what had happened.

"Oh, Jim," was all she could manage as he held her. The ever-present smile was absent and her eyes were puffy. She was always spirited and vibrant, the one to do anything on a dare. Her hair was normally neatly combed, but now it draped limply on her white shoulders.

"He's alive, Patricia," was all Campbell could come up with.

She could no longer hold back and tears began to run down her cheeks as her arms tightened around him. She clung to him momentarily, then let go and backed away.

"But, Jim," she said, "I have to know more. Please tell me everything you can about Larry."

"I will, but I think it would be better if we waited until we get back to the hotel." He started to lead her away, then paused, remembering Pancho and Swenson. He introduced them to her and they both told her how sorry they were about Larry.

Karen pulled a blue silk scarf from her purse and waved it overhead vigorously. Immediately a green-and-white Datsun pulled from the line of waiting taxicabs and stopped next to them. The short, plump driver got out and made a *wai*—the Thai gesture of greeting. He held his palms together and brought the fingertips toward his nose as he bowed slightly.

"I am Anuman Chakrabongse, best driver in all Bangkok." He pulled out a fistful of cards and handed one to Campbell. "Please call me Johnny." His smile seemed a perpetual part of his face. He had tried to let his sideburns grow and wore a thin mustache. His eyes seemed to twinkle and the corners were wrinkled from his continuous smiling.

Campbell took the card and looked at it, glad that the driver went by a simple American name. "I'm Jim Campbell, Johnny." He put the card in his pocket and shook hands with the driver.

"You ready go to the hotel?" the cabdriver asked as he

picked up the canvas travel bag that Campbell had brought with him.

"Johnny has been our taxi driver ever since we got here," Karen said. "He knows everything about Bangkok and all the good places to eat." The two girls had been in Bangkok for over a week, coming directly from Hawaii. They had met Johnny at the international airport and he had provided them with taxi service ever since. He took them on tours, to restaurants and places to shop. They couldn't believe they had been so lucky to obtain a driver as knowledgeable as Johnny.

"Yes, I think it's time we got out of this hot sun and headed for the hotel." Campbell opened the door of the taxi and waited as Patricia got in, followed by his wife.

The taxi driver immediately pulled out into traffic and tail-gated the car in front of him. He gave a continuous monologue of history and facts as they drove northward toward Bangkok. But during the long ride to the hotel Patricia stared silently out the window, preoccupied, her mind elsewhere. Little was said among the three, and Karen was content for her husband just to hold her hand.

Arriving at the hotel, they all immediately went up to the third floor. Patricia disappeared into the room next to the Campbells', sitting silently in a chair in the corner, smoking a cigarette and waiting patiently for Campbell to come and tell her about her missing husband.

In the adjoining room Campbell hung his overnight bag in the closet of the bedroom, then sat on the edge of the bed as he waited for Karen to come out of the bathroom. His wife's makeup items spread across the surface of a small dresser, cast an air of femininity he had not seen for some time. He went over and picked up a bottle of perfume, one he had given her in San Diego. Chanel, her favorite. The scent immediately reminded him of her.

She walked into the room from the bathroom. "You're not taking up wearing perfume, are you?"

He smiled and put the bottle down. "Only if it would give me a few extra days in port with you." He walked over to her and pulled her down on the bed with him, twisting her underneath him as they fell.

She pulled him closer and they kissed hard and long. The separation and war only added to the feelings they had for each other, and they both could feel a fire igniting within them. Suddenly she pulled back. "Patricia's waiting, Jim. We had better go to her."

Campbell rolled over on an elbow, looking at his wife, brushing away a lock of hair from her eye. "I know. I have to get it over with, but facing her may be the hardest thing I've ever had to do." He sat upright, then pulled his wife up with him and they started for the door.

When Patricia heard the knock on her door, she pushed her cigarette into the ashtray. She opened the door, then went back to her chair. Jim and Karen sat down on the bed across from her, silent for a moment. He could see her eyes were red and moist and a half-empty box of Kleenex sat on a nearby table.

"Please, Jim, tell me what happened. Tell me he's alive. Tell me that." Patricia kept her eyes glued to his.

Campbell looked over at his wife for a moment, imagining the roles reversed and Jordan talking to Karen. He wondered how Karen would have reacted. He could see traces of moisture glistening in his wife's eyes. Then Campbell turned back to Patricia. "Pat, he's alive. I saw him standing with uniformed North Vietnamese troops at the bottom of a hill. They captured him and there was nothing more we could do." Campbell reached over and took her hands, wishing there was something he could tell her, some way he could remove the pain she was feeling. He felt a tinge of guilt, knowing that if he could have gotten into a firing position just moments sooner, he might have shot down the pursuing MiG.

Patricia bit her lip lightly, grasping for something to say. Finally, her voice trembling slightly, she said, "Oh, Jim, he promised me he would always come back. In my heart I knew he was alive, but I needed to hear it from his best friend." She pulled one of her hands free and placed it on Karen's. "Please, Jim, I want to know all you can tell me. How it happened, even how he got shot down—everything."

"Wait here a moment. I've got to get something." Campbell got up and went to his room, returning with a small topographical map, which he spread on the bed. Karen moved closer as he put his finger on a blue area representing the Gulf of Tonkin. "This is a point known as Yankee Station—all the carriers circulate around this area. This is where most of the strike flights originate and where we departed from that day." He moved his finger to a point farther up on the map and closer to land. "This is where we have a guided-missile cruiser stationed. That's our point man, and with their radar, they watch everything the North Vietnamese do. They are also prepared to shoot down anything the Vietnamese launch at the fleet. They keep tabs on the MiGs and control all the flights going in-country. They were controlling us that day and also sent in the fighters when we were attacked by the MiGs."

"Didn't you have the fighters with you?" Patricia asked. "Larry said that he always had fighter protection when he went in to bomb."

She looked puzzled. Campbell was afraid she might ask questions he couldn't or wouldn't answer. He moved his finger over to a spot on a small river south of Hanoi. "That's true in nearly all cases," he said. "Sometimes, there are circumstances that are beyond anyone's control. That day we had four F-8 Crusaders flying MiG Cap for us. They were close by but just couldn't close on the MiGs fast enough. It wasn't their fault. It was"—he paused for a moment—"just a combination of factors." Campbell looked into his wife's eyes, trying to imagine what she was feeling.

Patricia looked at Karen and then back at Jim again. "Weren't the MiGs spotted before they got there? Didn't you know they were coming?"

"No. They were there before anyone had an inkling. We were already attacking the bridge and everyone was diving and just all of a sudden they were there. Two of them I think, maybe four. Some of the flight just panicked and jettisoned their bombs as soon as they saw the MiGs. Larry called me and asked if I was all right, and then we continued down and dropped our bombs on the bridge spans. After we pulled off target I looked up and spotted two MiGs about three thousand feet above us. They were going in the same direction as we were, and I knew they were going to make a run on us. The F-8s were inbound and I hoped the MiGs would turn and run. Anyhow, Larry and I were heading for the coast as fast as we could go when they rolled in on us. I yelled at Larry and he called for a break." Campbell began reenacting the scene, using his hands as all aviators seemed to do when describing aerial action. "One of the MiGs stayed with Larry and one took off after me. I was trying to maneuver behind Larry and get a shot at the MiG. Larry was trying to shake him but the pilot was good, very good. I later found out he is their top fighter pilot and usually comes out on top if the odds are in his favor. And besides that, the MiG-17 turns like nothing you can imagine. I couldn't get close enough to use my guns on him, and the only chance I had was to launch a Sidewinder heat-seeking missile."

Patricia's eyes widened when Campbell mentioned the missile. "But doesn't that missile lock onto a heat source, any heat source?" she asked.

Campbell could see in her eyes what she was asking.

"Yes, Pat, it does," he said. "And I know what you are thinking. It will lock onto the hottest source of heat around regardless of what insignia is painted on the side of the aircraft. But it was the only chance we had. Pat, there was a MiG on my tail at the same time, probably flown by an inexperienced pilot, but nevertheless, he was on me and firing his cannons. If it had been me, I would have wanted Larry to do the same thing." He paused for a moment to let it sink in, then looked at his wife. He could see her expression changing as she listened.

This was the first time Karen had heard him describe the conditions of combat they experienced. She had only been exposed to tales of simulated combat as bragged about by all the pilots. In the past it had seemed to her like only a game played with multimillion-dollar toys by boys well past their years of playing war. Karen sat attentively and listened as Jim continued.

"I told Larry to keep dragging the MiG out for me. I was so close—so close. Larry and I had worked out a plan where if one of us had to fire a Sidewinder at a pursuer, we would call out 'Hellfire' and that would be the signal to throttle back, leaving the attacking jet as the hottest source of heat for the missile to track in on. Pat, I almost had him lined up in my sights when the MiG fired a missile of his own. I warned Larry, but it was too late, the missile flew right up his tailpipe. I had to keep evading the one on me and finally lost him in a cloud. By that time the F-8s showed up and shot down the one chasing me and the other one disappeared. I turned back and spotted a chute and followed it down. I got contact with Larry and had him hide in the bushes while we kept any ground troops away."

Patricia's eyes widened again. "There were troops? What kind of troops—how many?"

Campbell put his finger back on the map and pointed to an area covered with lines forming uneven circles. "Here," he said, "this is the hill Larry was on. He landed about here and crawled into some bushes. I spotted him and made radio contact with him. I even told him to pull his chute in so no one could see him. Then I flew around the area. When I spotted men running down a hill, we strafed them. Any that survived ran away from the area. What we didn't know at the time was that there were regular troops in the area."

"You didn't see them?" Patricia asked.

"No, it's just too hard to see everything at the speeds we fly. I think they must have spotted Larry's chute when he came down and then sneaked up along the creek bed."

"But the rescue helicopter. What about the helicopter? Larry told me not to worry because a rescue helicopter was always nearby."

"It was shot down trying to rescue Larry." He paused for a moment. "The four men on board the helicopter were killed."

"Oh, my God," she said. "I didn't realize . . ." Patricia was silent for a few moments, staring at the wall across the room, and then asked, "Was the MiG pilot who shot down Larry a Russian?"

"I don't think so. I got to see a report of some of their pilots and I'm pretty sure it's a North Vietnamese named Quang."

"Quang? You actually know his name?"

"Yeah. Somehow they managed to obtain a reasonably good history on this guy—probably from newspaper clippings from the *Hanoi Gazette* or whatever they have. He's supposed to have had a French father and was educated in both France and Russia. From what I've heard, he's the best they have and is suspected of downing nearly a dozen of our planes." As Campbell talked, he leaned back on his arms, crossed his legs and tried to find a comfortable position on the springy bed. "I'm really surprised anyone would want to fly wing with this guy though. He has a reputation for

letting his wingman fly lead while he hangs back and picks
and chooses the shots. Sometimes the lead gets sacrificed.''
Campbell sat up on the bed and let his legs hang over the
side, then crossed them underneath him. ''One thing though,
if you end up in a hassle with this guy, you can bet the
advantage is his or he wouldn't be there. He cuts and runs
when the odds change. He's one smart fighter pilot.''
Campbell looked at his wife and she looked at Patricia, then
she reached out and took her hand, trying to console her.

''Patricia, Larry's alive,'' Campbell said. ''I talked to
him and he was okay. He banged up his leg a little on
landing in the brush, but other than that he was okay. The
North Vietnamese captured him and they will probably take
him to Hanoi or one of their other prisons.''

Patricia took a tissue from a box and began dabbing at her
eyes. Mascara had begun to seep onto her cheeks and she
pulled the dampened tissue across her cheekbone, blackening
it. ''I'm sorry, you two.'' She continued wiping at her eyes.
''It's just that I never expected it to happen.'' She looked
down at the map, which contained a small inset showing
most of Southeast Asia. ''It's just that he's so near yet I
can't go see him, help him.'' She placed one finger on the
coast of Thailand and another near the top of North Vietnam.
''Do you think they will torture him?'' Her eyes were
beginning to clear now.

Campbell wasn't expecting that question. ''I can't answer
that, Patricia. All I know is that the Vietnamese have been
somewhat secretive about their prisoners and use them for
as much propaganda as possible. Larry doesn't know anything they don't already know and isn't related to anyone
famous that I know of. So they will probably question him
for a while and then put him in with the rest of the POW
population to wait out the war or he may be included in a
prisoner exchange. I know that possibility is being explored
by our side.''

Patricia lit up a filtered Kent and leaned back, taking a large drag from the cigarette. She let out a lungful of smoke and then sat up. "Yeah, sure. The army officer that came to give me the news about Larry didn't know anything. All he had was a telegram that had come into the American embassy. I even went to the embassy but no one could tell me anything. All they did was suggest that I go back to my home in San Diego and go on with my life. They said everything possible was being done and they would let me know if they heard anything else. I think they spent more time with some tourist over here from New Jersey who had his wallet stolen than they did with me. I had my husband stolen from me and all they wanted to do was get me out of their hair." She leaned back into the soft-backed chair, her thoughts spanning back to happier times with her husband.

"Have you heard from the skipper yet?" Campbell asked.

"Yes, I'm to have dinner with him tonight here at the hotel. He asked me to ask you two to come also, but you don't have to. In fact, I want you and Karen to go out and have a good time while you're here. The very thing I don't want is to be a burden to you and expect you to be with me every minute of the day. If I'm having a particularly hard time, I know you'll be there for me." Patricia pushed her cigarette into an ashtray beside the chair.

"You can count on us," Karen said.

"I know," was all Patricia had to say. She stood up and walked toward the bathroom door. "I'm going to go clean up now. I'll see you two tomorrow."

After a quiet dinner and a few drinks, Jim and Karen returned to their hotel room. Karen hung a DO-NOT-DISTURB sign on the door, then locked it and faced her husband. She had a provocative look on her face, one that could only suggest that she wanted him, needed him. Campbell lay on the bed, his arms behind him, watching Karen as she moved around the room. A small lamp was on, barely lighting the room, and Campbell's face was concealed in shadows. His wife's light chiffon skirt clung to her thighs as she moved, twirling outward whenever she turned.

Campbell watched his wife slowly walking toward him, her hands behind her back. A seductive smile was forming on her lips, suggesting possibilities he had only dreamed about aboard ship. Suddenly she broke and lunged toward the bed, falling on him. He grabbed her, rolling with her. The modest and proper little girl her father thought was almost saintly squirmed underneath him as he lay on top of her pinning her arms back on the pillow. He could feel her thighs tensing, enfolding his as he pressed against her, kissing her fully on the mouth. He began tracing the outlines of her breast, tightly straining against the fine cloth of her blouse. It had been nearly a month since they had made love, and in the weak glow of the lamp, they explored each other, until finally they could no longer hold back.

All during the night they made love till they were both exhausted. Then they lay there, fulfilled, she in his arms, and both of them drifting in and out of sleep.

It was midmorning and Campbell reached out for her, his hand grasping empty space. He opened his eyes and blinked, trying to focus on the ceiling fan laboring above his head, its wooden blades slicing at the air. He stared at the blades momentarily, pausing while he attempted to figure out where he was. Karen leaned over him, her blond hair hanging limply across her ears. "Good morning, stranger," he heard a voice say. It took him a moment to place himself inside the hotel room and not inside his stateroom back aboard the *Barbary Coast*.

"Good morning." He raised up on one elbow, reaching for his watch on the nightstand next to the bed.

"It's almost ten o'clock," Karen said. "You were sleeping so soundly this morning I thought I would let you sleep in before you have to escort me around Bangkok proper.'' She sat down on the bed and pulled her knees up to her chin, hugging them.

"I haven't slept this good or long for months," he said.

"I figured as much. That's why I let you sleep in."

"What's on the agenda today?"

"I've already arranged for Johnny to guide us."

"You mean the taxicab driver that brought us in? I hate to think what that is going to cost."

"Just enjoy it. Remember, it's part of a delayed wedding present from Dad. He can afford it."

"Yeah, I know, he reminds me of it at every opportunity. Okay, where are we off to today?"

Karen pulled out a guidebook she had purchased in the hotel lobby and opened it on the bed in front of Campbell. "Patricia says she wants to be alone today and that she will see us tomorrow. I think the CO and some other high-ranking officers are going to be with her. She won't be without company, anyway."

Campbell thumbed through the book, studying pictures of life in a country that seemed strange to him. "What have you seen since you've been here?" he asked. He continued thumbing through the book, pausing at a map of the city.

"Oh, we went to see the Emerald Buddha. You've got to see that. Anyhow, Johnny says he will show us the best of everything. Bangkok as he puts it. Let's leave it up to him, okay?" Karen took the book away and pulled him up from the bed. "Now, jump into the shower and get ready." She began pushing him into the bathroom.

It was nearly an hour later when Johnny appeared downstairs in the Thai Room. He leaned against a wall inside the entrance, talking to a uniformed waiter as he waited. He spoke in hushed tones and glanced around nervously as the waiter pulled a rag across a carved teak bas-relief, applying an almost invisible coat of scented oil. Across the room, another bar attendant stood cutting wedges of lime. Johnny's smile reappeared as he spotted Karen coming down the stairs. "Ah, Ms. Karen, so happy to see you." He brought his hands up, making the traditional *wai* greeting. Bowing slightly to Karen, he then faced Campbell and repeated the gesture. He grinned as Karen returned the greeting.

Campbell, not sure of what they were doing, just said good morning to him.

"And good morning to you, Mr. Campbell. I hope you had a good sleep last night. Today, you have good *sanuk*."

Campbell looked at his wife, puzzled.

"*Sanuk* mean good fun," the taxicab driver chipped in. "Thai people believe life should be fun. That's why they smile all the time. They believe nothing is so bad that you can't find some joyful meaning. Today we *pai taeo*, just wander around for fun," he said. "Your government pick a good place for *sanuk*."

Campbell looked at his wife and grinned. "*Sanuk*," he said.

"*Sanuk*," she repeated.

They quickly boarded the taxi and Johnny pulled the Datsun away from the curb, darting in between another taxicab and a gaggle of motor scooters, easily blending in with the flow of traffic. "Too many cars," Johnny said. His smile was still frozen on his face. He turned right onto Charoen Krung and settled into the jumbled flow of traffic moving northward. "Ms. Karen say she want you to see the Emerald Buddha now. I take you there." He got as close as he could to the car in front of him, pressing down on the accelerator and braking at the same time.

Campbell turned to his wife. "Okay, I give up. What's an Emerald Buddha?"

Karen smiled, knowing her husband probably knew all along where they were going. "Patricia and I went to see it last week. It's so beautiful I want to see it again. It's only about two feet tall, but it's carved from a solid piece of jade. I just loved it.''

"It is located in Wat Phra Koe, which is where we are heading," Johnny said. He swerved to miss a motor scooter and then continued, "It is one of our most sacred objects. We believe it houses the guardian spirit of the city and was carved by a Thai craftsman a long time ago—maybe four-teenth century or earlier.''

Campbell opened the small "Guide to Bangkok" to the index and flipped through it until he found the section he was looking for. He laid the book open on the seat. "If you weren't over here with me, this is where Johnny would be taking me." Campbell was grinning.

Karen picked up the book, and seeing it was opened to the "Nightlife in Bangkok" section, she threw it at him just as he ducked and it flew out the open window.

Johnny turned off the main road and into a parking lot directly across from the temple. "I wait for you," he said. "Ms. Karen knows the way."

"I guess I do," she agreed.

Campbell and his wife made their way across the busy street, mixing in with the crowd there to see the temple. For the next hour the two walked through Bangkok's most revered *wat*, marveling at the splendid temple. Karen attempted to explain as much of the history as she could remember, trying to recall everything Johnny had told her and Patricia when they had first visited the temple. Afterward they made their way back to the taxi, where they found their driver asleep, a newspaper in his hands.

"Wake up, Johnny," Karen said, standing but a few feet from the open window.

The driver opened his eyes, a grin forming on his face. "Good tour?"

"Yes, good tour," Karen answered. "Now we want to get something to eat.

"I know just the place." Johnny started the motor as Jim and Karen got in, then turned out into the traffic, narrowly missing a group of orange-robed monks. "Too many monks," he said. "In Thailand, anyone can be a monk for a short time, even as little as two weeks."

Campbell twisted around to see the group of robed holy men regrouping themselves. "I don't think they were too happy over that, Johnny."

"They only novices—like in training to be real monks."

Campbell turned around again. Karen was looking out the window, engrossed in the sights and sounds of busy Bangkok. Johnny took them to a small restaurant belonging to his cousin, then after lunch and an afternoon of sight-seeing, he dropped them back at their hotel.

It was to be their last night together, and Johnny had promised to pick them up and take them to a popular restaurant off the beaten track. Karen had a nervous fear that it could be their last night forever, and though she tried to put the thought out of her mind, it would not go away. All she knew was that at ten o'clock the following morning her husband would be back on the *Barbary Coast*, returning to the war zone.

Campbell stood in front of the hotel with Karen next to the taxi station, waiting for Johnny to appear. Karen wore a simple light-yellow sundress, with small stringlike straps clinging to her honey-colored shoulders. She also wore the small emerald earrings Jim had purchased from a gem shop that Johnny had taken them to earlier, jewelry that complemented her blue-green eyes. Campbell had also bought her a large smoky-topaz cocktail ring, which she wore on the fourth finger of her right hand. Tonight, he thought, she looked especially beautiful.

"You're positive Johnny is going to pick us up tonight?" The preselected time for the taxi to arrive came and went as Campbell checked his watch and searched the street for signs of the green-and-white Datsun.

"Oh, don't worry, he'll be here. There is some kind of festival tonight and the traffic is probably terrible." Karen looked down the busy main street, crowded with cars and motor scooters loaded with smiling Thais, shouting well wishes to each other.

"There he is," Campbell shouted. The car darted into the passenger off-loading ramp at the front of the hotel, coming to a screeching halt. Johnny jumped out, hurrying around the still-running auto, and stopped in front of Campbell.

"*Sawadee*," Johnny said, making the traditional Thai greeting with his hands. "I'm sorry I late but I had to make a little side trip for something special tonight." He brought his hands down and opened the rear door of the taxi.

"What kind of 'special'?" Jim asked.

"You wait, you see. You won't be disappointed." Another taxi pulled up behind them, almost touching bumpers. "You get in and we go. I promise Ms. Karen the best table at great Thai restaurant. You won't be disappointed." Johnny's smile widened as he waited for Campbell to get in. Karen was already in the car, pulling at Campbell's hand. Campbell climbed into the backseat, feigning reluctance.

"Better hold on to me," Campbell said. "I have a suspicion our driver's ancestry might include an uncle in a Japanese kamikaze squadron."

Karen pulled in underneath his arm, snuggling in close as they darted in and out of traffic, working their way across the Phra Buddha Yodia bridge and then turning north until reaching a small parking lot next to a *klong*—canal—that led out to the Chao Phya River.

"We have to take short boat ride to reach restaurant," Johnny informed them as he stopped the car.

Jim held Karen's hand as she stepped down into a small wooden boat not much larger than a dugout. "We've come this far, so what the heck," Campbell said, holding Karen's hand as Johnny handed some small bills to the small-framed boatman. He accepted the money and smiled, revealing blackened teeth darkened from chewing betel-nut leaves. He started up the old outboard motor and pushed away from the wooden dock, heading into the middle of the *klong*. Johnny sat down in front of Jim and Karen, clutching a paper bag as they begin winding their way between houses raised up on stilts. They watched some naked, brown-skinned boys jumping from wooden landings at the bottom of a house, frolicking in the muddy water. The smallest boy in the group sat on the edge, brushing his teeth as the others splashed water on him.

In the rear of the boat, the boatman bailed water from the bottom with a rusty tin can and smiled when he caught Campbell looking at him.

"Just around next bend is restaurant," Johnny said. "Many parties tonight."

"Do you have any idea where we are going?" Campbell asked his wife. He felt safe in Bangkok only up to a point. The brochure that the ship's chaplain had prepared emphasized that southern Thailand was completely safe. The people were friendly as a result of their never having been colonized or uprooted like their neighbors. Jim began thinking about the northern part.

The beat of the one-cylinder engine stopped as the boatman rounded the last bend of the *klong* before it emptied into the Chao Phya River. Carefully he raised the outboard and attached a looped rope to the handle. He picked up a long pole and steered the drifting boat toward a long dock that extended down into the water.

Johnny turned around, facing Jim and Karen. "See, I told you so. You like this one."

Karen looked at her husband. He was staring at the many-tiered roof of the structure that seemed to hang over the edge of the *klong* and then spill out into the river on the other side. It was more than he had anticipated, and secretly he was glad he had trusted his wife's faith in their driver. "What does that sign say?" he asked.

Johnny was already out of the boat, standing on the wooden dock and holding the bow. "Garden of Waning Moon," he said, extending his hand and helping Karen step from the boat.

The Garden of the Waning Moon stood at the corner where the canal emptied into the river. It could only be reached by boat and was popular with local Thai and a few foreigners wanting to experience real Thai food.

To one side at the end of the dock, a garden area had been constructed, highlighted by a large banyan tree with gnarled roots twisting down the embankment underneath the building. Lush greenery clung to the slope, dotted with wild orchids and lotus flowers. The three made their way through the garden and up a flight of stairs leading to the main dining room overlooking the water and garden. They stood at the top of the stairs while Johnny talked to the manager of the restaurant.

"Oh, Jim," Karen said, "it's ten times more beautiful than I imagined it would be." She leaned out over the railing, staring at the magnificent view of the Grand Palace and Wat Phra Koe across the river.

Campbell looked around the room. Families sat at tables covered with bright tablecloths, laughing and eating, the children happily teasing each other.

"Jim, Karen, come this way. We have best table. You can see everything." The cabdriver motioned them to follow him. They were soon seated at a table for four next to the railing, overlooking the water and just above the garden. They could see everything on the river and the *klong*.

For a moment they were silent as they took in the huge room with its unique high-pitched ceiling of rafters made from hardwoods from northern Thai forests, the rafters crisscrossing in every direction and supporting the palm-thatched roof. Large rough-hewn timbers served as ceiling joists, holding the structure together and supporting the large number of ceiling fans, all turning at exactly the same slow speed.

Johnny turned their attention to the white-shirted waiter who had suddenly appeared and greeted them. Johnny returned the *wai* as the waiter stood smiling, first at Karen and then at Jim. "He is an old friend of mine. He promised to make sure we have best food."

"Are you sure I'll be able to make it back to my ship tomorrow?" Campbell asked.

Karen kicked him beneath the table.

"No problem. I promise you like. Little spicy but that's way we Thai like it. Don't worry." The cabdriver turned back to the waiter, conversing in Thai.

The waiter took Johnny's paper sack and the menus and left, leaving Karen wondering what was said.

"I have ordered a traditional Thai meal, fit for the occasion," Johnny explained.

Karen saw Jim cross his fingers.

"I also order a glass of palm wine to toast the festival of floating lights tonight."

"What is that?" Karen asked.

Johnny smiled. "It is a time when people help out their luck for the year. Tonight, everyone will launch a frail little handmade craft called a *krathong* out on the water. It is a small lotus-shaped float made of bamboo and leaves and colored paper. In the center is a candle and three incense sticks sticking out from a pod of flowers. Underneath this is two small coins. You light candles and launch boat at water's edge while you say prayer in hope it will float away from bank and sail out of sight. If it returns or is overturned, or if candle is quickly blown out, this means river gods won't allow owners misfortunes to be blown away. But if it bravely floats off with candles still burning, next year's luck will be very well. Sometimes," he added, "launching into river is risky because of all boats tramping up and down. Some people put their little boats into still pond so as not tempt fate."

"That's beautiful," Karen said. "When will it begin?"

"Soon, shortly after we finish our meal. You will be able to see many candles floating out on river."

The waiter returned with their drinks—a clear liquid Campbell had never seen before.

"Mekong," Johnny said. He held his glass up over the middle of the table.

"Mekong," Campbell said.

"No, 'Mekong' is name of drink, you toast."

"Peace," Karen said. She raised her glass to the others, letting them touch gently.

"Ah, yes, to peace," Johnny said.

"Peace." Campbell brought the glass to his lips, letting a small quantity of the strange liquid seep onto his tongue. Nothing like whiskey, he thought, but not bad.

"They also have American beer," Johnny said.

Campbell ordered a beer for himself and Karen before the first course came. He suspected he would need the cold beverage to help wash down some of the hotter dishes he was anticipating. He soon found himself enjoying a pleasant meal of fried shrimp pasteballs and then a crabmeat selection that was pierced with bits of pork and stuffed back into a crab shell. He tried some of the fried squid, but both he and Karen found it a bit too chewy. Johnny helped himself to it. The last dish set before them was a highly spiced soup made with shrimp.

"What is this called?" he asked Johnny.

Johnny elaborated. "It's called *tom yam* and is very delicious, but watch out for little peppers that hide beneath coriander leaves."

Campbell poked around with his spoon and not finding any peppers, ate half of the soup before reaching for his half-empty bottle of beer.

"Please order me another beer," he quickly said to Johnny as he ran the corner of his napkin inside his lips, trying to remove the stinging oil of the pepper.

Karen grinned at her husband. "He warned you."

"Not strongly enough. That's the hottest thing I've ever eaten!" His eyes were beginning to water.

"I know, even most Thais pick them out. They so small they hard to see." Johnny motioned to a waiter and another beer was set in front of Campbell. "Soon we'll have dessert. And then I go talk to my friends and you be alone for a while."

The waiter eventually appeared again, bearing a tray with several small boxlike sweets that Johnny had ordered. "This Thai favorite," Johnny explained when he returned.

Campbell studied the strange dessert dish. "What's in it?"

"It got coconut, powdered rice, and coconut cream mixed with sugar and is stuffed with jam made from beans and palm sugar. It stuffed inside the leaves from a *toie* plant and shaped like a box." He picked one up and placing it in front of his mouth, squeezed the sides, popping the contents into his mouth. "Don't eat the box," he said. He watched as Campbell tried one, managing to land the stuffing back on his plate.

Karen laughed a kind of giggle that Campbell loved to hear. He picked up another one.

"I leave you two now. I'll be down on the dock and see you just before the festival start." He got up from the table and walked away.

They both turned and looked toward the river. They could hear joyous shouts coming from the revelers inside the rented boats plying up and down the waterway. Karen slid her chair closer to her husband and reached for his hand. Neither one said anything and they continued looking out into the darkened waterway.

"I don't want you to go back to the ship," Karen finally said, still looking out over the water.

"C'mon, Karen. It's my job. You know that. You knew what I did when we got married."

"But it's different now. The rules have changed. If the other guy wins, he doesn't just get some points and a gold star, he gets you. *He takes you away from me*." She turned her head and looked straight at him. "I don't want you to be a navy pilot anymore. But an airline pilot, a crop duster, anything. I just don't want to ever lose you."

"Oh, Karen, you're just upset over Larry's getting captured."

"Captured!" She raised her voice, then lowered it again. "Our own people don't know if he's alive or dead. Patricia is pulling her hair out trying to get answers from anybody, and you're the only one who has told her anything. The navy, the army, the State Department, nobody knows or will tell her anything except to go back and be a good wife and keep quiet. Did you know she went to the International Red Cross yesterday, hoping they might have his name?"

"She did?"

"Yes. They told her the North Vietnamese had already been contacted and they revealed nothing about a Lt. Larry Jordan. My God, Jim, what if it had been you? I would be getting the runaround and not knowing whether you're dead or alive. I couldn't take it, I just couldn't." A trace of moistness appeared in the corners of her eyes.

Campbell didn't say anything for a moment. "So Patricia contacted the Red Cross. What else has she been doing?"

"I don't know. She only told me she would do whatever it takes to find out if he was dead or alive."

"I told her he was alive and generally okay when he was captured. We were out in the boondocks, honey. It probably will take them some time before they put him in their main prison. They like to parade our pilots around for a while, you know—make sure everybody gets his picture taken and all that. He's all right, I'm sure of it."

"Daddy says he would love to have you go to work for him if you would quit the navy. You could be the son he never had. You know how good his business is and you like Pensacola." Karen's expression changed. Her eyes were dry and she began to smile again.

Campbell bristled at the comment and refused to even discuss her father at the moment. He turned away and stared at the crowd in the room.

"Look, Karen, this war won't go on forever. After this tour I'll be back in the States."

"What about the next tour, and the next war?"

"Sweetheart, this is our last night. Let's enjoy it. When this tour is up, we'll talk about it."

They both lapsed into silence and turned to look out over the water. Small flickering lights began to appear along the banks. Campbell looked up as Johnny approached the table.

"These are for you," he said, setting two small hand-crafted floats down on the table in front of them. Each had the bits of colored paper and candles he had described before. "Take them down to the water like everyone is doing and say a small prayer before you light the candles and release the craft." He gave a *wai* gesture and departed before they could say anything.

"That was sweet of him," Karen said. She picked up the two boats and handed one to her husband, then took his hand.

Campbell reached into his pocket to make sure he had the

cigarette lighter he always carried even though he didn't smoke. Finding it, he led her down the steps and onto the floating dock in front of the restaurant. Already families and couples from the restaurant were lighting the candles and incanting small prayers as they released their craft, testing their luck. Campbell kneeled down next to a small boy who was attempting to light his candles with some damp matches. He handed him his lighter and the boy grinned, then lit the three candles easily, saying something in Thai that the boy's family repeated. They smiled at Campbell as he took the lighter back.

Karen bent over, getting down on her knees, and held the small boats for her husband to light. A breeze gently blew across the river, imparting a heady odor of incense from the boats. Soon six candles flickered in the breeze. Jim took her hand and together they said a silent prayer before setting their two frail craft down in the water. Campbell stood up and pulled Karen to her feet beside him. Together they stood on the dock and watched their boats slowly drifting away in the current. Some of the others weren't so lucky as their small boats returned and bumped against the water-logged pilings. They moaned at their misfortune. Others cheered theirs on as the miniature flotilla floated out to the center of the river, only to be swamped by a passing boatload of revelers. They cursed as they anticipated no further protection against a year of bad luck. Campbell silently held his wife as they watched their small craft rocking in the current. They stood there until the flickering candles were no longer in sight, hopefully a sign of good fortune.

"How is your luck?" Johnny asked, suddenly appearing from nowhere and standing next to them on the dock.

"We watched them as long as we could. The candles were still burning," Karen said.

"Ah, that is good. The deities of the river will watch over you for a year, but then you must test your luck again."

* * *

That night they made love again, then talked and made love once more. They stayed up late, talking into the night, reliving good times and bad until the first glow of dawn appeared much too soon and they watched it together on the small hotel balcony that overlooked the city. The bustling river traffic had already begun.

As the sun began to rise, Karen went to lie down for a moment and quickly fell asleep. Campbell remained on the balcony overlooking Bangkok and the river and watched the sun come up over the temples as she slept, a contented look on her face.

He hated to wake her but soon had to, then called Patricia, who wanted to drive with them to the Thai base. They all had a quiet breakfast together, then Johnny picked them up and drove them out of the city.

During the ride, Karen now seemed more withdrawn, saying little and clinging to her husband the whole way. The ride seemed short to both of them, and Johnny soon pulled off to the side to the entrance of the base.

Karen followed her husband out of the car while Patricia remained inside. Campbell draped his hanging bag over the top of the car, then turned to his wife.

"I've got something for you," Karen said. Reaching into her purse, she pulled out a small box and handed it to him.

"What is it?" Campbell took the box and removed the lid, revealing a small amulet she had purchased from a street vendor. It was gold and in a shape that he didn't recognize. Karen told him that the vendor, an old woman with teeth stained black, had promised in broken English that it would protect the wearer.

"For good luck," she said. "Please wear it until you get back."

Campbell took the small gold object from the box, unhooked the chain from around his neck, and slipped the amulet onto it next to his ID tags, then refastened the chain. "Don't worry. I'll come back. I promise." He paused for a moment, then took her into his arms, holding her to him. "I love you," he said, then gave her a long kiss.

"I love you, too," she said, embracing him, then giving him one last kiss. Then he was gone, blending in with the ocean of white uniforms heading for their home on the sea. She saw him board the landing craft, then its ramp was raised and she could see him no more. She watched the landing craft back away from the sandy beach, watching until it became a speck against the background of blue sea. On the way back to the hotel she quietly cried with her head on Patricia's shoulder.

7

The wind rushing by the open window and the tires rolling over the asphalt highway seemed deafening in the silence of the cab as Johnny drove away from the Thai navy base. The pudgy Thai had ceased his monologue almost as quickly as it began and concentrated on the traffic ahead. Glancing up into the rearview mirror, he could see Karen and Patricia both immersed deep in thoughts of happier times as each looked out of the windows and stared into the distance. Their eyes were puffy and splotches of mascara dotted their cheeks, though the wind had dried away their tears. The sight of the gangplank of the LCM being raised and sealing her husband from view had been especially hard on Karen, even more than their first parting at Pearl Harbor.

Finally Patricia broke the silence. "I talked with an International Red Cross person again yesterday."

"Oh," Karen said. "Did you find out anything more about Larry?"

"I found out they do try to keep up with the prisoners in North Vietnam, but their relations with the Vietnamese haven't been very good. They have absolutely nothing on Larry. But they did tell me the navy had contacted them." She paused for a moment, then looked out the window. "They said it was not unusual for the North Vietnamese to hold up identity. It doesn't mean he's not okay, it's just that they won't admit they have him—for whatever reason."

Karen reached over to Patricia and took her hand. "He's okay, Pat, I just know it. Have you talked to the embassy people again? Do they know anything?"

"Nothing. All I get from them is excuses and that I should return to my home and wait. I'll be contacted as soon as anything develops. In other words—nothing at all."

Karen tried to think of something she could say to reassure her best friend. All she could come up with were more questions. "Is there anybody else who could help? Isn't there somebody you haven't contacted?"

Patricia started to answer, then noticed Johnny looking in his rearview mirror. She looked away.

"Maybe you talk to people who have your husband," he said.

"What, what did you say?" Karen was surprised by his interruption.

The cabdriver repeated himself. "You go talk to North Vietnamese, ask them yourself."

"What do you mean?" Patricia asked. "You mean go to North Vietnam?"

"No, no, not North Vietnam. They wouldn't let you go

there anyway. You go to North Vietnamese embassy, speak to man in charge." He waited for his statement to sink in.

Karen spoke first. "I don't think that would be a very good idea, Pat."

"Where do they have an embassy? I haven't seen one in Bangkok." Patricia sat up straight, her attention suddenly focusing on the front seat.

"One in Vientiane," Johnny said. "Or Phnom Penh in Cambodia. Vientiane better."

Patricia's eyebrows arched up, forming short little wrinkles in her forehead. "But that's in Laos, isn't it?" She wasn't sure but thought her husband had once mentioned something about it.

"Yes, Laos. Just above border in northern Thailand. I have cousins there," he added.

Karen looked at Patricia, who was already looking at her. Neither one spoke for a moment and then Patricia asked, "But how would we get there? We don't even have a visa to enter the country. That would probably take weeks even if they'd let us." Her green eyes began concentrating on a small space directly in front of her.

"I know that look, Patricia. It's that look you get when your mind starts racing a thousand miles a minute."

Patricia blinked, then turned and faced Karen. She had not heard anything she'd said. "Oh, Karen, what would be wrong with talking to them? All I get from our own government is a constant runaround. I need to know that Larry is safe, no matter what I have to do." She paused for a moment, then took Karen's hand. "Can't you see?"

Karen was silent as she tried to picture where Vientiane was. "But what if someone tries to contact us? What if there is some word about Larry or Jim and we aren't at the hotel in Bangkok?"

"We can leave word with the hotel manager about where to contact us," Patricia said.

"No worry," Johnny said. "American embassy in Vientiane. Lots of embassies there, lots of Americans, too."

"How much would it cost?" Patricia didn't have a lot of money. She and Larry had scraped together what they could and borrowed the rest to finance this trip for her. Unlike Karen, her parents weren't wealthy and could never have afforded to just give them a lump sum to spend. Suddenly the thought that she couldn't afford the trip entered her mind.

"Five hundred American dollars."

"Five hundred dollars!" The amount was almost as much as her husband received per month.

"There's probably not even an embassy in Laos," Karen said, becoming more convinced by the minute that going to Laos was nothing more than a waste of time and money—and probably dangerous. "And it doesn't cost any five hundred dollars to fly there, either."

"That money if I drive you there—not fly."

Karen began shaking her head as she looked at Patricia. "There's no way in the world I'm going to take off across Thailand by taxi, no way."

Johnny listened to them arguing for a while then broke in. "You ladies discuss tonight. I make call to cousins and set up trip then call you tonight."

He slowed as he approached the road leading back to their hotel.

"How long would it take to get there?" Patricia asked.

"If I drive, I show you Thailand you never see staying in city. Take two days on Thai superhighway. That highway you Americans help build for us. It runs all the way from Bangkok up to Nong Khai on Mekong River just across from Vientiane. Take two days, you see plenty." The Thai driver slowed as they approached their hotel and began jockeying for an outside lane among the busy traffic.

"Oh, Karen, please," Patricia begged. "This may be the only way I can find out. I'd do it for you if it were Jim."

Karen felt the words like sharpened spikes being driven underneath her fingernails. "Let me think about it, okay? But not by car," she added.

Johnny pulled up to the curb in front of the hotel and twisted around in his seat. "You two stay hotel tonight and I call. I have to contact cousins and see what has to be done, but you two no worry. Everything okay. I get you into Laos no problem. I only charge fair amount and you can use traveler checks. Pay me one-third in morning, one-third at border, and one-third in Vientiane." He got out and opened the rear door, waiting for them to get out.

Patricia stepped down from the Datsun, followed by Karen, who handed Johnny a one-hundred-baht note. "We'll be waiting for your call tonight," she said.

Upstairs in their room Patricia lit a cigarette, then pulled out the map Campbell had left for her. Spreading it out on the bed, she sat down and traced the road that ran from Bangkok up the middle of Thailand to the northern border with Laos. She put her finger on Vientiane and called to Karen.

"Here, right at the top of Thailand," she said, waiting for Karen to come out of the bathroom, then holding the map up for her.

Karen took it and laid it back on the bed, staring at the inset of Thailand. To her it was a forbidding place, surrounded by countries she knew little about.

Patricia put one finger on Vientiane and stretched another to Hanoi. "It's probably not far from where they have Larry. I remember Larry talking about Laos—about all the people we have up there. I remember him saying we had more air bases in Thailand than we had in Vietnam." She looked at the map but saw nothing that indicated the presence of a single U.S. base.

"The U.S. government probably wouldn't acknowledge it anyhow. There are an awful lot of airplane symbols on the map. Those must be bases—they couldn't need that many places for airlines to land in Thailand. There's even a symbol at Vientiane." Karen continued studying the map.

"And one at Hanoi," Patricia added. "Oh, Karen, please," she begged. "This may be the only way I can find out. We may be his only chance."

By eight o'clock Karen had exhausted every argument she could think of. Patricia had made up her mind and was going with or without Karen. Finally Karen gave in and agreed to at least visit the Laotian embassy the following morning to see if they could obtain entry visas. Afterward they went down for dinner, then bought nearly a thousand dollars' worth of traveler's checks and made arrangements with the hotel to look after their baggage and handle any messages. When Johnny called later that evening, Patricia convinced him they would go by plane if they went at all. He agreed to pick them up in front of the hotel early the following morning and take them to the Laotian embassy.

Sleeping that night was difficult for both of them. Each had tried to empty her mind of unanswered questions. Both had lain awake, each wondering what success or disaster their journey might bring. Karen tried to envision her husband, now somewhere out in the South China Sea, heading north back to the battle zone. She silently prayed he would remain safe and come back to her, then fell asleep thinking of him.

The following morning, Johnny drove them to the Laotian embassy, where they were met by a representative who spoke of his acquaintance with the taxi driver. As they waited, he quickly typed up entry papers and made the appropriate notations in their passports, pocketing the twenty-dollar bill each had left inside her passport. Returning to the green-and-white cab parked out front, they went back to their hotel to purchase airline tickets on Air Lao for Vientiane for the following morning.

Seven o'clock came early. A light rain was falling and Karen and Patricia stood just inside the entrance of the hotel, looking out through the glass panels. They had slept little during the night. They had secured their extra luggage with the hotel and downed a light breakfast before waiting for Johnny. Each possessed one hanging bag for the trip. Karen looked up and down the street, searching for the familiar Datsun and almost wishing it wouldn't show.

They were dressed simply, each with low-heeled shoes, slacks, and large handbags packed with essentials for the trip. While they waited, they watched uniformed Thai schoolgirls passing in front of the hotel holding pieces of clear plastic over their heads and noisily chatting amongst themselves. They could see saffron-robed monks out by the curb ignoring the rain as they lined up to receive their morning breakfast provided by grateful Thais.

"There he is." Karen spotted Johnny trying to maneuver through the busy morning traffic from the far lane.

Johnny pulled up in front of the hotel and stopped. The rain was letting up and Johnny jumped out of the car and ran into the hotel, carrying a large unopened umbrella.

"Good morning, ladies." He made a *wai* sign and smiled at Karen. Both women returned the gesture. Picking up their bags, he led them out to the parked taxi, tossing the bags into the trunk, slamming it down several times before it would lock. "Do you have your passports?" he asked

Karen as she climbed into the rear seat. "You will need them at the airport to leave Thailand and hopefully enter Laos."

Patricia's eyebrows arched. "I thought you said you could guarantee us entry into Laos?"

"No problem," he said. "When you get to Vientiane airport, my cousin help. You see." He smiled at Patricia.

"Oh, well, we've come this far. And besides, we left word with the hotel manager where we were going and how we were traveling there."

Johnny jumped into the driver's seat and in an instant was back out in the swirling Bangkok traffic, headed for the international airport.

In less than an hour they were on the outskirts of the city. Traffic had thinned and Karen fingered the small cross she wore, wishing she had bought herself an amulet. The sign for airport appeared and she turned to look, troubled by second thoughts about the trip.

Johnny pulled the Datsun to a stop and pointed to a line of people departing Thailand where customs agents were busily checking passports and luggage. Getting out of the car, he handed their bags to them, then pocketed the fare Karen handed to him. Waving good-bye, he waited until they had disappeared inside the building, then hurried to a telephone booth and quickly made a call. Smiling to himself, he hung up the phone and hurried back to his cab.

The flight to Vientiane was uneventful and thirty minutes into the trip both women were nodding as the ancient DC-3 droned northward. They had quickly tired of looking out the window at the gridwork of rice paddies crisscrossing the flat terrain. The aircraft followed the new highway below, a thin ribbon of concrete built by the United States and connecting the south of Thailand to the Mekong River in the north below Vientiane in Laos. The lumbering aircraft skirted the air base at Nakhon Ratchasima, known as Khorat, as an F-105 mission got under way eight thousand feet below, loaded with bombs for targets inside North Vietnam.

Approaching the muddy Mekong River, the pilot began his descent and Karen and Patricia woke up. The river seemed larger than they expected and muddier. When they deplaned, they were immediately struck by the heat and humidity, and Karen was puzzled at the number and variety of parked aircraft. She saw American-built aircraft, although they had no markings she recognized. Across the field were other types of aircraft she had never seen before. In another group she spotted a T-28 that had Laotian air force markings.

"Passport," an agent said, handing Patricia a clipboard holding a form with instructions written in several languages. She took it and handed over their passports. The agent examined them, studying the photos laminated inside, then opened the hanging bags the women had placed on the counter. He seemed to be looking hard, first at Karen's and then Patricia's. Suddenly his face relaxed and he smiled. "Americans," he said, turning to Patricia. "All correct," he said, then handed the documents back to Patricia. "You pass, have nice day." His grin was almost infectious, and the women grinned back at him as they picked up their bags and walked to the front of the building. They paused when a young man wearing khaki pants and a white shirt stopped before them.

"I have taxi," he said. "I take you to hotel."

Karen looked at Patricia and shrugged. Together they followed him outside to a Datsun similar to the one Johnny owned. Soon they found themselves driving onto the dusty red streets of Vientiane, the administrative capital of Laos.

They stared out the window as new sights and smells of a

strange city passed before them. Dust rose from some of the unpaved streets, covering the parked cars like a thin skin of red suede. Karen noticed that many of the buildings were pocked with holes, while others were unmarked. "Did they have a battle here?"

The driver grinned. "Laotians like to sometimes vote with their guns on who running government. Don't worry, peaceful here, not so in north." He drove down Setthathirath Street past yellow stucco buildings with their French-styled red roofs. The street had been named Rue Maréchal Foch in French colonial times. Chinese merchants were hawking their wares from small shops along the street while refugees congregated nearby. Tribesmen driven down from the hills now embroiled in war were trying to eke out a living in a strange city. They gathered in groups, still wearing the bright costumes of their tribes. The taxicab continued past the hospital and several government buildings, past the police station and telephone and telegraph offices. He turned onto Lang Xang Avenue and drove down the superwide street until he came to the Lang Xang Hotel and pulled to a stop in front of the building.

"This is where you stay," he announced. "Many people of all countries stay here."

"Where is the North Vietnamese embassy?" Patricia asked.

"It not far away but you no contact them, not good idea. Too many people watch all the time. You wait, I contact, let you know."

Patricia wondered if he was the cousin Johnny had mentioned. She decided to let it pass.

"Is the American embassy around here? I want to let them know we are here," Karen added.

"It is near here but no good you contact them. They want to know why you here and then make big fuss." The driver got out of the car and opened the trunk, removing their bags. He set them down beside the car and motioned for them to get out. "Hotel have plenty room, you check in and you be contacted soon." He pocketed the American dollars Karen handed him.

Karen and Patricia got out and were about to question him about Johnny when he suddenly drove off.

"What's wrong with him?" Karen asked. She picked up her bag and started up the steps alongside Patricia, eliciting stares from several men coming out of the hotel.

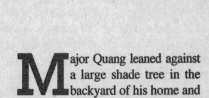

8

Major Quang leaned against a large shade tree in the backyard of his home and watched his son and daughter playing noisily next to their grandfather. The North Vietnamese officer was wearing a freshly laundered uniform complete with ribbons awarded for combat. His hat lay on the grass beside him, tossed there by his young son, who had quickly tired of wearing it down around his eyes. His wife's father sat on the ground opposite him, balancing a small butterfly on his finger. Entranced by the multicolored creature, Quang's daughter, Mai Ling, stopped chasing her brother and kneeled down beside the old man. Her expression widened, and her smile revealed a small gap between her two front teeth as she watched the black-and-yellow wings fold and unfold.

Quang endeavored to make the most of the few precious moments he was allowed with his family, and he cherished the time away from the war and death in the skies. He watched his son, Le Doc, pushing his toy plane around on the ground imitating the sound of the jet airplanes he often heard flying over the city. The boy was too young to have any real understanding of what was going on around him and to him, it was only a game, a series of diversions to be enjoyed. In his innocence the time spent in the bomb shelters only provoked amusement, not concern.

Inside the kitchen of their tiny stucco home, Kwan Chi busied herself preparing tea for their guest, who would be arriving at any time. Her mother was absent, gone to the black market to barter for scarce items unavailable from the government stores. A porcelain teakettle once belonging to Quang's mother sat on the stove, spewing out small puffs of steam, and Kwan Chi turned down the heat. She had selected the teacups she would use and placed them on the table. Her mother's rice cakes, baked only yesterday and showing signs of Le Doc's sampling, were neatly arranged on a platter. She removed one with bite marks, then placed the tray on a small table. Satisfied everything was ready, she walked out into the backyard to check on her children. "You look too comfortable—as contented as an old cow," she commented, walking over to the tree and sitting down beside her husband.

Quang picked up his hat and flicked off a blade of grass sticking to the brim. "If Le Doc were big enough, he could wear this hat and then I could retire underneath this tree." He placed his hat on his wife's head, then laughed as the rim came to rest on her ears.

"I think one soldier in this family is enough." She lifted the hat off and placed it on top of his head. "I hope when Le Doc is grown, there will be peace everywhere and he will be a teacher or a doctor."

The major put his arm around his wife as they sat underneath the tree, watching the children playing. "In my father's time there was not peace. In his father's time there was not peace. Maybe this time when we win this war there will be a peace for our children."

"Do you really think so?" Kwan Chi's face lit up as she looked up at her husband.

"Maybe, but not soon. There will be many hardships before it is over. We Vietnamese have a history of war and occupation. Our friends become our enemies and then become our friends again. It sways back and forth like the tides of the ocean. Only when the moon no longer shines will wars end."

Kwan Chi eased from underneath his arm and crawled over to her daughter. The youngster was still watching the butterfly resting on her grandfather's hand. Mai Ling crouched close to him, squealing with delight when he raised his hand near her face, causing the butterfly's fragile wings to brush against her cheek.

"Is the tea ready?" Quang asked his wife. "The major should be arriving at any time."

"Yes, it is ready." Kwan Chi raised up onto her knees. "I think I heard a car pull up in front of the house. Perhaps you had better go and see if that is your Russian friend."

Major Quang stood up, removing his hat and brushing himself off. He slapped away the remaining grass blades, then walked through the house, stopping at the front door and peering through a small glass set into the frame. He could see a black, Russian-made Volga sedan parked out front in the narrow street. The Vietnamese driver was leaning against the car, lighting up a cigarette. He was standing with his back to Quang, his face hidden. Halfway up the path leading to the front door a short, white-skinned figure was quickly approaching. His height made his heavy build seem even larger than it was, and his thick neck only added to his look of a weight lifter. Quang opened the door.

"Major Vassilov." Quang stood holding the door open.

The Russian stopped at the door, smiling at him, then held out his hand.

Quang could see he was wearing his usual baggy black pants and white shirt rolled up to his forearms. The last time he had seen the Russian officer in uniform was in Moscow. Even then he wore his uniform with less than care and it never seemed to fit. Maj. Sergi Vassilov was attached to the GRU, the Russian military intelligence directorate, and was assigned to Hanoi as an advisor. He had met Quang when the pilot was a student and they had renewed their acquaintance upon his arrival in Hanoi. On occasion the Russian would call upon Quang to interview one of the captured American pilots when it was thought he had information they wanted. Quang didn't relish the idea, but it did get him off flight duty for a day or two.

"Comrade Quang. It is good to see you." The Russian grasped Quang's extended hand firmly. "I hope our little journey is not going to inconvenience you from the war?" Major Vassilov stepped through the doorframe, following Quang into the house. He enjoyed visiting Quang's house and seeing his beautiful wife.

They walked into the kitchen and Quang turned, facing the Russian. "Comrade, my wife has prepared tea and cakes for us before we go."

The Russian smiled, then walked to the back door and looked out at the children playing with their grandfather. "Ah, Quang, you have such a nice family." He spotted Kwan Chi next to her children. "Good morning," he said in the few Vietnamese words he knew.

The grandfather looked up, spotting the GRU agent standing in the doorway. "Tell the Russian pig he stands lower than the ankles of a water buffalo," he called in Vietnamese.

Kwan Chi blushed as she gave her father a stare.

"My wife's father says you are looking well and wishes you a pleasant day." Quang put his arm around Vassilov and quickly guided him back into the kitchen, followed by Kwan Chi.

"Thank you," Vassilov said in Russian.

"The water is hot and I will serve you tea if you like," Kwan Chi told her husband in Vietnamese. She spoke little English and no Russian at all. She wanted the Russian away from her grandfather before he picked up on something the old man might say.

"That is a good idea, Kwan Chi." Quang led the major toward the table, offering him the best seat. They sat down while his wife busied herself preparing the tea.

"So, comrade, how does your squadron do in shooting down the American aggressors?"

Quang thought for a moment, trying to recall the latest kill-figure ratios of the air war. "Officially or unofficially?" he asked.

"Ah, yes." Vassilov paused for a moment. "Always two versions." He grinned at Quang, revealing a large gold cap on one of his front teeth. "Your papers say you have gloriously shot down more of the Yankee airplanes than they have ever launched at you. But you and I know you are bringing down about one for every two you lose. And in your case"—he smiled—"you have about eleven to zero." He leaned forward and winked, then let out a short laugh. "That is even better than the kill ratio we had in the glorious Korean war of liberation."

"Eleven is correct," Quang said.

"Don't become disillusioned that you are losing so many, my friend. You are almost always outnumbered. And I'm afraid it will have to remain that way at least for now. If we gave you more planes, then that stupid president of theirs would probably start attacking your bases. It is better this way, better to keep the flow of materials going to our heroic brothers in the south.''

Quang turned away without saying anything and looked to see how his wife was doing. "Kwan Chi, are you almost ready?''

"Yes, almost ready.'' She picked up a black lacquered wooden tray with a platter of rice cakes and the tea service and set it on the table. She placed a cup in front of the Russian and one for her husband, then began pouring the tea.

"Ah, rice cakes,'' the Russian said. "I have developed a certain fondness for these small Vietnamese pastries.''

"Thank you, Kwan Chi. Please leave us now,'' Quang said in Vietnamese.

After sampling several rice cakes Vassilov turned his attention back to Quang. "I heard your wingman got shot down and killed. I am sorry to hear that, but I know you were successful in disrupting the American war criminals attacking the bridge. Some of them were forced to jettison their bomb loads before they reached the target.'' The Russian wiped his arm across his face, then reached for another cake. "Good.''

"What?''

"Very good, these cakes. Why don't you have one?''

"No, go ahead, help yourself. I don't feel like eating.'' Quang shoved the remaining cakes toward the major.

"Ah, Quang, you should not let the war get to you. With our help you will win and be united with the south once again. You will be rid of the Americans, the French''—he paused to pick up the last rice cake and stuff it into his mouth—"and even the United Nations.'' Again he used his forearm to clean his mouth, knocking crumbs off his chin onto the table.

"Yes, we are very appreciative," Quang said thoughtfully. He was thinking of how they would then have to get rid of the Russians and the Chinese.

Vassilov wiped his hand on his pants, then gulped down a large slug of tea to chase down the remaining crumbs sticking to his teeth. "We must get on the road, Quang. We have a long way to go to the compound. Please express my thanks to your lovely wife." He pushed himself away from the table and stood up, waiting for Quang to follow.

Quang walked to the back door and motioned to his wife. He said good-bye to her and then to his children, who had suddenly run to the door. Promising to return safely, he turned and led the major outside.

The Vietnamese driver quickly started the Russian Volga sedan after closing its rear door. They traveled the short distance down the dirt side street before pulling out onto the nearly deserted highway that ran through Hanoi and eventually connected with Saigon in the south. The car belched smoke from the low-grade Russian gasoline. The driver had the window down, keeping one ear cocked for any sound of aircraft or warning sirens. His eyes watched the air as much as the road, though it was still early in the morning and no attacks were likely until later in the day.

Quang looked over at Vassilov. He could see the Russian was becoming nervous as they drove out onto the Paul Doumer Bridge to cross the Red River. The river ran through the middle of Hanoi, and the long-spanned and heavily defended bridge was one of the high-priority targets of the war. Somehow it had managed to withstand the barrage of attacks against it. Vassilov didn't like crossing any bridges and only relaxed as they neared the edge of the causeway on the other side.

"Don't worry, comrade, it's too early for an attack," Quang assured him.

"There is always a first time, Major. Just the same, I'm

glad to be off the bridge. At least in the open you can run for cover.''

Quang could see traces of perspiration forming around the Russian's neck. He guessed that the palms of his short, stubby hands were probably moist, too. Quang wondered if Vassilov had ever personally faced anyone in direct combat. Deciding not, he looked away and stared out the window as they left the outskirts of Hanoi and continued south.

Quang spotted a burned-out hulk of a locomotive, lying on its side. After workers had salvaged everything that could be reused, the remains had been abandoned until it could be cut up for scrap. Grass was growing around the rusting mass of twisted iron, and vines were reaching for its sides. Behind the narrow-gauge track were caches of spare railroad tracks and piles of gravel awaiting the next bombing and the instant repair that would follow. Farther along the highway were stacks of tires, then groups of fifty-gallon drums filled with gasoline and hidden beneath large leafy trees. The whole countryside was a warehouse beneath the fronds of swaying palms. War material was scattered upon receipt and only rarely did the bombers find it bunched up.

Vassilov was sleeping soundly, slumped in the seat, as they passed through the bombed-out city of Phu Ly. Quang studied the remains of the town that had virtually been destroyed from the bombing and never rebuilt. He could see mounds of rubble piled up, now hosts for vines and rats. He remembered when the attack came, less than a year ago. He and three other fighters had attempted to intercept the attacking force but had been turned back by their accompanying fighters. The Americans had dropped tons of bombs on the railway that ran through the town, destroying both the town and the railroad. Only the railway had been rebuilt.

The driver slowed as they passed another overturned locomotive with several tank cars piled around it. Farther along Quang could see burned-out and rusted trucks piled up and pushed aside. The only thing left standing was a large Catholic church, now abandoned. The driver sped up again, following the highway south for another hour before he turned off onto a dirt road heading west. The turn woke up Vassilov.

"Ah, comrade, that was a good nap. Did you have one yourself?"

Quang smiled at the major but said nothing.

"Have you been here before?" asked the Russian.

"No. But I'm sure I've flown over it many times."

Vassilov was looking through the windshield at the building down the road. "This was part of an old French plantation before your war with the French. I have been here many times and find it enjoyable to get away from that infernal bombing in Hanoi."

Quang stared at the upcoming building. It looked like an ordinary farmhouse common to the leftover plantations. "This place we are going to—is it one of the prison compounds where the captured flyers are kept?"

"Oh, no, comrade," the Russian answered proudly. "This one is a special camp accommodating only a few prisoners at a time. Today we will be visiting a rather stubborn American, an individual whom you've met before."

Quang seemed puzzled. "I don't understand."

Vassilov clasped his hands together. "This one you met in the air. He is the pilot from your last kill, the one responsible for getting your wingman killed."

Quang thought back for a moment, then remembered the figure ejecting from the burning aircraft. "Why is he important?" Quang asked.

"He probably isn't, but then again we know he was involved in some of the early testing. At least he was flying the plane carrying the weapon during at least one testing period. In time we will find out whether he is knowledgeable about the Americans' new Bullpup missile or not." A thin smile formed on his lips.

The North Vietnamese pilot felt uneasy. He had questioned captured pilots at Vassilov's request before and never knew of anything's coming of it. He knew his job would remain the same regardless of the weapons the Americans developed. He still had to shoot them down first.

"Sometimes talking to another pilot puts them at ease. We want you to ask him some questions pertaining to their delivery methods."

Quang said nothing and turned to look out the window again. In the far distance he could see the karst mountains rising from the lush green forests at the edge of the rice paddies, a pleasant backdrop for the old plantation house. "Is that it?" he asked.

"Yes, that is it. The Americans have flown over it dozens of times with their reconnaissance flights, but they pay it little attention."

"Why is there no watchtower?"

"No need. There are never more than two or three prisoners here before they are transferred to more permanent facilities. Some may go to Hanoi, some to other places."

Quang dropped the subject as the driver pulled up in front of the house, stopping beneath several large trees. The driver shut off the engine and jumped out, opening the door for the Russian.

Vassilov got out of the car, standing up on his toes to stretch himself. "I need more exercise, I think." He walked around the Volga and headed for the entrance, Major Quang following behind with the driver carrying Vassilov's briefcase.

A bearded, olive-skinned man wearing green fatigues and combat boots stepped up to the Russian, throwing his arms around him and kissing him on both cheeks. "Ah, Comrade Vassilov."

Vassilov stepped back, his hands still holding the man's

shoulders as he looked him over. "You look well, my friend. I have brought you something special." He motioned to the driver, who stepped up with the briefcase. Vassilov opened it while the camp commander eagerly watched, a look of expectation on his face.

"What have you got this time, my friend? You have more connections than anyone I know." His eyes eagerly followed Vassilov's hands as he pulled out a package.

The Russian stepped forward, holding up the package. "These are for you, comrade." He shoved five large cigars wrapped in tobacco leaves up to his friend's nose. "I got them from the captain of a Bulgarian freighter in Haiphong last week." He watched his friend remove one of the long cigars and hold it underneath his nose, inhaling deeply and then breaking into a wide grin. He watched the Cuban let out his breath and inhale again.

"Comrade, I will be forever indebted to you."

Vassilov suddenly remembered he hadn't introduced the North Vietnamese pilot. "Major Quang, ah, please forgive me. I have been so caught up in giving Gutierrez his cigars that I forgot to introduce you. Please meet Comrade Amelio Gutierrez of the Cuban Internal Security Force, on loan to your country. Amelio, Major Quang is their leading fighter pilot, with eleven kills to his credit. He also speaks English and French well."

"Major Quang," the wiry Cuban turned toward Quang and extended his hand as he clutched the Cuban cigars in the other. "It is a pleasure to meet such a distinguished flyer and for me to be of service to your country."

Quang took the hand of the Cuban. His handshake was light and felt cold to the major. "My countrymen appreciate your help in our long and victorious struggle," he responded. Withdrawing his hand, he discreetly rubbed it against his pants.

"Let's go inside. We can have some Cuban coffee and

one of these fine cigars.'' Gutierrez turned and led the others into the house, passing by a guard brandishing an AK-47. They went through what was once a living room still containing an old and faded rug on the wooden floor. Gutierrez opened a door and Vassilov and Quang followed him in. He motioned for them to sit down while he looked for coffee cups.

"Gutierrez, you never cease to amaze me. No matter what country you and I find ourselves in, you seem to manage to come up with some Cuban coffee or some other thing you think you can't live without.'' Vassilov turned to Major Quang. "When Amelio and I were in Africa, he always had cigars no matter how far out in the bush we were, right, Amelio?''

Gutierrez smiled and set cups on his desk. He poured each cup full then sat down in his chair.

The Russian's face suddenly turned serious. "Has he changed his attitude yet?'' He took a sip of the hot coffee.

Gutierrez gulped down a swallow of coffee, then paused, looking over the edge of his cup. "Not yet, but soon. Your trip with the major may have been a little premature. In a few more days, maybe then.'' He paused again before continuing, "There is only so far that we can go without serious problems.'' The Cuban stared into the Russian's eyes.

"I understand, Amelio. Perhaps Major Quang would like to see the man he shot down. Why don't you bring in this Yankee war criminal for us?''

"But of course.'' The Cuban stepped to the door, giving an order to the two guards standing outside the room. "It will take a few minutes to unshackle him. Would you like some more coffee, Major Quang?'' He brought the glass coffeepot over and topped off Quang's cup, then sat down behind his desk. The room turned silent as they waited for the prisoner.

In the tiny chamber down the hall at the far end of the farmhouse, a guard peered through a narrow peephole. Jordan sat on the floor in the corner, his back against the wall and his head lowered. His eyes were closed and his hands were at his sides, limply resting on the floor. Iron shackles locked his feet together, preventing movement within the room. A narrow straw mat lay to one side next to two containers, one for food and one for waste. A single light bulb burned continuously from the center of the high ceiling of the windowless room.

"You get up. You get up, no sleep." The guard unlocked the door, then kicked it and barged into the room. He paused for a moment then kicked Jordan in the upper leg, eliciting a muffled scream from him. The second guard entered the small room and bent down to unlock the shackles. The first guard kicked Jordan again. "You get up, you get up," he repeated.

With his head bowed, Jordan slowly raised up on his knee. The two guards grabbed him by his arms, jerking him upward and tearing the sleeves of the black pajamas he wore. He tried to raise himself up but only managed to fall back down on one knee, causing the shorter of the two guards to curse and grab his arm again, jerking him upright. This time he stood erect and put his weight down on one leg and glared at the guard. Jordan walked out of the small room, his arms hanging loosely at his sides. He flinched as the smaller guard prodded him with his rifle. Slowly he limped down the corridor of the French farmhouse.

Gutierrez put his coffee cup down and went to the door to see what was taking so long. He shouted something and Jordan felt the rifle butt strike him in the rear of his shoulder. He let out a small cry then continued.

"Ah, finally, my friend from San Diego." Gutierrez looked up at the sickly looking figure hobbling into the room. "I have visitors for you today." He stood up and sat on the edge of his desk. "Have him stand over there. . . . No, have him sit in that seat across from us."

Jordan looked confused and probed the room with his eyes, staring first at Vassilov and then at Quang before he sat down.

"Well, Major Quang, what do you think of the brave and dangerous American war criminal that bombs and kills your wives and children?"

Quang looked at the American sitting across from him. He felt uneasy looking at him. Here was someone who probably had a family, had trained just as he had and loved to fly. And yet here was someone who had caused the death of his wingman and dropped his bombs on his friends and countrymen. At first he felt pity, then feelings of hatred returned the longer he looked at him.

Quang was silent for a moment, then finally said, "I am the one that shot you down." He waited for a reaction and after a brief period the American slowly raised his head, a blank expression on his face. "What is your name?" Quang asked.

The American continued looking at Quang then answered slowly, "Jordan, Lt. Larry Jordan, United States Navy, six seven six nine three seven." He continued staring. He looked older, the dark circles beneath his eyes adding ten years to him.

"Why do you continue to bomb my people?" Quang asked.

Jordan shifted his stare to the Russian. He had seen him once before, right after he was captured. At first he had thought he was a journalist. He shifted his stare back to Quang. The situation was becoming more confusing to him by the minute as he looked at the Cuban, then the Russian, and then at the North Vietnamese officer, all of them able to speak English. He tried to raise his arm but it was limp and hung by his side. The Cuban had hung him by thin ropes that he had tied around Jordan's arms held behind his back by the guards. Then they had thrown the rope up over the rafters and pulled Jordan off the ground. This method of torture seemed to be a favorite of the Cuban, who seemed to take special delight in pulling on the rope and raising him off the ground.

The Cuban interrogation specialist suddenly wheeled in his chair, kicking Jordan and sending him sprawling to the floor. The POW moaned as he landed on his arm.

"I'm sorry, Jordan," Gutierrez said. "I didn't mean to do that. It's just that you are so stubborn sometimes, even in front of our guests."

Quang stood up. It was the first time he had actually seen mistreatment and it made him uneasy. "I would like to talk to the pilot alone for a few minutes."

Vassilov looked at Gutierrez, then back at Quang. "Of course. Amelio and I will be across the hall if you need us. Take your time." He put his hand on the Cuban's shoulder, guiding him from the room and closing the door behind him.

Jordan managed to climb back up into the chair, holding his arm and looking at Quang. "I know who you are," he whispered.

Quang could not quite hear him. "I do not understand you."

"You, you're the Gray Ghost, aren't you?" Jordan stared intensely at Quang, unable to take his eyes off him.

"Who is this 'Gray Ghost'? My name is Major Quang." He looked puzzled. It was the first time he had heard the name mentioned.

"Quang." Jordan's voice was raspy. "I thought you were just a rumor. But you're the North Vietnamese ace—the one with crosses painted on his aircraft." Jordan's words came slowly, his expression pained.

Quang looked down at him for a moment, saying nothing.

"It doesn't matter what you call me, or if you even know me. I fight for the same thing as my friends. You could help yourself by helping us."

"You know I can't do that."

Quang studied Jordan for a moment, neither saying anything. Finally Quang said, "The Russians have information on all your weapons systems. Whether you tell us or not they will find out. It would go better for you to cooperate."

"Sorry, pal, you'll have to buy it." He was sitting up straight but still holding his arm.

"Do you have a family?"

"Why?"

"I have a family—a boy and a girl. When I fight, I fight to protect them from men such as yourselves. What do you fight for?"

The room was silent for a moment as each of the men studied the other. "If South Vietnam had invaded North Vietnam, then maybe I would be fighting to save your side."

"You should not be fighting for either side. It has never been your war." Quang stood up, then walked out of the room, motioning to one of the guards.

Vassilov got up out of an overstuffed chair. "Did you have a pleasant conversation? I don't suppose he volunteered anything, did he?"

"No, nothing."

"I will just be a minute." Vassilov walked into the room with Jordan and opened his briefcase, taking a folder out and laying it on the desk. "I'm sure you will want to answer these simple questions that I am going to leave with you. Then you will be moved in with your friends and you can wait out the war in safety. And please don't think we are not serious. You will answer the questions. Amelio!" he shouted to the Cuban in the other room. "Escort the major out to the car. I will be out in a moment."

Quang followed the Cuban outside and waited.

Inside, Major Vassilov watched Jordan for a moment. Jordan remained silent, only his eyes following Vassilov's every move. Vassilov reached inside his briefcase and extracted a large envelope. Opening it, he produced an eight-by-ten, black-and-white photo and held it up before Jordan.

Jordan stared at the photo for a moment, trying to focus his eyes on the figures in the picture, then raised his eyebrows and gritted his teeth. "You bastards!" he yelled. He stared at the photo—clear and precise—showing his wife, Patricia, standing alongside Karen Campbell and next to a smiling Asian in front of a taxicab.

Vassilov closed his briefcase, leaving the photo on the desk. "It has been a pleasant visit, my American friend. Please give our little questionnaire your best consideration. And remember, if we want, we can keep you forever. Nobody even knows you are alive." He motioned for the guard, then walked outside to the car, stopping in front of Gutierrez.

"Is he cooperating?" the Cuban asked. "If not, I can promise you he soon will."

"I know he will, my friend. We will be in touch."

Vassilov and Major Quang got back into the car and their driver quickly started the Volga, which spewed a cloud of oily smoke as the engine caught. Nearing the main road, Quang asked, "Why is he not with the rest of the prisoners at the main POW complex in Hanoi?"

Major Vassilov was silent a moment, then said, "He is one of the special ones."

C aptain Pearson ordered the
Barbary Coast turned into
the almost lifeless air and
another boiler brought on line. In time the carrier would
pick up speed, charging, running head on with the bow
slicing through the flat, lakelike sea. Green water would
cascade into waterfalls and bottle-nosed dolphin would leap
through the froth just out of harm's way. Schools of flying
fish would flee, forming arcs in the air. A mound of white
froth would climb her bow as she pushed ahead, forming the
"bone in her teeth" that photographers loved to see. The
boilers would strain to produce needed steam for the launch
into nearly windless conditions.

On the port CAT, a VA-47 A-4 taxied into position,
dipping its nose as the linemen signaled the pilot to stop.
Another sailor darted underneath to attach the steel launching

bridle. Like a medieval dragon made of steel, the A-4 sat motionless, its talons sharpened and waiting, only needing release from its master to set it free and find its prey.

The second A-4 was already on the starboard catapult. It also sat still, its red collision lights rotating silently as the pilot inside waited for his wingman to acknowledge he was ready.

The sun was straight overhead in the cloudless sky, burning everyone on the flight deck. Some were napping out on the catwalks, while others were in the guntubs, still trying to rid themselves of the taste of Bangkok. A few still dreamed of the abundant sex, cheap booze, and good food they had enjoyed only yesterday. It would be the last opportunity to relax before round-the-clock flight operations got underway as the *Barbary Coast* hurried to reenter the war zone to the north.

With the wind adequate down the deck, the signal to launch was approved and a signalman ran a flag up the halyard followed by the skull-and-crossbones pennant. Captain Pearson sat in his captain's chair, watching the two A-4s on the bow cats. They were running behind schedule and he had issued orders to his officer of the deck to turn back to the north as soon as the jets were launched. The mission had only been approved that morning and was to be an indoctrination mission for the new pilot. All "green" pilots were required to conduct a sortie into South Vietnam into a relatively safe area before being allowed to go on the more dangerous bombing missions to the north. Ensign Swenson, assigned to fly wing with Campbell, awaited the signal to launch.

The launch officer extended his arm and pointed at the A-4 on the starboard cat, paused momentarily, then made an overhead twirling motion with his right hand. As he listened to Campbell he continued to twirl, all other sounds absent as the General Electric turbine wound up, creating a violent roar and sending hot exhaust gasses into the raised jet-blast deflector. Sailors lying on mattresses in the starboard guntub held their ears and cursed the war. Campbell wiggled in the seat one more time, then saluted the launch officer and faced forward, bracing himself for the jolt. The launch officer signaled his assistant. A tall, gangly youngster standing in the catwalk by the catapult panel pushed a button and Campbell felt himself being pushed into the backrest. The A-4 hunkered down as it traveled the length of the deck, then the shuttle came free and he was airborne.

Swenson already had his engine running at full power and was launched in an identical fashion. Swenson found himself airborne, banking to port in a climbing turn as he flew toward his leader.

"In sight, Blackbeard two four, join on me, over." Campbell was climbing into the hot, humid air that was extracting a toll on the climbing ability of their heavily loaded aircraft. He maintained a constant angle of bank as he turned to their vectored heading that would take them over the northern sector of South Vietnam. Campbell looked down into the cockpit, quickly scanning his gauges. Satisfied everything was working properly, he glanced back at Swenson. He could see him closing in on a constant bearing.

Eleven thousand feet below, the *Barbary Coast* was turning back to the north again, taking two of her boilers off line, reducing speed as she journeyed north to rejoin the *Bon Homme Richard* at Yankee Station. Flight operations were secured and again sailors gathered out on the flight deck. The *Bonnie Dick* was anxiously awaiting their return and looking forward to going off line in two weeks for R and R in the Philippines.

Campbell and Swenson continued their climb through 18,000 feet as the *Barbary Coast* disappeared beneath them. They flew westward until the coast of South Vietnam was in sight just ahead. Swenson was hanging tightly in formation as they switched over to Da Nang control and proceeded inland. They would wait for an assigned target from forward air control (FAC) aircraft working the South Vietnamese countryside.

The FACs were slow, prop-driven planes, usually OV-1 Bird Dogs or sometimes the later version OV-2 push-pull Cessna high-wing aircraft. They carried small wing-launched rockets that held smoke markers instead of warheads. The dangerous job of finding a hidden enemy earned them the highest respect of the navy pilots flying under their control.

A Bird Dog, flown by 1st Lt. Rick Hanover, flew a series of low-altitude passes back and forth across suspected areas of troop concentrations and recent activity, hoping to spot enemy movement. He dropped lower, raising the bet and hoping to entice someone to give himself away.

"Blackbeard flight, this is Coast Watcher." The ground controller handling the navy flight watched the small blips on his screen and made a notation on his clipboard. "Nothing yet—the FACs are looking hard to stir something up. Suggest you orbit two five five degrees four zero off Coast Watcher at Angels one five, over."

Campbell acknowledged the call and started a descent to 21,000 feet, adding the briefed 6,000 feet to the assigned 15,000. He swiveled around, checking on his wingman. Swenson was hanging motionless just below him and slightly aft. Campbell gave him a thumbs-up and turned back around, continuing the descent.

Over the horizon he could see karst mountains sparkling in the high sun. Riddled with caves, they had been home for soldiers of countless generations during hundreds of years of warfare. Campbell stared at them for a moment, then entered into the first turn of the loop in the racetrack pattern they would fly at reduced power to save fuel. He could see gray haze hanging over the mountains, dipping down into the jungles and countless checkerboard rice paddies criss-crossing the country. To the north he could see smoke rising from a target being bombed by aircraft from another carrier, controlled by a FAC.

Campbell flew the pattern for another ten minutes, droning on, occasionally checking on his wingman, who never seemed to be out of position. Their aircraft hung in the sky, the heavy bomb and fuel loads straining at the small wings, which were cocked up and generating lift from their high angle of attack.

Campbell looked far to the west and he thought he could see into Laos and he wondered if the hazy mountains in the far distance were in Thailand.

The voice booming over his headset startled him. "Blackbeard three one, this is the Watcher, over."

"Blackbeards up, go ahead, over." He acknowledged the call and shot a quick glance back at Swenson. His wingman gave him a thumbs-up, still in a rock-hard position off his wing.

The twenty-six-year-old air force sergeant leaned over his radar console, watching the flight of the two etching small circles on his screen. "Okay, Blackbeard, head two two zero to your briefed target. That's all we can find for you for now. Contact Cable Car on button nine upon arrival." He wrote down the time of contact.

Campbell acknowledged the instructions, visually indicating to Swenson to change radio channels. He banked toward the new heading, rolling out on 220 degrees. Edging up on the power slightly, he did a quick radio check with Swenson.

"Right with you, sir," Swenson checked in. In order to wipe out the landing mishap from everyone's memory, he wanted this mission to go perfectly. Campbell had assured him the flight would be just like a training mission back at the Chocolate Mountains out in the desert in California. He recalled Campbell's saying there would be no known opposition. They would probably try to knock down a hill that overlooked a trail used for bringing down supplies from the north, though the enemy would predictably dig it out overnight. Then they would get to bomb it again sometime. This would be his chance to exonerate himself, since before joining Campbell he had one of the best aerial bombing records any student had ever achieved. He was consistently able to place his practice bombs on target, day or night, never fixating on the target, and always pulling out at the right time. He wondered if now he could do it for real.

Campbell was flying the assigned heading that would take them into the bombing area, hoping it would be a simple drop with no opposition. They had been briefed to expect a milk run, but then the briefers never had to go on these missions. Maybe they should, he thought to himself. There were always a few guys taking potshots at them with rifles. He never saw them in the daytime, but he knew they were there. He keyed the mike, "Cable Car, this is Blackbeard three one, over."

"Hello, Blackbeard, this is Cable Car. Read you loud and clear. What do you have for me today?" The air force lieutenant pulled back on the control stick and pushed it against his right knee, banking the plane up and around until the wings were nearly vertical. He was searching for any sign of enemy activity or for the presence of antiaircraft guns that could fire on the jets when they began their bombing runs. He was an unusually easy target, one often tempting to gunners on the ground who hid from him beneath the trees. They held their fire under orders from their leaders, who knew the downing of one observation plane gained them nothing but a guaranteed bombing. They would watch silently, concealed in the shadows below as the OV-1 above them glided around like a hawk riding thermals and seeking its prey.

Campbell saw the area ahead was dotted with low hills

punching up from the almost solid jungle, an area that could hide almost anything, or swallow up a man if he had to eject. Previous bombings had opened up the tight canopy of jungle, revealing ponds filled by recent rains. They reminded him of the small catfish ponds he had seen around Meridian, Mississippi, during flight training.

"Roger, Cable Car, Blackbeard three one, lead for flight of two; Blackbeard two four is wingman. Have two one-thousand-pounders each. Can give you a total of two runs apiece and three one will make first run, over." Campbell continued toward the target, signaling Swenson to move out several thousand feet abeam and set his station arming switch for the release of a single bomb.

The OV-1 pilot made one last sweep over the target area, then flew off to the east where he could observe the bombing run. "Your target appears clean, Blackbeard. Lay your first bomb just above the road into the hill. That should bring it down on the road and give the slopes something to do tonight." He banked the tiny observation plane and started a turn back to the south.

"Three one's in." Campbell peeled off from Swenson and rolled on his back, pulling the nose down to a forty-five-degree dive angle, then rolling the A-4 upright again. He was concentrating on the hill but his nose was yawing back and forth. The hill ricocheted around the rings of his gunsight as the rising currents of humid air buffeted the aircraft. The ground was coming up rapidly and he concentrated on zeroing in on the target, holding the hill steady just long enough to release. He worked at the rudders, trying to keep the hill from wandering, then released the bomb from the carriage underneath his wing just as the hill passed through the gunsight pipper. He could feel the A-4 jump upward as the bomb came off. He pulled back on the stick, sending the small jet skyward again. "Three one's off," he called.

Cable Car watched the dark-green, oblong shape fall silently downward, then impact at the bottom of the hill just beyond the road, sending a cascade of earth into the air and out over the jungle. He could see the first drop had landed long and too far to the north. "The Future Farmers of South Vietnam will want to thank you for that new rice paddy you just created. Okay, Blackbeard two four, let's see if you can do any better. This time bring your aim point back up the hill about fifty meters."

"Yes sir." Swenson eased the Skyhawk around, lining up the hill, then rolling on his back as Campbell had. "Two four's in." Swenson concentrated on the hill and the rising cloud of dust at the north end. His descent was perfect and his airspeed at 450 knots, just where he wanted it. He flew downward through the upper level of the rising humid air, experiencing the same burbling Campbell had experienced. The hill was walking across the target, teetering around his gunsight. He worked the rudder pedals, anticipating each swing of his nose until he had the target almost stationary and superimposed under the gunsight pipper. Swenson glanced down at the rapidly unwinding altimeter and began counting to himself. "One thousand and one, one thousand and two," he said, counting off the seconds to the drop point before he depressed the button on the control stick between his legs. The bomb immediately fell away. He then put back pressure on the stick, sending the A-4 skyrocketing upward and toward his orbiting flight leader.

Cable Car was just above the treetops about one thousand meters from the target area, watching the impact of the bomb and the rising debris. He could see the bomb had landed right where he wanted as tons of earth flew upward from the ground. But because of all the dust in the air, he wasn't sure if the hill had collapsed on the road.

"Don't let that go to your head, two four, but I think it was right on. I can't tell if the road is buried or not, so give me another one same place. OK, three one, give me a drop right on the last cloud of dust your partner raised.'' The FAC pilot expertly rolled the OV-1 up on its wing and twisted around for another look.

Swenson joined up with Campbell, expertly tucking underneath his wing in close formation. The flight leader grinned to himself, proud of his wingman's accomplishment, but slightly embarrassed that he had been so far off himself. ''I didn't hear you call off target,'' he radioed to Swenson.

''Ah . . . two four's off,'' Swenson called, embarrassed he had forgotten the mandatory call.

Campbell signaled to Swenson and rolled in for his second run. ''Three one's in.'' Again he concentrated on holding the weaving hill in his gunsight as he descended into the rising, unstable air. He released just as the hill was passing across his nose, hoping he had timed it right this time. ''Three one's off.''

Cable Car banked his small high-wing Cessna, turning until he had a perfect view of the descending bomb, giving him the ''best seat in the house,'' as he like to brag to his buddies back at his home base. He watched the bomb impact with the hill. ''Close, but no cigar,'' he called. ''Three one, hold up on your next run until the dust settles. I want to go have a closer look at the target.'' He orbited to the south, waiting for the gentle breeze to clear away the suspended dust. A few minutes later he flew over the target area. Flying just above the road, he could see a large bomb crater at the bottom of the hill and one at the top. The explosions had rearranged the hill but had not brought the complete collapse he was seeking. He continued circling overhead. ''Blackbeard, make your last run but drop about twenty meters down the hill closer to the road from your last drop and . . . oh, shit.'' A quick burst of an automatic weapon caught his right wing, leaving a line of holes through it but doing little other damage. He banked and flew away from over the road. "I think you just pissed off one of the road repair guys—I'm taking hits from small arms. You are cleared to drop anytime." The FAC pilot quickly cleared the area.

"Okay, Swenson, let's see if you can do it again." Campbell watched his wingman break off and roll into his bombing dive, releasing the last one-thousand-pounder.

"Two four's off." Swenson's voice was strained and heavy as the high G load pulled at his body. He twisted his head around, straining his neck to see dust rising from the hill. He couldn't tell what damage he had accomplished.

"Looks like a good shot, Ringer, join on me." Campbell rolled into a shallow angle of bank as he watched his wingman rising up to him.

The OV-1 pilot waited for the dust to settle and then flew as close as he dared, not wanting to become a target again. He pulled out a set of binoculars he carried and held the aircraft steady with the stick between his knees. "The hill is gone—lying on the road below. Can you give me a strafing run down the tree line?"

Both Campbell and Swenson had a full load of 20-millimeter shells. "Affirmative, we can give you one pass down the road."

"You're cleared. Bend a few of their shovels for me."

Campbell rolled in with Swenson not far behind and off to the side. Going lower this time, they began firing a string of 20-millimeter shells into the tree line not far below, dropping treetops and tearing up anything nearby. "Blackbeard's off," Campbell called, and the two A-4s peeled off from their low-altitude strafing run and climbed back up again. "Returning to Motha, and we want to thank the air force for the use of their firing range," Campbell radioed to the FAC pilot.

"The pleasure is all mine—and a special thanks to your

wingman." FAC pilots loved to rub it in anytime they had the opportunity, especially with another branch of service. The FAC pilot knew that navy flights sent to him usually had at least one green pilot aboard. He watched them disappear and then turned back for Saigon and the dreaded paperwork that awaited him.

In a few minutes the A-4s were flying above the beach of South Vietnam and Campbell reported "feet wet" to Coast Watcher, telling him they were over the water and heading for their home base. They were given a vector and expected arrival time over the *Barbary Coast*. When they checked each other over for battle damage, Campbell discovered a couple of holes in Swenson's rudder but nothing dangerous. He calculated the time they could remain airborne with the fuel on board and headed out across the hazy-looking sea below.

They flew back in loose formation, Swenson hanging back in a comfortable position. He wanted to remain nonchalant, but he kept breaking out into a grin every time he thought about what they had accomplished. He was inwardly proud that he had been the one to collapse the hill and hoped that his performance would make up for the landing incident. He felt calm and confident. Campbell was just hoping the rest of the flight would go as smoothly.

Campbell signaled Swenson to close in and pull in tight as they approached the *Barbary Coast*. They were just above the wake of the carrier and were rapidly approaching the point where they would turn downwind. The carrier had already turned into the wind and called, and they were cleared for the "break."

Campbell was just above the carrier as he called, "Blackbeard, three one, flight of two, clean and minimum damage, one point five, over." Campbell put his gloved hand to his visor and saluted his wingman, rolling away from Swenson in a ninety-degree angle of bank.

As Swenson watched Campbell's A-4 pulling away from him, he counted silently to himself, then rolled into the same maneuver and made a hard break to port as he turned downwind behind Campbell. He saw the other A-4 well ahead of him and already turning toward final. He glanced down at the water and then at the sky, satisfying himself that conditions were right. Swenson heard Campbell call the ball, and he silently mouthed the landing checklist, then adjusted his harness as he started a turn toward final. He picked up the ball halfway through the turn. "Ball, A-4, one point two," he called.

Campbell had already made the trap, snagging the number two wire, cleared, and was taxiing forward. On the LSO platform, Pokey heard Swenson call the ball, then saw him immediately rise above the glide path. "Don't do it to me again," he muttered to himself. He watched the junior pilot make a power-and-attitude correction and grinned as the A-4 flew steadily down the glide path. With satisfaction he watched the jet catch the number three wire. Pokey let his breath out. "High at start, good correction, okay pass, number three," he told his assistant, who was copying the information into a small notebook. Pokey secured the LSO platform and headed for the ready room where he would make his customary comments on landing performances. He saw Campbell still sitting in his aircraft, grinning at him. The LSO shot him the finger as he walked by.

Most of the pilots had assembled in the ready room waiting for Swenson to return from his first mission. A large amount of money had been bet on the outcome of his landing performance, and now bets were being collected. All landings were recorded on a remote-control TV system, and they watched intensely as the small A-4 glued itself to the cross hairs on the screen. Pancho had even gone up and banged on the screen, thinking the picture was frozen. When the camera angle switched from deckline to overhead, cheers went up when they saw Swenson catch the number three wire, then moans as the losers dug into their pockets to pay off the skipper, who had bet on his most junior pilot.

On the flight deck a lineman hooked up a tow bar to the nose of Swenson's aircraft. A plane captain was already inside the cockpit to ride the brakes, and they waited for Swenson to complete his walk-around of his aircraft before they towed it away. He stopped near the tail section, looking up at the small jagged holes stitched into the rudder section. Welcome to the war, he thought to himself. He waved at the plane captain, then headed for the island where Campbell was waiting for him.

"Fantastic, Ringer, it couldn't have gone better." Campbell was all smiles as he went up to Swenson and put his arm on his shoulder. "But don't get too overconfident. Up north, things are going to be a lot hotter." They walked inside and were met by an airman from the maintenance shop who handed them each clipboards with the yellow-sheet maintenance forms that documented the maintenance history of their aircraft, which they quickly filled out. Winding their way down from the flight deck to the Combat Information Center, Campbell pushed open the door, revealing a darkened space dimly lit by red lamps and jammed with status boards and radar repeaters. A ship's company lieutenant junior grade immediately stepped in front of him.

"Sorry, can't come through here," he said. He stood firmly in front of Campbell, blocking his path.

"Since when?"

"Since the admiral laid down orders that CIC is not to be used as a passageway to debriefing, that's when." The junior office held his ground.

"Well, shit," Campbell said, loud enough for everyone to hear. He turned around, pushing Swenson back into the passageway. "Looks like we go the long way." He edged around Swenson and headed through another room, not even looking at the two occupants typing out reports, and stepped out the door on the other side into the passageway. "Short-cut," he explained. Swenson was hurrying to catch up. Campbell stopped in front of a door identified only by its compartment space and entered, confronting another lieutenant junior grade sitting behind a large gray desk. The briefing officer looked as if he had never seen daylight. Campbell thought all intelligence types liked staying hidden in their sealed spaces, never going out in the light.

"Mr. Campbell, right?" The small-framed officer looked up from the map he had spread before him. "Got a message in from Da Nang Intel and initial reports look good. Seems you two trashed the road real good." He handed them both a clipboard to fill out and pointed to two seats resembling school chairs over in the corner.

Campbell took the boards and handed one to Swenson. "Fill this out the best you can remember. By tomorrow, they'll have the road dug out and the holes filled in and ready for action all over again." He sat down, throwing his helmet bag to one side. They both were still wearing torso harnesses and G suits and sat uneasily in the too small chairs. Campbell quickly jotted down all the information he cared to and handed the board to the briefing officer. "Here you go, sport. See you back in the ready room, Swenson," he said, leaving the junior pilot trying to decipher the unfamiliar form.

By the time Campbell returned to the ready room, most of the pilots had drifted away with all bets settled. Only the duty officer was there along with Lieutenant Commander McClusky, the LSO, and a few of the junior officers who hung around to congratulate Swenson on his successful landing and bolster his confidence.

"Well, congratulations," Pokey said, grinning at Campbell as he came through the back door of the ready room. "Your number two finally got his act in gear."

Campbell headed directly to the rear of the room and threw his helmet bag upward, catching a peg with one of the bag handles. He hung his torso harness and G suit on a lower peg. The off-duty telephone talker handed him a cup of coffee and Campbell walked over to Lieutenant Commander McClusky.

"How did it go?" he asked. The operations officer stood facing Campbell with his legs spread apart. Lt. Comdr. Thomas McClusky was known as Red Robin due to his reddish face. He was responsible for putting the missions together after the orders went down for a strike. He had a talent for accumulating information from any and every source he could lay his hands on, and he enlisted help from anyone. It was a tough job and one he performed well. Everyone expected him to make commander the first time he went before the selection board.

Campbell smiled an embarrassed but confident smile. "It couldn't have gone better. Well . . . maybe a little better if I had been on target." He looked beyond McClusky to see if Swenson was coming through the door. "Don't tell him, but that little farm boy put his thousand-pounders right where the FAC wanted. Dropped the whole fucking mountain right down on the road. Even took a couple of small-arms hits in the tail feathers as a memento."

McClusky grinned back at him. "Well, at least we know he can bomb. Maybe his first landing was just a fluke, stage fright or something. But today was no fluke. He made one correction on the glide path and hung in there like glue." He cut off his words as the door behind him opened and Swenson walked in.

"Ringer, go hang up your gear, grab a cup, and we'll debrief." Campbell watched his wingman walk to the back of the ready room, where he was immediately surrounded by some of his buddies, who pounded him on the back as he hung up his flight gear.

"What do you think of combat now?" McClusky hollered back to him.

Swenson hurried down the aisle toward the front of the room, trying to suppress the grin forming on his face. "It was kind of like the training command in a way," he said.

Both Campbell and the ops officer looked at each other. "Wait until you get up north. Then we'll ask you that question."

★ 10 ★

During the dry season Vientiane could be extremely hot, broiling under the sun overhead and encrusted with the red dust originating from the mud of the river bottom, covering anything and everything. At other times, it was just plain sultry, stifling to those used to cooler climates and drier air. It was the mecca for displaced tribesmen, immigrants from their own land who were driven down from the hills and sought protection in the administrative capital of Laos. It was also a nest of spies, with agents from all sides either officially or unofficially represented.

To the immigrants, Vientiane was a strange and fascinating place. The strikingly decorated Meo tribesmen huddled together, the men dressed in black and their women nearby wearing eye-catching jewelry crafted by their ancestors.

Their children, wide-eyed at the crush of nationalities banded together, hid behind their mothers' skirts, peeking out at any strangers passing by. It was a concoction of hopes and wants, a blending of tribes that previously had rarely seen each other. Some eyed each other suspiciously, although their children would quickly find ways to communicate.

Not far from this mélange of humankind was the Lang Xang, the hotel most popular with foreigners. Located near the center of town and always filled to capacity, it was considered the best hotel in the city. It was also the best place in town to nose around for rumors or keep an eye on who was talking to whom. Here CIA mingled with KGB, and North Vietnamese paid courtesies to the Laotians they were trying to overthrow through support of the Communist Pathet Lao fighting in the north. The USAID was also here, as well as boys from 4-H Clubs of America who taught Laotian tribesmen how to raise fatter pigs. Subversion from within and without tore at Laos daily as various factions fought one another. Yet for the time being, the southern part of the country maintained an easy peace. As long as the Communist forces remained ten miles north of the Mekong River, which formed the border between Thailand and Laos, then the Thais agreed to stay out of the war.

The two navy wives sat in the hotel bar at a table near the windows. Each had a cold beer in front of her and Patricia chain-smoked her dwindling supply of Kents. They were patiently waiting, indulging in small talk and casting an apprehensive eye out the windows toward the street in front of the hotel. They hoped someone would appear in answer to their request to visit the North Vietnamese.

The hotel bar was typical of many found in Asian countries. Dark wood-paneled walls butted up to jalousie windows always opened to catch any breeze. Overhead the usual ceiling fans labored, moving otherwise still air around the room. Scotch, whiskey, or cold beer was the favored drink during the hot, dusty dry season, served with ice for the Americans and without for the British. On one wall a single painting was hung, large by most standards, featuring a group of war elephants charging through throngs of dark-skinned invaders. The artist depicted a scene in which the invaders were overwhelmed and crushed by the elephants as the warriors followed the towering animals into battle.

It was now three days since their arrival in Laos and they were becoming concerned. They had ventured out only once to walk down to the marketplace crowded with refugees, then quickly returning when they thought someone was following them. Several Americans had tried to strike up a conversation with them in the hotel, but they had refused to answer any questions about their reason for being in Laos except that they were in town to visit friends. They had met one man—Tom Spaecik. He had befriended them earlier, introducing himself as a member of the USAID mission in Vientiane. They thought it strange he had never directly asked why they were there, but when he had pressed for more information they had suddenly changed the subject. Another acquaintance, Harry Christian, claimed he was a stringer for *U.S. News & World Report*. He revealed to them his hopes to obtain a good story that would get him a job with the famous newsmagazine. He said he spent most of his time nosing around the city and sometimes went out to the countryside if something was going down.

Karen looked around the bar and out into the lobby. She hoped to spot their "would-be" journalist. Seeing no one, she turned back to Patricia, who was still gazing out the louvered windows. "Do you think he will show today?"

"Sure, he'll be here. What else does he have to do but try and pry information out of us." Patricia took a long drag from her half-smoked cigarette, as they both stared through the dusty panes.

A half hour passed, then another fifteen minutes before Harry stepped through the doorframe, scrutinizing the nearly empty room. It was early and only a few of the regulars had shown up, choosing to sit at the bar. He spotted the women sitting by the window and walked over. "Ah, my friends from the south," he said cheerfully, pulling a chair away from the next table and seating himself at the end of theirs. "Still haven't run into your friend yet?"

Patricia turned away from the window. "Hello, Harry," she said without enthusiasm. She had earlier confessed to Karen that she didn't know if she believed him or not. Everyone in Vientiane seemed to be something other than what they claimed to be. Karen had only shrugged her shoulders.

"Chasing a hot story today?" Karen asked, greeting the journalist with a big smile.

"Nah. Too hot to be out in the country. I think I'll just let the war come to me, which will be soon enough."

"What do you mean?" Karen asked. She had a hard time differentiating between all the warring factions.

Harry grinned at her and watched Patricia push her spent cigarette into the already overflowing ashtray. "Your friend doesn't say very much but she definitely likes Kents."

Patricia started to reach for another but changed her mind and picked up the bottle of Thai beer instead, finishing it off and pushing the bottle away from her. "Know where I could buy another couple of cartons?" she asked.

The journalist signaled to a waiter to bring another round. "Maybe," he said. He turned toward the waiter, nodding at him then back to Patricia. "What's it worth to you?"

Patricia smiled, then turned back to the window. She was in no mood to play cat and mouse with the reporter, so

Harry turned his attention to Karen. The Laotian waiter set three more beers on the table, adding them to Harry's tab.

After a few beers, Patricia began to mellow. She liked the correspondent well enough but was unsure of him. By the end of the afternoon, the three were telling each other stories like old friends, talking about their backgrounds and other trivia. Alcohol always made Patricia more agreeable, and the strong Thai beer had them all revealing more about themselves than she would have liked. She found out he actually was a writer and supported himself supplying off-beat stories to the wire services. He told them he had been raised in the Northeast and worked for a small newspaper before quitting his job, selling everything he owned and moving to Saigon. There he had hoped to work himself into a good job with one of the major news services. It was also there he decided he wasn't too crazy about accompanying platoons out on combat missions and decided to try his luck elsewhere, ending up in Vientiane where the competition wasn't as tough. Occasionally he managed to come up with a story that would pay his bar tab.

Getting information out of Patricia, on the other hand, hadn't been as easy, and she continued to resist. Karen had finally let slip that her husband was a naval aviator flying off a carrier in the Gulf of Tonkin, although she wouldn't say which one. She also let slip that Patricia's husband was missing, earning a stare from Patricia.

"I bet I know what you are really doing up here," Harry said. First he looked at Patricia and then at Karen. "Let me guess. The military has been giving you the runaround, right? They told you to go home and hang out a flag and be a good little wife until they tell you otherwise. In fact, the only reason I can think of that you would want to come up here by yourselves is that you want to talk to the North Vietnamese. Am I right?"

Neither of the women said anything but sat there silently with stunned looks on their faces.

"Don't feel bad, girls." Harry paused to swallow a big slug of beer. "Listen, you aren't the first to go seeking information from the source."

"How could you tell?" Patricia demanded.

"It's not hard. If you stay here long enough you develop plenty of sources for information. That's my business, you know. The whole town is nothing but a collection of people spying on each other. And Vientiane ain't on your regular world-tour schedule." He leaned back in his chair, allowing the two front legs to come off the floor.

Patricia lit another cigarette. "Are we the first ones . . . I mean, am I the first wife of a missing flyer to go straight to the North Vietnamese?"

"Maybe, at least up here anyway. I heard some have been pestering the North Vietnamese embassy in Paris but hadn't made any headway yet. You can bet the North Vietnamese aren't going to see you unless it's to their advantage. That's probably why you haven't been contacted. You are waiting for someone to contact you, aren't you?" He rocked his chair forward.

Patricia looked at Karen again. She felt like a bit actor in a cheap movie script. "Why would we have a contact up here? You and Tom Spaecik are the only ones we know in Vientiane."

Harry laughed. "Tom Spaecik. I might have known." He leaned back in his chair again and glanced around the room. "You might as well have befriended the head of the CIA. It's well-known by virtually everyone around here that Tom's employed by the USAID as an agricultural liaison officer with the 4-H Clubs of America. Yeah, can you believe that? A bunch of American youngsters out here teaching some tribe how to grow corn. Anyhow, Tom's a good boy, but he can have you shipped out of here in a minute if he wants. Just a word to the Laotian government and you are suddenly persona non grata.''

"Do you think he knows why we came up here?'' Karen asked.

"Probably not at first. More than likely he got your names as soon as you showed up and ran a check on you. He probably found out you were wives of navy pilots and by now he knows more about you than your husband does.''

"Then why have they let us stay?'' Patricia asked.

"Curiosity most likely. They want to see what the North Vietnamese will do. Once they suspect the advantage goes to the other side, out you go. That's usually the way it works.''

"But what about my husband?'' Patricia clenched her fist as she spoke. "All I'm trying to do is find out if he is alive or not. Is that too much to ask?'' She could feel tears welling up in her eyes but willed herself not to cry.

"In World War Two, no; now—yes.''

"Why is now any different?'' Karen asked.

Harry lay his crossed arms on the table and rested his chin on them. "It wasn't always true, but for the most part, prisoner information used to be traded soon after capture. Then you were just out of the war as far as the Americans and Germans were concerned. The Japanese weren't quite as nice. They seemed to have a different outlook on things. Korean war, same thing. What you've got to understand is that North Vietnam is a very poor country. And from what I've seen, they are very clever and ingenious when it comes to finding ways of getting their own way. They have the Russians and Chinese supplying them, but how they will get rid of them someday will be a problem for them. America is a very powerful country. She has the best and most powerful weapons, plenty of manpower, and tremendous industrial capacity. But we have a problem.''

"What's that?'' Patricia asked.

"We're a democracy. That means trouble when half the country is trying to do one thing like fight a war and the other half has other ideas. I've been watching those wily Communists at work for a couple of years now, and I think I see where they've found a crack in our dam. It's just a trickle now, but leaks have a way of becoming torrents in no time, and pretty soon the whole dam comes tumbling down and then you can't reverse the process. You may be part of the trickle."

"I don't understand," Karen said. "What trickle?" Harry leaned back in his seat again. "Before I left to come over here I used to cover some of the student demonstrations back in the States and got to know a few of their leaders. Now I'm seeing them show up in places like Vientiane and Phnom Penh on their way to Hanoi to discuss antiwar movements. The Communists are exploiting them for all they are worth. What I'm saying, my dear unfortunate souls, is that one of the accepted rules of winning wars is the support of the people. If you don't have it, you don't win, period. And that is why I think the North Vietnamese are trying to figure out what they can gain from you. I'm sorry to have to say this, but if they have your husband and haven't released his name, they darn well know who you are and are going to try to use you in some way that is advantageous to them. And it won't be the first time, I'm sure."

Patricia brought her hands to her face, clasping her cheeks and preventing herself from gasping. A thousand questions were racing through her head.

"If that's true, then there is nothing we can do," Karen admitted.

"Oh, sure, you can cooperate with the North Vietnamese and get the State Department on your backs. But more important, what would your husband want you to do? That is something only you can answer." Harry paused for a moment. "Whatever you decide, I'd like to be able to tell your story."

Patricia seemed crushed, consigned to possibly never knowing the fate of her husband. She sat silently, thinking of what she could do, unsure of what direction to take.

Outside the hotel a taxi covered with red dust pulled up in full view of the windows at the bar and stopped at the curb. The taxi sign was barely legible, and the same driver who had brought them to the hotel pulled out a newspaper, began reading, and waited for them to spot him.

Inside the bar, Karen noticed the sudden appearance of the Datsun and nudged Patricia beneath the table. Patricia looked out the window, then pulled out a handful of the local currency, dropping it on the table. "That should cover our part." She pushed the pile in front of Harry. "You're great company, Harry, but we've got to go." She was up and out the door before he could say anything. Karen followed behind her, waving to the reporter as she left.

Outside, the driver spotted them walking down the steps and put his paper down, smiling.

"We thought you had forgotten us," Patricia said. She slid across the backseat, followed by Karen.

"No forget, just take time. You first ladies want to visit North Vietnamese in Laos and they have to discuss your case. My cousin Johnny convince them they must see you."

"Where are we going?" Karen said, uneasy as the driver swung the cab out into the nearly carless street, glancing into his rearview mirror.

"I take you North Vietnamese. They see you now." He began driving to the end of the block, then turned left, following a narrow street paralleling the river until he reached a block containing several two-story stucco buildings built by the French.

Karen looked at Patricia apprehensively as they stopped in front of a building with cracked and peeling stucco.

"This where North Vietnamese see you."

Patricia peered out from the taxi up at the top of the steps a few feet away. A single short Asian man stood at the door. He was wearing an ill-fitting gray suit with trousers too short and was neither smiling nor frowning, his features expressionless. Patricia couldn't tell whether he was Laotian or Vietnamese.

"You go to top of steps. They expecting you." The driver twisted around and was now facing them.

Patricia looked at Karen, hesitating. "Oh, what the hell." She got out of the Datsun, followed by Karen, and walked to the top of the entry steps, stopping in front of the guard. She looked back at Karen, seeking reassurance.

"We've come this far," Karen said.

Patricia turned and faced the guard. He said nothing and she watched him knock on the door. He waited a moment, then opened the door, holding it open for them.

Patricia stepped cautiously inside, her eyes diverted downward away from the guard. Karen followed behind her, curiously staring at the guard as she went in. They both turned around upon hearing the taxi drive off and saw the guard close the door behind them.

A frail-looking girl, not quite five feet tall and wearing black, loose-fitting pants, entered the room through a door at the far end. She stared at them as she approached, her face devoid of expression. "You please to come in," she said, then walked across the room, stopping near several straight-backed chairs next to a small wooden table. "My name Mai Vo Vung. I will translate for embassy representative Doan Quang Nhut. You sit please, he be here soon."

The two Americans looked at each other guardedly then sat in the chairs next to the table, thanking the girl as they sat down. The Vietnamese girl said nothing.

The room was large, the ceilings over twelve feet above the few pieces of furniture. A single credenza rested at one end. The space overwhelmed the few odd pieces of old furniture that made up the reception area of the official legation of the government of North Vietnam.

They both stared at a portrait that hung above the credenza, of the North Vietnamese leader Ho Chi Minh. Patricia looked at the picture, wondering what a kindly-looking old grandfather could be doing leading his country through so much pain and suffering. Both women felt the same strange sensation come over them as they waited in the house of their husbands' enemy. Not sure of what to do, they both sat silently, alone with their thoughts. Patricia looked at the portrait once more, then heard a door opening at the end of a hall. The translator immediately walked toward the opening door.

"What do you think, Karen?"

"I don't know what to think. Are we safe here?" She thought of the atrocities she had read about in the papers.

Suddenly a middle-aged man with slightly graying hair appeared at the far end of the room. His hair was cut short on the sides and he wore a nicely tailored gray suit of better material than the guard out front. He was not smiling as he walked toward them with the translator at his side, speaking to him in Vietnamese. He motioned for them to sit down.

Karen and Patricia eased back into their chairs, glancing nervously between the translator and their host. Neither had known what to expect—whether their reception would become a shrieking confrontation or a futile encounter. They looked up into his eyes and he into theirs.

"Mr. Doan welcomes you and asks if you will take tea with him." The slender translator remained standing.

"Yes, thank you," Karen said. She watched the translator quickly leave as the official took a seat across from them, sitting back and crossing his legs at the knees.

The three sat in silence with Doan smiling at them whenever their eyes met. It seemed to take forever until the girl returned with a tea service tray and a plate of small pastries. She quickly poured each a cup of tea and placed it before them, then stepped back.

"Mr. Doan ask how he may be of service to you."

Patricia looked at the girl for a moment, then turned to the official. She hesitated, wanting to choose the right words to express her feelings to a representative of the government holding her husband captive. Her mind was going blank. "All I want to know is . . ." She groped for the right words. "Do you have my husband as a prisoner?" she blurted out, surprising herself. Not knowing what else to say, she waited for his response.

The representative wasn't surprised by her question and continued to watch Patricia, his expression remaining the same as he stared straight into her eyes. He knew who she was and where her husband was being held, and where she had stayed in Bangkok. He knew many things about the two women—even where they were married and who their fathers were. The information had been supplied by Johnny, the Thai cabdriver who had driven them around Bangkok.

Everything Johnny had managed to find out about them, he had furnished to the North Vietnamese, as he often did with other servicemen and their wives in Bangkok. He found it easy to obtain bits and pieces of information about husbands, the military, the ships they were on and the aircraft they flew, as well as the squadrons they belonged to. What he couldn't find out for himself, his network of hookers and hustlers could. It was simply his job to collect as much as possible while driving the women around and making sure they had a good time without any harassment. His information had been turned over to the man in charge of the legation as soon as the women arrived in Vientiane, and the next few days were spent correlating and cross-referencing the information they already had. Much of it had been sent by radio before Karen and Patricia had landed at Vientiane.

The translator bent over, listening intently as Mr. Doan spoke, his voice lowered and the Vietnamese words meaningless to the women.

The young girl straightened up, facing Patricia. "Mr. Doan says it possible your husband could be a prisoner but hard for him to say. We consider all prisoners to be criminals since they are killing and maiming innocent people in our country. He says you should tell your president to stop this criminal war and then there would be no more killing." Her face remained stoic and she seemed to feel no emotion at all as she waited for Patricia's answer.

Patricia looked at the North Vietnamese intensely. She was beginning to shake a little. The room seemed cold, like a cavern deep underground. She saw a change of expression in him, but his eyes still burned into her as he waited for her answer. For a moment she let herself wonder if he had a family, then decided he did not. "I am just a simple housewife," she began. "I think all war is evil." She paused as she groped for her next sentence. "I also think no one has the right to tell others how to live for that matter. All I ask is that you tell me or tell somebody that my husband is alive. I was told by the man who flew with him that my husband was shot down and captured and he saw him being led away by your own troops. Why haven't you released his name as a prisoner of war? He can't hurt you now." Her eyes were pleading now and she was squeezing her own hand as she sat up, waiting for his answer.

Doan studied her for a moment. His expression hadn't changed and the girl stood silently by his side. Finally he spoke.

The girl translated immediately, "We have no prisoners of war, only air pirates who bomb our country and kill our children."

Karen could see the thin smile leaving his face momentarily, then returning. She said nothing.

"You should go home and denounce the war," the translator began again. "You should go home and tell your leaders that this is not their war, that they are wrong and many innocent lives will be lost. Then perhaps your husband's name might turn up. I cannot guarantee it, but it is your only hope."

Patricia felt as if the air had been squeezed right out of her. She slumped into the chair and stared back at the representative, his smile unwavering. She turned to Karen and then back to him. "I could never do that," she said. "Larry would never want me to do that. It would be treason and—"

"You should think about it, Mrs. Jordan," Doan interrupted, speaking in English for the first time. "You should think about your husband." He stood up and smiled, then walked away from her, disappearing through the same door he had entered by.

The translator began picking up the tea service, then looked up. "Best you go now," she said. Then, carrying the tray, she left the room, leaving the two girls alone.

In a moment she returned. "I am sorry but you must leave."

Patricia got up, followed by Karen. They stood there for a moment not knowing what to do, then the girl disappeared through the door at the end of the room.

"I guess the interview is over," Patricia said.

They walked out through the heavy entrance door, stopping at the steps. The guard was gone and the street was empty. They looked up and down, hoping that the cabdriver was nearby. He was nowhere in sight.

"Now what do we do?" Patricia thought she could hear a car. "Maybe that's our taxi coming back."

They both looked in the direction of the sound. Instead of

a Datsun, a light-tan British Land-Rover covered with red dust was approaching. They were astonished when it stopped in front of them.

"You'd better get in," Harry said. "I'll give you a lift back."

That night at the hotel, Harry invited himself to dinner, meeting them in the hotel dining room. After their encounter with the North Vietnamese, Patricia was glad to have someone to talk to and told him everything that had occurred. He could offer no encouragement but she felt better for having at least tried. She felt that at least they knew that the U.S. considered him safe when captured, and the North Vietnamese would have to account for themselves someday if he failed to return after the war was over. After Patricia finished explaining their visit to the embassy, Harry told them their visas were being canceled by the Laotian government for improper entry into the country and that they could expect to be put on the next flight to Bangkok.

Patricia was stunned. She sat there angrily cursing her own government for having so much control over their lives—then conceded her business was finished in Vientiane. The next morning they left for Thailand.

★ 11 ★

The *Barbary Coast* was scheduled to arrive at Yankee Station the following morning, but a minor mutiny was in the making. The officer responsible for movies on the ship had screwed up, and *Goldfinger* was scheduled for the third night in a row. In his first six weeks aboard the carrier, young Ensign Carroway had managed to become the most unpopular man in the wardroom, having consistently mixed up the movies sent over for exchange. The assignment of getting movies was always given to the most junior officer, but bungle the job and fail to come up with movies that pleased nearly everyone—and your name was quickly known aboard ship.

The few officers who hadn't seen the film and with nothing better to do remained in the dining room after dinner and waited for the stewards to clear away the dishes so the movie could start. The wardroom adjacent to the dining room could accommodate about a dozen tables of ongoing games of bridge, backgammon, poker, cribbage, pinochle, and a game called smoke that was played almost entirely by naval aviators. In the middle of the room were two large one-hundred-gallon aquariums bolted to steel stands. They were filled with tropical fish at the beginning of the cruise and were now home for several large cichlids who were quickly devouring the smaller fish. The tanks served as inclinometers, the angle of the water surface giving perfect indications of the condition of the sea. When Swenson had had his landing mishap, water was spilling out the top. Tonight the water was calm.

The wardroom was filling fast. Officers leaving the dining room staked out seats for card games or gathered in small groups, griping about the movie or reliving tales of Bangkok. In less than eighteen hours, aircraft would again be armed and flung into the air to attack the transportation arteries of the north. Only the two fighters, sitting ready alert on the forward catapults, indicated any possibility of flight operations. The two pilots sitting in their planes passed the time by reading paperbacks beneath red-lensed flashlights.

Campbell had seen the movie the first night it was shown and like everyone else, was not willing to sit through it again. He stood in the corner, holding a cup of coffee and talking to Lieutenant Commander McClusky about the mission scheduled for the next day. He was concerned about taking his green wingman into an area with known SAM defenses. All afternoon long he had been reviewing procedures with Swenson, going over each detail of defensive maneuvering against tracking missiles, formulating the plan for what each would do when the missiles were launched at them.

McClusky filled his cup again from the urn sitting on top of the credenza, then faced Campbell. "He has to go north sooner or later. It might as well be on this one." McClusky was a quiet man, usually somber before a sortie but always fair in mission assignments. He had written the flight schedule and after it was signed by the CO, sent it to administration for printing and distribution.

"I just hope the F-8s take care of the defenses before we get there. I don't want to see a repeat of Canh Tra," Campbell said, concerned about Swenson, but realizing he would have to go anyway. The knowledge that the F-8s would be preceding them as flak suppressors and would be available for defense against MiGs made him feel a little better about the mission.

McClusky took a final gulp of coffee, then put the cup down. "Gotta go check on the schedule." He quickly left the wardroom, leaving Campbell standing by the credenza.

Across the room at a table in the corner, Pancho sat at a card table alone, unfolding a long green felt cloth. He floated it across the table on the first try, then smoothed out the wrinkles with his forearm.

Campbell walked over to the table, pulled out a chair, and sat down. "Little early to start a smoke game, isn't it?"

"When everybody sees what the movie is for tonight, we'll get one going. Just hang loose. Where's that wingman of yours? Isn't it about time we busted his cherry?" The Mexican American pilot surveyed the room as he continually shuffled a deck of cards. "Now, bring on the sheep," he added. "It's time for the slaughter."

"He'll be along."

"*Fantástico*, man, I can't wait to get in his knickers. Hey, maybe he'll liven up this game. I sure do miss old Jordan. That old gringo could play smoke like nobody else on this tub." Pancho dealt out a hand to Campbell as they waited for their regular group of players to show up. Their usual procedure had been to watch the movie, then start a game with Jordan, Campbell, Pancho, Larue, Aggie, and occasionally one of the other fighter pilots on board. Additional players would sometimes join in, only to be seen storming away angrily, swearing they would never again play with this bunch of cheats.

Swenson walked into the room and spotted Campbell. He walked over to the table.

"Hey, tiger, what's up? You going to play with us tonight?" Pancho asked.

Swenson took a seat across from Pancho. "Yeah, I guess so. But I'm not very good at cards."

"No sweat. I'll give you a quick briefing before the others get here," Pancho said, then dealt out three hands and rolled over a card from the deck. "Simplest game in the world. Object is to play like spades but score like golf. The lowest scorer collects ten cents a point from everyone with scores higher than him. IOUs are acceptable and due at the end of the cruise except from the worthless fighter pilots, whom we demand cash from on the spot." He raised his voice as Dan Hanson stepped up to the table and sat down beside Swenson.

"Easy, I thought this was a friendly game," Hanson said. He was one of the F-8 fighter pilots on his first WestPac cruise, and he had learned the game during carrier qualifications. He played with them whenever he could get away from his collateral duty assignment as administration officer.

"Always a friendly game. Got a new man who wants to be a smoke player," Pancho said.

"Now go easy on my wingman, guys," Campbell interrupted.

"Don't worry. Guaranteed." Pancho lay the deck in front of the fighter pilot and waited as he cut the cards. Scooping the deck up, he turned to Swenson. "Okay, kid, now pay attention. You get five cards dealt to you and it's up to you to take one trick or all five of 'em. If you don't take any, you get five points tacked to your score. One or more is a point apiece."

"That's simple enough," Swenson said.

"Wait. There's more. Here you have to use the correct names of the cards or you're fined five points every time."

"What names?"

"Oh, like the cards are called papes and trump is called smoke. And the suits are sparklers, puppy feet, diggers, and bleeders," Pancho said, flipping a diamond, club, spade, and heart from the deck onto the table to make his point. He watched Swenson's eyes widen slightly as he did, then continued sailing the cards faceup across the table, calling out the names as each landed in front of Swenson.

"Top of the loop, double asshole, teats of puppy feet," called the fighter pilot as he named the nine, eight, and queen of clubs.

"And here comes the hook, another double asshole of bleeders, a trip, and a deuce," Campbell said, naming the jack, eight of hearts, a three, and a two for his wingman.

"You getting the idea, Swede?" Pancho fanned the rest of the deck out on the table and searched out the yet-to-be-named cards. "Okay, here's the ace, four, five, six, ten, and king—better known as the blade, quad, nickel, bottom of the loop, tracks, and cac. You can actually call them anything you want except by their real names or you get five points tacked on. Any questions?" Pancho raked in the pile of cards and began shuffling again.

Swenson looked at Campbell and then Pancho, wondering if he was going to figure out this game. "I guess not."

"And one more thing—cheating is legal unless you fall

out of your chair trying to sneak a peek at your neighbor's papes. In this game, luck and superstition are worth more than skill and science." Pancho spotted Aggie Anson coming out of the dining room. "Hey, Aggie, get your worthless body over here. We're about ready to start a smoke game."

Anson immediately headed for the table, pushing a chair in against the end card table. "I don't know who's responsible for the movies, but if he shows *Goldfinger* one more time, he's going over the side." He suddenly spotted Campbell's wingman sitting in. "Hey there, Swenson. I hear you've been dropping bombs inside your section leader's impact craters. That true?"

Swenson suddenly felt embarrassed. "Just rumors. I've been a little lucky, that's all."

"Don't worry, Swede," Pancho said. "Campbell considers it a good day when his bombs hit the right country." Pancho winked at Swenson and began dealing out the cards, sending them flying across the table to the other four players.

"Where's Larue?" Campbell asked.

"He's still in the dining room jawing with another jarhead. He'll be along." Aggie picked up his cards and held them close to his face, quickly looking them over and then placing them facedown on the table.

Pancho rolled the top card to the bottom of the deck, then held it up for everyone to see, then rolled another and placed it on the top of the deck. "Puppy feet," he called.

Swenson sat third down from the dealer, holding his cards tightly to his chest. Aggie sat to his left, and Swenson had caught him trying to peek at his hand. He held a trump king, an ace, and three smaller cards. Not sure of what to do, he waited.

"Okay, I got the blade. Who wants to talk?" Campbell advertised his power, hoping to convince someone that he had more than the single nontrump ace that would be his only chance of capturing a trick.

"You are a lying sack o' shit," Pancho said. "How can you have the blade when I got it?" His raised voice caught the attention of a couple of ship's company officers and they moved in closer to watch. "I got all the power. Who wants to talk? We'll cut everyone's nuts."

"You got the blade, *amigo*? Well, that's just peachy, *bueno*. I've got his royal ass and two smaller ones. You let me take the first trick and then we'll cut everybody."

The helicopter pilot's quick peek at Swenson's cards had revealed a single trump. With a void suit, he hoped to talk himself into taking a trick.

Aggie led with the ace of diamonds and Swenson, not quite sure of what he should do, played his highest diamond—a ten. Campbell and the fighter pilot followed with lesser diamonds, leaving Pancho to make the last play.

During the second round, Swenson caught a trick without picking up a penalty as he adjusted to the flow of the game. By the fourth hand he was confidently lying about his hand and catching on to the finer points of the game. For the next several hours they played, joined by another regular player, Captain Larue. Occasionally an outsider would sit down and play a few hands, only to jump up and leave swearing never to sit down with another bunch of aviators.

As ten o'clock, the agreed upon time to quit, approached, a last hand was called for. Campbell shuffled the cards, then stopped as the 2200-hour briefing over the wardroom PA system began. It was Admiral Laceur's idea to have the latest Viet Cong atrocities read as part of the nightly intelligence briefing for the crew. He had his staff scanning all sources for any information, and most of it came from daily DIA and CinCPac intelligence briefings. Campbell fixed his eyes on the green felt table covering as he listened.

". . . And today it was revealed that a village chief was disemboweled by Viet Cong raiders during a nighttime raid on a small village in the Ashau Valley. Official sources said that the entire village was forced to watch, including his pregnant wife and two small children. Reportedly the leader of the Viet Cong force was a former member of that village and said he would return, promising the same fate to anyone siding with U.S. forces attempting to use pacification methods in the area. U.S. forces were attempting to appoint a new leader in the village as of last report." The voice droned on with additional reports, including the daily body count, from the overhead speakers.

Pancho reached over and made a deep cut of the cards. He seldom listened to the nightly reports, finding them too horrible to believe, nor did most of the other crewmen aboard the *Barbary Coast*, who felt the voice coming over the PA system could be reporting on a war from another planet. They rarely saw the light of day from their work stations deep within the bowels of the ship; they usually only saw the planes taking off and coming back. It was just too hard for them to relate to something they never came into contact with. Only the pilots had contact with the enemy.

The last hand finished, Campbell placed the deck of cards in the middle of the table. "Okay, gents, time to settle up." He waited while Pancho subtracted his low score from the others, then listened as Pancho read the results. The only moan came from the fighter pilot, who had been the night's big loser. "Gentlemen, I'm turning in," Campbell said. "Swede, you and I are on the schedule for tomorrow afternoon, so get a good night's sleep." Campbell pushed away from the table and headed for his stateroom, leaving Pancho arguing with the fighter pilot over his debt.

* * *

Campbell woke the following morning to the sound of his windup alarm clock, and as he got up, he realized his stateroom still seemed eerie, devoid of anything belonging to Jordan—all his personal belongings had been removed and stored. After breakfast, Campbell had paperwork to complete before the afternoon mission, work he had put off to the last minute and could delay no longer. He hurriedly completed it that morning, ate lunch, went back to his room, and changed into a clean flight suit before heading for the ready room.

The briefing went quickly and the launch was routine, each aircraft heavily loaded with enough high explosives to destroy the train switching station that was their target for the day. Blackbeard flight found itself leveled off and quickly heading for the coast of North Vietnam, flying west in cloudless skies. The F-8s were already working over the antiaircraft positions and SAM sites around the station, endeavoring to make the A-4s' mission easier. Red Crown had authorized the F-8s to enter the target area and reported no MiG activity. Campbell guessed the MiGs would elect to remain on the ground with F-8s now in the area.

Blackbeard flight quickly found itself approaching the IP, the initial point, and experiencing heavy antiaircraft fire. The flight division leader, Lt. Comdr. Duke Majors, and his wingman, Pancho, were ahead of Campbell and Swenson. Both sections jinked hard as they attempted to spoil the aim of the AAA that the F-8s had failed to destroy. They headed for the train switching station, which had been bombed earlier in the week by planes from the *Bon Homme Richard*. Recon photos taken earlier by an RF-8 revealed the damage to the switching station tracks had been repaired and that additional guns were now installed around the train yard.

The F-8s continued making passes, attempting to neutralize the fire and give the A-4s a better chance of taking out the station completely. One F-8, high overhead, was hit by triple A and headed for the Gulf, trying to make it back to the ship. As the A-4s rolled in, the remaining F-8s exited the target area and orbited nearby.

"Two one's rolling in hot with two. Stick close to me, Pancho," the flight lead said, rolling inverted, pulling the nose downward and picking out the center of the tracks. Pancho was just off his wing and holding his position as the two aircraft started down.

Campbell watched the two A-4s ahead of them on their backs, entering a steep dive. Exploding flak left puffs of gray-black smoke surrounding them, a gift from the gunners the F-8s had missed. He could smell the cordite burning in the air as he rolled inverted.

"Three one's in hot with two. Okay, Ringer, here's where you earn your flight pay." Campbell couldn't see his wingman but knew he would be right with him. He held the nose down until satisfied with the dive angle, then rolled the aircraft upright again and put the gunsight pipper on the tracks. He had lost sight of Majors momentarily and concentrated on his dive, jinking as they dropped downward through the wall of flak the North Vietnamese were sending up.

In a densely wooded area several miles north of the switching station, a mobile trailer lay hidden beneath several trees. Camouflaged and undetected by the earlier recon flight, the trailer was the command center for the SAM battery hidden in the wooded site. Inside the trailer, several Vietnamese technicians watched intently as their Russian advisor, cursing out loud in Russian, frantically reset dials after temporarily losing power to the trailer. The radar would take a few minutes to come back on line, and he impatiently watched the voltage meter as the Vietnamese corporal worked on the generator outside.

The Russian technical advisor had been in North Vietnam less than six months and hated it. It was always hot and there was little to do beyond training the Vietnamese on the complex surface-to-air missiles that dotted the country. To add insult to injury, Lieutenant Mikalivich seemed to find himself assigned to the most remote sites and concluded he had somehow said something that displeased Major Vassilov. Only the fact that the experience would be good for promotion kept him away from the bottle. A few of his fellow advisors were already drinking heavily, even more so as the attacks escalated. As far as he was concerned, the lanky Russian looked forward to being transferred out of North Vietnam.

The power was up and he signaled Lieutenant Bo to switch on the Spoon Rest radar. Instantly the E-1B orbiting offshore detected the signal, and a general warning was quickly issued alerting all aircraft that the North Vietnamese had turned on their acquisition radar and were attempting to acquire a target.

The youngest of the Vietnamese technicians called out to his officer in charge. He had locked onto the targets attacking the train station again and was tracking them. Lieutenant Bo studied the scope for a moment, then turned toward the Russian, getting a nod from him. Quickly he called for the fire control radar to be turned on. Across the room a small, owlish-looking boy activated the Fansong targeting radar. The boy had been out of high school less than a year and had been assigned to a missile battery shortly after completing technical training. The boy studied the console, his eyes narrowing on the signals representing aircraft. The Fansong, tied in to the acquisition radar, used a narrower beam, feeding information to the tracking and target computers. One man worked with the altitude presentation and another with the azimuth while the Russian watched, scrutinizing their every move and patiently waiting as the targeting information was updated. He nodded approvingly as Lieutenant Bo encouraged his crew, a number of them green and fresh out of school.

Lieutenant Bo had been in the missile batteries for a year now and had credit for six kills. Barely five feet tall and slightly built, he wore his hair cut short on the sides and had a slight hump in the bridge of his nose. When the war ended, he hoped to attend school again. Patiently he waited for the bombers to come off target and go into their climb.

"The beam is tracking well, Lieutenant Bo," the Russian said in Vietnamese. He was anxious to fire the missiles resting on their mobile launch pads several hundred yards away, connected by long, heavy black cables.

The North Vietnamese officer sensed his advisor's anxiousness, but he was not yet ready. He wanted a perfect shot. "Stand by on missile one and two," he ordered. Yellow lights changed to green on the first and second firing panel. The two missiles rotated downward, then slowly pointed upward as the launchers followed the flight paths of the bombers. The control fins on each missile moved as they attempted to correct their stationary attitude and home in on their target. The launcher swung slowly as the jets pulled off target and began a climbing turn. The igniters were already arcing, lacking only fuel to light off the missiles.

The early-warning E-1B flying offshore broadcast another warning as it detected the targeting radar of the Fansong unit. Every pilot in the sky was twisting his neck as he looked for a missile flying through the air or dust blasting out as a missile launched. The attack pilots pressed their attack. The sounds of an imminent missile launch pulsated in their headsets.

"Three one's off," Campbell said, glancing over his shoulder and spotting Swenson. Out of the corner of his eye he picked up the unmistakable cloud of dust of a surface-to-air missile lifting off. Though only a few feet in the air its booster rocket was already accelerating it in a quest for supersonic speed. "SAMs at eight o'clock low," he called. Again every pilot swiveled his head back. Campbell went into a hard left turn with Swenson hanging on his tail. He pushed his nose over and watched the lead missile follow his move, pulse quickening as he realized he was the target. Campbell pushed the nose over farther and watched the missile move down with him. "Ringer, they've got two with our numbers on them. When I call, I want you to go into a high-G barrel roll to the left." Campbell raised his nose back up. The missile followed.

"This is three four. Got it, boss." Swenson eased back from Campbell as he anticipated the move.

"Now!" Campbell said.

In the trailer, Lieutenant Bo watched the blips on the screen and studied the targeting information. The Russian-built SA-2 Guideline missiles were set to explode in close proximity of their target or from a signal sent up from the ground. Bo had his finger on the detonation button of the second missile following behind the first, waiting to see what evasive maneuvers the jets would attempt. Bo knew the flight limitations of his missiles, and he also knew what maneuvers the enemy employed to escape. The missile's small tracking fins were incapable of flying it through a high-G barrel roll, and he anticipated the Americans doing just that. "Change the second missile to manual," he said. He watched the technician reset the controls as the second missile stopped tracking its target and continued on the last targeting information. He avoided looking at the Russian and continued with his plan.

Upon hearing the call from Campbell, Swenson pulled hard, forcing his aircraft into a climbing left turn. He rolled around an imaginary point forty-five degrees off his nose. The missile attempted to duplicate the maneuver and the small control fins went to their maximum deflection as it followed Swenson through the maneuver. As Swenson passed through the horizon inverted, the SAM was at the edge of its tracking envelope. It passed well to the side and exploded behind and above him. Swenson looked back, then let out the breath he had been holding in.

Lieutenant Bo counted silently to himself, then depressed the red firing button, instantly exploding the second SAM. He grabbed binoculars and ran outside the trailer with the Russian behind him. Together they searched the sky, then both shouted with delight when a burning aircraft was spotted descending in several pieces and trailing smoke. Bo focused on the area of the wreckage until he spotted what he was looking for and ran back inside. "Call battery headquarters and report a parachute about four miles to the southeast. Use the last targeting information!" The Russian was pounding him on the shoulder, overjoyed at downing another American aircraft.

Bo started to say something but was cut off in midsentence as the technician working the acquisition radar shouted, "They are coming in low, too low. I can't get the Fansong to lock on!"

Lieutenant Bo ran to the radar console and watched the blips on the screen moving rapidly toward the center. Suddenly he wheeled around and leaped to the fire control console, rapidly spinning the azimuth and declination dials on the three remaining SAMs and pointing them in the direction of the closing flight. "Stand by on all three."

"But we have no targeting information and—"

Bo pushed the nervous technician aside and selected ARMED AND READY on the control panel. He began counting to himself as he watched the green blips on the screen. Light was streaming in from the door left ajar as Mikalivich ran from the trailer.

The two F-8 crusaders were flying inbound at treetop level, less than three miles from the SAM site. The lead pilot watched intensely for the first sign of any SAMs lighting off. "Bingo, here they come," he said. "Let's go starboard." The two F-8s rolled into a sharp turn away from the path of the missiles lifting off their launch pads at minimum trajectory. The pilot leveled his wings and watched the three missiles accelerating. He saw the missiles pass behind them and explode as Lieutenant Bo manually detonated them. "Okay, sucker, now it's our turn," the pilot said. "Let's come around and level that bastard. If he has any more, we'll sidestep them, too." The flight leader pulled hard as they headed inbound toward the target.

Lieutenant Bo said nothing as his worried technicians looked up at him with ever-widening eyes. He continued watching the green blips changing direction on the screen and turning toward the center. For a mere fraction of a second, the occupants of the launch trailer heard the scream of the jets passing overhead. Then their world disappeared as the cannon shells exploded, obliterating the trailer and mobile launchers.

In the meantime, Swenson was becoming frantic. He hadn't seen Campbell take a hit and presumed the burning wreckage falling downward was part of the exploding SAM. Ringer turned seaward, expecting to hear Campbell call him and chew him out for becoming separated. "Blackbeard three one, this is three four, over." He listened for a response but heard only the E-1B cancel the SAM alert.

"Blackbeard three one, this is three four. Where are you, Soupy?" Swenson puzzled over not hearing Campbell answer him.

"Blackbeard three four, this is Blackbeard lead. Is three one with you? Over."

"Negative, sir. We were both busy dodging SAMs and I lost three one." Swenson banked the A-4 around as he continued looking for Campbell.

"Okay, three four, see if you can spot any wreckage." He switched over to the E-1B and requested the SAR helo approach the beach and stand by while they searched. None of them had heard a beeper go off.

Overhearing Blackbeard's last call, the two F-8s broke off and headed for the rising black smoke they could see in the distance. They banked as they flew over the wreckage site, staring down at the pile of junk on the ground. The flight leader recognized a piece of an aircraft wing and called Blackbeard lead, informing him of the discovery.

Campbell looked up and watched the aircraft flight crisscross overhead several times and assumed they were making low passes over the burning wreckage, looking for him. He was in water and below a bluff that extended out over the river he had landed in. He could only catch fleeting glimpses of the jets as they combed the area then finally departed, leaving him with only the sounds of the river. He clung to a handful of reeds growing at the edge while he tried to catch his breath and pull himself together. Campbell ran his hands over each limb until he was sure nothing was broken. He was breathing hard, taking huge gulps of air, the shock of the exploding SAM, ejecting and then landing in the water leaving him gasping. He was beginning to shake almost uncontrollably. He took a deep breath and then bit his lip, afraid someone would hear him panting.

The water was warm and the current was gently pulling at

his body as he crouched among the reeds, his feet barely touching the sloping bottom. He could see his parachute out in the middle of the river streaming with the current, its risers entangled with a submerged log. But he was too weak to go out and cut it loose. After the landing in the water, it had taken most of his energy to free himself from the log, and at one point, he thought he would drown. The current had stretched out the chute, causing the submerged tree to rotate and pull him under. When he unhooked the attachments, he had broken free and shot to the surface, gasping for breath. He took off his helmet, letting the current carry it downstream, and chose not to inflate his flotation device, instead paddling furiously with his hands to remain afloat. Campbell was deathly afraid of being spotted, and the personal flotation device would keep too much of his body out of the water. He'd finally reached a bend in the river, where the pace of the muddy water was slower near the edge. He'd paddled over to the bank and pulled himself up into the reeds, breathing hard.

Now it was quiet except for the sounds of distant jets—and even that was beginning to fade. Campbell looked across the river to the opposite side. A high bluff seemed to run only on one side, and it was too much to scale. Confused and unsure of what to do, he pulled himself farther into the reeds, his knees barely touching the clay bottom. He thought back to the descent and tried to remember what he had seen as he watched the ground rising up. All he could remember was a mélange of rice paddies and mountains in the distance. He knew he was in a remote area somewhere on the river that ran under the bridge at Canh Tra, and without the use of the radio he was isolated and would have to move to an area where he could signal an overhead flight. One thing he was sure of—he would have to get away from the parachute as quickly as possible before he was discovered.

Maybe they'll think I drowned and dive down and retrieve the parachute to see for themselves, he thought to himself. That would keep them busy for a while. He pulled out his portable radio and tried it again. Not even a hiss. He put it back inside its case and secured it in his pocket. It was nearing sundown and the shadows were long on the water. Spotting an old log wedged into the bank, he pushed it into the current, holding on to it for support. Slowly he drifted downstream with the current. The quicker he got away from the visible parachute the longer he would have before they came looking for him; that is, if he wasn't spotted first by some villager. He decided it was a chance he would have to take.

Offshore, the three remaining A-4s flew silently back to the *Barbary Coast,* several miles behind the faster F-8s. None had battle damage. Swenson moved into echelon as they turned up the carrier's wake and approached the break point, his mask off and hanging to one side. He monitored the radio traffic but was thinking about Campbell, finding it hard to believe that one minute he was there and the next he was gone. Swenson hooked up his mask as the flight leader called for them to tighten up the formation. Swenson was the last to land and was glad to feel the abrupt stop as his tailhook caught the number three wire. As the A-4 stretched out the cable, Swenson let out his breath and pulled the throttle back. In a few minutes he was down in debriefing with the rest of the flight and the skipper as they all racked their brains trying to figure out if Campbell might still be alive.

After the debriefing, Swenson returned to the squadron ready room and flopped into a seat in the back row, tired and depressed. He knew a flight would be sent out tomorrow to check out the area and that listening watches were continuously monitoring the emergency channels. The young pilot tried to imagine what it would be like out there in the jungle, in a strange land, with the enemy looking for him. He fell asleep in the ready room thinking about it, hoping they'd find Campbell, but wondering if he was going to be next.

Campbell looked at his watch and shivered. The luminous hands indicated 3:19 A.M. and he was chilled. To warm himself he put one arm between his legs as he hung on to the floating log and drifted downstream with the current. Above him were the countless stars of the Milky Way twinkling in the ink-black sky. The moon, in its quarter stage, hung low in the sky as it prepared to hide beyond the horizon. The stars and the moon were his only companions during the slow and arduous journey downstream, but Campbell no longer looked at them. The low-intensity light of the stars was almost too good, and he felt as if he were beneath a spotlight, visible to everyone in North Vietnam. In a few hours dawn would come, and Campbell hoped to drift as far south as possible before seeking refuge in the forest along the riverbank. It was silent now; even the rhythmic baritone cadence of the river frogs had ceased.

Campbell had been in the water nearly four hours, drifting steadily with the one- to two-knot current. He didn't know how far he had traveled, only that he was putting distance between himself and the chute and the area the Vietnamese would probably begin searching. He had expected immediate capture as soon as he hit the water, and still couldn't believe he had evaded them this long. During the night he'd heard voices along the riverbank and had submerged himself with only his nose above water. When he'd cautiously raised his head above water, it was silent again and no other sounds of humans were heard. Whether they were soldiers searching for him or only villagers, he never knew. At first light, he expected the North Vietnamese to start their search in earnest. He was convinced divers would search the area around the chute and discover he wasn't tangled in the shrouds at the bottom of the river.

Campbell scanned the bank for signs of life and a place to go ashore, wishing he had some kind of camouflage paint for his face. Although the water temperature itself was warm, he was shaking and felt he had to get out. He was hungry and wanted one of the packages of peanuts in his survival kit but decided to wait.

For the tenth time he fingered the standard navy-issue Smith & Wesson .38-caliber revolver secured in the side holster sewn into his survival vest. Then he would run his hand inside his torso harness and feel the concealed .22-caliber special automatic with a long barrel that no one in the squadron knew he carried. He carried two boxes of .22 magnum long-rifle shells and two clips, taking up little room. In the same pocket was a cylindrical barrel as long as the gun itself that he'd bought from a friend who knew a gunsmith. The silencer cost as much as the gun, but he figured it would allow him to shoot without being detected.

He looked at his watch again—almost five. The chilling effect of the water was taking all his energy and he began paddling, kicking his feet to create body heat. He would do this until his muscles felt warm again, then rest, holding on to the log. His legs were beginning to cramp, and after rounding the next bend, he paddled over to a stand of trees growing at the edge. He could feel clay underneath his feet and let go of the log, pushing it out into the current. Cautiously and quietly, he waded toward shore. As he reached the bank, the bottom changed to sand and small rocks and he grabbed on to a branch, pulling himself up into a tree. It took all the strength he could muster and he feared he would break some of the small branches, alerting anyone looking for him. Slowly he inched his way down the trunk and onto the ground away from the waterline.

The stand of forest seemed to grow down into the water. It was still dark and the tree line seemed to thin out, then thicken again thirty meters from the water. Everything was in shadows, but he could see well enough and worked his way up the slight incline into the second tree line, stopping and resting against a big tree.

He decided to wait until dawn before selecting a place to hide during the day, since there was a faint light glowing downstream, one he assumed belonged to a village. The fear of capture returned, and he realized it was up to him alone to conceal himself effectively enough to determine the outcome. His left leg was cramping and he rubbed it with both hands until the kink was gone. He was dripping wet and slipped off his survival vest, then removed the G suit and torso harness. The chill had left him and he pulled out a candy bar from one of the waterproof packets and ate it hungrily, washing it down with water from the tiny bottle he carried. He carefully placed the wrapper back in the pouch along with the bottle and secretly longed for a hot cup of coffee.

In the faint light, Campbell could make out a sheer bluff across the water. The far side of the river seemed elevated, with gnarled roots and twisted vines creeping down the side. His side was low, gently sloping down to the water and heavily forested with clumps of brush growing in clear areas. Cautiously he eased down the slope to the river, carefully making his way through the brush, clinging to fallen trees until he found one extending out into the water. Climbing out to the end, he filled a collapsible canteen with water, then made his way back through the brush and into the forest, careful to avoid leaving any signs or tracks. The ground was covered with fallen leaves and rotting vegetation over a soft, dark, loamy soil. His steps were silent and he worried that he might not hear anyone moving in the woods. Campbell looked for any signs of trails. Seeing none, he selected a well-concealed site underneath some brush, hidden from chance view. With his survival knife, he dug out a shallow depression. Mosquitoes were quick to locate him and he took out his mosquito net, pulling it over his head. He placed the wet torso harness and G suit at one end of the depression and lay down, pulling loose leaves over and around him. Finally warm from the blanket of leaves, he fell asleep, exhausted by the all-night trip down the river.

That afternoon while Campbell slept, a North Vietnamese search party discovered the remains of his parachute pulling at a submerged tree trunk. Its panels were ripped and the current had torn part of it away. Not finding a body attached, they immediately began a search around the area and downriver. A crewman aboard a small patrol craft discovered Campbell's helmet a short distance away, tangled in some brush. The searchers probed the riverbank, only half-heartedly pushing their long sticks into the brush. They believed Campbell had drowned and his body would be found within a few days. If he was still alive, someone would see him and he would be captured.

The sound of an outboard engine at low speed caused Campbell to wake with a jerk. He froze, afraid to move as the sound grew louder, alerting him to the Vietnamese searching for him. He could hear the high-pitched voices of men talking to each other, voices that were different from any he had ever heard. These were the first words he had ever heard uttered in Vietnamese. The language seemed strange to him—the pitch seemed to change in midword. Then he remembered an instructor saying that the ending pitch of a word spoken in Vietnamese determined its meaning. He listened as the crew of the boat talked and joked among themselves. Finally the sounds grew fainter as the boat worked downriver.

He lay motionless for fifteen minutes, listening. Only the mosquitoes and flies buzzing around his head spoke to him, and he slowly brought his arms up and brushed away the leaves from his face. As he raised up, his eyes darted back and forth, scanning the forest for signs of life. Seeing nothing, he rubbed his eyes and then his shoulder. It was stiff from lying on the hard ground, and his mouth felt dry and fuzzy. Attracted by his breath, insects continued to circle outside the net, probing for an entrance. A few found their way in and immediately drew blood, causing him to put his gloves back on and tuck the netting in around his collar.

It would be dark in a few hours and Campbell decided it would be better to stay hidden. He eased back into the depression and covered himself again. As he lay there, he began to think about Karen and anything that would pass the time. He needed to relieve himself and his mouth felt parched. Without thinking, he relaxed and felt a warm sensation between his leg as his bladder emptied itself, wetting his flight suit down to his calves. He grinned, wondering what his mother would think about her son now having to piss in his pants. The warm feeling was quickly gone and then it felt cooling to him. He had begun to sweat and the urge to jump up and run down to the water was almost overwhelming. He forced himself to think again, about anything, just to pass the time until dark. He let his mind drift as he lay there, thinking back to Bangkok and Karen. Then he thought of what Larry was probably going through right now, and how he might be heading for a similar fate. The vision only hardened his resolve to get out of North Vietnam alive.

The hour passed slowly and finally shadows were overtaking sunlight in the forest. Campbell sat up and drank some water from the bottle, then pulled out a peanut candy bar and ate. He tried to remember what was being served for dinner back on the *Barbary Coast*, then gave up, still wishing he had a precious cup of coffee.

Finally it was dark enough to make it difficult for anyone to see him in the shadows, even if they walked right by him, and the thought made him feel more relaxed. He spent considerable time removing all traces of his presence, then moved back to the water and climbed up in the tree bending out over the river. It was dark and the moon was nearly invisible. The glow downstream was still there—probably a village, he decided. Eventually he would have to chance it, slipping by undetected.

By eleven o'clock he felt it was time to reenter the water, and he pulled a piece of driftwood from the bank's edge out into the current. Again the stars were out in a cloudless sky and the current was running at one to two knots. He estimated he had covered eight to ten miles the night before and hoped to do the same again. He decided his only chance was to reach a bend in the river with an island that they had used for an IP during some of the bombing missions. There he could try to signal some of the jets that flew overhead daily. His radio was useless, yet he still carried it with him. He still had all of the gear he had ejected with except his helmet, but planned to ditch some of it if he had to cross overland. Now the gear helped hold in body heat as he drifted slowly in the current with only his head above water. Though it seemed dark enough, he knew anyone with good night vision might spot him.

Time was the enemy in the water and it passed slowly as he worked his way south. After several hours, the faint lights in the distance grew brighter. As he got closer, he could make out the shape of a large-spanned bridge stretching across the water. A chill ran through him as he realized what it was—the bridge at Canh Tra, the one he and Jordan had bombed the same day Larry was captured. He dog-paddled over toward the bank until his feet rested on the bottom, then eased up to the edge. For a moment he studied the bridge and the buildings around it. A few dim lights flickered in windows from behind drawn curtains. Campbell decided that either all the inhabitants were asleep or it was a ghost town, abandoned because of the bombing that went on around the bridge. He would have to take a chance.

It was well past midnight and he pushed off the bank out into the current. As he approached the bridge, he paddled toward the shadows, biting his lip as he got closer. He knew there must be soldiers and probably laborers to keep the much-bombed bridge repaired. He decided they must be sleeping soundly after a hard day's work. In the dim light he could see stacks of stockpiled material along the sides, awaiting future use. In sandbagged revetments, a few gun crews smoked cigarettes as they quietly passed the night, their only duty being to stay awake. No night attacks had ever been flown against the bridge.

Campbell breathed in short gasps as he drifted underneath the main span of the bridge. At the river's edge he spotted a patrol boat tied up to a makeshift pier, probably the one used to search for him, he thought. He looked up at the bridge, but it was too dark to tell whether it was damaged or not. At the least, he decided, he would note the positions of the gun emplacements. Quietly and slowly he drifted away from the abandoned town and bridge, then disappeared around the bend. He let out a large breath of air. Now he knew exactly where he was. If he could make his way to the IP downstream, he might be able to signal an aircraft with the signal mirror he carried in his survival kit. To reassure himself, he rubbed his hand over the pocket containing the small glass, feeling the shape within. The mirror itself was only about three by four inches and had a hole in the middle for aiming. It could be seen by an aircraft for miles, as well as by any enemy on the ground if it was flashed at too low an angle.

He was shivering again as the hours of submersion took their toll. It was several hours from dawn and he calculated he was seven or eight miles short of his destination. He would have to spend another day hiding. The tree line along the river was becoming thinner and the banks lower as Campbell drifted into flatter country. In the distance he could make out what looked like a large stand of trees going down to the shoreline and he paddled over into a stand of reeds growing from the shallow bottom. Releasing the log into the current, he eased into the shadows of the trees. It was still too dark to see, at least an hour before the first light would be visible. He sat down on the ground and pulled out his canteen and another of the candy bars. His hands were wrinkled and he rubbed them, both feeling like rubber to him.

As light slowly crept in among the trees, he could see large ferns growing around their thick trunks, the forest floor covered with undisturbed leaves and vegetable matter. At the base of a tree he dug a shallow hole, again covering himself with leaves as he lay down. Exhausted, he slept instantly.

Late in the afternoon Campbell awoke. For a moment he lay there motionless, his body stiff and sore from the hard ground. Without moving he rolled his eyes around, searching. Seeing nothing unusual, he slowly rolled over on his side, resting on one elbow, then froze. Something had moved. His eyes darted back and forth as he scanned around him. Seeing nothing, he slowly raised up on his arm, then froze again. Less than two feet from his head he could see a black, forked tongue sniffing the air, darting in and out of a spade-shaped head. Campbell gritted his teeth and took a slow, deliberate breath as he watched the snake. He could see the cold black slits of eyes staring at him, the body coiled and tensed, and remembered some of the snakes he had seen at the reptile house at the San Diego Zoo, snakes the signs at the windows labeled "extremely dangerous." He remained frozen, staring at it, in no position to move. The snake would hit him before he could jump in any direction, and he would probably be dead instantly. The snake continued to watch him, its head slowly moving sideways as its sensors picked up his body heat, and Campbell broke out into a sweat, which dripped down into his eyes. But as he blinked to clear them, he saw a blur heading for his face.

★ 13 ★

A sudden downpour had taken everyone by surprise, forcing several couples waiting for taxis outside the hotel to seek refuge inside the Ambassador. Dressed in evening wear, they huddled together off to the side as the Thai doorman called for the next cab in line to edge closer to the entrance. The rain lasted but a few minutes, leaving steam rising from the heated asphalt and adding to the prevalent humidity in Bangkok. ·

Inside the hotel the manager was hunched over a small desk behind the counter, filling out a form. Air rushing by the heavy glass entrance doors caught his attention and he looked up, staring over the bifocals on the tip of his nose. Seeing two Americans approaching, he automatically smiled, then his eyebrows arched up as he noticed the trail of water

Patricia and Karen were leaving with each step. A small boy wearing a dark hotel uniform quickly mopped up the puddles, scooting onto the floor behind them and quickly blotting the stains with a large towel.

Patricia let her wet hanging-bag slump to the floor, her dark hair soaked and stringy from the heat and the rainshower. Karen stood beside her still holding on to her bag. The sudden rain had caught them both in the open as they left their taxi across the street from the hotel. To them it seemed as if they had been riding cars or airplanes all day long, and both were weary from the trip. Patricia had been anxious to return to the hotel to see if anyone had been trying to contact her about her missing husband.

"I'm Patricia Jordan. You promised to save a room for us when we returned."

The immaculately dressed Thai looked at her for a moment, then smiled. "Oh, yes, I remember. You two ladies go up north and come back. I have message for you."

Patricia's eyebrows shot up as she took in a deep breath, then looked longingly at Karen as he turned to retrieve a slip of paper from a slot. Neither one said anything as they watched him return with the folded slip.

He handed it to Patricia, then placed both hands on the counter. "This gentleman call several times. He say it important you contact him."

Patricia unfolded the note, her hands beginning to shake with anticipation. There was only a name and a number written down.

"What is it?" Karen was almost afraid to ask, fearful it could be bad news about Larry Jordan. She took the note from Patricia. "Would you like me to call?"

Patricia looked away for a moment, lightly biting her lip. "No, I'll do it." She faced the manager again. "Is there a phone?"

He pointed to a phone on a table in the corner, then asked for the number she desired.

Both of the navy wives walked over to the table, dumped their wet hanging-bags on the floor, and sat down. In a moment the phone rang and the clerk pointed to them.

Patricia hesitated for a moment, then picked up and answered, "Hello, I'm Mrs. Larry Jordan. You have a message for me?" She listened as the distant female voice mumbled while she thumbed through a list of instructions left by various personnel attached to the American embassy. It was Saturday and most of the staff had gone home, leaving only a few working late and someone to handle the phone.

"Yes, here it is. Captain Cramer wants you to contact him right away," the voice at the embassy said, then read the number while Patricia fumbled for a pencil.

"He didn't say what he wanted?" Patricia seemed annoyed but thanked the woman and hung up the phone, turning to Karen.

Karen was almost afraid to ask and took Patricia's hand.

"Wouldn't say. She said just call the number. This guy is an attaché at the embassy." She got up and handed the number to the clerk and waited while he placed the call. There was no answer, and after several tries they checked into the hotel again, deciding one would clean up while the other kept trying. At nine-thirty, Captain Cramer called them.

"Yes, this is Patricia Jordan." She sat on the bed holding the phone while Karen stood next to her, toweling her hair. The conversation was short and Patricia, looking puzzled, put the phone down and looked up at Karen. "He wants to meet both of us here. He refused to reveal what he wanted, but said he would be here in less than thirty minutes."

"They're mad because we went on our own," Karen said, trying to offer a fragment of encouragement for her friend, though in fact she was worried herself. As they finished dressing, the two continuously offered encouragement to each other as a shield to mask their fears. Fifteen minutes later they were seated at a booth in the hotel bar, waiting for Captain Cramer.

Traffic was heavy as usual and the army officer was delayed. He parked the dark Chevrolet staff car in the hotel parking garage and briskly walked into the hotel. He wore civilian clothes: a dark suit, plain thin tie, and dark shoes. He was short. At five foot six and stockily built, Cramer made the shorter Thais feel more at ease with someone they didn't constantly have to look up to. And his rudimentary grasp of the Thai language was helpful in his duties.

Standing in the doorway, he canvassed the room, quickly spotting the only two women, alone at a table. He walked over and introduced himself, then sat down.

"Would you like a drink, Captain?" The two had ordered a second drink while waiting for the officer, unsure of what he wanted.

"No, thanks." He looked at the two wives, each with her eyes fixed on his, anxiously waiting. "Look, Mrs. Campbell, I don't know how to say this, except, we received word yesterday that your husband is missing." He watched as Karen gasped and brought her hands to her mouth. Patricia was stunned. She had thought it would be news about Larry, not Jim. Patricia grabbed Karen and pulled her to her.

"Is he . . . ?" Patricia asked. Karen could not even look up as she quietly sobbed on Patricia's shoulder.

"We don't know, Mrs. Jordan. Information is sketchy. The message that came in from the navy only indicated he had been shot down and was considered missing in action. His plane was thought to have been downed by a surface-to-air missile fired during an attack. That's all I have for now. I wish I had more."

Karen lifted her head up, looking at the army officer. Her

eyes were red and puffy and tears had streaked her makeup. She stood up, staring at the young officer. "Where was he shot down?"

"There was no information—only that he was downed on a raid against a rail line. That's all I have, Mrs. Campbell. Please believe me. I would gladly tell you more if I knew. I understand how you must feel."

"You don't even have a clue," she said, wiping her eyes while both wives left without saying another word.

Campbell felt no pain as he shot backward over the ground. He landed hard on his butt and opened his eyes, staring straight into the opened jaw of the viper that was desperately trying to extract its long fangs entangled in the mosquito netting. He could feel the snake's body wriggling against his chest, then the netting being pulled away. Without thinking, he tore the netting and his baseball cap from his head, grabbing the snake's body with his other hand, and threw them to the ground. Campbell dug his heels into the ground and kicked with both legs, propelling himself backward and scooting across the ground until he was safely away from the snake. The viper continued to writhe as it tried to extricate itself.

Campbell sat up straight, the muscles in his body jumping

uncontrollably as he shook. He was shaking so hard that the leaves still covering his body fell to the ground. He could feel his heart pounding hard within his chest and realized he was hyperventilating. He bit his lip trying to control his breathing.

Campbell sat on the forest floor captivated by the scene a few feet away. He watched the viper wrapping its coils around the long-billed baseball cap underneath the netting, trying to pull itself loose.

He examined himself closely and finding no sign of snakebite, wondered how the snake had failed to sink its long fangs deep into his body. When the snake had struck, Campbell had been unable even to bring his arm up, only managing to kick with his legs and close his eyes, awaiting the death he knew would be his.

Campbell picked up a broken tree limb lying nearby and stood up, keeping his eyes on the snake. He approached cautiously and began beating it, striking it repeatedly until its movements slowed, then ceased altogether. He extracted his survival knife from its sheath and pushed the blade through the snake's head, pinning it to the ground. It coiled itself weakly around the knife, then its movements stopped.

Campbell's shaking slowly receded and he stared silently at the reptile. Its only movement was a slight twitching as its involuntary muscles jerked its body. Campbell prodded it with the limb then put his boot on the head and extracted the knife. He severed the head which remained entangled in the mosquito netting. Carefully he cut the netting from around the head, leaving a three-inch gap in the barrier. The head looked evil, spade-shaped with slits for eyes. He tossed it aside and examined the four-foot body. Without the head it didn't look as menacing, and he gripped the skin at the cut end and began stripping it away from the body. Underneath the skin, transparent linings held the viper's intestines and other organs in place, but a purple sac nearly fourteen inches long puzzled him. He quickly pulled the entire mass loose and threw it into the hole he had slept in.

The time he had spent on survival training had convinced him he could eat anything if he was hungry enough. The white flesh was firm and elastic, similar to that of snakes he had sampled during survival training and found especially good if prepared properly. He had sampled roasted worms, and some of his instructors swore that insects were a way to provide needed protein when other food was unavailable. He poured water over the meat, rinsing away bits of residue and leaving white, clean-looking flesh. Campbell cut away a small piece and popped it into his mouth, swallowing as much as he could without really tasting it. It reminded him of undercooked chicken breast he had once sent back to a restaurant kitchen. Now he wished he had packed a supply of salt and pepper and maybe even some of Pancho's Tabasco sauce. Eating as much as he could, he cut the rest into smaller portions and stuffed them into his pockets, feeling lucky to be alive after the encounter. Then Campbell sat down and extracted one of the precious candy bars he carried. He wanted something to get rid of the taste of the snake in his mouth and broke the bar in half, saving the rest for later.

The sun was still overhead and filtering down through the thick canopy of the trees, quiet except for the sound of an occasional bird. Sometimes he imagined he could hear voices beyond the ridge above him and he decided to investigate. First he covered his gear with leaves, then eased up the hill to just below the ridge and into the shadows. He could definitely hear voices now beyond the trees at the top of the ridge and some distance away.

Campbell dropped to a crouch, listening. The voices seemed stationary and distant. Cautiously he eased up to the top of the ridge. Stopping behind a large tree, he eased his head out and peered beyond the tree line in the direction of the sounds. He could see the roof of a large white stucco building. Campbell crept closer until he had a full view of the house. Crouching low in the brush, he stared at the building across a road that ran nearby, a structure that reminded him of a farmhouse. The back of the house faced the river, and he could see a garden under cultivation while two uniformed Vietnamese guards carrying automatic weapons stood beneath a large shade tree. Three men dressed in black, loose-fitting garments and wearing conical Vietnamese peasant hats were bent over hoeing between the rows. Campbell assumed they were Vietnamese prisoners, although they seemed much taller than their guards. Two of the prisoners were very thin but one seemed heavier. Campbell lay on the ground watching the scene across the road, wincing when one of the guards lunged at the larger prisoner and knocked him down with a blow of his rifle butt to his shoulder. He could see the worker struggling to get up, then stand upright and bow to the guard as the other guard began laughing. Campbell started to inch his way down the tree line until he could see directly across into the garden.

He could hear the guards laughing again, making a game out of harassing their charges. Campbell watched as the shorter of the two guards handed his AK-47 to the other, then went over to the tallest prisoner, punching him in the stomach. The blow bent him double, sending his hat flying and bringing him down to his knees. The figure slumped over holding his stomach while the guard looked on, laughing. Slowly he raised up on one knee, then brought himself into a standing position.

Campbell watched intently, his body concealed by the foliage and his eyes peering out from between the branches. He could not take his eyes off the scene before him. It was something he had only seen in movies and never thought about; only the survival training courses he had taken had given him an idea of what might lie ahead. All of a sudden, one of the men looked familiar—his movements, the way he stood. Then it hit him like a gunshot. "Larry!" he whispered. He was convinced the figure standing before the guard was Jordan. The sight made him more confused, his mind reeling at the scene before him. He had a sudden overwhelming desire to take out his gun and charge across the field, killing the guards and rescuing the three POWs. But tempting as the idea was, he knew it was impossible and reconciled himself to just watching. He didn't recognize the other two prisoners, but there was no mistake about the third one. It was Larry—and he was alive! Although his weight was down and he looked haggard and moved slowly it was Jordan. Campbell was sure of it.

The back door to the farmhouse opened and he heard someone shout in Vietnamese. The two guards looked toward the house, then began shouting at the prisoners, quickly prodding them inside the building. The door slammed shut, leaving Campbell with only the sounds of the forest. He sat there thinking, finally coming to the conclusion that the thing he had to do was somehow get back to the carrier so a rescue operation could be organized. He studied the building and surroundings intensely, memorizing every door and window, every stand of trees, and everything he thought significant. He was puzzled at the lack of security, expecting it to look more like a conventional POW camp, with guard towers on every corner. He lay there until twilight, watching the activity of the guards, their movements and anything he thought would be helpful. He could account for fewer than five guards. He crept back to his campsite to prepare for the trip down the river.

By 2100 hours Campbell had finished a meager meal, concealed his campsite, and eased into the water, hanging on to a floating log. There was no moon, but the sky again summoned the stars for him and they glimmered overhead.

He would have preferred an overcast sky. To minimize a chance of detection he let his body ride low in the water until only his face was exposed. At first the water felt warm and relaxing. He had on all of his gear to conserve the body heat he would eventually lose, and tonight he had rubbed mud on his face as camouflage.

The farmhouse was not far from his entry point and he passed nearby. He could see a dim light in the window and he watched the house as long as he could, noting the small boat dock that extended out into the water. Slowly but steadily he drifted away, and then he thought he heard screams. They were muffled and seemed to come from the direction of the house. Campbell was unsure of the source of the sound and the thought only added to his resolve to get back to the carrier. He was determined to make it to the island. It was his only chance.

He drifted all night, stopping only twice to get out of the water where he thought it was safe and regain some of the body heat he was losing. As he drifted, he was alone with his thoughts and the stars. For the first time he was having trouble staying awake and sometimes found himself slipping from the log. He was afraid that if he slipped under the water and began coughing, he would alert someone. Campbell decided to risk climbing up on the log, where he promptly fell asleep.

The next thing he knew, the sun was blinding him and he could hear voices. Cautiously he raised his head and looked around. The log was wedged up on a sandbar, about sixty feet from an island. The voices were coming from the other side of the island and he assumed he had not been seen. Easing into the shallow water, he crept toward the spit of land protruding up into the middle of the bend in the river. Crouching down, he cautiously stepped out onto the land and moved toward the bushy interior. Halfway up he realized he was leaving large footprints in the sand. To cover his tracks, he turned around and walked back to the water's edge, then brushed his footprints with his hands as he moved backward. Reaching a section of grass, he turned and walked into the brush- and weed-covered island. A few trees had high-water marks and some driftwood still clung to the lower branches from a previous flood.

Campbell had finally reached the island used as an IP against the bridge at Canh Tra, where Campbell felt he had his best chance to signal an aircraft flying overhead. He knew that the land became flat with countless rice paddies and little cover south of the island, making it useless to try further evasion. He tried but failed to recall any villages around the island and pushed farther into the undergrowth. Nor could he remember exactly how large the island was, and he kept walking inland until he stumbled over a log concealed in the grass. Picking himself up, he looked around. There were no signs of anyone's having been there, and it was well concealed from the river. Campbell was bone tired and wanted to sleep, but first he would have to investigate the voices beyond the island. The voices were different from those of the guards he had listened to, sounding more like villagers'. Hearing the sounds of children playing, he crept through the brush until he could peek out on the other side of the island.

Cautiously he separated several blades of the high grass along the riverbank and looked across the river. There were fishermen, several families it seemed to him, working their bamboo fish traps and apparently unaware of his presence. The traps were secured to poles pushed down into the mud. Some of the fishermen were pulling floating baskets and filling them with the contents of the traps. The children were splashing each other as they followed along behind the men. A few women were also on the beach, working on the morning's catch. Campbell could hear the men shout whenever a large fish was pulled from a trap. There was nothing he could do but remain hidden and hope they stayed on the other side of the river. Letting the grass close together again, he slowly crept away from the bank to the center.

He was too tired to worry about snakes and sat down at the base of a log and soon fell asleep, concealed from anyone on the river by the shrubs growing in clumps that dotted the island.

He slept soundly but was soon awakened by the voices of the fishermen shouting something he could not understand. When he opened his eyes, the blinding midmorning sun was burning into his skin. Confused, he twisted his head from side to side, surveying his surroundings and trying to put things in order. Around him were high bushes and a few trees that had taken root. He had fallen asleep against a large rotting log and he slowly stood up, still.

It was hot and humid, making him sweat. He eased out of the torso harness and G suit, stuffing them underneath the log. Slowly he crept to the edge of the bushes and peered out across the river. The families of fishermen were still working their traps, less than one hundred feet away. If a patrol boat came by or any of the fishermen came over, he would be discovered.

Slowly he crawled backward to the log and sat down, pulling out what food he had left plus the remains of the snake. He placed the pieces of meat on top of the log for the sun to dry and nibbled on a candy bar. The signal mirror lay beside him as he waited for an aircraft to fly over, hoping the brush would conceal the mirror flash from anyone on the ground.

By nightfall he had flashed his mirror every time he saw a contrail overhead, but unable to signal anyone, he resigned himself to another night in North Vietnam and lay back against the log. A gentle breeze picked up the odors from cooking fires across the river, making him hungrier and he forced himself to gulp down some of the snake, which was now hard and chewy from lying in the sun. He washed it down with the treated canteen water, then lay back against the log, staring up at the stars and thinking of better times. All was quiet and he pulled some brush over himself and went to sleep, hoping the next day would bring some luck.

Aboard the *Barbary Coast,* Joe Kissinger sat in an uncomfortable chair in the intelligence debriefing room filling out his strike report. He had been a helicopter pilot and had somehow gotten himself transferred into jets, quickly gaining the nickname "Whirly." It was his first tour as an attack pilot and he was assigned to the sister A-4 squadron. Kissinger got out of the chair and walked over to the staff intelligence officer's desk, laying the form down and then stepping back and crossing his arms.

"What's this you wrote in the miscellaneous block?"

Whirly had to think for a minute and then smiled. "Oh, yeah, a strange flashing light I spotted down on the ground. It looked like a signal mirror."

"Near the target?"

"No, over by that big bend in the river with the island that everybody uses for an IP."

"Anybody else see it?"

"Nah, I mentioned it while we were flying but nobody saw anything. Funny though."

"What do you mean?"

"A few minutes later I looked back and I could see that same flashing light, which had to be coming off a mirror. Maybe some slope shaving himself, I don't know." Whirly picked up his flight bag and headed out of the room, wanting only a shower and a meal. He had missed breakfast when he overslept that morning.

The intelligence officer laid the report aside until that evening when he stopped at a file detailing the sketchy information on Jim Campbell. He was listed as "MIA,

Unknown.'' He knew Campbell and paused for a moment as he read the report, then put it back in the file, deciding the location was wrong. He picked up a clipboard listing the recon flight schedule for the next day. The RA-5 Vigilante was scheduled to make a photo run through the area at eight the next morning. Pulling a recon form from the drawer, he filled in a request for additional photo coverage of the IP near the bridge, then called up the recon squadron duty officer. He would inform the admiral's staff officer later.

Campbell woke early the next morning stiff from sleeping on the hard ground. He could feel the mosquito bites on his neck where the insects had worked their way in. At least somebody is eating well, he thought. The pangs in his stomach told him he needed food. His supply was nearly gone, only a few pieces of the dried snake and a candy bar left. He decided to eat the snake first and kill the taste with the chocolate bar. He would have given anything for a cup of coffee.

The sun was creeping over the tree line as he finished his meal. The last pieces of the snake were tough and chewy with almost no taste. He ate half of the bar and the sugar seemed to give him a rush. The welts on his neck were bothering him and he poured water on them to relieve the itching. The relief was only temporary and he rubbed his neck with the palm of his hand, hoping he wouldn't break the skin. The rubbing felt good and he rolled his head around, then suddenly stopped. Campbell was startled to see a figure squatting several yards away, watching him. He reached for his gun, unstrapping the leather strap securing it to the vest. His eyes darted from one side to the other as he stood up. Seeing no one else, he replaced the gun in its holster and refastened the strap. Barely ten feet away was a small boy, squatting down at the edge of the brush and staring at him. He couldn't have been more than four. The boy had very light skin and piercing black eyes.

Campbell was in a quandary and he knew it. The boy could give him away in an instant. It would do no good to harm him, though he could never do that anyway. If he held the boy, he would be missed and the adults would come looking for him. He reached inside his pocket, extracting a small piece of candy he had saved. He removed the wrapper and held it out to the boy.

For a moment the boy continued watching him, hesitant to come any closer. He had seen soldiers before, but none were dressed like this nor looked like the American. Reluctantly, he crept forward and held out his hand, taking the piece of candy. Slowly he moved away, squatting and eating the candy as he continued watching Campbell.

A sudden overhead roar startled them both, and the boy ran into the brush and Campbell dropped to his knees, knocking over his canteen. My God, he thought, now I know what it's like when the North Vietnamese get hit when they aren't expecting it. The boy was gone and Campbell picked up his mirror, scanning the skies for another aircraft. Deciding there was nothing he could do if the boy revealed his position, he picked up the spilled canteen, recapped it, and leaned against the log. Pulling out his pistol, he held it in one hand as he waited for another jet to pass overhead.

"Make copies immediately and send them to the admiral's staff." The intelligence officer pulled an eight-by-ten photo dripping from the tray and headed for the admiral's staff room, leaving a trail of water behind him.

In flag quarters just down the passageway, he laid the still-wet photo on the chief of staff's desk. "Excuse me, sir, but this is important. I think it's one of our downed pilots."

Captain Briggs looked annoyed at being interrupted but took out a magnifying lens from his desk and examined the photo. "Notify the admiral," he told an orderly standing nearby. "When was this taken?"

"About an hour ago."

Admiral Laceur stormed into the room. He had just finished a midmorning snack. "What do you have that's so hot?" he asked, walking directly to Briggs's desk. He picked up the photo, squinting as he looked at it.

"There's no doubt, is there?" the admiral said. Under magnification, the photo plainly revealed a figure in flight gear standing near a log with a torso harness lying across it. The boy was hidden by overlying brush.

The young intelligence officer nervously asked if he should notify the SAR coordinator in Thailand.

The admiral looked up, his eyes narrowing. "No, no, we'll do it." He turned to his chief of staff, directing him to start rescue efforts immediately. No SAR coordinator was going to take credit for this rescue.

Captain Briggs made calls to each of the participants who would be involved in the actual rescue. The CO of Jordan's squadron, Commander Lorimar, would fly cover with his wingman, and Aggie would take in his Sikorsky helicopter for the pickup. Almost immediately the A-4s were armed and on the cats. Aggie was already inbound.

Campbell crouched down in the brush, watching the fishermen work their traps. He could see the small boy who had visited him playing with some of the other children in the water downstream from their parents. Campbell was surprised the boy had not gone straight to his parents and told them what he had found. He continued watching, then looked puzzled as the group of small children suddenly started swimming out to the island. Soon Campbell found himself surrounded by more small children, who watched him with bug-eyed curiosity. He broke up the last piece of candy into equal portions and handed one to each child, then stepped back and watched them eat. Suddenly they leaped up, shouting and running back to the water and swimming across.

Campbell expected the parents of these children to grab machetes and charge across the river, but an hour passed and they had not crossed. He nervously faced one direction then the other as he waited, and suddenly he heard the sound of an outboard motor. The fishermen finally did inform someone, he thought. He heard the patrol boat that had been searching for him, now approaching from upriver. Well, at least I tried, he thought to himself.

Campbell straightened up when he heard the familiar sound of A-4s nearby. He looked up, spotting an A-4 circling overhead. Frantically he flashed his signal mirror at the aircraft and broke into a big grin when he saw the jet dipping its wings.

"No fire observed, Loosefoot," Commander Lorimar called to the helicopter just minutes away from the island. "You are cleared in and good luck." The A-4 pilot jinked his aircraft as he crisscrossed the area, looking for any sign of enemy activity. Aggie was flying a short distance away waiting for A-4s to check out the area before he went in. Aggie's rear crewman was already lowering the jungle penetrator as Aggie swept in across the river. The other crewman manned the rear machine gun, straining hard to see anyone taking aim on them. Aggie spotted Campbell standing up on a log as he approached the island. He could also see the fishermen across the river and a small boat rapidly approaching.

"I've got a boat on the river," Aggie yelled into his lip mike. "Keep an eye on them." The boat was close and he could see the soldiers on board and they were firing.

"Taking hits, going around." Aggie pulled up on the collective and dipped the nose down as he aborted the approach. His gunner was trading fire with the boat crew, and the rear of the helicopter was showing holes as the riflemen found their mark. "Somebody has to take out the boat!" Aggie flew over the bluff just above the fishermen, who were quickly dispersing into the forest.

"Stand by, Loosefoot, until we get rid of the boat. Did you see anyone on the island?" Commander Lorimar and his wingmen were bending around hard as they approached the island. They ran a line of 20-millimeter shells that left splashes at the edge of the bluff and ran right across the boat. It promptly exploded, sending burning fragments of its wooden hull into the air.

"You got him. Nice shooting, Commander." Aggie wheeled the helicopter around and began another approach to the island. "I saw someone. Keep me covered. I think that's him."

The jungle penetrator was dragging through the water as Aggie came to a hover above the beach. The wash from the huge rotor system was uprooting some of the drier brush and the blades were nicking at some of the tree limbs. "That's as close as I can get. Grab him and let's go!" Aggie shouted over the intercom.

Campbell ran into the edge of the water and opened up the penetrator and climbed onto the open arms. He was immediately pulled upward and went into a slow spin as the crewman operated the hoist. Campbell could see some of the fishermen on the opposite banks staring out from the brush at them.

"He's aboard. Let's get out of here!" The third-class sonarman reached down and grabbed Campbell with both hands, gripping him by his flight suit, and pulled him aboard while the other crewman stood behind the minigun and watched the fishermen.

"We got him!" Aggie announced over the UHF. "Let's move it!"

Campbell crawled forward to the cockpit, grinning like a Cheshire cat. He recognized Aggie at the controls and put his arm around his shoulders. "Thanks," he shouted.

Aggie winked at him then turned around and called Commander Lorimar. "Blackbeard, this is Loosefoot five four. You're not going to believe this, but we got Campbell." He waited for the expected response.

"Campbell?"

"That's affirm. Not Jordan, *Campbell*. I guess Pancho will go to any lengths to collect on a smoke debt." He heard Pancho chuckle over the radio as they headed for the *Barbary Coast*.

★ 15 ★

Turn that thing off. I've seen enough." Admiral Laceur sat back in the big easy chair his staff had purchased for him. His feet were propped up on the footrest and a half-smoked cigar dangled limply from one hand. He had been watching a replay of the helicopter landing aboard the carrier and Campbell stepping out on deck. The scene was being played over and over again on closed-circuit TV for the benefit of the officers and men aboard the *Barbary Coast*. A thin smile crept onto his face then disappeared as he uncrossed his legs and stood up. He turned around, facing his staff, and began drumming his fingers against the back of the chair. Never knowing what to expect from him, his staff officers waited.

"Gentlemen, that little rescue has shot morale up one

hundred percent." He rolled his cigar back and forth be
tween his fingers and pondered his next statement.

'Yes, sir, you're right, absolutely right," Captain Briggs
responded. "And coming well into the cruise."

Laceur tapped the cigar end against an ashtray, then took
a deep drag, blowing smoke across the room. "But there
still is that little problem with Jordan's wife, and with
Campbell's wife, for that matter. Do you have a copy of the
message with you?"

"Yes, Admiral." Briggs opened his briefcase, extracting
the message they had received from Naval Intelligence
Headquarters in Washington.

Laceur accepted the copy and took another drag from his
cigar, slowly exhaling as he reread the message, looking at
it for a long time. It was a long, detailed message regarding
the women's trip from Bangkok to Vientiane and back
again. There was no mention of the Thai cabdriver. Laceur
looked up at Commander Lorimar and handed him the
message to read. "Campbell doesn't know what his wife
has been up to, does he?"

"I doubt if he has any idea. I personally think the women
just tried to find out something about Lieutenant Jordan on
their own. I would never have expected them to head off to
a country like Laos and visit the North Vietnamese."

"Why not? Some wives have been pestering the North
Vietnamese in Paris." Laceur shook his head again. "But
wives don't belong over here. When we hit port, I want you
to have a heart-to-heart talk with Campbell and his wife, if
necessary. I want those women on the next plane back to the
States."

The attack squadron commander nodded his head in
agreement and handed the message to Captain Briggs.

There was a knock at the door and the marine sentry
stuck his head in and announced Lieutenant Campbell and
his party of officers had arrived.

"Show him in," ordered the admiral. He walked toward the door and shook Campbell's hand when the pilot stepped inside. "We are certainly glad to see you back safe and sound," the admiral said. "Did the doc get you something to eat?"

Campbell looked around the room for a moment. He had never been inside the admiral's quarters and was amazed at how much it resembled a posh hotel room. "Ah, yes sir, he, ah, he started me on a special diet right away."

"That's good, son, that's good." Laceur studied Campbell for a moment, not sure if he had seen him before, then decided he hadn't. "You know Captain Briggs, of course?"

"Yes sir." He shook the chief of staff's hand.

"And you must be Lieutenant Anson, the young helicopter pilot who picked up Campbell."

"Yes sir." Aggie shook hands with the admiral and then Captain Briggs.

"Well, you did a fine job. You are all to be congratulated."

Campbell looked away from the admiral as Laceur talked to Aggie. He could smell someone cooking steaks, the aroma coming from the adjacent kitchen reminding him of his mother panfrying T-bones in butter when he was a teenager. He was sure of it. His sense of smell had intensified with the time spent out in the woods. It was driving him crazy now.

"Lieutenant Campbell. Lieutenant Campbell," Laceur called.

"Oh, sorry, sir. Yes sir."

"I was saying that we would like to talk to you alone for a moment if the doc and Anson will be so kind as to wait for you out in the passageway."

"Ah, yes sir," he said while the flight surgeon and Aggie stepped out of the room.

Laceur handed him the two-page message and Campbell began reading. He turned to the admiral after he finished. "I don't understand. Karen is in Bangkok."

"She is now, but after we left Bangkok your wife and Jordan's wife did exactly what the message says they did."

Campbell looked puzzled. "I can't believe those two. Not my wife. She wouldn't have the guts to try something like that."

Admiral Laceur took the message from Campbell, leaving the pilot standing there trying to comprehend the meaning of what he had read. He looked at the admiral and then at Commander Lorimar. "I really don't know anything at all about this and almost find it hard to believe. But then knowing Patricia as well as I do, I can understand her reasons. It's just my wife that surprises me. I would have never thought she had the guts to take off and do something like this."

Laceur pushed his cigar into the ashtray, quickly filling the room with an acrid stench. "Do you think Jordan's wife will try anything else?"

Campbell thought for a moment. "If she can't find out anything about Larry, she probably will. She's no pushover. I wouldn't blame her, would you?"

The admiral remained silent for a moment, waiting for Campbell to continue.

"I know where Jordan is," Campbell suddenly blurted out. He had just finished debriefing with the intelligence officer about his discovery of Larry Jordan in the POW camp. When the admiral didn't respond, he repeated himself. "Sir, I saw Larry Jordan in a POW camp just up the river from where I was picked up. It wouldn't take much to assault the camp and get him out."

"How did you come by that information?" Laceur asked. He was skeptical and didn't try to hide it.

"When I hid out by the river on the second day I came up on a small farmhouse. I saw Jordan and two other American prisoners being worked by two guards. One of the guards punched Larry and he stood up, giving me a good look at him. I couldn't recognize the other two. If my radio had been working, we could have gotten them out."

The admiral stared at him for a moment. "Son, I can understand how you feel about one of your squadron mates, but a rescue mission against an armed POW camp takes large-scale intelligence and planning. And besides, it takes approval from the highest levels of authority and none have been approved so far." Laceur moved closer to Campbell. "I wish it could be done, but it's just too risky. We believe their guards have orders to shoot the prisoners if a rescue attempt is made, so that's that unless orders come down from Washington. And if you're positive it was Jordan, then perhaps the bureau can release that information to Mrs. Jordan."

"Perhaps release it! My God, it was *Larry*! All it would take is a few armed troops. They could get in and out before the Vietnamese knew they were there. The camp is not like a full-fledged POW camp with watchtowers and all that—just a few armed guards."

Commander Lorimar put his arm on Campbell's shoulder. "Jim has been through an ordeal, Admiral. I can sympathize with him and I wish to God we could go in and get Jordan out, but I think Lieutenant Campbell needs some rest. I'm sure he will talk to his wife when we pull into port."

Realizing he wasn't going to get anywhere, Campbell thanked the admiral for the rescue effort on his behalf and walked out the door where the flight surgeon and Aggie waited with Pancho. The three accompanied Campbell back to sick bay where he was to spend the night. He wasn't looking forward to all the tests the flight surgeon had ordered for him.

That evening, Pancho and Aggie snuck into Campbell's room in sick bay. Campbell was lying in bed, writing a letter, when the two walked in and set a tray on the table next to him without saying a word. He looked up at them and started to say something but paused as he sniffed the air.

"If that's what I think it is, you two just got included in my will." Cautiously he pulled back the tinfoil covering the plate, revealing a freshly cooked T-bone fried in butter with french fries and sweet peas on the side. "I don't think I want to know where you got this." Grinning from ear to ear, he happily dug in. His earlier meal had consisted of Jell-O and soup, which the flight surgeon felt would be better for him the first day back.

"Let's just say that the admiral probably won't miss one little piece of meat from his freezer for a while," Pancho said, having snatched the special meal that afternoon while he waited outside the admiral's quarters, sticking it inside his shirt.

Aggie sat on the end of the bed while Campbell continued eating. Pancho found a chair and brought it into the tiny room, sitting down across from Campbell.

"Man, we thought you were a goner for sure. When they started filling the sky with SAMs, everybody was scattering and nobody saw you get hit or even a chute. No beeper or nothing."

Campbell swallowed a piece of meat, then washed it down with water. "Yeah, I know. I never thought a SAM would get me. I always thought I could outmaneuver the damn things."

"Did you really see Larry? I mean, you know, it was him for sure?" Pancho found it hard to believe that Campbell had just happened on him out in the jungle and wondered if he hadn't hallucinated at some point.

Campbell stopped eating, setting the plate on a table beside him. "As sure as I know it's you I'm talking to, I'm sure it was Larry. There is no doubt whatsoever. It was him. He was being worked in some kind of a garden along with two other Americans out behind an old farmhouse down by the river. When the guard hit him, he knocked Larry's hat off and I got a good look at him.'' Campbell's face tensed as he recreated the scene for them. It was still vivid in his mind, the picture permanently etched and easily recalled.

"Did he look all right? I mean, was he injured or anything?" Aggie asked.

"He seemed to be favoring one arm and his weight was down. The other two prisoners with him looked pretty bad. The thing I can't understand is why there were so few prisoners or guards around. Maybe it was some kind of collecting point for POWs. But then those other two looked like they had been there for a while. God, it would be so easy to get him out. It's remote, plenty of cover to sneak up on them. It pisses me off that the admiral is content to just let it pass while some GS-1 in Washington does a feasibility study.''

"When the word comes down to go in," Aggie said, "I'll volunteer. That old bastard still owes me six bucks from a smoke game.''

★ 16 ★

The *Barbary Coast* pulled against her massive anchor buried in the mud, stretching the heavy chain taut in the gentle current. The morning was still cool from the cloak of heavy mist that lay over the water and edged into the city, a last respite before the sun turned the humidity into a blanket that would cling to the skin like a steaming barber's towel.

The carrier was surrounded by clusters of brightly painted fishing craft bobbing gently alongside coastal trawlers hanging on to their anchors. The *Barbary Coast* was too large to anchor at the quay wall or at the British naval base. She had been assigned to the roads, a point offshore marking the entrance to the harbor, while her accompanying destroyer escorts were able to tie up at the British Naval Base.

Street lights still glowed eerily beneath the heavy gray mist. Street vendors were racing to set up their stalls and begin a day of trade, frantically cutting their prices to entice the American sailors to buy something on their last day of liberty. Shopkeepers rolled up the steel protective screens to display their wares while smaller entrepreneurs pushed small carts laden with cheap trinkets into the alleyways. Others were busy cooking on open braziers awaiting hungry patrons. By midmorning the streets would be transformed into a capitalist's nightmare.

Within minutes after liberty call, liberty boats from the carrier began their runs shuttling sailors to the beach. As always, the men of the *Barbary Coast* were ready and willing to sample any thrills or attractions offered up to them. The British had been on the island for years, and ample opportunities for pleasure and endless drinking had been established long ago.

By midmorning, Singapore was thriving with American sailors in uniform and the officers identifiable by the multi-colored Hawaiian shirts purchased in Pearl. By noon, the white uniforms had been swapped for civilian dress, and only the boyish-looking faces singled out the American sailors as they spread out into the city seeking bars and gawking at the strange mixture of Chinese and Malay women.

At the bar in the old Raffles Hotel, the rail was lined with pilots from the air wing and a few of their British counterparts, trading jokes and gambling on drinks. Karen sat toying with a Singapore sling at a table across the room, making designs in the dew collecting on the outside of her glass. Campbell sat next to her, deep in thought and looking out at the boats in the harbor. She watched him staring at a colorful fishing vessel pulling up its anchor as it prepared to get under way. For a moment she wished it was them

going on a fishing trip instead of her husband going back
to the war in a few days. She wanted him out of the
war.

"A penny for your thoughts."

Campbell took a deep breath, then turned away from the
postcardlike view. "I was just imagining what it would be
like to be a fisherman out at sea all day and then coming
home to a big family."

"You mean like those fishermen out in the harbor?"

"Yeah."

"They probably work twelve hours a day to catch a few
fish and then come home to a fat wife screaming at ten
kids."

"That's what I mean—a simple life with no complica-
tions, no wars, no wives running around pestering embassies."

"I hope you're not going to start on that again, especially
with Patricia about to show up at any minute."

"No, ma'am, not a chance. I've said my piece and now I
can tell the skipper that I raked you over the coals."

All eyes in the room shifted to the front as Patricia
entered through the double-door entrance. Wearing a strap-
less white cotton sundress and sunglasses, she marched
across the teak flooring, ignoring the men following her
movements. Spotting Jim and Karen near the window, she
walked over to their table.

"A gin and tonic—a big one," she said, making an effort
to smile at the waiter as she ordered, then turned back to her
friends.

Campbell could see she was upset. He watched her reach
into her purse and pull out a pack of cigarettes.

Karen pushed her glass away. "What's the matter?" she
asked. "The admiral wasn't too receptive this morning—
right?"

Patricia finished lighting her cigarette and took a long
drag, blowing smoke toward the window and looking out

into the harbor. "That bastard wouldn't even see me. I had to talk to his chief of staff. He said the admiral deeply sympathized with me but there is nothing they can do. He said they were lucky to find out he had been taken prisoner at all." She faced the window again, staring out at the boats in the harbor.

"Did you talk about anything else—you know, rescue or anything?" Karen asked.

Patricia turned toward the table again. "I tried to, but he kept evading me. Finally he said something like that would have to be a decision from higher up. *Higher up,*" she repeated, raising her voice and then lowering it again. "It doesn't take much to figure out that a rescue attempt was not on their agenda and that my husband is now a statistic. All he could talk about was how I could really help Larry by going back to the States and being a good little housewife until he comes home. That I should let them run the war and not get involved."

"What are you going to do?" Campbell asked.

Patricia turned and pushed her smoldering cigarette into the ashtray. "Go back to the States. There is nothing more I can do over here." She paused and leaned forward, crossing her arms. "But I promise you this—I'm not going to sit around and be quiet. I'm going to yell and scream at every politician and group that will listen to me. I'll join every association that can help me, and if there aren't any, I'll start some. I don't think the public really knows what is going on over here."

Campbell looked at her and grinned. "I believe you will, too. Larry would be proud of you." He paused for a moment and turned to his wife. "Then you two can go back together."

Patricia looked at Karen. "I thought you were going to stay for the whole cruise."

"No, I've decided it would be best for both of us if I

went back to Pensacola and my parents and waited there. I need to be near my family and . . .'' She lapsed into silence.

Patricia looked at her for a moment and then at Jim. She could feel there was something different about them, that something had changed in them since the start of the cruise. She started to speak but then didn't.

"Yeah, right," Campbell said. The three lapsed into silence as the waiter arrived with Patricia's drink.

That evening, Campbell sat on the bed in their hotel room tying his shoelaces while Karen busied herself applying makeup. They were readying themselves for the party hosted by the British at the naval base. The next morning the carrier and her destroyer escorts would depart for Yankee Station and the last part of the cruise. Campbell intended to escort both his wife and Patricia for a short appearance at the party, then return to the hotel for a quiet evening alone with his wife.

"Honey, are you about ready?" He looked at her reflection in the mirror as she applied the last bit of eyeliner.

"Almost. Give me another minute."

Campbell sat on the bed watching his wife. He had seen her do the same thing hundreds of times, but tonight she was looking especially beautiful. Her honey-colored hair was pulled up in a French twist, exposing her delicate earlobes and the two earrings he had purchased for her in Bangkok. Around her thin neck rested the matching necklace that sparkled every time she moved in the light. He knew he would have his hands full keeping sex-starved officers away from her, but at the same time he would be proud of the beautiful woman he would have on his arm for the evening. He went over to her and put his arms around her, looking at her reflection in the mirror. "You could be a goddess."

She looked up at his image and put her hand on his arm and smiled but said nothing.

"It's our last night—let's make the most of it," he said, then walked over to the closet and selected the white dress jacket he would wear, silently wondering what the state of their marriage really was. At the beginning of the cruise it couldn't have been better. Now, his wife seemed to have undergone a change since Jordan had been captured and he himself had nearly become a POW. She had been exposed to the realities of war and his profession and it had changed her. At times it seemed as if she wanted to be held all the time, and at others he felt she was afraid to let herself get too close to him. Her message seemed to be that he would have to choose between the loves of his life—her or the navy. The choice was his.

Karen sat on the edge of the bed quietly watching her husband as he stood in front of the mirror adjusting his black, snap-on bow tie. He looked so handsome to her, erect and only a little thinner than she remembered him before the cruise began. She thought back to when she first saw him in uniform and remembered how he looked and how he had invited her to a party at the cadet club on the base at Pensacola.

She had grown up in Pensacola, a navy town dotted with cadets learning to be officers and pilots. It had always seemed so storybook to her. Young men in uniform, daring and romantic. It was every little girl's fantasy to be swept up and carried off by a gallant knight, but she had confused knight with naval aviator and the parties and pomp of a naval life had only reinforced her feelings. The separation and death were never part of her fantasy, and facing it had changed her. She wasn't sure if she could live up to her part. She would need some time to think it out.

* * *

The cricket field behind the officers' club at the British naval base had been cleared and tables with white table-cloths and individual place settings rested on the large expanse of green lawn. An open bar had been set up for the officers and their wives and guests. Early arrivals already crowded around the bar, ogling the wives of the British officers as they strode onto the grounds. The freshly mowed lawn was dotted with splotches of white as the officers arrived in formal dress. A quickening breeze from a passing thunderstorm out over the bay stirred the air and cooled things down, yet made life difficult for the coxswains guiding the liberty boats out to the carrier through the choppy waters. Lightning and thunder that reverberated across the bay threatened to end the party if the storm moved inland, but the British took the daily thunderstorms in stride and mingled with their guests, speaking in their clipped accents and causing many of the Americans to lean closer to understand them. Among the British were a sprinkling of Malaysians from the Malayan military units in the north, and in further contrast were the American naval aviators, their chests supporting rows of medals representing battles fought over the North Vietnamese skies. Their British counterparts, on the other hand, wore one or two service medals at most.

Finally, scattered throughout the gathering were the wives of the British officers. Though a few were young and beautiful, a good many were common-looking women. They had decided to come and see for themselves what the Americans were like and stood by their husbands as the American officers were introduced, trying not to stare.

A portable bar constructed from bamboo and plywood stood at one end of the yard with an identical one across from the tables. Like a magnet, it had attracted Aggie as soon as he spotted it, and he had immediately taken up residence at one end, standing next to Pancho and Swenson, who was nursing a gin and tonic and looking slightly out of place.

"I think I'm in love," Aggie said. He pushed his empty drink glass toward the bartender while he continued to stare at a terrific-looking girl sitting nearby. "Gin and tonic," he ordered.

Pancho turned back to the bar and leaned on the counter, taking a swig from a beer bottle. Pancho looked sharp. His military presence was as honed as a cadet's at inspection at the naval academy, and even the creases in his highly starched trousers were holding up. "You're always in love," he told Aggie. "I think that constant *wop-wop-wop* sound of the rotor blades in your ear has affected your brain."

Aggie continued staring. "I think that lady wants my body," he said. He felt the bartender slide the refilled glass into his open hand, and he brought it up without looking, taking a long swallow.

"She's not even looking at you."

"She did once."

"Probably thought you were one of the bartenders and wanted to order another drink."

The Australian bartender leaned over the counter between the two pilots. "I wouldn't be getting me hopes up if I was you."

Aggie turned around to see who was talking. "And why not?" he asked.

"Well, mates, that one belongs to Major Culkinny."

Aggie turned around to look at the man standing next to the girl. "Doesn't look so tough to me."

"That bloke ain't her husband you're looking at, mate. Her husband is head of the Royal Marine Recon Group on this here rock. And he's a bit fond o' that lass, he is." The bartender grinned and left to wait on another customer.

"Nice pick," Pancho commented.

"On second thought, she's kind of bony, don't you think?" Aggie said, turning back to the bar.

Working his way through the crowd toward the bar, Captain Larue spotted Pancho and Aggie.

"Well, if it isn't the *Barbary Coast*'s number one killer," Aggie said. "Hey, Larue, over here. I just found out that a big ugly British marine said he could whip your ass." Aggie held out the bottle of ale he had ordered for him.

"Pay him no attention," Pancho said. "He just found out the love of his life is married to a big British marine and he wants you to take him out."

Larue took a long swig from the bottle then turned and looked out at the crowd. He was taller than Aggie and towered above the helicopter pilot when Aggie slouched down at the bar. His marine dress whites were immaculate and his shoes looked brand-new. Only the minimum number of medals on his chest revealed his lack of combat. "Ah, lukewarm. Haven't the British discovered ice yet? What's she look like?"

The helicopter pilot pointed his glass at the girl. "There she is. See for yourself."

The marine captain turned and faced the group a few yards away, studying the lithe figure standing sideways to him. "Might be worth it if I get the girl, but not too good for our foreign relations. Cheers." He lifted the warm bottle of British ale to his lips and downed half of it.

"Have you seen Soupy?" Aggie asked.

"Yeah, saw them up front. They are working their way through the crowd. I think they nominated Swenson here to sit with Patricia. This big dumb Swede should be able to keep everyone around her at bay, except maybe for you, Anson. But if you even think about it, I'll let my men use you for bayonet practice."

"Hey, there are plenty of British wives to keep me

occupied tonight. I may be bad but I ain't dishonorable—well, not completely—well, maybe a little," he added.

Across the yard, Campbell and the two wives worked their way through the crowd, stopping to introduce the women to friends, then moving on toward the open bar.

"Hey, amigo, long time no see," Campbell shouted at Pancho.

"Yeah, at least since this afternoon. Hello, Karen, Patricia." The two stood up as the group arrived.

"You girls are really looking especially nice this evening." Pancho said.

"Thanks," Patricia responded

"For some reason, the word 'spectacular' comes to mind," Aggie added.

Larue put his arm on the helicopter pilot's shoulder, resting his thumb and middle finger on Anson's collarbone. "Aggie was just saying he was going to buy the first round. Right, Aggie?"

"Right. Absolutely." He dropped down slightly from the pressure against his collarbone.

"What'll it be, mates, another round?" The Australian bartender leaned over the bar, grinning as he waited for their orders.

Aggie ordered drinks for everyone and smiled at Larue, who relaxed his grip. "And make sure that beer for the captain is cold."

Clutching their drinks, the group made their way over to a corner and found an empty round table. The men waited until Karen and Patricia sat down, then took their seats.

"I'd give anything if Larry could be here tonight," Patricia wished.

"Patricia, if you start thinking about Larry again, you won't be able to think about anything else." Karen put her hand over Patricia's.

"It's hard not to, but I'll try. I know he'd want me to."

Then, trying to work herself out of her mood, she turned to Swenson, who was sitting on her left. "Can you dance, Swede?"

"Yes, ma'am." His voice was thick, the early rounds of booze lightly slurring his words.

"How do you get this guy to quit saying 'ma'am'? He makes me feel like I'm twice his age."

"He says that to everybody." Karen said.

The band began a faster number and Patricia turned to Swede and took him by the hand, coaxing him out onto the patio while Jim took Karen's hand and guided her out as well. The beat was fast but familiar and he could easily dance to it. He held Karen close to him, guiding and spinning her around the patio.

Patricia looked up at Swede as he danced in place, twisting and turning to the tempo. She followed his lead and the grinning pilot quickly picked up the beat and began to spin even faster, Patricia doing her best to stay in unison. But turning her head away from him momentarily, she didn't see his outstretched arm come around as he spun, and she caught the full force across the side of her head. She stood there stunned and missed seeing Swede fall to the floor, landing flat on his back.

Campbell immediately rushed to Patricia and guided her back to the table. Larue and Pancho ran out and quickly got Swede on his feet and half carried him to his seat. Several tables of British officers held up their glasses and toasted them.

Karen found some ice and rolled a napkin around it, holding it to Patricia's head. "That was some exhibition you two put on."

"I saw a few stars for a moment—but I'll live." Patricia held the ice to her head, then looked over at Swenson. He seemed unsure of what had happened and continued to sit and stare off into space. "Could we go back to the hotel now? I think I've had enough."

Aggie, who had nearly passed out, sat slumped in his chair at the table. With the assistance of several Royal British Marines, Aggie and Swenson were loaded into one taxi with Larue and Pancho, while Campbell, Karen, and Patricia followed in another.

At the hotel, Swenson was quickly shuttled up to his room and put to bed, though Aggie woke up eventually and now sat at a table near the bar with Larue, wanting another drink. Patricia decided she had had enough fun for the night and begged off, returning to her room, while Karen decided she wanted to be with her husband and was not ready to turn in.

They made their way to the bar, now almost empty of American and British servicemen, and took seats at the same table by the window overlooking the bay that they had sat at that afternoon. An evening of drinking had taken its toll on them, and Karen suspected this was how men always spent their last night in port—living this life as if there were no other. She granted them that.

"If Larry were here, he would probably be climbing and holding on to the ceiling fans until one broke or Patricia knocked him down with something." Campbell stared into the drink the waiter had just placed in front of him.

"Yeah, it's not right that guys like that go down," Aggie chipped in, sitting right near them.

"We ought to go get him," Campbell said, staring into his glass.

"What's that supposed to mean?" Pancho asked.

"Go get him—get him the hell out of that prison camp." He forgot his wife was there for a moment and lowered his voice. "You haven't seen the camp—I have. I watched it for an hour—I watched them beat Larry to the ground right in front of my eyes, and I saw so few guards, your grandmother could take them.'' The table had gotten quiet as he spoke and Karen was hearing things she had not heard before.

"There must be a reason for so few guards,'' Larue said. He was the only one trained in ground assault and he combed his mind to come up with a reason. "We've never assaulted any of their camps before, so why should they use up manpower guarding a bunch of weakened prisoners? I don't know why, but I bet it could be done.''

"I'll do it,'' Aggie said, lifting his head up. "You get the troops and I'll fly them in. Can't be any different from picking you up out of the middle of that little firefight. What would it take?''

Larue thought for a minute. "Minimum—a few men—a sharpshooter to pick off the guards—a quick shock team to get in before they know what's going on, and more important, some up-to-date intelligence. That's the key.''

The table was quiet, each man deep in thought. Finally Karen broke the stillness. "Jim, let's call it a night. I'm ready to leave.''

Larue was the most sober of the bunch and quickly jumped up, excusing himself and saying good-bye to Karen. The others followed suit and Campbell found himself alone with his wife.

Outside the window, in the distance, the *Barbary Coast* hung at anchor, brightly lit for everyone to see.

"She's pretty, isn't she?''

"Yes, I guess she is, in her own special way,'' Campbell said. He twirled the melting ice around in his glass as he stared out the window at his ship.

"If I close my eyes, I can imagine it's a big Scandinavian cruise ship. And we're tourists in our last port waiting to sail home again. But then I open my eyes and I don't see bright lights and lighted swimming pools on the deck. All I see are planes in neat rows parked up on top, one of them waiting to take my husband away. One of them waiting to take him away from me forever.''

"Karen, please don't think like that. I promise you I will come back to you.'' He attempted to take her hand but she pulled it away.

"You promised me that in Bangkok, but you almost didn't. Jim, it's just too hard on me. I guess I got close to the war and saw too much. I see what Patricia is going through and then I see me. It's just too much.''

"Larry *is* coming back.''

"What do you mean?''

"Don't ask me how because I can't tell you, but Larry is coming back and so am I.'' He pulled her to him and she cuddled up on his shoulder, tears streaming down from her eyes and falling to his coat. He held her for a few moments, then they got up and left, going to their room in the hotel where they made love and fell asleep in each other's arms. When he left for the carrier in the morning, she did not accompany him to the docks as she had in Bangkok. They had both said their good-byes in the room before he left. At eight o'clock she and Patricia both watched the *Barbary Coast* weigh anchor and steam off. They cried and then packed and caught Air Malaysia back to Bangkok, where they changed to an international flight heading for the States. Karen said nothing to Patricia about what Jim had told her the night before.

★ **17** ★

Major Quang leaned against the doorframe inside his kitchen exhaling smoke from an American cigarette. The cigarettes were given to him earlier in the week, a gift from the Russian GRU agent. The Russian brands tasted harsh and he disliked them as much as the Russians did, preferring American brands whenever he could get them. Quang ground out the stub in a clay ashtray on top of their small stove, watching his wife scurry around in their tiny kitchen.

Kwan Chi busied herself putting away the morning dishes and straightening up after her children. Their daughter was in another room preparing to attend a half day of school. Normally her grandmother would be there to help her get ready for school, but she had left early for the market to barter. Kwan Chi's father was in the backyard, smoking his pipe quietly underneath his favorite tree where he spent most of his day.

The children ran excitedly into the room and then into the backyard, shouting at their grandfather. They kissed him on his cheek, then ran noisily into the kitchen and stopped by their father, waiting to say good-bye. Le Doc stood by his sister, clutching his toy airplane and holding a cloth bag containing his sister's school supplies. Mai Ling and the boy were dressed in dark school uniforms, supplied by the state. Le Doc was too young to attend regular school and sometime spent part of the day at a state-supported care center.

Major Quang reached down and took the plane from the boy, holding it up before him. The boy bit his lip as he watched his father.

"You must leave your plane, Son. I will put it here on the table and you can play with it when you come home. Even my plane has to rest sometime."

Resigned to leaving without his favorite toy, Le Doc shrugged and grunted, staring down at his feet.

"You are going to be late for school. Tell your father good-bye." Kwan Chi grabbed her daughter and pushed her toward her father.

Quang bent over and kissed his daughter, then his son, and watched the two youngsters disappear through the kitchen door. Quang watched for a moment, then said, "I have been talking with the administrator for schools again, Kwan Chi."

His wife said nothing and continued with her tasks.

"He has convinced me that it is imperative that we place the children in the country school system where they will be safe."

"They are safe here," she said without looking up.

"No, they are not safe. They only appear to be safe. I

have made up my mind, Kwan Chi. The children will leave the day after tomorrow.''

He waited for a response from his wife but she said nothing, only dusting faster.

"I have also made arrangements to move you and your parents out into the country. I know your father won't mind nor will your mother. It is only you that is so stubborn.'' He put his hand on her shoulder, forcing her to stop flitting around the room.

Kwan Chi stopped her cleaning and put her hands on the back of a chair and looked up at him. "I don't like living in the country. I don't like working the rice fields, I like it here.''

"I know you don't, but we have no choice. I would rather have you alive with blisters on your hands than take a chance of losing you to a stray bomb.'' He knew how stubborn she could be at times, even immovable, but it was becoming too dangerous in the city.

Kwan Chi looked at her husband. She knew it was useless to argue with him when his mind was made up. She went to him and put her head on his chest, leaning against him. "I will go, but I won't plant rice,'' she said.

Quang only grinned. "We will move this weekend then.'' He kissed his wife on the top of her head and gave her a squeeze. "I have to go now. I am on duty for the rest of the day and will be home tonight.'' He kissed her again on the cheek and grabbed his hat from the kitchen table and went out the door.

She watched him start his motor scooter and ride off down the dirt road for the base.

Off the coast of South Vietnam over the waters of the South China Sea, a flight of Republic F-105 ''Thunderchiefs'' was engaged in inflight refueling. The last ''Thud'' pulled away from the fuel drogue after taking on a full load of fuel.

258 ☆ Charles Stella

The pilot, Capt. Jack Benning, watched the long fueling line snake itself back inside the KC-135 ghosting along in the smooth air, then eased his aircraft away. Benning was part of a twelve-plane flight out of Takhli Air Force Base in Thailand that had taken off less than an hour ago loaded with 2,000-pound delayed-fuse bombs.

He watched the huge transport converted into an airborne fueling station gently bank and turn back for its home base at Clark AFB in the Philippines. Benning added power and moved back into position behind his element leader's wing. It would be less than an hour before they would be over their target—the underground radar complex at Bak Ca outside of Hanoi.

In the remote radar site, Major Bhi leaned over his desk and lit up another Russian cigarette, then sat back surveying the scene around him. The ex–fighter pilot rested his now useless arm in his lap, rubbing it to alleviate the throbbing. His face was drawn and dark circles formed beneath his eyes. Bhi was spending long hours underground coordinating the defenses in his area, yet he still longed to be back in the air flying MiGs. As that would never be possible again, he reconciled himself to his important job, trapped inside the bunker from morning till night.

The Russian technical advisor assigned to him was out of the room for the moment, which relaxed him. Bhi didn't care for the Russians and felt ill at ease with them around, thinking them no better than the French or any other group seeking to exploit them. He looked across the room at the map of North Vietnam with luminous markings drawn on a large Plexiglas sheet. A special light made the lines glow in the subdued light, and he watched a corporal writing in the coordinates of the large force they had been tracking as it left Takhli AFB in Thailand. Major Bhi knew the Thuds had flown across South Vietnam to refuel out over the ocean,

then turned north as always. The flights were almost predict-
able. He wondered what their target might be.

The flight was spotted the minute it took off from the
jungle base in Thailand. The command center had received
a radio transmission reporting the bomb loads, aircraft type,
and direction minutes after the last aircraft had retracted its
gear. The information was immediately passed to Bhi's site.
The people they had stationed around each air base in
Thailand then went back to their cover jobs as laborers in
the fields after burying their equipment in the rice paddies
or underneath pigsties or in other places no one was likely
to discover.

Major Bhi thought to himself for a minute. He had to
agree with the command center that with so many planes
inbound, they were probably going after the steel plant, the
power plant, or even the Central Military Complex itself,
although he didn't think so. He knew it had escaped detection so far and he didn't think the Americans even knew
where it was, although they certainly knew of its existence.
From the surface it looked innocent enough, hinting at
nothing more than a typical village above ground, but it had
false streets, cars and houses, and even fruit orchards
planted with fake trees. It was the North Vietnamese equivalent of the American command center at Cheyenne Mountain, the huge underground complex in Colorado, with its
widespread radars and satellites keeping track of airborne
threats to the United States.

Bhi leaned back in his chair and studied the Plexiglas
battle zone for a moment, taking a drag from his cigarette.
He motioned to an enlisted man wearing a headset with
communication directly to the operations room of the MiG
fighter squadron that was under his control. "Tell the
operations officers that we have twelve F-105s inbound from
the Gulf that are probably going for the steel mill. Tell them
I will expect them to launch in less than forty minutes. I

want a four-plane flight airborne at our signal." Major Bhi listened to the orderly repeat the order over the phone. Satisfied, he went over to the search radar repeater and looked down into the greenish screen. His face glowed eerily in the light as the tracer made several sweeps around the screen. No blips yet, he thought to himself, and went back to his desk and sat down, twisting out the cigarette stub into the ashtray made from a spent 37-millimeter shell casing. He watched the orderlies updating the board for a moment, then lit up another cigarette and opened up his intelligence briefing book lying on his desk.

Inside the thick looseleaf notebook was intelligence on all the forces operating against their country, including equipment and weapons. He turned to the section marked "Takhli AFB, Thailand," and continued turning the pages until he came to the section on the F-105. Many of the pages were copies out of *Jane's Fighting Ships*. Others were clippings from American magazines that had been supplied by the Russians. He continued turning until he came to the weapons system used by the F-105 and placed his middle finger on a picture of a 2,000-pound bomb. If only I knew the kind of fuse they were armed with, I could guess the target, he thought to himself. He continued staring at the picture until the phone talker put his hand on his shoulder. "What is it?" He sat up straight, closing the book.

"Sir, Command Central called and said they are sending up a four-plane MiG-21 flight near the ridge. You are to hold your flight on the ground for now." The corporal stood rigid, waiting for an answer.

"Tell them I will hold the flight," Bhi answered, then opened up the intelligence book again and went back to staring at the picture of the 2,000-pound bomb.

At the MiG airbase, Major Quang stepped down from the Chinese-built flatbed truck used to haul pilots out to their aircraft. His aircraft was parked in the sandbagged revetment closest to the runway and visible only from the front. Only a direct hit would destroy the MiGs parked inside their protective shields. Stretched overhead each revetment was camouflage netting, captured from the French during their war with the Vietnamese. The aircraft was nearly invisible to fast-moving aircraft flying overhead.

Quang spotted his favorite mechanic working on his plane and dictating orders from underneath the fuselage to workers as they moved about the MiG-17. A long black cable ran from a start cart to a plug on the side of the aircraft, standing by to provide the power to start the powerful engine spinning. Quang smiled to himself, knowing he had the best man on the field taking care of his aircraft. Walking up to the left wing, he set his bag of flight gear down and began a walk-around of the aircraft, a ritual conducted by all aviators since the beginning of flight.

He stopped beside his mechanic's feet, sticking out from underneath the tail section. "Sergeant Tuang, if you make any more adjustments, this aircraft will probably be able to fly itself."

His mechanic looked up and grinned, then went back to working on the idle fuel flow adjustment. Quang had complained about it on his last flight and Tuang was determined to correct it. The mechanic pulled his slightly bowed legs underneath him and raised to a squatting position, looking up into the opened engine com-partment. He placed a cotter pin into the nut he had tightened then twisted safety wire onto the nut. Smiling, he backed away, leaving the panels for his men to reinstall.

"Now, Major, it will not run so fast while you are sitting out there waiting for the signal to launch. We ran it up an hour ago and this last adjustment should do it."

Quang nodded his head in agreement and continued his walk-around of the jet, shaking the controls and checking the Atoll missiles hanging on the aircraft. He stopped his walk as the sergeant approached him wiping his hands with a rag.

"And how is your little girl doing?" Quang asked. He knew the enlisted man's baby daughter had been hit by a piece of shrapnel, probably the result of a spent bullet. Although the wound was not serious, Quang was concerned.

"She is fine," Tuang said. "She heals fast and will only have a little scar. She is young and I hope she will not remember it." He stopped several feet from Quang, waiting for him to continue his inspection.

"Your family is in the country now?"

"Yes, my wife and my daughter."

"That is good. I am moving mine out this weekend." Quang bent down to examine the landing gear.

"Five minutes to start engines, sir," a phone talker wearing a headset called out to Major Quang. "The bombers are passing over the coast in sector five."

Quang nodded to the enlisted man and walked around the nose of the MiG, placing his right foot into the first step in the side of the fuselage. He climbed into the cockpit, followed by the sergeant, who began helping him strap in, then handed him his helmet. Another enlisted man quickly pulled the arming safety pins and held them up for Quang to see. The major nodded and flipped on the battery master switch and quickly set the other switches for the engine start. He motioned to Tuang to engage the start unit. In less than a minute he watched his RPM gauge with Russian markings come alive. He moved the throttle out of the cutoff position to the first detent, then shifted his stare to the exhaust gas temperature gauge. As the needle started to climb, he could hear the sound of exploding fuel in the tail and the engine sprang to life, spinning up rapidly. Quang signaled to Tuang to disengage the start unit, then concentrated on his instruments and quickly completed a mental checklist.

Sergeant Tuang ran to the side of the aircraft. Quang nodded to him and Tuang spread his hands, signaling two younger soldiers to remove the chocks. He guided Quang out of the revetment and saluted him as he taxied out to the end of the runway, followed by the other MiGs.

The flight of American bombers approached the North Vietnamese coastline and moved into combat spread. Leading the flight in were four specially equipped F-105 Thunderchiefs known as Wild Weasels. The four two-seater aircraft moved ahead of the flight, slowly leaving the main body of aircraft.

The lead aircraft was piloted by Capt. Lawrence Massa, a slightly balding officer of Italian descent and an Air Force Academy graduate on his sixty-eighth mission. As was his habit, he twisted around to check on the aircraft behind him. In the second seat of his aircraft, 1st Lt. Bobby Walker concentrated on the screen in front of him while he listened to the enemy radar signals coming through his earphones. The mission of the four lead aircraft was to locate and attack SAM sites, and they carried special electronic gear for detecting the special radar signal emitted by the radars of the missile sites.

Walker adjusted the volume of his headset, listening to the different sounds emitted by the radars. He had played the game before and ignored the acquisition radars and listened for the fire control radars. That was his target—the tracking and targeting radar that fed information to an airborne SAM.

Massa flew deeper into North Vietnam, inviting a SAM launch so they could go to work. He had a reputation for being able to outmaneuver the SA-2 Guideline SAMs with the best of them. He was the bait, the target for the SAMs stationed around Bak Ca, which he hoped to take out with the radar homing missiles he carried. Massa approached the target area wide-eyed, his head constantly moving as he looked for threats from all quarters. Only the drumming beat of the Firecan radars came through his headset as Vietnamese gunners trained their radar-controlled guns on him. He continued inland, jinking hard to dodge the flak that was edging up at them. He had also received a call that MiGs were airborne.

To the east, a flight of four MiG-21s orbited at high altitude near the ridge of rock northwest of Hanoi, waiting for their GCI controller to order them to attack the inbound flight. Like vultures riding the air currents, they circled and waited, hoping to find a wounded Thud when it tried to escape, and finish it off with high-speed attacks as the Thuds ran for the safety of the ridge. Superior at altitude, the MiG-21 was extremely fast and was used for slashing attacks on the fleeing Americans after they came off target. The low-altitude work was better suited for the slower MiG-17s. The flight was being rigidly controlled by the ground controllers in their underground command facility at Bak Ca.

"Okay, green 'em up," Captain Benning heard Captain Massa call over the UHF. Benning quickly flipped the armament switches and watched individual green lights flash on. Glowing steadily, the lights indicated the circuitry was complete and the two 2,000-pound deep-penetration bombs with delayed fuses were ready for release. Out of habit he rubbed his sweat-stained rabbit's foot for good luck. The flight was splitting up and he hung tightly underneath his element leader's wing preparing for their attack. Benning could see clouds of black smoke dotting the sky above and below them, and the smell of burning explosives seeped into the cockpit, filling his nostrils. He could hear the noise patterns of the Firecan radar coming over his headset as they probed for him. Benning jinked his aircraft harder and stroked his rabbit's foot again.

At the MiG base south of Hanoi, the flight of four MiG-17s lined up on the runway with their engines idling while the pilots anxiously awaited the order to launch. Heat from the four exhausts was causing the air to ripple, distorting the view across the runway. In the lead aircraft, Major Quang relaxed with his steel-toed boots lodged against the brake pedals. The canopy was open and he was monitoring operations, listening to the constant upgrading of information going out on their tactical frequency. He could hear the controllers talking to the leader of the MiG-21s, advising them of the progress of the incoming flight. It was no secret to anyone that the flight was heading for Hanoi and one of their approved targets within the city limits. Quang hoped they would launch soon and break up the flight. Lately it seemed they were relying more on their ground gunner crews and the SAMs as the Vietnamese technicians became more proficient at controlling the missile.

Quang acknowledged the launch order, lowered the canopy, then glanced back at his wingman. Seeing a thumbs-up signal, he turned around and smoothly added power as he released the brakes. Heavy with fuel and the weapons load, he accelerated slowly at first, then gained speed rapidly as he thundered down the runway. His wingman was close behind and the second section followed a few hundred meters behind. Quang pulled the stick back in his lap and felt the nose gear extend on its oleos as his aircraft rotated. He eased the stick forward as the jet became airborne, rapidly accelerating with his wingman tucked close beneath his wing. They were now fair game according to the U.S. rules of engagement, and Quang moved his head from side to side, scanning the skies as he climbed. He raised the gear handle and then the flap handle. They were soon joined by the second two aircraft. Following the controller's instructions, they headed for the Americans, who were preparing for their attack. The controller advised them the guns would be silenced just as they engaged the Americans, then gave Quang his vector heading. He was to make one firing pass through the Americans, then fly beyond the antiaircraft area to pick up any stragglers coming off their bombing runs. The MiG-21s would use their speed advantage to pursue the Thuds that escaped the MiG-17s.

Quang was rapidly approaching the flight of F-105s and could see them starting their diving runs. He selected the lead aircraft as his target, hoping to bring down another Thud and increase his tally. The North Vietnamese ace adjusted the flight path of his aircraft, holding the diving Thud in his gunsight and holding his finger to the gun button. He would have but a moment to fire at the lead before switching to the next aircraft. Even if they failed to bring down a single plane, the pass would force some of the Americans to miss their target. He squeezed the gun button.

"Bandits, two o'clock low," someone called. The lead Thud banked away from the line of fire and his wingman jerked his aircraft hard to keep from running into him.

"How many?" someone asked.

"Two, no, four MiG-17s, and they're splitting up."

The flight opened up as they tried to dodge the tracers pouring past their aircraft, making it difficult to keep an eye on the MiGs and the target ahead.

"I'm hit," the pilot of the fourth Thud called as he made a quick scan of his instruments. He saw his hydraulic pressure decreasing rapidly and jettisoned his bomb load. The pilot pulled off target, bending the Thud around while it was still controllable. Out of the corner of his eye he caught a glimpse of two MiGs turning to reengage him and realized it was only a matter of time before he either lost control of the aircraft or received a coup de grace from the pursing MiGs.

"Can't control it any longer, gotta go," was the last anyone heard from him until moments later when the squeal of the radio carried in his ejection seat began automatically broadcasting, announcing to all that a pilot was going down. The pilot hung on to the riser cords of his parachute as he watched the MiGs fly by. The descending parachute was highly visible from the ground, and he could see people gathering below looking up at him. He pulled on the risers, hoping to change his direction, but the crowd below changed directions with him and he thought he could see some of them holding pitchforks. He fingered his pistol, assuring himself it was there.

Quang regrouped his flight and watched the gaggle of aircraft heading downward trying to regain flight discipline. His pass through the Thuds had scattered some of them. He heard his controller ordering his flight out of the area and they turned away, hoping to catch the Thuds on the other side of the target area. Quang realized it was doubtful they would be able to catch any of the faster Americans.

In the bunkers at Bak Ca, the controllers suddenly realized they were the target. Fansong fire control radars began lighting off as technicians in the remote trailers followed the orders of the panic stricken controllers in the bunkers. Moments later the first telltale cloud of dust stirred by the booster rocket was visible to the F-105s above.

"Shops open," Captain Massa announced. His rear seater was too busy watching his scope to see the lift-off, but the familiar squeal of the radar was echoing in his headset. On the instrument panels of both pilots, a flashing light announcing "launch" blinked on and off. Massa knew the

Vietnamese would launch everything they had when they discovered what the target was.

"Okay, boss, come right thirty degrees and bring the nose up. Stand by to fire." The second seater had his first missile locked onto the signals being emitted by the Fansong radar.

Massa rolled the aircraft and adjusted his nose upward, hitting the arming switch at the same time. He watched three of the earliest SAMs altering their flight paths as the controllers zeroed in on him.

"Fire!"

Massa pressed the button on the stick and the missile dropped away from his aircraft and ignited its rocket motor, quickly whooshing away as it homed on the controlling radar below. He could see additional clouds of dust rising from the ground as the Vietnamese continued launching their missiles. He pulled up hard and barrel-rolled to confuse one tracking dangerously close to him. It was unnecessary as the SAMs had already lost their controlling signal. His radar-seeking missile had found the antenna below and destroyed it. The three SAMs detonated automatically and his back seater tuned in another radar. Massa's Wild Weasel flight was having a field day with the SAMs.

Several miles back, the descending Thuds were taking hits from the heavy AAA fire. The leader had holes in his wing from flak that seemed everywhere. The heavy defensive fire and MiGs had broken up the integrity of the flight and they were coming in from six different directions. Several of the Thuds had jettisoned their bomb loads and pulled off target. The others continued downward as the ground gunners frantically tried to bring them down.

"Lead's off," the first of the attacking aircraft said, pulling hard off target after releasing his two bombs. He could feel the aircraft jump as the 4,000-pound load left his ejector racks. Behind him, a struggling Thud dropped its bombs and pulled off target, accelerating as rapidly as possible and heading for the safety of the ridge to the northwest of Hanoi.

"Four two is hit and losing power!"

"Can you make it to the ridge?" someone asked.

"Maybe, but I'm slowing down. Easy meat for the vultures around here."

Captain Benning spotted the sick Thud, reduced power, and dropped behind the stricken craft, taking up a defensive position. "I'm above and behind you. I'll cover your six." Benning scanned the skies looking for the MiGs he knew were up there somewhere. He spotted them peeling off from above the ridge and heading for the slower Thud. He armed the single Sidewinder missile he carried, while above him the remains of the Wild Weasel flight had spotted the MiGs and flew head-on at them, hoping to dissuade them from their weakened quarry. Benning saw the Thuds knife through the diving MiGs, scattering two of them. The remaining two MiGs continued their run, and Benning found himself under fire as the MiGs passed by at a closure rate of over a thousand knots. The sight of tracer bullets caused him to break hard and turn away from 42, and he caught a glimpse of the other two MiGs engaging the remains of the Wild Weasel flight above him. He turned hard to engage the MiGs who he thought were below him, but when he looked, he could not find them, then felt bullets striking his aircraft. Benning quickly pulled hard to the right in a desperate attempt to escape the MiG that was outturning him, pushing the nose down and the throttle into afterburner. Accelerating rapidly, Benning could easily outrun the MiG; they were both down on the deck now and the tracers had stopped. Suddenly his headset came alive with the familiar sound of the Fansong radar being activated. The word "launch" flashed on his instrument panel, then someone called, "SAM launch." He heard the same voice call, "Aircraft on the deck. There is a SAM in pursuit." His heart rate doubled and he put the aircraft on the deck just above the treetops, banking hard to the right, looking behind him as he pulled. The long, white, tubular body was zeroed in on him and accelerating, countering his every move and gaining on him rapidly.

"Five one's got a SAM on my ass. Can anyone see it?" He reversed his turn back to the left. The missile followed.

"Five one, the SAM is coming right up your ass. Give me a hard high-G barrel roll to the right—understand—to the right!" The pilot saying this didn't think the Thud had a snowball's chance in hell of eluding the SAM, but he knew it was his only chance. He watched Benning pull the Thud up and roll to the right and saw the missile almost on him trying to follow his maneuver, its booster rocket still accelerating the missile. Soon Benning was upside down and looking at trees that seemed as if they were growing inside the cockpit, convinced he would never survive the maneuver and that both he and the SAM would crash into the wooded terrain. Out of the corner of his eye he glimpsed houses on the ground, then completed the maneuver, rolling out just above the rooftops below. From above, the pilot watching the maneuver couldn't tell if Benning had survived or not. He saw the missile pulling up as it attempted to follow Benning and then explode, hiding the aircraft in a shroud of fire and smoke.

Benning felt the explosion as the fireball flashed to the side of his aircraft. He glanced at his instruments—and saw nothing abnormal. He couldn't believe it, he had survived.

"If I hadn't seen it, I wouldn't have believed it," the pilot above him called. "You okay?"

Benning rubbed his rabbit's foot and started a climbing turn to catch up with the rest of the flight. "Yeah, I'm okay."

The remaining Thuds joined up beyond the ridge and headed back for Thailand. Some in the flight were struggling to remain airborne, and several of the F-105s flew cover above and behind them.

The MiGs had been recalled to their bases and Quang led his flight as they approached the runway. He would be the first to land and he turned on final with full flaps and gear down. Quang touched down lightly and rolled to the end with the other three MiGs following behind. Each had faced combat and for once had come back with all members of the flight and little battle damage. Quang had bagged another aircraft and he felt good, even exuberant. He was happy the SAM crew had also gotten one of the Thuds. Retracting the flaps and speedbrakes, he opened the canopy and loosened his mask as he rolled down the long taxiway to the revetment. As he approached the tow vehicle, he pulled the throttle into cutoff and coasted to a stop. Quang quickly secured the remaining switches and climbed out of his aircraft while his maintenance chief stood waiting.

"The engine idles fine," Quang said. "You have done a good job. You can paint another symbol next to the others." He smiled, then completed a postflight inspection. Satisfied there was no battle damage, he walked to the truck waiting to carry the pilots to their operations building.

Sergeant Tuang smiled as Quang walked away, then shouted to one of his assistants to bring the brush and paint. He would personally add another cross to the second row on the side of the MiG beneath the canopy, bringing the total to twelve.

★ # 18 ★

The all-clear siren wound down slowly, signaling the end of the attack and hostile aircraft over the city. Inside the underground shelters scattered around Hanoi, anxious residents looked at the clocks near the entrances and marked the time. Before they could exit out onto the streets again, they would have to allow time for the exploded antiaircraft and surface-to-airmissile debris to rain down on the city. The pieces of metal that fell from as high as 50,000 feet after a battle were sometimes a greater hazard than the bombs that were dropped. No one left the shelters until the rain of metal had ceased.

Quang was riding his motor scooter home several miles outside the base. He could hear the sirens of fire trucks as they raced through the city to reach the American jet that had exploded on impact. The aircraft had crashed in an open field and threatened a rice-drying shed nearby. A vacant home closest to the crash site was on fire, and flames leaped high into the air as the fuel from the jet burned furiously. The fire fighters concentrated on containing the fire and protecting the shed, ignoring the burning house.

Quang pulled off the road and looked back at the smoke rising from a SAM battery near the airfield. From his idling motor scooter he could make out the twisted ruins of the launchers and mobile trailers that had been the target of the antiradar missiles. He wondered to himself how long it would be before the American president would authorize the bombing of their air bases. It had to be soon, he decided.

With one foot Quang pushed himself forward until the underpowered bike accelerated enough for him to balance himself. There were a few pieces of spent ammunition lying on the road, probably pieces from the antiaircraft fire. He maneuvered around them, avoiding any that could pierce his tires. The road was relatively empty of traffic but would soon be filled with trucks moving replacement missiles and ammunition across town. Quang was anxious to reach his home and opened the throttle until the small engine vibrated from the strain. He quickly approached a group of workers with shovels and hoes working on a section of the road damaged from an exploding bomb. A worker holding a flag waved at him and he slowed as he drove around them. In a short time, the damage would be repaired using material stockpiled along the roads.

Quang could hear a high-pitched siren wailing in the distance, and he twisted around to look behind him. A single fire truck was rapidly gaining on him and he pulled off to the side. The truck was one from the base, a gift from the Russians, and it quickly sped by and disappeared around a bend. He knew they were rarely used outside the base unless there was a serious fire or military emergency. Quang pulled back on the road as the noise of the siren quieted, slowing down only once for a slow-moving flatbed truck hauling SAMs.

Approaching the dirt road leading to his neighborhood, Quang slowed again. He expected to see more people out in the streets than the few visible. Concrete lids lay scattered on the ground alongside the road, pushed to the side of the concrete vessels buried in the ground. The one-man shelters were large enough for a person to crawl into and pull over the lid, giving protection from all but a direct hit. Many had been occupied during the air raid and now looked as though each had been rapidly vacated. He could see the last of several families scurrying out of a public underground bomb shelter, hurrying across the street toward their homes. He paused for a moment to see if Kwan Chi might be among the group abandoning the shelter, then decided she and his family were already home.

Quang squeezed the black throttle grip on his scooter, but it would go no faster and he eased up. Approaching a curve, he put his foot down, letting it slide along the ground and taking the turn at full speed. He was on the next-to-last street before his and he smelled smoke—an acrid odor similar to the one he had experienced when he witnessed a SAM blow up on its launcher, a smell that reminded him of a mixture of kerosene and high explosives. He twisted the throttle again, pushing the small one-cylinder engine to its limits.

Most of the residents of his street were outside, some milling around while a few wandered aimlessly. Dodging pieces of debris lying in the road, he swerved to miss the control fin still attached to a piece of badly twisted and burned fuselage from the SAM lying in the gutter.

The North Vietnamese pilot felt his heart rise up into his throat. His heart pounding, he viewed what had once been his neighborhood and his home. The house next to his was gone and others were in ruins, their roofs collapsed and smoldering, and Quang's house was burned to the ground; only charred and smoking wood remained. A civil-defense fire truck was parked nearby, hosing down the area, the rising steam creating a surrealistic landscape. The white stucco fence that had once stood in front of Quang's house was almost leveled. Only a pile of rocks strewn about marked the spot where it had once stood.

Quang slammed on the brakes, skidding to a stop next to the fire truck in his front yard, then jumped off the bike and let it fall to the ground with the engine still running. His mind was racing as he frantically searched the gathering crowd for his family but couldn't find them. There was nothing left at the scene—only pieces of burned and melted material. Even the large shade tree in the backyard was destroyed. The tree his children had played under was now only a smoldering stump.

As Quang turned away from the devastation, something caught his eye and he bent down to examine it: the toy airplane he had made for his son, now less than half of it intact. He cried as he stood up and walked away from the smoldering piles of ashes, toward the black tarp stretched out near the fire truck.

A cold chill formed inside him and his stomach wanted to empty itself while he stood there for a moment with tears running down his cheeks. He reached down and jerked back the tarp, and just as quickly he fell to his knees and threw up. He remained in the same position for a few minutes, taking deep breaths and staring at the hideous creatures lying on the ground. What he had seen were now only blackened, unrecognizable forms, and he bit his lip to keep from throwing up again, staring at the lifeless shapes. A rescue worker pulled the tarp over the bodies and helped Quang to his feet, leaving him standing there. Stunned, he walked away, looking for anyone who might tell him of his family.

Reaching the other side of the truck, he spotted Kwan Chi's father sitting near the cab, his legs crossed and rocking back and forth. The old man was holding his small grandson across his lap, the lifeless form hanging limply from his arms. The boy's head tilted backward and his mouth gaped open, mocking death. Kwan Chi was kneeling beside him, alongside her mother, who was wailing incoherently. Quang ran to the old man, then collapsed to his knees. He said nothing for a moment, just stared silently at his son, at the dried blood blotting his face. Quang reached for Le Doc's hand, then gently closed his gaping eyes. With his head tilted upward and his eyes closed, the North Vietnamese fighter pilot let out a long moan, a primal sound that echoed across the yard.

The grandfather continued to rock, quietly sobbing to himself as he held the lifeless body across his lap.

Quang opened his eyes and looked at his wife. "Where is Mai Ling?" he asked, in fear of what the answer might be.

Kwan Chi kneeled next to her mother, her head bowed, then slowly looked up at him. "She is safe at school."

He could see a small cut across Kwan Chi's temple and blood oozing slowly into her hair. Her mother was unharmed but seemed in shock as she rocked back and forth on her knees, quietly moaning. His wife looked at him for a moment, then began sobbing uncontrollably and moved next to her husband, wanting the comfort and security of his arms. After a moment she told him what had happened, how they had failed to hear the warning, how something had exploded nearby and fire had quickly spread. She told him her father had run back into the burning house to find Le Doc. The old man had been badly burned searching for the boy, who was already dead from the explosion. He pulled the boy's body from beneath the rubble and carried it outside. She told him she and her mother had been knocked down by the blast, but were unharmed.

Quang held his wife close to him as he looked at the old man. He could see the deep cut across his forehead, the blood trickling from his mouth down into his beard, staining the white hair scarlet, and the burns covering the left side of the old man's face. But the old man continued to rock back and forth, now humming the song he often sang to his grandchildren.

Quang placed his hand on his shoulder. "Grandfather," Quang said as he looked him straight in the eyes. "What's wrong?" The old man suddenly began making gurgling sounds that came from deep within his chest, and soon his eyes looked straight ahead but stared at nothing. Quang started to say something again, then stopped as the old man, whose heart had stopped beating, slumped over his grandson's body.

★ 19 ★

One hundred and fifty-three days after leaving San Diego, the end of the WestPac cruise was in sight, and the officers and men of the *Barbary Coast* were anticipating departing Yankee Station. To hasten the end of the cruise, calendars with the days carefully crossed off adorned lockers and office spaces. Many betting pools were started, with the prediction closest to the actual docking time in San Diego to take the pot.

But the pilots charged with stopping the flow of materials to the south still faced increasingly heavy defenses. North Vietnam was continually upgrading the number of SAM and radar sites and bringing more radar-controlled antiaircraft guns into operation. By the end of the year, surface-to-air missile sites alone would more than double. And even more deadly to the pilots were the increased radar installations, nearly tripling in number by the year's end and the majority tied in to the radar-controlled antiaircraft guns. The defensive weapons used against the Americans attacking bridges and storage facilities were devastating and accounted for most of the losses of the war. In addition, bad weather was frequently a blessing to the enemy, and postponed flights gave the Vietnamese time to rebuild defenses and move equipment to the south. The rules of engagement—ROE— dictating what targets could be hit, when, and how, were frustrating to the American pilots, and its rules equally baffling to the leaders of North Vietnam but nevertheless frequently taken advantage of. MiG bases were off limits, as well as a zone at the Chinese border. Rolling down the runway or fleeing across the imaginary line below China gave the MiGs American-endorsed protection, a luxury guaranteed to cost American lives and give the Vietnamese needed time to strengthen themselves.

The *Barbary Coast* had lost six aircraft to enemy operations and two to operational accidents, fitting somewhere in the middle of the statistics book for WestPac cruises. One pilot was a known POW, two were listed as killed in action, and one was MIA. One had died when the catapult failed to develop full power and the pilot went over the edge into the water, failing to eject. Another had simply disappeared on a training operation and was never heard from again, swallowed up by a vast, unforgiving sea.

It had been three weeks since the *Barbary Coast* weighed anchor and departed the roads at Singapore, returning to Yankee Station and the final period in the war zone. And now bad weather was becoming a factor.

The bridge at Canh Tra, in the meantime, had been repaired again and was on the priority list for a bombing mission. Attacked periodically throughout the war, it was always rebuilt and supplies shuttled across it when supply lines were cut in the west. Admiral Laceur decided it was a matter of pride and wanted one more crack at it before turning it over to the replacement air group and having to admit defeat to some of his former Annapolis classmates.

Campbell and Swenson had flown several missions since leaving Singapore—limited attacks against petroleum storage facilities outside Haiphong, some rail lines running out from Hanoi, and a few missions against transportation sites scattered to the southwest of Hanoi.

It was Sunday afternoon and a low, squally overcast hung over the ships orbiting Yankee Station. Not a single mission had been scheduled that day because of the weather over the target area. But if the weather improved, a sweep against truck traffic was planned plus several sorties against suspected truck parks. Campbell was scheduled for either one.

Alone in his stateroom, he leaned back in his chair, silently gazing at the picture of his wife. His tape recorder was belting out Peggy Lee's "Tennessee Waltz" and his copy of the waltz step chart was spread out on the floor. It was showing signs of wear and he had taped several tears in the corner with Scotch tape. An enlarged photograph of the French plantation where he had seen the POWs was lying on his desk. Campbell picked up a magnifying glass and held it above the photo, concentrating on the blurred figures he thought were Americans. Of the five figures, three wore the typical Vietnamese hats, making them appear like field-workers. Two figures held something in their arms that he knew were the guns the guards were holding on the POWs. Even to a talented photo expert, it would be hard to tell who the figures were. To Campbell there was no doubt.

He stopped the tape and rewound it until he found the starting part of the same song and pushed PLAY on the recorder. Peggy Lee began her song of waltzing again and he leaned back in his chair, closing his eyes and visualizing the steps it would take to get Larry out. Campbell had given up hope on anyone's trying a rescue attempt, convinced everyone from the admiral up had written Larry off and no rescue was being planned. He imagined Larue and several men and himself at the edge of the tree line, watching the building just as he had. Then storming the old farmhouse before anyone knew they were there and busting out Larry and the other POWs. He imagined Aggie there right on time to pick them up and fly them back to the carrier and a hero's welcome. He was just imagining the landing when Pancho walked in, destroying the image.

Pancho was his new roommate and had moved in with him soon after Larry was lost, although he spent most of his time in the ready room, sleeping in air-conditioned comfort. He was rarely there and his bunk showed little sign of having been slept in. Pancho came back to change in the morning when it was cooler.

"Hey, man, you still thinking about getting old Larry out?" He spotted the photo lying on Campbell's desk and picked it up, looking through the magnifying glass. All he could see was a building with some figures outside.

"It could be done," Campbell said.

"Every time you show me this photo, it still looks like these figures could be anybody. You just can't tell who they are." He tossed the photo back on Campbell's desk and sat down on the lower bunk.

"Look, I saw him with my own eyes and that's the difference." Campbell reached over and stopped the recording. "Pancho, if someone asked you to volunteer and help get Jordan out, would you do it?" Campbell waited while Pancho sat down on the bunk again.

"You mean like an official mission?"

"Not exactly."

The two men were silent and looked each other directly in the eye for a moment. "You're crazy, man. I don't know what you're thinking, but you better put it to rest." Pancho picked up the travel kit he had come after and left the stateroom for the head just down the passageway, leaving Campbell alone with his thoughts again.

Campbell had spent some time hanging around the intelligence spaces, shooting the breeze with the planners and nosing around when he had time. He had found out a bombing mission against the bridge at Canh Tra was in the planning stage and that an F-8 flak suppression mission would go in the day before. The following day his squadron would bomb the bridge. The intelligence planners had assured him it would be the last mission of the cruise. It was his last chance to try to get Jordan out of North Vietnam—if he was still there.

Campbell hurried down to see Commander Lorimar and volunteered for the last flight against the north. Lorimar thought he was crazy but agreed to let him go. He left Lorimar's stateroom and rushed down to the helicopter detachment and into Aggie Anson's small, crowded office.

Seated behind a gray desk badly in need of painting, Lieutenant Anson was bent over a clipboard twisting a ballpoint pen in and out of his fingers as he studied the maintenance gripes on one of his two helicopters. He looked up as the door swung open. "Soupy," he called out. "What the hell are you doing down here in 'swing-wing land'?" He laid the clipboard down.

"Came to talk." Campbell pulled out a chair from the corner and eased into it.

"Sounds serious."

"Aggie, let's go get a cup of coffee." Together they left the detachment space and walked down the passageway, then down one level to the hangar deck.

"What's up?" Anson stopped at the foot of the stairs and looked back at Campbell.

"Is there any place we can talk—alone, I mean?"

"Yeah, I know a place. Let's go back to one of my helos buried in the pack."

"I'm right behind you." Campbell followed Aggie as they dodged around and under the wings of the aircraft packed together on the crowded deck. They worked their way aft to the end of the hangar bay where one of the two helos was parked. Aggie opened the hatch behind the copilot's seat and pulled down the two-piece door. He climbed inside the helo and walked to the rear of the helicopter with Campbell right behind him.

"Okay, what's so important?"

Campbell looked around to ensure no one was working on the helo. Satisfied, he placed a foot up on the troop seat and leaned closer to Aggie. "Remember that conversation we had back at the hotel in Singapore? The one we all agreed could be pulled off without a hitch?" Campbell waited as Aggie's expression changed from a smile to puzzlement.

The helicopter pilot looked dumbfounded for a moment and just stared at Campbell. "That wasn't just Scotch talking back then, was it?"

"No, it wasn't. This may be Jordan's only chance to get out alive. Laceur isn't going to risk his precious career to get Jordan. We are the last hope he has and maybe the only hope." Campbell looked straight at Anson and waited for his answer.

"You're crazy. What you're thinking could get everyone including Larry killed, not counting the jail time we would all get if we managed to pull it off. We don't make the rules, we just carry them out."

Campbell looked perplexed. Aggie had seemed the most enthusiastic at the table until he passed out. Campbell tried to think of something to say. "We are his only chance."

"Look, I know the way you feel. Larry was my friend, too, and if the admiral authorized a rescue attempt, you couldn't stop me from going. But he didn't and probably isn't going to. Larry will come back someday. This war can't go on much longer."

"What if Larue would be willing to go? Would that change your mind?"

"Look, Jim, it's just no good. Forget it." The helicopter pilot opened the rear hatch of the helicopter, climbing down to the deck and leaving Jim standing inside. He walked quickly out of sight, leaving Campbell alone.

Campbell watched Aggie for a moment, then climbed down and started across the hangar bay. Reaching a door-frame, he stepped through and started down. He was unsure of the exact location of the marine spaces and spent some time wandering through the maze of passageways and blind alleys until he found himself facing a huge Marine Corps emblem painted on the panel. Walking inside, he was greeted by a corporal sitting behind a desk with a duty band stretched around his arm.

Spotting the naval officer approaching his desk, the marine stood up. "Good morning, sir. Is there something I can help you with?"

Campbell stopped in front of the desk. "I'm looking for Captain Larue. Is he here?"

The corporal moved forward a step, squinting as he examined Campbell's name tag. "Yes sir, he is. Just wait here and I'll tell him you are here to see him." He turned smartly and disappeared through a doorway, leaving Campbell looking around the room. He was always impressed with the differences he found between a marine space and navy one. The room was ringed with photos and old prints of marine heroes of long ago. Half of the room was cordoned off with white rope drooping between polished 55-millimeter shell casings. Off to one side the American flag hung from a staff mounted inside another shell casing. He thought of his own workspace, a dingy cubicle with two desks, both badly needing paint, and a couple of old filing cabinets.

"How do you like our little detachment?" Larue asked as he came into the room, stopping just short of the ropes. He held a pipe in his hand.

Campbell turned to face Larue. As usual, the marine captain's uniform was flawless. The military creases in his shirt that ran vertically from the beltline to the shoulder and down the other side reminded Campbell of the recruiting posters he had seen in his hometown post office. Campbell felt more at ease with Larue in the wardroom when his uniform had given up to the humidity. "This place is spit and polish as usual. Any chance you could show me around? I've been dying to see all the toys you guys get to play with."

Larue puffed on his pipe for a moment trying to coax smoke from the bowl, then gave up. "Sure, no problem. I'd be glad to." He turned to the corporal standing off to one side. "Corporal, give me the key to the armory."

Campbell watched the young marine unlock a key box and hand another key over to Captain Larue.

"The lieutenant and myself will be in the back if we're needed," he said to the duty NCO. "Jim, want to follow me?" He laid his pipe down and went through the door and down the passageway until he came to a steel door with a large chain and lock securing it. Larue unlocked the door. "After you," he said. He followed Campbell through the doorframe and into the sealed but well-lit room.

Immediately Campbell spotted a row of M-16 rifles lined up and secured to the wall by clips. Below each, a tag identified the owner and serial number of the weapon. In open cases at one end of the room, tagged automatic weapons lay ready for instant use. On the floor were several 7.62-millimeter machine guns resting on their tripods. Larue told Campbell they were the same type of gun Aggie carried in his helicopter. A single .50-caliber machine gun on a tripod sat in the corner next to cases of ammunition. In the far corner were boxes with military markings stenciled on the sides. Campbell opened one up.

"M-79 grenade launchers," Larue informed him.

"Very impressive. Now I feel safer. Can we talk here?"

"Yeah, we're alone. What's up?" Larue closed the lid to the grenade launchers.

"The thing we talked about back in Singapore. I just finished talking to Aggie and he says it won't work, that you couldn't pull it off."

The marine lowered his eyes and pushed the box against the bulkhead with his foot. "Aggie should stick to flying helicopters. I think it would work. If it's exactly like you say, then I could do it. If the admiral authorizes it, we can get him out."

Campbell's shoulders sagged and he sat down on an ammunition case. "The admiral is not going to authorize it. Jordan can stay there and rot as far as he is concerned."

"Then that's that, I suppose."

"But how would you do it, if it *were* authorized?"

The marine captain sat down on a box next to Campbell. "It would have to be a two-day affair: one day to observe and the next day to assault. The extraction would have to be timed to perfection."

"If Aggie could get you in on the tail end of a flak suppression mission and pick you up the next day during a strike on the bridge just above the camp, would that work?" Campbell waited for the marine's reaction.

Larue didn't say anything for a moment. "The whole outfit would volunteer if I make it public. I did discuss it with two. One of them is the corporal you met coming in."

"That guy out front?" Campbell arched his eyebrows. "He doesn't look like he could hurt a fly."

"That guy can shoot a fly off your ear at six hundred

yards. He's the designated sniper for our detachment. That guy is the one that would pick off the guards if we made it that far.''

"What do you mean *if*? Are you having second thoughts?''

"No, if the camp is like you say it is, then we could pull it off. If we get in and find it's got guard towers and more troops than you saw, we would have to kiss it off and get out of there. That would take more men and equipment. Something the planners could spend months on. You do understand that, don't you?''

Campbell remained silent for a moment. "I knew that all along. The final decision would be yours and yours alone.''

"If we could do it, we would. If it's an abort, then Aggie would have to pick us up and get us out.''

"I know it's a long shot, but if you only knew how unprotected that camp is.'' Campbell wasn't quite sure of what to make of Larue's comments. At one time it seemed as if he would go in a minute, if only Aggie would fly them in. At other times it seemed as if he was just humoring him. "How would you and Aggie communicate?'' Campbell asked.

Larue got up and walked over to the corner, pulling back a tarp covering several radios. "We would be carrying one of these. You could give me the call signs and freqs for the bombing mission before we left.'' Larue threw the cover back over the radios. "You know my men and I could be up shit's creek if Aggie were knocked down. No one would even know we were there until the Vietnamese announced it to the world—and that's why you wouldn't be one of us.'' He watched Campbell's face sag. He knew Campbell would want to be in on it. "You would be the only one that could convince anyone to get us out—if they would. They probably would just leave us hanging.''

"You would probably have to get out the best way you could—but let's hope it won't come to that.'' Campbell continued to explain the details of the operation as Larue studied the map and photos he produced. Campbell could tell Larue wasn't completely convinced it would work.

"It sounds like Aggie would have one busy day," Larue observed.

"I think we would all have a busy day."

"Have you figured out how we're going to explain all of this if we managed to pull it off, or have you been thinking about how you would plead at your court-martial?"

"I don't want to think about it, but I do think we could drop this one in the admiral's lap and make it look like it accidentally happened. Then he could claim all the credit."

"In a pig's ass. Look, I hope the rocks at Leavenworth are soft."

"Yeah, right." Campbell left for his stateroom. In his mind he had accomplished little. He felt Aggie had turned him down completely and Larue was only humoring him. And there was little time left.

★ 20 ★

Sergeant Tuang stood off to the side of the MiG-17 and took a long look at the damaged fighter. Just minutes before, the wounded pilot had been removed from the cockpit and placed on the back of a flatbed truck and spirited away for treatment. The fighter was riddled with holes and ripped metal, causing Tuang to wonder how Quang's wingman had even managed to make it back. Luckily, the aircraft had received most of the damage, not the young pilot, who had caught a small piece of shrapnel in his arm. Tuang shook his head as he continued his examination. It was the same type of damage that had occurred the preceding week—flak damage from their own guns and always to the wingmen flying on Major Quang. If the officer in charge didn't ground Vietnam's leading ace soon, it was just a matter of time before Quang was killed, and some of the junior pilots as well. Already the younger pilots were making excuses not to fly with him. They thought Quang was crazy. From the moment his son was killed, he began disobeying orders, engaging in combat when the odds were too high and pursuing aircraft into the flak concentrations in complete disregard for his or his wingman's safety. Tuang just shook his head.

It would take him all week to repair the damage even if he had all the spare parts he would require. He turned and walked to the edge of the piled-up sandbags and watched the second MiG turning off the runway and taxiing in, his eyes straining to see any damage.

The rhythmic pulsing of the Kilimov VK-1F engine was mimicking the throaty roar of a finely tuned dragster as it approached the sandbagged revetment. Its deep bellow overwhelmed anyone nearby as the North Vietnamese plane captain confidently guided the MiG-17. His elbows were extended out to his sides, locked in place and shoulders high. Only his forearms were moving slowly up and down as he directed the returning fighter. The fighter pilot braked and the nose of the jet dipped as he halted. Two linemen barely seventeen scrambled to place wooden blocks snugly against the wheels as the plane captain drew his hand across his throat, signaling the pilot to secure his engine. The canopy of the aircraft remained sealed and the pilot sat motionless as the engine continued to idle. The plane captain repeated the cut signal, then with a shrug of his shoulders looked over to the chief mechanic.

The pilot still had not moved and Sergeant Tuang grabbed a boarding ladder and hurriedly pushed it against the side of the still-running aircraft. He pushed the external canopy button as he scaled the ladder, energizing the canopy motor. The concerned mechanic anxiously looked for signs of blood, thinking Quang was injured, though the only damage he had seen were some minor rips in the tail section. Though he could see no blood, Quang was still, only staring ahead as if in a trance. Suddenly Quang jerked his head and looked up. His oxygen mask hung down to the side and his visor was up. His face looked vacant then suddenly tensed up, and he reached over and pulled the throttle into the cutoff position, instantly killing the engine. With a few quick motions he secured the aircraft, then handed his helmet to the mechanic as if nothing had happened.

The mechanic reached in and withdrew the rolled-up safety pins and inserted them into the ejection seat and canopy. Sergeant Tuang waited for Quang to climb down, wondering why he had remained in the aircraft with the engine running for so long. Quang had a habit of always shutting the engine down as he taxied in, rolling to a stop with the systems already secured. Then he would bound out of the aircraft as soon as the ladder was within reach. But now something was wrong. Quang's temper had become shorter and Sergeant Tuang noticed he was snapping at his younger mechanics over minor things. He had even asked Tuang to increase the power of his engine beyond the recommended maximum, arguing that he needed the extra power. He seemed fixated on doing battle with every American jet that crossed the beach and became disgusted whenever he was held back from launching. He was taking risks beyond ordinary daring. Tuang wondered if Quang was suffering from some kind of battle fatigue.

Quang dismounted from the MiG and began his customary walking inspection of his aircraft. He spotted several rips in the tail section, damage from their own ground gunners. Quang had pursued an F-105 through a field of antiaircraft fire against the orders of his GCI controller.

The damage caused him to suddenly remember his wingman. "Where is Second Lieutenant Vung? He landed ahead of me and should be here.'' Quang continued staring up at the damage to his aircraft.

Sergeant Tuang was already making notes of the damage. "Lieutenant Vung's arm was injured. They have taken him to the hospital.'' The mechanic didn't mention that the youngster's aircraft had received considerable damage and that he was lucky to have made it back. Quang could see only the nose of the MiG sticking out of the next revetment. The mechanic had already been on the phone with the ops officer and had described the battle damage to the MiG.

Before he left, Quang asked his mechanic if he could increase the power of his engine once more, which would threaten its remaining life. Tuang agreed to look into it.

Satisfied, Quang turned away and headed for the truck waiting to carry him to the small operations building at the end of the field.

The mechanic watched the truck drive away, then turned to his two assistants. The younger of the two had been there the longest and he looked bewildered.

"There is definitely something wrong with Major Quang.''

Tuang finished scribbling on his status board then turned to the boy. "It is his loss that is affecting him. He hasn't been the same since his boy was killed. The operations officer told me Quang thinks the Americans deliberately dropped bombs on his neighborhood, but it wasn't so. We think it was an accident, an exploding missile, but he refuses to believe it. Now he flies with a vengeance. I don't think he can go on much longer.'' The mechanic shrugged his shoulders and turned away, preparing to patch up the damaged jets, his two assistants close behind.

At the concrete-block operations building, a clerk was pecking on an old typewriter captured from the French. He barely noticed Quang as the pilot entered and stopped in front of his desk. As with paper pushers the world over, the importance of properly dotted *i*'s and columns filled in took precedence over everything else, and he continued to work on the form he was filling out for the operations officer. Quang lay his helmet bag atop the form.

"Where is Colonel Doc?" Quang leaned over the desk, glaring at the corporal. "I was informed he wanted to see me."

The clerk looked up, then pushed Quang's helmet bag aside. "He's busy and said you are to wait for him." He went back to filling out the form again.

Quang grabbed his bag and walked over to a nearby chair. He was still wearing his flight gear and began pulling at the many zippers of his G suit until he had it and the torso harness lying on the floor. Relieved of the uncomfortable garb, he sat down, wondering why he had been called in.

After a few minutes he was ordered into the small office, where a large map of North Vietnam dominated one wall. The other wall had equally large maps of the surrounding countries and a Plexiglas status board with opposing forces, their own forces, and maintenance and pilot status. This information would be found in any operations center. A small desk was covered with forms and a clay ashtray was filled with cigarette stubs.

The officer in charge stood up when Quang entered. He was much shorter than Quang, as nearly everyone was, and he wore glasses. He had been a pilot once but no longer flew and concentrated on getting the most out of the air force supplied to them by the Russians. "Major Quang, I am pleased you returned safely." He decided not to mention Quang's wingman for the moment and shook the pilot's hand.

Pointing to the chair directly in front of the desk, he waited until Quang sat down before seating himself. He looked directly at Quang. "You look like you have given up sleep, Major Quang. Are you not resting well?"

Quang looked back at him and forced a smile. "When

does one ever get enough sleep? Anyway, you wanted to talk about the flight?''

"Yes, the flight, and your flying. Did you know your wingman was injured?''

"Yes, my mechanic told me when I landed.''

"Did he also tell you that both of your aircraft were damaged by flak—our own flak?''

"No, he . . . ,'' he began, then caught himself.

"You were pursuing the Americans right through our own fire against our orders. I talked to Major Bhi and he told me you refused to respond when you were ordered to veer off. Our own people were shooting at you as well as the Americans when they could have been concentrating only on the Americans.'' The officer's face began to redden as he criticized his best pilot, but then after a few quiet moments he calmed himself. "Major, I think it would be best if I took you out of our area for a while.'' He paused again. "You are pushing too hard and taking too many risks. Your hatred is overcoming your judgment. You are the best fighter pilot we have, and now you risk everything trying to down every enemy plane in the sky. But we can't afford to lose you, so I'm ordering you to our southern defense command.''

Quang looked up at the officer, his face saying what his voice wouldn't. "For how long?''

"Indefinitely. I'm ordering you and a new pilot to take two aircraft to the airfield and await orders. Only when the GCI controllers order you into the air will you launch. Is that understood?'' The officer stared straight into the eyes of the fighter pilot, calmly waiting for him to answer.

"Just the two of us?''

"Just the two of you. The Americans get nervous every time we position aircraft on that field, and it forces them to alter their plans even though they won't attack your aircraft on the ground. If the opportunity presents itself, you will be ordered to attack, but only then will you launch. At all other times you will be sitting in your aircraft every time an attack is picked up. Do you have any questions?''

"No, Colonel, no questions.''

"Good, you will leave tomorrow morning." The officer stood up and silently indicated the meeting was over. He waited for Quang to leave, then called Major Bhi.

★ 21 ★

Campbell was alone in his stateroom sitting at his desk. He repeatedly tapped a pencil against the desk top as he worked on a letter of resignation from the navy. A small wastebasket was pulled up close to his chair, now filled with crumpled sheets of paper. Each time he had started to write, the words seemed wrong to him, although a simple declaration was all that was required. After the first few lines he would wad the sheet up and throw it away, only to start over again. He had spent a sleepless night thinking about his future: a naval career without his wife or a married life without the navy. At the corner of the desk lay the one letter he had received from Karen, a short note announcing she was in Pensacola. She mentioned that Patricia was in San Diego forming an association of wives whose husbands were prisoners or were missing in action. Although she didn't come right out and say it, he was sure she was offering him a choice—her or the navy.

He folded up a draft of his letter of resignation and slipped it into his breast pocket, deciding to finish it later. Looking up, he saw Aggie standing at the door. "How long have you been standing there?" Campbell asked.

"Not long. Mind if we come in?"

"Who is 'we'?" Campbell asked, leaning back in his chair to see who else was in the hall. He watched Aggie walk into the stateroom, followed by Larue.

Aggie sat down on the lower bunk bed while Larue stood at one end. "I've changed my mind."

"What do you mean, changed your mind?"

"Larue and I have decided to give it a try," Aggie said, watching Campbell, waiting for the statement to take hold.

"Why the change of heart?"

Aggie looked up at Larue then back at Campbell, smiling. "This may be the only chance I ever have of collecting the money he owes me from smoke."

"You two bastards may be the best friends I'll ever know. So when do we go?"

"Day after tomorrow—but you're not going."

"What do you mean I'm not going. I'm the only one who's seen the camp. I have to go."

"You're not going, period. If I'm going to risk my ass, then I don't need someone to get in my way. No offense, old buddy, but there is nothing you could do. You're the only one that may be able to get my ass out if everything falls apart, and I want you on top of things while I'm in country. Besides, you're part of the mission. You're going to cover my ass if I need you when you make your attack on the bridge."

"Canh Tra?"

"That's it, the big mission planned against the Canh Tra bridge. The F-8s are going in the first day to hose the area down for flak suppression, and the next day you and your CO and the rest of the flight are going in to take out the bridge." Larue bent over and picked up the photo Campbell had stuck in the corner of his desk. "I need two days to make it work. One to get in and check the compound out, and the next day for extraction."

"How do you get in?"

"That's where I come in," Aggie said. "After I fly plane guard for the F-8 launch, I'll move closer to shore to cover them. Larue and his men will be on board and I'll report a false beeper and go inland to investigate. That's when I drop Larue off in the river."

"Okay, great, you drop him and his party off in the river above the camp. How are you going to put several marines into a helo without anyone seeing them?"

"We'll give them flight suits and put them aboard the Sikorsky while it's still in the hangar bay," Aggie said. "They can hide behind the curtain in the rear. It's mostly empty except for some electronic black boxes and controls going to the tail section. Then after we're on deck and about to launch, they can step forward and strap in."

"What about your crewmen?"

"We can trust them. One of them will probably want to go with the marines."

Campbell smiled and looked at Larue. "Great, but who's going in with you?"

"Two men. The marine you saw standing watch in the armory and my gunnery sergeant. Both of them understand the situation and volunteered."

Campbell shook his head, then watched the marine captain unbutton his top pocket and pull out a folded map, spreading it out on the desk top.

"Now here's what we are going to have to do." Larue

put his finger on a river junction on the map. "Here's the bridge. It's not far from the coast, Aggie, so you shouldn't have more than a twenty- or thirty-minute flight to reach the river. It's about eight or nine miles below the bridge."

Campbell studied the map for a minute then pointed. "This is the prison camp, right here near the water."

"Not too far from where we picked you up, is it?" Aggie asked as he moved closer to the desk and studied the map.

"It seems farther when it takes all night to get there floating on the river," Campbell said, opening up his desk safe to remove another black-and-white, eight-by-ten photograph. "This is the latest recon photo of the area, but it doesn't tell us a thing about the camp. From the air it always looks like one of those old French farmhouses."

Aggie picked up the photograph. "It's really pretty simple. All I have to do is get him to the river undetected and then pick him up the next day. The slopes will be too busy shooting at the F-8s on one day, and at Campbell the next, right? Yeah, sure," he answered his own question. "It all sounds too easy to me. I know in my heart it will work, but something is bound to go wrong. You know, Murphy's Law."

Larue dropped the photograph on the desk. "Look, when the fighters go in to hose down the area next to the bridge, all hell is going to break loose around there. If Aggie can claim he's picked up a beeper or something, he's got the perfect excuse to go inland. He can fly five or six miles upriver from the camp, low and slow over the water. We'll jump into the river and hide until dark, then drift down into position just like Campbell did. The camp won't have the foggiest notion anybody is even around. The following morning we'll be in position to recon the camp."

"It still sounds too easy."

"Look, Ag, nobody knows about this but you, me,

Larue, and maybe a couple of his men. That's the beauty of it, no big brass to screw anything up.''

''What if something goes wrong? Maybe one of the guys gets shot down or I get replaced or something?''

Campbell sat back down. ''If the mission gets blown or compromised at any point, we have no choice but to tell higher authority. But we have to get Larue and his men out in any case. If it gets compromised, my ass is going to be hanging from the highest antenna they can find on this ship, and I'll be swinging all the way back to San Diego. And probably with the rest of you, too. That's the risk we all have to take.''

Aggie looked at the map for a moment, then folded it up. ''All right. Count me in.''

''Great. Now, here's what we'll do. Tonight, let's meet up in the fo'c'stle to go over the details. You, me, and Larue right after the movie starts—by the anchor chain.''

At midafternoon the next day, two F-8 Crusaders lined up on the port and starboard catapults. Two more were behind them, awaiting their turn for launch.

Farther back on the flight deck Aggie picked the Sikorsky helicopter up into a hover and quickly scanned his instruments for signs of abnormalities. Satisfied the engines were running normally, he rocked the helo forward and flew down the angled deck gaining speed, then returned to port and eased away from the deck, flying behind the carrier. His primary function during the launch was to recover any of the F-8 pilots who crashed. A destroyer also serving as plane guard trailed to the rear of the carrier, ready to rescue anyone needing help. It was not uncommon for an unsuspecting sailor to be blown off the carrier deck by a jet blast.

Aggie flew around to the starboard side of the carrier and put the helo into a hover. He matched the carrier's speed and pushed the left rudder in slightly, side-slipping the helo and drawing in air through the opened side window while he observed the launch.

Captain Larue and his men were stripping off their flight suits, revealing the full-camouflaged battle dress they wore underneath. Aggie twisted around to view his passengers and gave them a thumbs-up, grinning from ear to ear.

In a matter of minutes the F-8s were airborne and climbing, quickly disappearing from sight. The carrier turned back to its original course and reduced speed. The officer in PriFly secured flight stations and released Aggie from his plane guard assignment, and the helicopter headed west, moving closer to the North Vietnamese mainland.

Aggie banked the huge helicopter and switched over to Red Crown, checking in with the controller aboard the guided-missile cruiser. Twisting around to check on Larue and his men, his eyes widened when he saw the three, their faces now masked in hideous shades of greens and browns, with slashes and jagged marks adorning their skin from the neck up. The face paint made them look crazed and wild, and Aggie could hardly recognize the man he played cards with.

Larue saw Aggie looking at him and smiled, revealing shiny white teeth that stood out against the darkened skin. The marine captain was sitting on the bench holding an automatic weapon between his legs with the butt resting on the floor. A large backpack with its contents wrapped in waterproof material sat in a heap at his feet.

Aggie grinned back at him, then returned to his duties. He told his copilot to have everyone test their guns before they neared the beach. Ensign Franks turned around and motioned to one of the crewmen. Smiling, he told him to pass the word to check their weapons. The third-class petty officer opened the cargo hatch, then got behind the gun and slammed a shell into the chamber. He began firing off a few rounds while the other crewmen tested the forward gun.

Even the sound of the machine gun could not be heard above the noise of the helicopter transmission. Satisfied, he signaled to Captain Larue, and the marines moved over to the opened hatch and test-fired their weapons except for the .30-06 that Corporal Jones left in the case. Satisfied, everyone sat down and waited for Aggie to cross over the beach and take them to the river.

High overhead, the flight of Chance Vought Crusaders sped toward the beach and the waiting gun crews surrounding the bridge at Canh Tra. With little fighter action for the MiG Cap patrols, the F-8s had been pressed into an attack role to supplement the attack squadrons. Armed with four 20-millimeter guns and Sidewinder missiles, most pilots considered these aircraft the last of the true gunfighters, even though the Crusader pilots had few opportunities to engage the North Vietnamese fighters, and they welcomed the opportunity to bomb.

The F-8s carried CBU cluster bombs, which would separate into hundreds of small bomblets that were effective on gun crews. A second wave of F-8s carried bombs to destroy the guns themselves and, hopefully, make the job easier for the bombers going after the bridge itself the next day.

Aggie approached the beach and made a call to Red Crown, telling him he was picking up a beeper signal from a SAR radio and proceeding inbound to investigate. Before the officer aboard the cruiser could respond, the helo pilot turned his radio volume down and continued westward. He was flying just above the water and below the North Vietnamese radar coverage. Aggie turned his SIF/IFF gear to standby then concentrated on crossing a section of beach that contained few villages or known guns. His copilot switched over to the F-8 discrete frequency and made a quick call advising them that they would be inland if needed. The puzzled flight leader acknowledged but was too involved dodging flak to question the call.

The helicopter was designed by Sikorsky and sold to the navy to hunt and kill submarines. Captain Larue and his men looked completely out of place in the rear of a helicopter that should have been over the open ocean hunting Russian submarines instead of flying into the unknown over the jungles of North Vietnam.

Corporal Jones removed his glasses, closed his eyes and leaned back into the seat strapping, letting his mind wander to what he would be facing. He thought of the ordeal the POWs must be undergoing and steeled his mind to what he would have to do. Jones was frail-looking, too tall for his weight and a poor match in hand-to-hand combat, but he was deadly behind the sights of a sniper rifle and that was why Larue wanted him. His eyes still closed, he cradled the camouflaged case containing the sniper rifle and scope in his lap, the service-issue M-16 between his legs.

To his right, Gunnery Sergeant "Bat" Masterson sat holding a small plastic, waterproof map, comparing the terrain he could see through the open hatch with that depicted on the map. His body was lean and the veins in his neck popped out when he turned his head sideways. This was not the first time he had operated behind enemy lines, nor was it the first unauthorized mission he had made into North Vietnam. As they crossed the beach, he looked at his watch, and shouted the time to Larue, silently estimating when they would be over the river.

The marine captain put his hand to his ear in an effort to hear above the high-pitched whine of the main transmission and two jet engines above their heads. He looked at his watch and nodded at his sergeant. It was nearing five o'clock and the sun was low in the western sky.

In the cockpit Ens. Gary Franks carefully watched the land checkpoints and compared them against the map spread across his lap. He had made the trip inland with Aggie during Campbell's rescue, and this time he was not nearly as nervous. "Twelve minutes to the river," he said over the intercom. "We're right on course and should come out where Campbell said there was good cover."

"Yeah, right. So far, so good." Aggie made a quick zag to throw off any small-arms shooters. He was more concerned with them than the larger guns that dotted the country. In a minute he zigged the other way, then adjusted his course over countryside that was rapidly changing from the swampy areas near the beach to the familiar grid patterns of numerous rice paddies. He headed across the middle of a paddy, causing some of the planters to look up as they flew by. Beyond the tree line a village leader had sighted the helicopter and was reporting it to his aircraft spotting coordinator. The information would be called to Hanoi where a response would be coordinated.

"That looks like a village up ahead. Better swing south."

"Nah, too small. Most likely just a few hooches for the rice farmers out here in the woods." Aggie continued on, pushing the Sikorsky to its maximum speed.

"Oh, shit!" Franks looked up startled. He could see flashes coming from the shadows near the huts and pushed back into the armor-plated seat.

Aggie banked the helicopter sharply and dropped down even lower, flying away from the muzzle flashes. In a few moments he turned back on course. "Too far away to be effective. Mark that down on the chart so we don't fly over it again."

Aggie could make out distant plumes of smoke rising from the ground off to the right, probably, he guessed, from the fighters attacking the gun crews. He turned up the volume on the UHF and listened to the chatter from the fighter pilots engaged in their bombing runs. For a moment he wondered what it would be like to fly one of the sleek jets against heavily defended targets, then he decided he would never know. "Tell Captain Larue and his men we are five minutes out. When we approach the river, I will turn north and fly it for a short distance to the drop zone."

Franks switched to the crew intercom and passed the message back, giving a thumbs-up sign. He watched them strapping on their backpacks, checking each other until satisfied that they could jump into the river with assurance of success. He was glad he wouldn't be spending the night behind enemy lines. "They're ready," he said to Aggie.

"Good, I see the tree line at the river up ahead. These rice paddies go right up to the riverbank on this side. Tell Larue we'll be monitoring his freq as soon as he leaves the chopper. That's your job. I'll stay with the fighters on the other radio in case one goes down. Boy, will they be surprised if one of 'em goes down and I'm sitting in a hover waiting for his parachute." Aggie grinned to himself thinking about it, then banked the helicopter to starboard as he approached the tree line. "Two minutes," he said. He could see the bend in the river coming up fast. Campbell had marked an area on the map he felt would have the best coverage and Aggie could see it up ahead. "Tell 'em to stand by."

Franks passed the order over the intercom and turned to look in the rear. The three marines were standing by the door, holding on to its sides. Sergeant Masterson had binoculars out and was sighting along the riverbanks. The men gripped the sides of the door as Aggie raised the nose sharply, making a quick stop to hover fifteen feet above the muddy waters below.

Larue took a quick breath and jumped, crossing his legs and holding his equipment tightly as he fell the short distance to the water. Jones and Masterson followed, landing a few yards upstream from Larue.

"They're out," the rear crewman called. He got back on

his door gun and cleared the chamber one more time. The swimmers below quickly disappeared from his sight as Aggie pushed the nose over and accelerated, continuing up the river for a short distance before turning to the east.

Captain Larue and his team watched the chopper for a moment then swam to the bank. Gunny searched the bluffs behind them for signs of people. In a moment they were in heavy reeds along the bank and listening for any sounds. Sergeant Masterson opened up the radio and made a quick, coded call.

"Blue Lightning."

Almost instantly he heard the word "Thunder" and repackaged the radio, sealing it in its waterproof container.

It was deathly quiet and only the sounds of river frogs could be heard as they started their mating rituals again. The sun was reaching for the horizon and the trees were casting long, dark shadows into the water. Concealed by the reeds, the three waited for complete darkness before beginning the slow drift downriver to reach the same area where Campbell had spent the night and discovered the camp and where they would hide until daylight.

That night as they drifted with the current, each man was alone with his thoughts and fears, wondering if Aggie had made it back to the carrier.

★ 22 ★

Dawn crept slowly over the North Vietnamese landscape, and dense fog hugged the river in patches, making the reeds growing along the riverbank appear as if they were sprouting from low-lying clouds. The sun peeking through the tops of the tree line would soon absorb the fog.

Captain Larue pressed against the ground blending in with the leafy brush growing in the stand of thick trees. He peered through high-powered binoculars at the two prisoners hoeing in the garden next to the farmhouse. The three marines had positioned themselves across from the farmhouse during the night, taking turns watching the camp. During the night a single guard walked the grounds, then at first light was replaced by two more who stepped outside and leaned against the building, smoking cigarettes. Not long after, two prisoners marched out in single file, carrying baskets and dressed just as Campbell described them. The prisoners were immediately put to work in the plot of garden behind the building.

Larue winced as he watched the guards prodding at their charges with rifle butts. It seemed strange to him that the POWs were pulling up half-grown plants by the roots and piling them into a basket. Larue handed the glasses to Sergeant Masterson, whispering, "Something doesn't seem right."

The sergeant looked through the glasses, focusing on the distant figures. "Maybe," he said. "They seem to be tearing up the whole garden. I see only two guards. No, wait, another is coming out the back door." Masterson studied the new guard intently, watching him pause for a moment and then go back inside. "Must be one of the honchos."

"Why do you say that?"

"Had a different type of uniform on. Some kind of rank on his collar that I couldn't make out, and a fancier belt buckle." He continued watching the guards through the glasses.

Directly behind them and a few feet down the hill, Corporal Jones was covering their rear, concealed in brush and watching the river area. His sniper rifle lay beside him, loaded and ready with a high-power scope and silencer mounted on the end. Jones lay low on the ground, wearing a headset and monitoring the discrete frequency they had earlier agreed on, hearing only static.

Larue slid silently down the bank and tapped Jones on the shoulder. "We can pick off the two guards easily," he said quietly. "But Jordan isn't in sight and it's too early. You keep watching our flank and let me know if you hear anything on the radio."

Jones nodded, and Larue eased back up alongside his sergeant. "Anything new?"

"Nothing." Masterson continued watching the guards.

"This may be our best chance to take out the guards," Larue whispered. "If they go back inside, we'll have to storm the building. That might give them a chance to kill the prisoners before we get to them." He paused for a moment, looking back at Jones. "What do you think, Gunny? Can Jones take them both out?"

"No question."

Larue twisted his body around. "I hear something." His eyes darted back and forth as he searched for the source of the sound. "It's a truck—up the road." The two slid farther down the bank as the two-and-one-half-ton truck drove past, its open flatbed empty. Larue looked at Masterson. "What do you think?"

"I don't know." Masterson inched up the hill and to the edge of the brush. He eased the binoculars back up and watched the truck as it pulled to a stop in front of the house and out of sight. He could hear two doors slamming shut and whispered to Larue, "There were two in the cab." He paused for a moment. "Could be they're coming to pick up the POWs and move them, or it could be just a change of the guards."

Larue thought for a moment, his face twisted slightly as he struggled to decide. "If the truck is here for the prisoners, we'll lose them if we wait." Silently he eased down the incline next to Jones. "Have you heard anything yet?"

"Nothing, sir."

"See if you can raise anybody." He waited while Jones called several times on their assigned frequency.

"Nothing yet, sir."

"It's too damned early. They haven't even launched." He paused, thinking hard while staring down at the river. "Jones, secure the radio—you're going to take out the two guards." The marine captain eased back up to the tree line next to Masterson.

Jones stuffed the radio inside the backpack and pulled some brush over it. He carefully removed his rifle from its case and eased up the slope, moving in next to Sergeant Masterson. Gunny handed him the binoculars and he quickly scanned the yard behind the house. Satisfied, he handed the glasses back to Masterson, then assumed his favorite prone shooting position. Slowly he eased the barrel up above the grass and sighted down on the guards, who were still standing in the garden. Jones swung the rifle to the right and sighted a POW still pulling up the half-grown vegetables. He adjusted a knob, bringing his face into focus as the cross hairs intersected on his cheekbone. Jones grimaced as he studied the man's gaunt and tired face. He swung the gun to the left and centered the cross hairs on the first guard standing by a tree, then to the other guard, who seemed to be watching the prisoners more closely and was holding his rifle braced in his arms. Jones made a small adjustment to compensate for the one-hundred-yard distance, then slowly pulled back the bolt, extracting a shell from the clip. He pushed the bolt forward, chambering the hollow-point, high-grain bullet. "Ready," he whispered.

Masterson glanced at Larue, who was looking through the binoculars.

He nodded to the sergeant. "Take them both."

Jones placed the cross hairs on the man's chest and took a slow breath, held it for a moment, then gently squeezed the trigger. The muffled sound was barely audible, and he chambered another round and sighted on the second guard, pulling the trigger again.

The prisoner nearest the first guard looked up, startled after hearing the deep thump made by the bullet striking the guard. He had a puzzled look on his face as he watched the guard gasping. He stared silently as the short Vietnamese raised both hands to his chest, dropping his rifle to the ground. The POW watched the guard fall, still clutching his chest, his eyes glazing over as he fell. The startled prisoner turned to the other guard standing near the tree. The guard was bringing up his rifle when there was the sound of another thump and he, too, fell to the ground, making gurgling noises. For a moment the POW stood there, staring at the dead guard lying facedown on the ground. Confused, he went back to picking vegetables. The other POW was looking in the direction of the river.

"They're down, let's go!" Captain Larue was already up and running, half crouching as he moved across the open ground toward the building. Ten yards behind him Sergeant Masterson was sprinting, his eyes darting back and forth as he ran. A few yards behind him, Corporal Jones followed, holding his M-16 rifle tightly across his chest. He left the .30-06 behind, and out of habit, he looked both left and right before crossing the road.

Larue reached the garden first and pulled the two stunned prisoners to the ground between the rows of vegetables. "Where are the rest?" he asked. He was appalled at the condition of the two POWs. "Lieutenant Jordan," he blurted out, "where is he?"

The second POW began grinning as he realized what was happening. "Inside."

"Inside where?"

"Near the front—in the Cuban's office—near the front door. Are you marines?" he asked. He seemed bewildered at the sudden appearance of American soldiers.

"Yeah, U.S. Marines here to get you out. Go with the corporal back there. That's Corporal Jones and he'll take care of you." Larue motioned to Masterson, pointing to the curtained windows along the side of the building. The career sergeant moved quickly to the rear door and waited, covering Larue as the marine captain sprinted across the yard to the door.

"Ready?" Larue asked, stepping away from the door. "Then let's do it." He watched the sergeant turn the doorknob slowly.

It was unlocked and suddenly Masterson shoved the door, pushing his rifle inside. He caught a glimpse of someone turning the corner at the end of the hall and then disappearing before he could fire. "We're spotted," he said. Gunny ran down the hall with Larue right behind him. Reaching the corner, he came to an abrupt stop and slowly stooped down. He looked around the corner cautiously, then instinctively opened fire when he spotted two men with rifles, killing one instantly. Bullets stitched into the wall as the second guard ran for his life, bolting through the front door. "One going out the front," Gunny called.

"I'll go after him and then come back in the front." Larue wheeled around and ran to the back door, bursting into the yard and pursuing the fleeing guard. Jones had fired at him and missed.

Masterson inched forward, pausing to check the area where the guard lay dead. The body lay in a pool of blood that was spreading across the floor and staining the worn carpet. Cautiously he crept forward again, easing toward the closed door near the front of the room. He grasped the doorknob and gently turned it. It was locked. Masterson backed away from the door then fired a quick burst into it, blowing the lock to pieces and blasting away large chunks of the wood. He paused for a moment, listening. Hearing nothing, he kicked the door open and stepped to the side as pistol shots echoed out from the room. Masterson backed away. He could see three bullet holes in the wall opposite the door. Taking a deep breath, he pointed his rifle inside and held down the trigger, then moved away from the doorframe and loaded another clip. Hearing a groan from inside, he timidly peeked in. Inside the room was a desk with parts of its top splintered. The chair had been overturned and he could hear moaning coming from behind it. Quickly he withdrew.

Larue entered through the front door, stepping over the dead guard and stopping beside his sergeant. "He got away. Got in his truck and took off like a bat from hell. What do you have here?" He was breathing hard from running after the truck and leaned against the wall beside Masterson.

"At least one with a handgun that's down. I heard him moaning."

The marine captain eased nearer the door, peeking inside. His stomach tightened and suddenly he felt sick. At one end of the room he could see a man hanging with his arms tied behind him and pulled together at the elbows. The man was trying to speak but an iron bar in his mouth allowed him only to grunt. Larue watched him violently shaking his head in the direction of the desk and he thought he could hear someone talking in a foreign language he didn't recognize. Someone had a pistol pressed to the head of the dangling figure. The marine captain slammed a fresh clip into his rifle. "I think it's Lieutenant Jordan tied up and hanging from a rafter. One of the guards is holding a pistol on him. I think you clipped one—he's behind the desk moaning."

Masterson thought for a minute. "Didn't have time to look around the room. You want the guard?"

"Yeah, I want him. You ready?"

"Ready!"

"Cover me."

Masterson crouched by the doorway as Larue leaped into the office and dove to the floor next to the desk. He trained his rifle on the guard holding a pistol to Jordan's head. He could hear someone speaking in Vietnamese on the other side of the desk. Masterson stood above him, pointing his rifle at the figure on the floor behind the desk. Larue raised to a standing position and crept toward Jordan, his gun aimed at the exposed body of the guard.

The gunnery sergeant eased toward the desk, pointing his gun at the man sitting on the floor and leaning against the wall. He was holding the bleeding stump of his left arm. The phone was cradled in his lap and fell to the floor as he looked up. Masterson fired a burst into the phone receiver. He grinned when he saw the man's severed hand lying on the floor still clutching the pistol that had fired at him.

Larue realized that Jordan's guard was not Vietnamese but white, and he was wearing a uniform the marine had never seen before. "Do you speak English?" he asked him, moving even closer, holding the rifle pointed toward the strange guard's body.

"I speak excellent English, and if you move any closer, I'm going to fire a round into the back of your friend's head." He had the pistol barrel pressed hard into the back of Jordan's head, forcing him to lean forward.

"Who are you—Russian?" Larue studied Vassilov as he continued to move closer slowly.

"That's quite close enough, my friend." Vassilov moved more to the side, using Jordan's body as a shield.

"We are taking the prisoner back, one way or the other. So the only decision is whether you want to live or not." Larue continued creeping closer to the Russian. "What's your situation, Sergeant?" he shouted at Masterson.

Gunny had kicked the pistol with the hand still gripping the handle out of the reach of the moaning figure on the floor and held his rifle pointed at his head. Blood was gushing from between his fingers as he clutched at the stump of his hand and looked up at Masterson. "This one is going to bleed to death soon."

"It's your move," Larue said to the Russian, now within three feet of him and with a clear shot at his head. His finger rested on the trigger as he looked into Vassilov's hard eyes.

Vassilov smiled. "One American pilot is not worth my life. Here, I give him to you. Take him and go. You will never get out of Vietnam anyway." The stocky Russian eased his gun down, then handed it to Larue, butt first.

The marine captain nodded his head and accepted the pistol while he continued pointing his rifle at him. "Now cut him down."

Vassilov dropped his smile and slowly pulled out a pocketknife, cutting the rope looped through a ring nailed to the wall. Jordan collapsed to the floor with a crash. The Russian squatted down and removed the ropes binding his hands behind his back and the metal bar in his mouth, then stood up.

Jordan lay on the floor feebly rubbing his arms. Unable to stand up by himself, he pulled up into a slumped sitting position, trying to get circulation back into his arms and legs. He looked up at Larue as if he were having a dream, then smiled for the first time in months. "Thank God," was all he could say for the moment.

"You okay, Larry?" Larue asked, squatting down next to Jordan, trying to help him get up while he watched the Russian. "Who are these bastards?"

Jordan's strength was returning and he looked up at Larue, then blurted the statement out in one gasping stream of words. "This one's a Russian advisor and the other one is a Cuban." Jordan rose up from the floor into a crouch. He tried but couldn't extend one of his arms. He hobbled over to the Cuban and stood at his feet, staring at the person who had caused him and others so much pain.

Larue looked down at the Cuban, pointing his rifle in the Cuban's face. "What is he doing here?"

"He's a special interrogator—named Gutierrez. He and the Russian only work with POWs that they think have some kind of special information. That's why we're kept separate from the rest of the POWs." Jordan paused for a moment. "Have you seen Patricia?"

"Yeah, I saw her and Karen. They're both fine. They're back in the States. Listen, we'll talk later. Right now, we got to get out of here."

Masterson looked at Larue. "What should we do with the Cuban? Bring him with us?"

Larue thought for a moment and then turned to the sergeant. "No, he'll probably bleed to death. But we are taking the Russian for insurance."

"You can't do that," Vassilov interrupted. "If you take me back as a prisoner, the consequences from my government will far outshadow anything you may think you are gaining. Think about it."

"I've thought about it. The only reason I don't shoot you now is that you are our ticket out of here. So make sure you stay in front of me at all times or I'm going to blow your ass back to Russia. Now move." Larue watched Vassilov shake his head, then move toward the door.

Masterson looked at the blood cascading from the Cuban's arm. "This one's fading."

Larue grabbed Jordan around the waist and together they slowly made their way down the hall and exited through the rear door, heading for the river with the Russian a few steps ahead of them.

Across the road, Corporal Jones guided the other two confused POWs toward the river, stopping to retrieve the radio and his special rifle. Not far behind, Larue and Masterson half carried the weakened Jordan as they made their way toward the cover of the trees with the Russian complaining the whole way.

"Any contact?" Larue asked as they caught up with Jones.

"No sir, but I'm picking up some chatter on their strike freq. They must be inbound."

Larue looked at his watch and then at the three POWs, who were swigging down some of the fruit juice the marines had brought with them. "They're not due over target for another forty minutes. That puts the helo at an hour and fifteen minutes at least before it gets here." He then looked up at Sergeant Masterson. "Gunny, we may have to hold off whoever shows up," he said, also noticing the two AK-47s Jones had dragged down the hill.

Masterson looked through his binoculars, canvassing the terrain around them. "Captain, we can't defend ourselves from here. I suggest we move downriver a piece and up on the other side. Most likely they'll come from the road side and it will kill some time while they try to find us. When they do, we'll have a good field of fire for them to wallow in."

Larue looked up at the bluff across the river. "Agreed, let's move out." He picked up a spare rifle and grabbed one of the POWs by the arm, leading him down to the water. After covering their tracks on the leaf-strewn beach, they floated an old log and pushed it into the water. Each marine held on to one of the POWs as they drifted downstream, wanting to put as much distance between themselves and the camp as possible. Since the Russian wasn't a great swimmer, he gripped the log as if his life depended on it.

High above the Vietnamese terrain and inbound to the target IP, Commander Lorimar was leading the last mission of the cruise against the bridge at Canh Tra. Pancho, Campbell, Swenson, and Commander Lorimar made up the rest of the final flight from the *Barbary Coast*. Lorimar planned to make one pass, dropping everything they had, and depart the target area forever, he hoped. The *Barbary*

Coast was due to leave Yankee Station at midnight, official-ly ending their six-month WestPac deployment.

Lorimar jinked hard as they approached the IP, not wanting his flight to be brought down by some teenage ground gunner. The morning was bright and clear and he could see the sun reflecting off the rice paddies, appearing as if it were following him. He looked at Pancho, flying loosely off to one side. He still found it hard to believe that the Mexican American had never taken even a single round in his aircraft. He considered him a good-luck charm to have on his wing. On the other side he could see Campbell's plane farther back, bobbing up and down with his new wingman following his every move.

"Okay, guys, green 'em up and assume the position. If I miss anything, Swenson, you knock out the rest." Lorimar reached down and flipped the armament switches up, obtaining several green lights. "IP coming up."

Campbell was busy switching back and forth on his UHF, attempting to make contact with the helicopter. Finally he heard Aggie calling him. "Where the hell have you been?" he shouted into the mike in his oxygen mask.

"Had a little problem, but it's okay now and I'm ten minutes from the beach. Heard from Larue?"

"Negative. We're pushing over now and will call later. Out." Campbell switched back to the flight frequency and rolled over on his back at the same time. Too many things were happening at once, he thought. He put everything else out of his mind and concentrated on the bridge span weav-ing through his gunsight, then began dodging the exploding flak that the F-8s said they'd knocked out the day before.

Nearing a bend in the river, Larue pointed to the high bluff overlooking the water. Masterson nodded in agreement and they steered the log toward the bank. It was steep but climbable with the aid of protruding roots, the tree line reaching nearly to the edge of the bluff in places. Approaching the bank, they stood up on the clay bottom and waded ashore. Jones pushed the log out into the current and it quickly drifted out of sight. As they struggled up the bank, Jones removed the radio from its waterproof case and extended the antenna. He could hear call signs in bits and pieces over his earphones.

"Sir, someone is trying to call us but I can't make it out. I've got to get up on top of the bluff."

"Get up there as fast as you can," Masterson said, then grabbed the other POW by the hand and pulled him up, struggling with the slippery roots. Jordan had regained some use of his arms and was climbing by himself.

Nearing the top, Jones cautiously peeked over the rim, looking through the sparse trees. It was quiet and there were no signs of anyone. He pulled himself over the edge and squatted down next to a big tree, quickly extending the antenna to its fullest. "Loosefoot, this is Flintstone, over." He waited, hearing only static and then a voice.

"Flintstone, this is Loosefoot, over," Aggie answered.

Jones responded, "I've got Thelma plus six."

Aggie thought for a moment and then said to his copilot, "I hope he means he has three extra POWs and didn't capture a couple of slopes for trophies."

"Loosefoot, this is Flintstone."

Aggie recognized Larue on the radio.

"We're at X-ray three point five slash Charlie seven point five. Possible load of hornets out of their nest, and oh, yeah, our smoke-playing friend says hello, over."

"Roger, Flintstone, be seeing you in forty."

"Don't be late, out." Larue handed the headset back to Jones and moved near Masterson to discuss their situation. Masterson had given Jordan and one of the other POWs the Russian-made rifles. The third POW was basically incoherent and would be of no use in a firefight, and Vassilov sat silently as Jones held a rifle pointed at him. "What do you think, Gunny?" Larue lay down on the edge of the bluff looking along the river with the binoculars.

Gunny moved close to Larue, lying down on the grassy edge alongside him. "If they find us, they'll probably come at us from three sides. I don't think they'll try the open fields behind us. We'll be firing down on them and across the river. We can hold them off for a while—at least until the helo gets here." He took the binoculars from Larue and eased back to the edge of the bluff, concentrating on the road leading to the farmhouse. Several minutes passed, then he spotted several trucks dropping troops off alongside the road, then moving down and dropping off more. He punched Larue in the side with his hand. "They're here and they're looking hard." He handed the glasses over to the marine captain.

Larue refocused the binoculars and watched the North Vietnamese troops scatter along the river, probing cautiously. He could see they were regulars and not the ragtag locally appointed militia. "I make out thirty, forty men that I can see. Probably more at the farmhouse and even more on the way." He watched two wading out into the river toward the log they had used to float downstream. It had grounded itself on a sandbar and a soldier was bending over examining the broken limbs. Suddenly he turned and ran up the bank to another soldier with a radio strapped to his back. "Oh, shit. They've found us!" Larue said as he watched the soldier with the radio holding the phone to his mouth, gesturing wildly with his arm. "Have Jones call Loosefoot and report 'Hornets out of their nest.'"

The two MiG-17s were fueled and armed, each with
a pair of Atoll air-to-air
missiles hung underneath the wing. Each plane was in top
running order, and an aging auxiliary power-starting unit
idled at low rpm, standing by for a quick boost to start the
aircraft, preparing it to be airborne within minutes if the
order came down. The jets were parked in separate revetments and rimmed with sandbags piled high above them.
Camouflage netting stretched across the top, concealing the
jets from above, although their existence was well-known to
the American fleet offshore. The field was constantly monitored
by Red Crown to the north and airborne surveillance aircraft
from above. Voice and radar transmissions or anything that
would indicate MiG activity were closely studied from all

available sources, and the airfield was constantly bombarded with radar waves for any indications of a pending launch.

"What is happening now?" The sergeant in the revetment in charge of maintenance asked, wiping a cloth over a wrench and watching the radioman.

The radioman was pressing his headset closer to his ears attempting to better hear the commentary from the operations building. "Wait!" he said, holding up his hand as he strained to hear every word, all of the linemen and mechanics gathered around him anxiously waiting. The young man pushed up one earpiece over an ear. "The Americans are attacking the bridge at Canh Tra again!" he exclaimed.

Across the field inside the small concrete-block building serving as an operations center, Quang and his young wingman stood next to a corporal wearing a headset. He was connected directly by landline to the communications command center outside Hanoi, and he was listening to a running commentary on the attack against the bridge and relaying to the men down on the line. Suddenly he jumped up cheering. "They have shot down one of the attackers and his parachute is drifting down." A grin broke out on his narrow face. "Soon they will have him." Excitedly he pulled the earpieces tighter to his ears, wanting to hear every word.

Quang began anxiously pacing back and forth. He was wearing his torso harness and G-suit as he always did whenever an attack was in progress. Major Quang would have preferred to be sitting in his aircraft waiting for the word to launch, but higher command had issued orders for all pilots to remain clear of their aircraft whenever enemy planes were nearby, which was nearly always. They were afraid the rules of engagement would be changed at any minute and the aircraft would come under attack on the field.

Quang's copilot moved over to the corner of the small

room alongside several other enlisted airmen listening to the running commentary and watched Quang pace back and forth. They had seen him repeat the same routine each time an attack was under way. As always, he nervously walked around the room for a while, then calmly sat in the corner on the floor, his legs crossed and his arms folded as he quietly waited for the word to launch.

The corporal's face suddenly turned ashen and he turned to the operations officer leaning against a desk.

Getting up, Quang asked, "Why have you stopped talking? Have all the aircraft been shot down?"

The corporal turned toward Quang. "Headquarters reports that the missile station near the bridge is silent and no longer reporting and that—"

"And they still do not want me to launch?" Quang interrupted, disgusted as he turned away and walked to the window. He stared at the two jets at the end of the field, gripping the windowsill tightly with his hands.

Suddenly the room went silent for a brief moment. Their radioman looked at the operations officer, then at Quang. "They have invaded us!"

"What? That is impossible." Quang wheeled around. "They would never do that." He was silent for a moment. "I must launch."

"Sir, you have been ordered to remain on the ground," the corporal said. "Troops from the army barracks are being dispatched to repel the invasion."

"Where?"

"I don't know, sir. Only pieces of information are coming over the lines. Everyone is talking at once." The airman pressed his headset tighter to his head in an effort to make sense of the garbled reports.

Suddenly the front door flew open and a young private wearing an army uniform burst in. The left shoulder of his fatigues was stained with blood and still damp. "The Americans have stormed the camp. They have invaded us!"

The senior officer ran to the private, catching him as he weakened and slumped to the floor.

"What are you saying?"

"The Americans have invaded the prisoner camp near the bridge!"

"We have no prison camp near the bridge. What are you talking about?" The officer turned to another clerk and ordered water for him, then let his head slump to the floor.

Major Quang moved to the soldier's side, bending down on one knee. "Did you say the prisoner camp near the bridge? The old French farmhouse that Captain Gutierrez is in charge of?"

"Yes, yes. That's it. The Americans have overrun the camp. They shot most of the guards and wounded me. I barely got away in time." A soldier had returned with a cup of water and the wounded man gagged on it when he tried to drink.

"I know the camp. I have been there," Quang said to the officer in charge.

The officer stared at Quang for a moment, then at the wounded soldier. He was still dazed at the thought of American troops on North Vietnamese soil. By the time he turned around, Quang and his wingman had slipped out the door and made a run for the truck the wounded soldier had driven up in. The radioman, trying to decipher the conflicting reports, never noticed Quang's departure.

The keys of the flatbed truck were still in the ignition. Quang cranked the engine, then sped off, heading for the two waiting MiGs off the end of the runway, leaving a trail of rising dust. His wingman held on to his helmet bag and the seat as the truck bounced them about as Quang cut across the field.

The trail of dust coming from the operations building

caught the attention of one of the linemen and he pointed toward the wildly bouncing truck. Approaching, Quang stood on the brakes, causing the truck to slide to a stop near the sandbags.

Quang jumped out of the truck, pushing the door so hard it bent the frame when it flew open. Running, he passed the first MiG and ran to the second, tossing his helmet to a startled plane captain and bouncing up the boarding ladder.

The plane captain seemed stunned and shouted at the major, but receiving no reply and assuming Quang was cleared for launch, he turned and ran for the starting unit and increased the rpm until enough amperage was available to crank the engine. He heard the start unit speed up again as Quang hit his start switch. Another lineman quickly ran up and took over the cart, and the plane captain ran back to the boarding ladder to assist the pilot as he prepared for launch. In the adjacent revetment Quang's wingman was preparing as well.

The linemen pulled the chocks as Quang and the junior pilot who had yet to taste combat hurriedly taxied out to the end of the runway. They quickly tested the controls, as each pilot rapidly ran through an abbreviated takeoff checklist. They pulled to a stop and the canopies closed, the second lieutenant giving a thumbs-up as the power came up on both aircraft.

Quang pushed the throttle forward and even with the slow acceleration, felt the forces pushing his body back into the seat. The full fuel load made the jet feel sluggish at first, and he glanced back to check on his wingman, who was right on his wing, his eyes bore-sighted on his leader. Out of the corner of his eye Quang spotted the truck crossing the rugged field, bouncing and raising an even higher trail of dust than he had. He continued his takeoff run.

The truck bounced up on the runway as the operations officer turned the wheel, attempting to head off the two aircraft. He was only a few meters from the accelerating MiGs before spinning the wheel to the right and skidding hard, turning the wheel back as the truck began to roll over. As he turned the wheel to the left and slammed on the brakes, the flatbed truck skidded near the exhaust of the jets, heated to a thousand degrees at the tailpipe tip. Luckily for the driver, the truck flipped over and rolled into a ditch, coming to a stop resting on its side, far enough from the planes' exhaust not to turn the truck into an inferno.

The operations officer slowly pulled himself out of the cab, his face cut and his shoulder badly bruised. The windows of the truck were cracked and the paint was scorched from the flash of heat from the jet blast. As he struggled to get up, the two MiGs lifted off the runway.

★ **24** ★

Lead's hit, pulling off target," Campbell heard Lorimar call before he lost sight of him. He could see Pancho diving on the bridge and then lost him in the heavy smoke. He continued downward, sneaking a quick glance at his rapidly unwinding altimeter. He heard Pancho call off target and a moment later, released his load of bombs and pulled back on the stick. The view in his gunsight was mostly smoke.

Not far behind him, Swenson made a last correction and squeezed the button on the control stick, releasing his load of bombs. He felt the aircraft become lighter and he pulled back on the stick, sending himself zooming upward and away from the flak-infested target. "Three four's off," he called, unable to see his bombs as they struck the center span, hitting dead-on. The bridge buckled but the span remain upright.

span, hitting dead-on. The bridge buckled but the span remain upright.

Campbell twisted around in the cockpit, looking over his shoulder for the lead A-4. He spotted an aircraft circling off in the distance and headed for it. "Blackbeard lead, this is two seven, over," he said, flying away from the bridge with Swenson joining him on the way.

"Soupy, this is Pancho. Listen, man, they got the skipper. He's down and I ain't talking to him."

Campbell thought for a moment, his eyes searching for signs of a burning aircraft on the ground. "Did you see a chute?"

"Yeah, a good one. I think he made it out okay."

Campbell spotted a rising column of smoke coming from the ground, then noticed Pancho circling several thousand feet lower as he searched for Lorimar.

"I'll call in the helo." Campbell switched channels on his UHF and raised Aggie on the radio. "Loosefoot, this is Blackbeard two seven, over."

Aggie responded immediately. "This is Loosefoot. I've been monitoring you and I'm on the way. Give me a tone." Aggie reached down and selected the UHF homer, then watched the needle swing. "Got it. Listen, Soup"—Aggie paused for a moment—"Flintstone just called and the 'hornets are out of their nest.' They're a couple of miles downstream. Can you help?"

"Yeah, I can help. Contact Pancho and work with him. If you need us, we'll be at the hornets' nest. Come as quick as you can." Campbell signaled to Swenson and they veered away toward the river, leaving Pancho and Aggie to get Lorimar out. He switched over to Larue's frequency and called, "You up, Flintstone?"

"Yeah, I'm up. Where have you guys been? We've got some very unhappy troops trying to cross the river and some more working their way up our flanks. I'll light a smoke marker and you make a run about two hundred meters on either side.''

"Roger," Campbell said, switching back to Swenson. He had him change frequencies. ''Ringer, get on my wing. When you see the smoke marker, set up a pass about one hundred fifty meters to the right. I'll take the left. NVA are crossing the river. Do not, I repeat, do not fire on top of the smoke.'' Campbell waited for Swenson's acknowledgment. He had not told the junior pilot of their clandestine mission, only that they might have alternate targets. Campbell selected guns on his armament panel and set up for a strafing run. In the distance he spotted a smoke marker and eased the nose to the left and entered into a shallow dive. Approaching the river, Campbell squeezed the gun button, letting loose a fusillade of 20-millimeter shells that stitched across the ground.

Below, Larue watched the two A-4s scream past on both sides, sending up clouds of dust as the 20-millimeter shells tore through some troops hugging the ground. Vassilov was rolled up into a ball with his head buried beneath his arms.

"Nice pass," Larue called on the radio. "That should hold off their advance for a while." He flinched and hugged the ground as a bullet struck near them. "Try a run parallel to the river on the other side," he added.

"Will do," Campbell responded. "Swenson, let's make a pass from the south and then swing around and come back from the north." Campbell banked the A-4 sharply and set up for another run.

Several miles from the bridge Aggie had spotted a chute lying in a rice paddy. The chute was stained and crumpled up into a pile, half submerged in the muddy water. A short distance away Aggie saw Lorimar running as fast as he could, sending up big splashes of water as he charged through the paddy. Aggie watched him trip once and fall headfirst into the shallow water, then jump up just as quickly. Aggie air-taxied the helo toward Lorimar and stopped, holding the bottom of the helicopter just above the water. Lorimar seemed to be running around the helicopter and Aggie had to move forward to line him up with the cargo hatch. As soon as he was within reach, the rear gunner grabbed Lorimar by the seat of the pants and pulled him inside in one motion. Aggie heard the crewman yell over the intercom and he pulled up on the collective and eased the cyclic forward at the same time, accelerating away from the paddy.

Directly above them, Pancho said a small prayer of thanks and pushed the throttle forward, but then did a double take as he scanned his instruments and spotted the fuel gauge indicating almost empty. He would have to find a tanker fast or punch out over the gulf. He called Aggie, then quickly headed east, leaving the slower-flying helo behind.

Aggie switched back to their discrete frequency, advising Campbell that he had Lorimar aboard and would be there in ten minutes. He pushed the helo as fast as it would go and concentrated on flying around the villages in their flight path. "What's that damn smell?" Aggie asked, looking at his copilot, then at Commander Lorimar, who was standing between them behind the center console, dripping wet and patting Aggie on the shoulder, happy to be alive. When he realized Lorimar was soaked with water from the rice paddy and smelled like an outhouse, Aggie grinned and pushed on the left rudder pedal, side-slipping the helicopter to allow more air into the cockpit.

"What's your posit?" he heard Campbell calling him.

"Five out. I got your old man aboard," he answered.

"Does he know?"

"Negative. He thinks we're heading for home base. He seems okay but he got some burns to his face and can't see so good." Aggie could see the two A-4s making passes over the river. "Got you in sight now. Tell Flintstone to get ready."

"You don't have to tell me, I'm ready," Larue interrupted. "We're at the smoke and taking fire." Larue tossed the headset to Jones and rolled over, firing at the troops trying to work their way across the river. Several bodies lay at the water's edge where they were cut down, while Jones picked off anybody who stuck his head out from behind a tree, forcing the troops to cross under cover well above and below them.

Vassilov looked up when he heard the sound of the helicopter. Since Jones had taken his eyes off the Russian for a moment and was looking at the helicopter, Vassilov seized the opportunity and jumped up and ran for the edge, leaping over the edge and stumbling down the root-infested bank, screaming a mixture of Russian and Vietnamese toward the troops across the water.

Jones wheeled around and crawled to the edge and took aim at the Russian struggling toward the river, but Larue put his hand on Jones's rifle and shook his head.

"We don't need him now, let him go," Larue said as he watched Vassilov stumble into the shallow water and pick himself up, running along the side and screaming at the troops. But before he had traveled ten yards, a North Vietnamese bullet entered Vassilov's left shoulder, knocking him down. Larue watched him get up again, then another bullet hit him and he fell facedown in the water.

"Serves the bastard right. Let's get the hell out of here." Masterson grabbed one of the POWs and moved toward the approaching helicopter.

Aggie ignored the wind direction and headed directly for the smoke marker, raising the nose of the helo up sharply as he made a quick stop over the bluff. He quickly set the Sikorsky down on the ground away from the edge.

Larue and Jones grabbed the other two POWs and ran to

the cargo door, pushing them inside. They threw their equipment in and leaped aboard, shouting at the rear-door gunner to take off.

Aggie pulled up on the collective and rocked over on his nose as he transitioned to forward flight. The helicopter slowly accelerated as Aggie pulled maximum torque on the transmission. The North Vietnamese stood up and opened fire, pouring everything they had at the fleeing helo. Small holes began appearing in the skin of the helicopter and the third-class sonarman opened up with his door gun. Larue and his two marines poured fire from the cargo hatch. Lorimar just sat there, partially blind and stunned. He had no idea what was going on.

"Ouch!" Franks called out after a bullet passed through the Plexiglas side window nicking him slightly in the hand. He pushed himself farther back into the protective armor-plated seat.

"You all right?" Aggie asked, busy trying to get them out as holes appeared all over the helicopter. "We're taking hits, Soupy. Can you hose those guys down one more time?" he asked over the UHF.

"You bet," he heard Campbell call.

"Better back off a little, you're overtorquing," Franks said as he monitored the gauges while Aggie flew. He was afraid his pilot would pull the guts out of the main transmission.

"Anybody hit?" Aggie asked.

Franks twisted and looked into the rear, getting a thumbs-up from Larue. "Nobody yet," he answered, turning around again. His eyes stopped on the warning light on the caution panel as it blinked on and off. He scanned the instrument panel. "Number two's going." He pushed the power lever of the other engine up.

He didn't have to tell Aggie that he was losing an engine. Aggie could see the torque gauge jump on the remaining engine and needles splitting as he lowered the collective and slowed the helicopter.

"I smell smoke," the rear crewman called out over the ICS, then pulled a fire bottle from its mount and searched for the source.

"Pull the fire bottle on number two and secure it," Aggie ordered his copilot. After the fuel was shut off to the engine, the smell of smoke ceased.

Commander Lorimar sat erect in the troop seat, gripping the sides with both hands. He seemed stunned and makeshift bandages covered his eyes. He was still shaken up by the sudden ejection and unsure of what was happening.

"Soupy, we've lost an engine," Aggie called.

"Can you make it?" Campbell asked as the two A-4s crisscrossed above the stricken helicopter monitoring its progress. "Long as I keep moving, we're all right. Just don't ask me to go into a hover."

"Well, I guess it's time to spill the beans," Campbell said with mixed emotions about the call he knew he now had to make. When he announced they were accompanying a helicopter inbound with three live POWs aboard, all hell was going to break loose.

"Yeah, I guess it is," Aggie responded. "Enjoy your last flight in a military aircraft."

"Right," Campbell said, then switched over to Red Crown and paused, still trying to decide what he was going to say. He swallowed hard and pressed the mike button. "Red Crown, this is Blackbeard two seven, over."

The chief petty officer immediately came on line. "Blackbeard, I've been trying to contact you. I picked up MiGs departing the airbase above you. They've disappeared from the scope. MiG Cap has been advised, over."

Great, Campbell thought. He looked to the north and then down at the helo well below him. He froze when he spotted two MiGs heading straight for the slow-flying helo. He flipped back to their tactical frequency and shouted into his mask. "Aggie! MiGs your nine. Get on the deck!" Campbell rolled on his back and pulled hard, hoping to distract the North Vietnamese jets from their attack. The pull-up would be very close to the ground.

But the lead MiG lined up the slow-flying helicopter and held it in the concentric rings of his gunsight, rolling, then stopping upright and opening fire.

Campbell heard Aggie call out, then silence.

25

Pieces of shattered Plexiglas flew into the cockpit, covering Ensign Franks with shiny slivers. He could only stare at what was left of the instrument panel. The first tracers had slammed into the front of the helicopter, destroying most of the Plexiglas windscreen and covering the two pilots with fragments and blowing pieces into the rear. Ensign Franks wedged himself farther into the armor-plated seat as Aggie bottomed the collective, sending the helicopter into autorotation and a steep descent. The sudden change in the flight path threw off the aim of the attacking MiGs and the tracers disappeared overhead.

Aggie's sonar operator had manned the door gun behind Franks like an accomplished belly gunner on a B-17. Throughout the short attack run, he had squeezed the trigger so hard his finger was now bleeding, having fired an entire belt of 7.62-millimeter shells at the jets, aiming the tracer rounds well in front and hoping one of the jets would fly through his point of fire. He continued squeezing the trigger long after the ammo belt emptied and the jets had disappeared overhead.

Aggie pulled up on the collective as he approached the ground and started a hard skidding turn to the right. He knew he was lucky on their first pass, but the outcome of the second was going to be a foregone conclusion unless Campbell could get them off him. Now he was flying the helicopter by instinct, paying scant attention to the damaged instrument panel.

"How bad?" Campbell asked, his voice straining from the force of gravity on his body as he rolled into a vertical pull-up. He looked over his shoulder and spotted a single MiG pulling into a vertical along with him.

"We lost most of the front of the helo, but we're still flying," Aggie told him, surprised the radio still worked. "If you can get 'em to go play someplace else, we'd appreciate it." Aggie shook his head as he stared at where the windscreen had been. The overhead throttle quadrant was intact but most of the instruments were destroyed. Wires hung down like limp spaghetti and most of the circuit breakers had tripped. The torque indicator still worked, but the airspeed and altitude indicators were hopeless pieces of junk. He was lucky the shells were not a few inches lower or his knees would be gone. His years of flying and training were being put to the test as he nursed the bullet-riddled helo eastward.

Less than a mile from the helicopter, the MiG pilot continued his vertical climb and concentrated on his adversary. Major Quang watched the two A-4s climbing several thousand meters from him, then twisted his head from side to side looking for his wingman, whose MiG had vanished during the pass on the helicopter. Quang called several times but could hear only the controllers desperately trying to contact him, ordering him to return to base. He turned the volume down again, leaving only the steady hum of his armed Atoll missile whispering in his ear. The major continued to watch the A-4s, waiting for them to make a mistake.

"You still with me, Swede?" Campbell asked, easing his nose down as the energy bled off from his zoom climb.

"Right behind you, boss," Swenson answered.

"Okay, great, all we have to do is keep this guy off Aggie until the fighters get here."

"Roger," Swenson acknowledged, dropping back behind his section lead, ready to turn on the MiG if it rolled in again.

Campbell watched the solo MiG pilot roll inverted and head for the deck. "He's going after Aggie again. Let's bust him up." Campbell waited until the MiG was passing in front of him and rolled inverted, following him down with Swenson right behind.

But instead of continuing after the helicopter, the MiG pulled into a vertical again, rolling over the top and coming back on the two A-4s.

"You see him?" Campbell asked. He swiveled his head back and forth looking for the jet.

"No, I lost him when he pulled up over us and . . . oh, shit!" Swenson watched Campbell's right wing get shot up as the enemy tracers hammered into it. He pulled hard, hoping to get behind the MiG-17. The tracers only danced around him, easing closer, then out again.

"I'm hit!" Campbell called. "The MiG's behind us!" Campbell rolled to the right, looking over his shoulder at the same time. His neck felt as if it were being compressed into a pretzel as he searched for the MiG. Tracers streaked by his right wing and he quickly reversed, pulling the tiny Skyhawk into a hard turn to port. Feeling the aircraft buffeting as it went in and out of high-speed stall, he eased up on the stick. Tracers were flying off to the side, close but missing. Then Campbell twisted his head to the right, and his mouth dropped open. The MiG-17 was flying close formation just off his wing. He remembered the several rows of crosses painted on the side of the MiG just below the canopy and watched the North Vietnamese pilot raise the darkened visor of his helmet with one hand, smiling at him.

"Motherfucker!" Campbell shouted, rolling into the MiG, forcing Quang into an evasive maneuver to avoid a midair. He pulled the A-4 into a climbing right turn, straining his neck to keep the MiG in sight. Swenson, in the meantime, had separated from him and was maneuvering to gain an advantage on Quang's plane, while Campbell pulled up and back to come around on the MiG once more.

But Campbell's Skyhawk was slowing, the airspeed bleeding off rapidly. Campbell rammed his hand against the throttle. It was stuck. He hit it with all his force, succeeding only in bending it. He tried pulling it back but it was wedged and not budging. Now the power was stuck at a low rpm and he was losing airspeed, while below him he could see Swenson and the MiG flying away from him. He lowered the nose of the A-4, regaining some of the lost airspeed, and as the two aircraft passed in front of him, the Sidewinder tone came alive in his headset, startling him, as the memory of Quang's MiG pursuing Jordan reappeared in his mind. Without further thought, Campbell launched the missile. "*Hellfire—hellfire—hellfire—Fox two.*"

Quang's first sensation of being hit came with a deafening sound and his head was knocked into the headrest with the control stick vibrating in his hand. The caution panel began lighting up and a red fire light blinked on and off at the top of his instrument panel. With little control of his aircraft, Quang unloaded from the turn and pointed the MiG away from the departing A-4. He tried to cope with the controls, but they seemed to have a mind of their own, becoming more sluggish by the moment. Campbell's heat-seeking missile had blown off most of his tail section, leaving barely enough airfoil to keep the aircraft controllable. Quang pointed the aircraft to the west. But that wasn't good enough. A long plume of smoke poured from the rear of the fuselage—and then the MiG exploded. The Gray Ghost was gone.

"Soupy, you still with me?" the junior pilot asked, shaking. He pushed the throttle up again and listened to the pitch of the engine increase. For the first time he had an opportunity to scan his instruments. The fuel gauge had settled to an alarmingly low reading and he tapped on it several times, hoping it was only stuck.

Several thousand feet below, Campbell hammered at the throttle, succeeding only in bending it further. It was jammed and there was nothing he could do, the engine rpm pulsing just above idle, his airspeed deteriorating rapidly. He eased the nose down as he approached the maximum-range mark on the angle-of-attack indexer and trimmed the A-4 for the descent.

"Yeah, I'm still with you. Did it work?" Campbell asked.

"You bet it worked. Your Sidewinder did him in."

"That one was for Larry."

Major Bhi felt a sudden throbbing in his crippled arm again, and he gripped the edge of the radar screen tightly with his good hand. He stood rigid, solemnly staring down at the remaining blips on the screen. The room was quiet except for the sounds of his controllers desperately trying to raise Quang on the radio. The Russian advisor, who had been standing off to the side, silently shook his head as he looked at the North Vietnamese officer. Without saying anything, he turned and left the room. Bhi stared at the radar repeater for a moment then slipped off his headset and lay it on the console. Without looking up, he turned and walked to his desk, sat down and lit up a cigarette, taking a long drag. He exhaled a lungful of smoke out in front of him, then for a moment watched it refract the light from the radar repeater. Suddenly he stood up and slammed his fist down hard, causing some of the controllers to turn and look at him, then at each other, before returning to their duties. Without saying anything, he walked outside the bunker into the hot sun beating down on the fake buildings. Their best pilot was dead and there was nothing more he could do.

Aggie's helicopter was several miles off the beach and heading for the *Barbary Coast*. Aggie had contacted Red Crown and requested an additional helicopter. He had been advised that the SAR teams in the area had been alerted but the nearest helicopter was still forty minutes away and that two F-4s from Da Nang were inbound.

Aggie pressed his mike button. "Soupy, this is Aggie. I'm out over the water."

Campbell watched his altimeter slowly unwinding as he continued eastward. "Aggie, I've got a stuck engine and Swenson is running out of fuel. He can probably make the water, but I'm doubtful." Campbell could see the white breakers of the beach dead ahead as he flew nearer to the ground. He tightened his shoulder straps as tight as he could and began going through his ejection checklist. "Can you pick us up?"

Anson turned the helicopter around and headed back for the beach. "Yes and no," Aggie said. "I've only got one engine working and won't be able to hover with all this weight. The beach sand is probably too soft to make a rolling takeoff." He thought for a moment as he eased the helicopter closer to the water. "The best I can do is a slow flyby. If you can grab the sling as it comes near you, I think we can bring you aboard. It's that—or wait about forty minutes for the other helo."

It wasn't what Campbell hoped to hear and he turned his attention to his wingman. "How are you doing, Swede?" He could see his wingman ahead and above him as his stricken aircraft flew closer to the ground.

"She just flamed out on me," Swede said, sweating while he watched the breakers passing beneath him as the engine spun down. He could see the helicopter ahead, giving him a measure of relief as he trimmed the aircraft for a steady descent. He finished going through his emergency checklist and turned slightly to keep the helicopter in sight. "Aggie, this is Swede, do you have me in sight, over?"

"I've got you, but I can't hover to pick you up. We can try a slow flyby and it might work. In any case, get as far away from land as you can." Aggie turned the helo around as he watched the Swede pass overhead, flying lower and lower, then watched the canopy come off and then the seat firing upward. He could see the drogue chute firing out of the ejection seat, pulling the main chute out, and then Swede gently drifted downward as the chute opened.

Campbell lost sight of his wingman's aircraft and concentrated on preparing for his own ejection as he neared the ground. He could see the breakers in the surf about a mile in front of him and realized his stricken aircraft would make the beach but no farther. He had one hand on the face curtain ring and the other on the stick as he squeezed out everything he could from his aircraft. Out of the corner of his eye he saw a small village flash by beneath his wing. "Aggie, I'm passing by a village on the beach, but—I can't make the water." He pulled the nose of the A-4 up, momentarily slowing his descent but rapidly bleeding off airspeed. He pulled the face curtain.

Several miles offshore, Aggie dropped the helicopter down to within a rotor width of the sea's surface, obtaining the translational lift that required less power to keep the helo airborne. He slowed as much as he dared with the single engine running at full-rated military power, but it was a struggle just to remain airborne at the slower speed. Aggie could see Swenson floating in his flotation device. As they flew by, the rear crewman kicked out a smoke marker and Aggie twisted around in his seat to see the direction of the smoke. Guessing the wind direction, he turned downwind and passed abeam of Swenson, who was bobbing in the water and waving with both hands. Aggie continued downwind for several hundred yards, then rolled into a turn and pointed the helicopter into the wind. His rear crewmen were busy preparing to take Swenson aboard, and they quickly attached the horse collar to the rescue ring.

"Hoist going down, Mr. Anson," the rear crewman said, watching it dropping away as he let out cable from the hoist. Aggie was using all his skills as he slowed the helicopter as much as he could. Ensign Franks monitored the torque gauge closely, calling off the numbers as they approached Swenson. In the rear, the hoist operator was leaning out in his harness playing out cable, while Larue sat by the door ready to give him a hand.

"Torque's coming up," Franks announced. He could feel the helicopter vibrating as it approached the edge of the envelope. Anson was reaching the point where it would require more power than he had available to him to go any slower. "We're too heavy, I'm going around." He eased the nose forward and picked up enough speed to stop the vibrations, then climbed up to a hundred feet above the water with the horse collar dragging behind them.

"Throw everything overboard that's not tied down. And

anything that you can break loose," he added. "We've got to get lighter." He began a gentle orbit around Swenson.

Franks turned around and shouted to one of the crewmen standing behind him. "Start throwing everything overboard—fire bottles, guns, ammo, the sonar if you can break it loose—everything." He watched the sailor go over to Larue and shout into his ear, then unmount the rear-door gun and throw it overboard. They threw out all the marines' ammo, radios, and backpacks, sending them flying out the cargo door. He could see Corporal Jones let out a sigh when Larue pitched his sniper rifle and case overboard. In less than five minutes time they had the large sonar receiver out of its mounts and were tossing it out. Aggie vetoed cutting the sonar transducer loose, deciding it would not deteriorate in the salt water and could possibly be recovered by the Vietnamese in the shallow water. Instead, they tore up the motor and threw it out. Aggie could feel the helicopter becoming lighter and he set up for another pass.

Swenson decided against inflating his raft. He could barely see people on the beach and decided to keep as low a profile as possible. As the helicopter approached, he held one hand aloft, hoping to grab on to the sling. The horse collar was dragging behind the helicopter and Aggie flew even lower, kicking up a mist of salt spray into the air. Swenson could see Larue leaning out of the open cargo hatch as the helicopter flew nearer to him, then watched it veer away with the sling just out of reach.

"We can't hover so I'm going to fly a circle around him and drag the cable," Aggie said, then banked the helo to the right and circled the figure bobbing in the water.

Swenson drifted in the gentle swells and watched the helicopter drag the cable just out of reach. Behind him he could see the floating rescue sling dragging through the water. He lunged for the cable.

"He's near the cable, Mr. Anson. The collar is coming

up to him real slow. You're looking good, sir, just keep the turn in.'' The crewman was looking nearly straight down at the water from the steep angle of bank. He watched Swenson pulling the cable in, bringing the collar toward him and then grabbing it. "He's got it! He's got it!" he called excitedly.

"Okay, see if you can pull him up with the hoist motor," Aggie said, continuing flying the tight turn, pulling maximum torque to keep the helicopter from descending.

The sonar technician pushed a rocker switch on a panel near the opened hatch, engaging the hydraulic motor. The cable started reeling in, then bogged down as Swenson held on. "He's dragging through the water. We've got too much forward motion."

Aggie strained his neck looking back at Swenson, making a small wake as they pulled him through the water. "This isn't going to work," he said. "Okay, let out some more cable. I'm going to fly as tight a circle as I can and then start climbing when the cable tenses. If we're lucky, you can pull him up then."

Beneath the helicopter, Swenson clutched the horse collar that surrounded his upper body. He could not understand why they had been unable to pull him up, and he was coughing from the seawater he was swallowing. The kerosene fumes from the helicopter were also making him ill. Suddenly the spray subsided. He could see the helicopter overhead making a tight circle and attempting to climb. Swenson felt himself moving slowly through the water, then a sensation of being lifted up. For a moment he skipped across the surface, then swung in wide arcs from the cable that stretched out its full length. He looked up at the chopper overhead. Underneath was a big painted sign saying REMOVE CHUTE, and he could see Larue leaning out of the cargo door. The helicopter straightened out and began a climb with the huge attack pilot swinging like a pendulum underneath. Above him hands were hauling in the cable.

"He's coming up, Mr. Anson. Hold her straight and level for a while."

Aggie looked out the side window, catching a glimpse of Swenson as he swung out in front of the nose in a large arc over a hundred feet below. "I bet he never forgets this ride," he said to Franks. He was all grins again. He had been listening to the automatic beeper for a few minutes and knew that Campbell had ejected. He selected his UHF homer and watched the needle swing toward the beach.

Puffs of white dust kicked into the air as bullets impacted into the sand close to Campbell's feet. He was running as fast as he could, leaping from side to side to throw off his pursuers' aim. He was desperately trying to reach a series of small sand dunes less than fifty yards ahead of him, and he could hear the sounds of rifle fire two hundred yards behind as several dozen men from the nearby village pursued him, shouting and firing as they ran. Reaching a mound of sand, he leaped over the top and wheeled around, then fired off a few rounds from his service .38. Each time he stopped and fired, the village home guard would dive for cover, waiting to see what he would do.

Cautiously he peered over the top. A single soldier ran forward firing. Campbell squeezed off a round and the soldier dove for the ground. Campbell felt inside his pockets for the few remaining rounds. He ducked behind the mound again and pulled out the small portable radio from his vest and hit the PRESS TO TALK button. "Aggie, where are you?"

Anson's heart quickened when he heard his friend's voice. "Thought they had you for a while. Listen, I've got Swede aboard and I'm about two miles off the beach inbound to your beeper, over." Aggie pushed the nose of the helo over, picking up as much speed as he dared.

"Great. I've got troops north of me on the beach trying to run me down. They appear to be some kind of home guard or something, not very disciplined but persistent. Can you work them over and pick me up?" He peered over the dune, firing another shot as some of the troops began moving again.

"Listen, Soupy, the F-4s are supposed to be inbound but I haven't heard from anybody. We had to throw all our firepower overboard." Aggie was close enough to see some of the troops lying down in the sand. "We can't hover. All we can do is make a low-speed flyby. Your only chance is to grab something when we go by. If you want to try, Soup, you are going to have to run like you've never run before."

Campbell paused for a moment watching the troops cautiously moving closer. "Guess I don't have much choice." He was about to get up and start running again but paused when he heard another voice on the emergency radio.

"This is Peregrine seven two with a flight of two. Helo in sight and numerous troops on the ground. Best I can do is light off a Sidewinder and spook 'em." The leader of the F-4 flight armed one of his two missiles and prepared to fire. He hoped the troops on the ground didn't know the missile would probably do them no harm.

Just great, Campbell thought to himself, fighters with homing missiles and no guns. He was watching the two Phantoms coming in at almost wavetop height in burner when he felt something prod him in the back, pushing him down into the sand. Slowly he twisted his head around and saw a lone North Vietnamese soldier. He was about five feet two inches tall and wore a faded-green uniform and no shoes. He had a bandolier of rifle ammunition slung across his chest and was smiling at Campbell.

Campbell slowly rolled over on his back and raised his arms in the air, still holding the pistol in his hand. He watched the soldier intensely, listening to his strange but meaningless words.

The village soldier watched Campbell for a moment, then

indicated for him to stand up. Pointing the tip of his AK-47 rifle right at Campbell's stomach, he held his finger on the trigger. After Campbell was standing, he pointed to his gun, motioning for him to give it to him. Cautiously, Campbell stretched the gun out to him, handle first, and watched the guard slowly take it, breaking into an even bigger grin. For a moment they both just stood there.

The soldier pointed the pistol at Campbell's chest, letting his rifle drop to his side. The soldier's eyes widened as he pulled the trigger. Hearing only a click, he pulled it again and then again.

At the first snap of the trigger, Campbell's heart jumped into his throat. He could not remember how many shots he had fired with the .38, but at the second snap of the trigger, he reached inside his survival vest and withdrew the .22-caliber pistol he carried, pointing the barrel at the soldier's face and pulling the trigger again and again. The stunned look on the soldier's face lasted for a moment before he fell to the ground. Campbell turned and ran, heading away as fast as he could and holding the radio to his mouth.

"Get me out now!" Campbell said, his broken voice coming through Aggie's earphones.

Aggie saw a solitary figure running down the beach with troops in pursuit.

"Listen up, Soupy, I'm rolling in from behind you. Get on the port side of the helicopter and grab anything you can. The boarding ladder will be down on the port side." He wasn't sure if Campbell heard him or not. Already the boarding steps were down and Larue and the marine corporal were hanging out the entrance hoping to snap him with the horse collar they had taken from the hoist. Swenson was holding on to them both.

The Vietnamese troops were running and shooting, slowly gaining on Campbell. Aggie rolled in on top of them, lowering the gear as he attempted to run some of them down. A few fired at the helicopter as he flew between them, while others were crushed as they fell beneath the main gear. Campbell was less than a hundred yards ahead and Aggie was closing on him. The helo pilot lightly touched his main gear to the sand, kicking up clouds and letting it slow him. He lined the helicopter up on Campbell until the pilot was running to the left side. Aggie could see him looking over his shoulder as the helicopter got nearer to him.

"If you get any slower, we'll never get out of here," Franks called to him.

"We'll get out," Aggie said, coaxing every bit of power from the engine he could. Aggie watched Campbell coming up on the left side, then turn and dive for the hatch. He could no longer see him and gently pulled up on the collective, afraid to look.

In the doorframe, Larue was hanging on to Campbell's hand with all the strength he could muster as Jones hung on to him. Swenson reached down and grabbed Campbell's free hand and together they hauled him aboard.

"We got him!" Franks shouted.

Aggie glanced over his shoulder, sneaking a peak at the figure being hauled into the helicopter. Smiling to himself, he milked the controls until the speed was up again. Turning seaward, he handed the controls over to Ensign Franks. It was the first time he had relinquished control since their takeoff nearly two hours before. In spite of the air rushing in through the missing windscreen, Aggie was drenched with sweat and suddenly very thirsty. He twisted around in his seat and looked at the three men lying on the floor. They were just holding on to each other and not moving. Campbell was panting from running and trying to catch his breath. When he saw Aggie looking at him, Campbell broke out into a big grin and grabbed his hand.

Aggie shook his hand vigorously then pointed to the rear

of the helicopter. Reaching behind his seat, the helicopter pilot withdrew a bottle of champagne he kept on board for special occasions. He uncapped the cork and watched it bounce around the cockpit. Pink liquid spewed from the bottle, streaming over the three on the floor. He handed the bottle to Swenson and watched him take a long swig, letting some of the liquid run down his chin.

Jordan had been sitting in the rear of the helicopter the whole time, stunned by what was happening. He crawled forward and sat beside Campbell, taking the bottle offered to him. "What took you so long, Soupy?" Jordan said, grinning, before taking a long swig from the bottle. Then the two friends embraced and tears filled both their eyes.

Ensign Franks nudged Aggie when he spotted the second helicopter ahead. They watched as the Sikorsky SH-3A joined up on their starboard side, flying formation with them as they returned to the carrier.

★ 26 ★

Rumors were running rampant, rapidly spreading throughout the ship as word got out that something big had happened. It had been less than an hour since Pancho returned to the carrier after refueling with an airborne tanker. His was the only one of four A-4s to return from the last mission of the *Barbary Coast,* adding further grist to the rumor mill. The Skyhawk had immediately been stuck below and towed to the back of the hangar bay and Pancho escorted to flag quarters for debriefing.

Only Cecil Washington had had a chance to talk briefly with Pancho as he had helped him out of the A-4. What little information he had gained he shared with his plane captain buddies, and now rumors ranged from one end of the carrier to the other. Some believed all three pilots had been captured and were now POWs. Another rumor was that someone had overheard a transmission between the helicopter pilot and a marine and that some kind of POW rescue operation was under way. The rumors spread quickly until everyone believed a rescue operation was going on in downtown Hanoi. Finally the public affairs officer was forced to announce that three pilots were down and rescue operations were under way with a second helicopter launched to assist in the recovery.

With nothing to do but wait, Washington slouched in the well-worn seat of the engine-starting unit. It was parked behind the island on the flight deck and his feet were propped up on the steering wheel with his hands clasped behind his head. The plane captain was thinking about what he had gleaned from Pancho while helping him unstrap in the cockpit. What he had heard had not sounded good to him. The cruise was coming to an end and he wondered if the aircraft he had so carefully nurtured were now a pile of charred junk on North Vietnamese soil and Lieutenant Campbell or even Ensign Swenson and the skipper were POWs like Lieutenant Jordan. Now he just watched the crowd that was gathering on the flight deck, milling around and speculating on the fates of the pilots. He closed his eyes and said a prayer.

Admiral Laceur sat in his command chair looking down on the crowd gathering on the flight deck, watching the throngs of sailors milling as they waited to greet the returning POWs they heard were coming aboard. The officers and men were talking and joking among themselves, a sea of multicolored uniforms thickening by the minute. Some had come all the way up from work spaces deep within the ship to see for themselves the results of the war that they had only heard others talk about.

The admiral's chief of staff stepped up to the admiral and

leaned over his chair. "Ten minutes out," he said. Laceur nodded and Briggs returned to his discussion with the flag lieutenant.

Laceur studied his watch for a moment, then raised his binoculars and aimed them to the west. The admiral twisted the adjustment back and forth, trying to spot the returning helicopters, but saw only empty sea. He put the glasses down and turned back to the crowd of sailors and officers gathering on the flight deck in ever-increasing numbers. Laceur had hoped there would be minimal personnel to witness the return. Grudgingly he relented and rescinded his order to clear the flight deck after an animated discussion with Captain Briggs.

Frank Rawlins and two additional flight surgeons attached to the air wing stood by quietly talking next to "Tilly," the big crane used to pick up wrecks on the flight deck. Standing behind them were several corpsmen and a dozen sailors designated as litter bearers. No information had reached them on the condition of the men. They were told that POWs were on board, possibly wounded, and that the helicopter was badly damaged. With little information to go on, they had brought enough medical supplies with them to make it appear as if they were opening up a clinic.

The carrier started into a turn and a sailor grabbed the portable rack holding several IV bottles swinging beneath it, preventing it from tipping over. Lieutenant Rawlins stopped talking to one of the corpsmen and turned and looked across the bow. The squadron flight surgeon could feel the carrier leaning slightly as it began its turn into the wind. The carrier was increasing speed, something it usually didn't do for helicopter recoveries.

"Stand by to recover helos," the announcement said. "All nonessential personnel will move to the forward one-third of the flight deck and stand clear of flight operations. The helicopters are one mile out and turning final.'' Everyone turned to look for the returning helicopters, facing the rear of the carrier. The announcement was repeated again and the crowd of spectators moved to the front of the carrier as ordered.

Pokey took his position on the LSO platform and stood next to one of the helicopter detachment pilots who was holding the wave-off trigger housing in his hand. Corbousier seldom went up on the platform during helo recoveries, wondering why an LSO was even required. Now he felt he should be there even if there was nothing he could contribute. There would be no wave-off and he stood off to the side, intently watching the two SH-3A Sikorsky helicopters, which were less than a mile out, one behind the other. He stared in disbelief as he monitored their progress through binoculars and let out a gasp as he studied the damage to the front section of the first helo.

''Eighteen knots down the deck,'' the helo LSO transmitted over the UHF radio. He was unsure if Aggie could even hear him. He smiled when he spotted the landing gear coming down on the lead helicopter.

The second helicopter flew slightly above and aft on the starboard side of Aggie's helo. The pilot could see lines of holes stitched across the tail section and the mangled engine housing where it had been hit. He couldn't believe that they had taken so many hits and the tail-rotor drive shaft had not been severed. He was too far aft to see the missing front section or see Aggie looking as if he were driving a convertible. The pilot of the second helicopter intended to fly formation with him until Aggie was safely on deck. They had switched frequencies and the LSO was now talking to Aggie. There was nothing to do but watch Anson make a single-engine roll on landing and then it would be over.

The two helicopters were in sight and anyone that could get away from his duties wanted to be on the flight deck when they landed. Sailors were pouring out of every access that led up to the flight deck. The catwalks along the side of the carrier and the forward guntubs were jammed. Dr. Rawlins was becoming concerned about moving his staff through the crowd out to the helicopter.

The closed-circuit TV system was zeroed in on the arriving helicopter, and any officers or sailors who couldn't make it to the flight deck gathered around available monitors and stared in disbelief at the damaged front end of the helicopter that was clearly in focus. They watched the Sikorsky Sea King approach the round down of the flight deck with less than ten knots of forward speed. Everyone became hushed as Aggie came over the end, touching down lightly on the main mounts. He rolled smoothly to a stop abeam the island, and two linemen ran out and placed chocks around his wheels. The roar of the main rotor blades drowned out the cheers that resounded across the flight deck and below.

Admiral Laceur silently watched the landing. "Well, they made it " He was not smiling.

"Yes sir, they made it," the junior flag lieutenant quickly answered, dropping his smile when he looked over at the admiral.

"Briggs, I want a meeting with all the members of that helicopter at fourteen hundred hours in my quarters with the exception of the POWs and the enlisted crewmen." Stepping down from his chair he walked directly to the door and left without saying another word.

Aggie quickly secured the single engine as rapidly as he could, pulling the fuel cutoff and then jamming on the rotor brake. He let out a sigh and just sat there for a moment as the five massive rotor blades quickly came to a halt.

Someone else could worry about folding the blades, he decided.

In the rear of the helo, Captain Larue and his two marines climbed down from the cargo bay, ready to assist the others. Campbell and Jordan stood at the open doorway as a staircase was being pushed up to the helicopter. Jordan looked out over the crowd and he began to feel traces of moisture seeping into his eyes. Inside, Commander Lorimar was still sitting with the air force POW, who seemed bewildered by it all.

Dr. Rawlins and his corpsmen pushed forward to the steps as sailors made room for them to pass through the growing crowd. Rawlins climbed into the helo behind two corpsmen carrying litters. He glanced around the cargo bay, then directed the corpsmen to place the air force lieutenant on the litter. The flight surgeon then looked Jordan over, his eyes stopping briefly on his twisted arm. He put his hands on his shoulder, eliciting a yell from Jordan. Rawlins turned and called for one of the litters.

"No thanks, Doc. I'll walk if you don't mind." Jordan smiled, then turned and followed the two corpsmen carrying the air force lieutenant down the steps. He stopped for a moment and looked out over the crowd that had turned silent. All eyes were on him as he slowly turned his head, surveying them. Jordan broke into a big grin as he slowly raised his arm, then gritted his teeth from the pain. He made his hand into a fist and extended his thumb up, sending the crowd into an uproar as they clapped and cheered. Jordan stepped down with Campbell at his side, followed by the other POW. Slowly they moved forward and the crowd separated, opening a wide path for them to pass through.

As they neared the door opening into the island, Cecil Washington stood at attention, smartly saluting. Campbell paused for a moment, then returned the salute, winking at him. "I liked your old salute better," he said, then stepped inside the island. He held Jordan's arm as they made their way down to sick bay.

Aggie was making a walk-around of his helicopter, shaking his head as he discovered one area after another where the helo had been hit. He wondered if the cost of the helicopter would be added to his fine and jail sentence—but then decided it was worth it.

After all the POWs were moved to sick bay, Dr. Rawlins ordered their ragged clothes removed and shots of vitamins administered. The air force lieutenant was hooked up to an IV and lying down as corpsmen hovered around him, cleaning away the repellent clothing he wore. Jordan sat on a bed sipping a glass of fruit juice and waiting to be x-rayed, while a corpsman examined Swenson on a table nearby. At the far end of the room, Commander Lorimar winced in pain as a doctor peered into the pupil of his eye with an examining light. The flight surgeon examined one eye and then the other. Lorimar waited as the doctor stepped back and pulled off his sterile gloves, throwing them into a basket. The medical officer put his hand on Lorimar's shoulder, announcing he would be fine, that the blindness was temporary. He directed a corpsman to apply some salve and wrap bandages around Lorimar's eyes.

The X-ray machine was ready and Dr. Rawlins nodded to the corpsmen then continued his examination of Jordan's arm. Jordan noisily sucked down the last of his fruit juice and threw away the straw, gently lowering his arm so Rawlins could continue his examination.

"Ouch," he protested when the flight surgeon lifted it up again. "Can't you just take my word for it that it's sprained? The slopes had me hanging for hours."

"Sorry," the doc responded. "Let's get you x-rayed before we do anything else." He helped Jordan from the bed and guided him toward the machine. Jordan had already been given shots of vitamins and gamma globulin, and blood and urine samples had been taken, which a corpsman was already examining beneath a microscope.

Jordan grabbed a bowl of Jell-O from a tray as they walked over to the X-ray table. "This is not what I've been dreaming about, although a few days ago I would have traded my mother-in-law for this bowl." He stopped at the table, where a corpsman helped him up onto the cold slab and positioned him beneath the gimbaled machine.

"Hey, Soupy," Jordan hollered from the room lined with hanging lead panels. "Who decided to send in the cavalry? That had to be a top-level decision." He lay motionless as the machine hummed into action.

Campbell and Larue were standing off to one side of the examining room and moved nearer to the corpsman operating the machine. "Not too high up the chain," Campbell answered. He could see Jordan stretched out on the black tabletop.

"It's just lucky you came when you did. That Cuban bastard was going to move us. Wouldn't say where, except that I was going to be one of their permanent guests. Who was it, the President, CinCPac?" The corpsman repositioned him for another shot.

Campbell and Larue looked at each other grinning. "None of them," Campbell said.

"Wasn't?"

"Nope."

"Then who was it? I know it wasn't Admiral Laceur. He wouldn't risk an operation like that unless he could count on a high body count or a bridge span falling."

"Right again."

Jordan stiffened and held his breath as he heard the X-ray machine coming on.

"That's enough for now," the flight surgeon said, stepping into the partitioned room. He helped Jordan sit up, and Campbell and Larue walked over to the table.

"Then who?" Jordan asked again, looking at each of them for a moment and then grinning as the realization hit him. "Nah," he said, shaking his head.

"Yep."

"You guys? You did this for me?" His eyes were beginning to mist over. "Son of a bitch!" he exclaimed.

Campbell prodded Larue as Pancho and Swenson walked in behind a smartly dressed marine, one of the admiral's orderlies. The marine stopped in front of Captain Larue.

"Sir, Captain Briggs, the admiral's chief of staff, directed—"

"I know who the admiral's chief of staff is, Marine. What does he want?" Larue interrupted the nervous soldier.

"Sir, you, Lieutenants Campbell and Anson, Lieutenant Junior Grade Gonzales, and Ensign Swenson are to report to his quarters at fourteen hundred hours this afternoon for an informal inquiry into this morning's mission, sir." He stood at attention waiting for a response.

"All right, Hansen, I have your message." Larue watched the corporal do an about-face and disappear out the door.

Jordan looked at the strained expressions on their faces for a moment. "You guys hung it on the line for me, didn't you?" The gravity of the situation was beginning to come home and all stood silent.

Campbell reached into his pocket and pulled out a letter Patricia had given him to deliver to her husband if he should ever see Jordan again. He handed it to him. "Yeah, we did, and you would have done the same for us."

Jordan took the letter and read it while the others stood in silence. "She was in on it?" He held the pages in his hand and looked up at Campbell.

"Not exactly, and you don't know the half of it, but now's not the time to fill you in."

"Where is she?"

"She's back in San Diego, waiting for word, which should already be on its way. You'll be seeing her soon enough."

"How about Karen?"

Campbell shuffled uneasily. "She went back to her folks in Pensacola. She was with Patricia the whole time and knew what we were planning to do."

"She didn't approve, did she?"

Campbell paused for a moment. "She would have wanted you to try the same thing for me."

That afternoon at two minutes before 1400 hours, Campbell stopped before the marine guard. The corporal was standing smartly just outside the entrance to the admiral's quarters and came to attention when the officers arrived. He knocked on the door, then entered the room and announced their arrival.

"Send them in." Captain Briggs looked stern as he watched the marine wheel around and step out of the room. Campbell was the first to enter, followed by Captain Larue, Swenson, Anson, then Gonzales. The marine sentry pulled the door closed behind him, leaving the five standing stiffly at attention in a line across the room. The air hung heavy with silence and each stared straight ahead at the wall laced with pictures.

"Stand at ease, gentlemen." Admiral Laceur stepped over to his favorite chair as the five spaced their feet slightly apart and clasped their hands behind their backs. Small wrinkles began forming on Laceur's forehead as he silently looked up and down the five officers standing before him. He studied each man intently. No one dared say anything while he continued his examination.

"Gentlemen," the flag officer finally said, "where would you like me to begin?" He paused. "Should I begin with the conspiracy to conduct unauthorized operations against the enemy? A privilege reserved only for those in command with explicit authorization, I might remind you." He paused again, looking at each man directly with penetrating eyes that seemed to burn through to the bulkhead behind them.

"Perhaps you would prefer to begin with destruction of naval property—or maybe theft of naval property—or absence without leave—or insubordination—or—or . . . ," he continued, his voice rising with each accusation. The room became silent again as he stopped talking. Laceur paused in front of Campbell and stared directly at him, then moved in turn to each officer as he continued throwing every charge he could think of at them, quoting from the *Manual for Courts-martial*. His voice rose and fell with each charge.

"Gentlemen"—his voice calmed down—"what you did broke every law of the United States Navy that I can think of. Who was the brilliant mastermind behind this unauthorized incursion into North Vietnam? You, Captain?" Laceur stepped in front of the marine and stared silently at him. Larue said nothing.

"I was, Admiral." Campbell came to attention. "I take full responsibility for the whole operation."

"Go on." The admiral turned his attention away from the marine and looked at Campbell.

"Sir, the others only thought it was official because I told them it was. I told them only a few would be involved for the sake of secrecy—that discussion would only lead to compromise and jeopardize the mission. Sir, they all thought they were following orders." Campbell could feel the admiral move to within inches of his face.

"I don't believe that, son. I think you planned it, but I

also think the others knew it wasn't approved or authorized and decided to go ahead anyhow. Isn't that how it was?'' He continued staring into Campbell's face.

''Ah hmm,'' Aggie mumbled, then cleared his throat.

''What was that?'' Laceur asked, looking away from Campbell. He stepped back and approached Aggie. ''You're the helicopter pilot, aren't you?''

''Yes sir.''

''What do you want to say?''

Aggie took one step back, feeling the admiral was too close to him. ''Admiral.'' He paused. ''The way I see it is like this. We are going to make you famous.''

Laceur put his hand in the side pocket of his jacket and moved closer to him. ''Famous?''

''Yes sir, famous. You are going to be known as the admiral who broke out the POWs from the enemy right on their own turf. Every paper in the States is going to carry your picture right alongside ours. Morale among the pilots will go up one hundred percent. Up till now, most of us felt that if you were captured, you were just written off and either died or waited out the war. And judging from the condition of the three we brought back, I certainly wouldn't want to go through what they did.''

Laceur stared at the helicopter pilot for a moment, watching Aggie's smile gradually fading. ''Mr. Anson, Captain Briggs talked to your copilot and we know everything you did, even when it was planned and how and who was involved. We can throw the book at you.''

Aggie thought for a moment, then began smiling again. ''Admiral, this cruise marks the end of my obligated service to the United States of America. I volunteered, served my time, and did you a good job. After we return to San Diego I've got two weeks of active duty left, after which I plan to buy a car, enroll in the next semester of college back at Texas A & M, and finish up what I started five years ago.

Now, the way I figure it, there's two ways to go. You can be a hero and take all the credit and do everybody some good." He paused for a moment to catch his breath. "Or you can throw the book at us and send us to jail. But you've got to consider the headlines on the nightly news and the magazine and newspaper stories that are going to come out of it. The American people may not be crazy about the war, Admiral, but they sure as hell don't like seeing their boys—especially boys who rescue POWs—doing time either." Having said all he was going to say, Aggie's face relaxed and he waited for the flag officer's reaction.

Laceur stared at the helicopter pilot for a moment, then turned away, telling Captain Briggs to dismiss them for the time being then meet him in his room. He stepped into his private stateroom, closing the door behind him.

The officers popped to attention as the admiral left the room. Captain Briggs dismissed them and they quietly and quickly headed for the door. Everyone exited down the passageway except for Pancho, who cut through the kitchen when Briggs's back was turned.

By the time they reached the ready room, Campbell was drained, slumping into his assigned seat. Swenson was at the coffee urn getting coffee for them. Ringer handed him a cup of coffee then sat down next to his wing leader. Campbell accepted the cup then leaned back into the chair. "Well, Swede, your first cruise is about over. Was it worth it?"

Swenson rubbed the patch the flight surgeon had taped above his eye. "Yeah, it was worth it." He took a sip of the coffee. "I haven't had time to thank you for saving my bacon this morning. Guess I owe you a bottle, at the least." He paused for a moment. "You know who it was you knocked down this morning, don't you? That was Quang, the Gray Ghost."

"Yup. And he had it coming. A lot of our guys are still in the Hanoi Hilton because of him."

"Well, you got him, sir. You got the Gray Ghost." Swenson watched his flight leader break into a big grin, and they sat for a while, retelling the story of the rescue over again every time another group of pilots came in to congratulate them. Finally they went down to sick bay to check on Jordan, who'd moved on from Jell-O and was now happily gorging himself on a T-bone steak.

EPILOGUE

One day out from San Diego . . .

Campbell jerked upright, gripping the sides of his chair. He was sweating and felt disoriented as he looked around the room, blinking his eyes in the darkness. The air wing had flown off the *Barbary Coast* that morning, leaving a sprinkling of pilots aboard the carrier to ride the ship into port. Only the most junior pilots or those without aircraft to fly had to remain aboard ship, giving them an extra day at sea. Campbell had volunteered to stay, wanting an extra day to think things out.

He sat upright, stretching his arms and legs, now stiff and cramped from his falling asleep in the chair. The small desk lamp was still on and he looked at his watch, which said half past ten. Campbell had missed the evening meal and would have to wait until the kitchen opened up later that evening, when fast foods and snacks would be available to those unable to sleep, sailors who were anticipating the following day when the carrier would dock in San Diego. They were the ones who had "channel fever," an affliction affecting anyone returning to the States for the first time in six months.

The letter from Karen lay unopened on the desk where he had left it before falling asleep. Campbell picked it up and put it in his pocket, turned off the lamp, and walked out of the room into the red glow of the passageway, making his way to the hangar bay and then up to the flight deck. As he stepped through the opened hatch, a long-forgotten sensation took hold of his nostrils, one he had not experienced for some time. He walked out on the empty deck and the smell became stronger, definitely not like the sea air he had grown accustomed to. For the first time, he felt he was home and free again.

The night was clear and black above the *Barbary Coast*, with endless stars spread across the sky. The moon was full and bright enough to read by, hanging above the island superstructure and casting shadows across the deck. Only an occasional red glow from a cigarette would mark the location of sailors passing the time, talking long into the night of tales of the cruise and families and girlfriends waiting for them in port. Most would be up all night, playing endless card games and talking, unable to sleep because of the excitement of coming home.

Campbell made his way to the fantail and sat down near the round down, now guarded by a fence erected across the end. He leaned against the fence and watched the glowing phosphorescence dancing in the carrier's wake, which to him seemed like a million fireflies stretched out to the horizon. He imagined the flying fish that were leaping through the air to escape the onrushing carrier as it cut through their countless schools. And of the dolphin riding the bow wave, catching a free ride in the moonlight. Campbell sat there with his legs stretched out in front of him, then leaned back on his hands. His thoughts turned to Jordan and he imagined him at Balboa Naval Hospital in San Diego, Patricia at his side every minute. He thought about Aggie for a moment and then laughed to himself, remembering the scene with the admiral and the little helicopter pilot standing up to the pompous flag officer.

He reached inside his pocket and pulled out the letter from Karen. He had started to read it several times, but each time put it away, afraid of what it might contain. Slowly, he tore one end open and pulled out the single page.

My dearest Jim,

It seems like only yesterday we were together in Singapore, and yet so much has happened since then. I really thought that would be the last time I would see you, knowing what you were planning to do at the time. I've spent so many days going down to the beach out on the island and just sitting, staring at the waves and thinking about you. It took me several days to really come to a decision, and I've had to relive all the events that occurred during the last six months of our lives. It's helped me to come to a decision about us. And it's that I'm hopelessly in love with you and that I was just being selfish and didn't want to lose you to the navy, the North Vietnamese, or anybody. I guess that during the time I spent chasing around Thailand and Laos with Patricia, I had a chance to grow up. It made me more aware of your wants and needs and the needs of others as well. I guess I was just blinded by the navy you introduced me to and couldn't see any of the warts that went with it.

What I'm trying to say is that I love you very much and want to be your wife whether you want to stay in the navy and be a jet pilot or want to sell shoes at K Mart. It doesn't matter, just as long as we love each other. Please forgive me for indicating otherwise and just write it off as the wishes of a very young and naive little girl.

I can't wait to see you when you pull into San Diego aboard the *Barbary Coast*. I'm going to be one proud little girl standing on the pier waiting for you.

My love,

Karen

P.S. If you don't find me on the pier, look for me in the bar at the Del Coronado Hotel. I'll be the horniest-looking girl at the bar.

Campbell folded her letter and put it into his pocket, staring out at the moonlight reflecting off the water. He pulled out the letter of resignation from the navy he had carefully composed and held it up to the light, reading the first line: *It is with deep regret* . . . He paused for a moment, then tore the letter into small pieces and flung them into the air, watching the bits of paper flutter down into the sea until he could no longer see them.

"Everything okay, Mr. Campbell?" a voice asked from behind him.

He turned around and looked up, seeing his plane captain standing there. "You bet, Cecil," he said. "Everything's just fine. In fact, things couldn't be better."

GLOSSARY OF TERMS

A-1 SKYRAIDER: also known as "Spad" and "Sandy," it was the perfect aircraft for accompanying rescue helicopters into North Vietnam.

A-4 SKYHAWK: Also known as "Scooter," "Tinker Toy," and "Hinnemann's Hot-rod," the smallest attack jet in the navy. Served as the workhorse of the fleet, delivering bombs on North Vietnamese targets whenever required.

AA-2 ATOLL: The Soviet version of the Sidewinder missile.

AAA: Antiaircraft artillery.

AK-47 ASSAULT RIFLE: Common rifle used by all Communist bloc countries.

ANGEL: A rescue helicopter.

ANGELS: Altitude in thousands of feet.

AOA: Angle of Attack—A cockpit instrument showing

the relationship of the angle between the wing and the relative air passing over the wing.

APU: Auxiliary Power Unit—The startling unit for aircraft.

ASW: Antisubmarine Warfare—Hunting and killing enemy submarines with aerial, surface and subsurface forces.

BALL: The round spot of yellow light reflecting fromt he mirror of the carrier landing system, used by the pilot as an indication of his position relative to the glide slope.

BACAP: Barrier Combat Air Patrol—An assigned area for fighter aircraft whose specific mission is to protect the fleet from enemy aircraft.

BARREL ROLL: An aerial acrobatic maneuver in which the aircraft is rolled around a point 45 degrees up and 45 degrees away from the nose. Sometimes employed by aircraft as a defensive maneuver against SAMs.

BOLTER: An attempted carrier landing in which the tailhook fails to engage an arresting cable and the aircraft continues in flight.

BREAK: (1) A term used to depict a point in which an aircraft rolls into a steep angle of bank and turns downwind for landing. (2) A break in communications in which the next transmission will be for the next recipient.

CAT: Catapult—A system designed to enable an aircraft to obtain flying speed in a short distance from an aircraft carrier.

CBU: Canisterized (Cluster) Bomblet Unit—An aerial weapon containing a larger number of smaller bomblets.

CHARLIE: The signal clearing an aircraft to land aboard the carrier.

CIC: Combat Information Center—The heart of a military vessel, into which all information relative to combat or defense is fed and utilized.

COD: Carrier Onboard Delivery—An aircraft designated to deliver materials and men to and from the carrier.

CVA: Aircraft Carrier, Attack—An aircraft carrier designated for an attack role.

CVS: Aircraft Carrier, ASW Support—An aircraft carrier designated for an ASW role.

DRV: Democratic Republic of Vietnam (North Vietnam)

E-1B TRACER: A twin-engine ECM aircraft operating in conjunction with fighter and attack aircraft during a mission to provide various communications and electronics countermeasures.

ECM: Electronic Counter Measures—Any technique used to confuse or neutralize enemy radar and communications.

EGT: Exhaust Gas Temperature—An aircraft instrument providing temperture readings of the exhaust gases of a jet engine.

F-4 PHANTOM: A twin-engine jet aircraft flown by the navy, air force, and marines in the various roles of fighter and bomber. A Mach 2 two-place aircraft, it has a RIO (radar intercept officer) in the rear seat who provides a second pair of eyes during dogfights as well as operating the weapon and radar systems.

F-8 CRUSADER: A single-engine, single-pilot, carrier-based fighter.

F-105 THUNDERCHIEF: Known as the "Thud," this was a large fighter-bomber used against North Vietnam by the air force.

FAC: Forward Air Controller—A pilot designated to control aerial strikes who usually flew in an OV-1 Bird Dog armed only with smoke rockets for marking target areas.

FAN SONG: North Vietnamese acquisition radar used in conjunction with a SAM missile battery.

FIRECAN: North Vietnamese AAA radar used for tracking aircraft and aiming the weapons.

FOREST PENETRATOR: A device carried by rescue

helicopters to penetrate down through heavy foliage and enable a downed pilot to ride the unfolded legs of the device back up to the helicopter.

FORMATION: (1) Section: a two-plane flight composed of a leader and his wingman. (2) Division: two or more sections.

G: A unit of measure describing an acceleration of gravity and the effect most often felt by pilots when suddenly displacing their aircraft from a steady flight path.

G SUIT: A piece of flight gear similar to a corset and worn by pilots to offset the effect of high G loads.

GCI: Ground Control Intercept—A ground-based system consisting of radar and personnel to provide relative altitude, azimuth, bearing, and other information about enemy aircraft to fighter intercepters.

GROUND EFFECT: An aerodynamic phenomenon in which an aircraft or helicopter (translational lift) realizes a decrease in the power required to maintain steady flight. It is accomplished whenever the aircraft or helicopter is usually within a wingspan (or rotor blade) distance from the ground.

GRU: Glavnoye Razvedyvatelnoye Upravleniye—The Russian military equivalent of U.S. military intelligence and the counterpart of the KGB.

HORSE COLLAR: A yellow padded ring, shaped like a horse collar, used to rescue downed aviators.

ICS: Inter-Communications System—A phone system used by aircrews to talk to each other.

IP: Initial Point—The preselected point that marks the beginning of a bombing run or other preassigned function.

JOLLY GREEN: Usually meaning the CH-53 helicopters based in Thailand and assigned for rescue duty of doiwned pilots in North Vietnam.

KC-135 STRATOTANKER: The military version of the Boeing 707 and used as an airborne filling station to provide fuel to whole formations of bombers en route to their target and requiring refueling under way.

KIA: Killed In Action.

LSO: Landing Signal Officer—An officer chosen for his superior knowledge of flying and his ability to help pilots make safe landings.

M38/39: A 37-millimeter anti-aircraft gun (usually mounted in pairs) with an effective range of 1,640 yards and firing 180 roiunds per minute.

M60: A machine gun used throughout the Vietnam war; common on helicopters. Fired 7.62-millimeter rounds.

MK 82, 83, 84: 500- to 2,000-pound aerial dropped bombs.

MIA: Missing in Action.

MiG-17 ''FRESCO'': The mainstay of the North Vietnamese air force, this highly maneuverable single-engine aircraft was armed with one 37-millimeter and two 23-millimeter cannons and Atoll air-to-air missiles.

MiG-21 ''FISHBED'': An extremely capable aircraft, typically carrying a 23-millimeter cannon and a pair of Atoll air-to-air missilkes. Capable of speeds up to Mach 2.1, its initial climb rate was around 30,000 fpm.

MIRROR LANDING SYSTEM: A system enabling pilots to visually follow a light source down the glide path to an arrested landing. Composed of a curved mirror and a datum bar of reference lights plus a source light, the gyroscopically balanced system allows the pilot to maintain his position in relation to a ball of light.

NVA: North Vietnamese Army

O-1 BIRDDOG: A slow, high-wing aircraft used to spot targets and control bombing missions.

PIPPER: The adjustable gunsight aiming dot used by the pilot against his aerial or ground target.

PRI-FLY: A space located in the rearward part of the carrier's superstructure (island) where the Air Ops officer overlooks the flight deck and controls all flight opertions in the vicinity of the ship.

R and R: Rest and Relaxation—A port selected for visits by off-duty sailors.

RA-5C VIGILANTE: A two-seat, twin-engine carrier-based reconnaissance aircraft.

RPG: Rocket-Propelled Grenade—A shoulder-fired weapon designed for use against tanks.

RVN: Republic of South Vietnam.

SAM: Surface-to-Air Missile—The Russian-built SA-2 Guideline was the primary missile used against American aircraft.

SAR: Search and Rescue.

SH-3A SEA KING: A large twin-engine helicopter used by the navy primarily as an ASW helicopter.

SHRIKE: Radar-guided, air-launched, anti-radar missile designed to home in on SAM guidance radars.

SIDEWINDER: An air-to-air, heat-seeking missile, which accounted for most of the downings of North Vietnamese aircraft.

SPOON REST: The initial acquisition radar used to track aircraft and provide information to the computers of the SAM site.

TILLY/CHERRY PICKER: The large crane usually parked behind the island of a carrier; used to pick up aircraft.

TORQUE GAUGE: An aircraft instrument commonly found on helicopters, indicating the amount of power brought to bear against a particular system, such as the main transmissioin.

TORSO HARNESS: A piece of equipment worn by jet pilots, containing fittings that are attached to the parachute and ejection system of the aircraft.

TRACER: A round of ammunition that burns as it moves through the air, so the gunner can see where the round is heading. Usually one of every dozen or so rounds is a tracer.

USS CHICAGO (RED CROWN): A guided missile cruiser armed with surface-to-air missiles. It contained the controlling agency for flights going in and out of North Vietnam and provided up-to-date information on MiG activity.

YELLOW SHEET: A form filled out by a returning pilot indicating any problems with the aircraft.